THE ROSE AND THE THORN

"Well, I hope you learned your lesson."

Royce raised an eyebrow. "Me?" He untied his horse and climbed on.

"You said the world is a cold, ruthless place."

"It is."

"You also said Albert would die from starvation in that barn—that no one would help him." He smiled broadly and reached out to the viscount. "Care for a hand up, Albert?"

"I'm only helping him for the profit he can—"

"Doesn't matter. You were wrong."

"I was not. I—"

"Even if you're doing it for selfish reasons, you're still helping to save his life. It just goes to show that good can come from helping a stranger, and it proves that the world isn't so bad after all."

Royce scowled. He opened his mouth to speak, then stopped and scowled again. Finally he just raised his hood and kicked his horse into a trot.

"I'll make a human being out of him yet," Hadrian said to Albert as they trotted off.

By Michael J. Sullivan

The Riyria Chronicles

The Crown Tower

The Rose and the Thorn

The Riyria Revelations

Theft of Swords

Rise of Empire

Heir of Novron

THE ROSE AND THE THORN

Book Two of the
Riyria Chronicles

MICHAEL J. SULLIVAN

www.orbitbooks.net

ORBIT

First published in Great Britain in 2013 by Orbit

3 5 7 9 10 8 6 4 2

Copyright © 2013 by Michael J. Sullivan

Map by Michael J. Sullivan

Excerpt from *Promise of Blood* by Brian McClellan
Copyright © 2013 by Brian McClellan

A CIP catalogue record for this book
is available from the British Library.

ISBN 978-0-356-50228-1

Printed and bound by CPI Group (UK) Ltd, Croydon, CR0 4YY

Papers used by Orbit are from well-managed forests
and other responsible sources.

MIX
Paper from
responsible sources
FSC® C104740

Orbit
An imprint of
Little, Brown Book Group
Carmelite House
50 Victoria Embankment
London EC4Y 0DZ

An Hachette UK Company
www.hachette.co.uk

www.littlebrown.co.uk

Contents

Contents

TRENT

GHENT

ERVANON

SHERIDAN
UNIVERSITY

NORTH RIVER

LOWLANDS TRAIL

ASPER

HIGH
MEADOWLANDS

LONGWOOD

EAST MARCH

MELENGAR

MEDFORD

SEON
UPLANDS

LAKE
WINDERMERE

WEST MARCH

DRONDIL
FIELDS

HIGHLANDS

GALILIN

CHADWICK

FORD

GALEWYR RIVER

GLOUSTON

AMBER
HEIGHTS

ALBU

WARRIC

FAENDELDREAL S

COLNORA

SHARON
SEA

AQUESTA

NORTHERN DUNN

RATIBOR

NORTHPOINT

BERNUM RIVER

RHENYDD

KILNAR

VERNES

CHAPTER 1

THE BATTLE OF GATEWAY BRIDGE

Reuben should have run the moment the squires came out of the castle keep. He could have easily reached the sanctuary of the stable, limiting their harassment to throwing apples and insults, but their smiles confused him. They looked friendly—almost reasonable.

"Reuben! Hey, Reuben!"

Reuben? Not Muckraker? Not Troll-Boy?

The squires all had nicknames for him. None were flattering, but then he had names for them too—at least in his head. "The Song of Man," one of Reuben's favorite poems, mentioned age, disease, and hunger as the Three Cruelties of Humanity. Fat Horace was clearly hunger. Pasty-faced, pockmarked Willard was disease, and age was given to Dills, who at seventeen was the oldest.

Spotting Reuben, the trio had whirled his way like a small flock of predatory geese. Dills had a dented knight's helmet in his hands, the visor slapping up and down as it swung with his arm. Willard carried combat padding. Horace was eating an apple—big surprise.

He could still make it to the stable ahead of them. Only Dills had any chance of winning in a footrace. Reuben shifted his weight but hesitated.

"This is my old trainer," Dills said pleasantly, as if the last three years had never happened, as if he were a fox who'd forgotten what to do with a rabbit. "My father sent a whole new set for my trials. We've been having fun with this."

They closed in—too late to run now. They circled around, but still the smiles remained.

Dills held out the helmet, which caught and reflected the autumn sun, leather straps dangling. "Ever worn one? Try it."

Reuben stared at the helm, baffled. *This is so odd. Why are they being nice?*

"I don't think he knows what to do with it," Horace said.

"Go ahead." Dills pushed the helmet at him. "You join the castle guards soon, right?"

They're talking to me? Since when?

Reuben didn't answer right away. "Ah...yeah."

Dills's smile widened. "Thought so. You don't get much combat practice, do you?"

"Who would spar with the stableboy?" Horace slurred while chewing.

"Exactly," Dills said, and glanced up at the clear sky. "Beautiful fall day. Stupid to be inside. Thought you'd like to learn a few maneuvers."

Each of them wore wooden practice swords and Horace had an extra.

Is this real? Reuben studied their faces for signs of deceit. Dills appeared hurt by his lack of faith, and Willard rolled his eyes. "We thought you'd like to try on a knight's helmet, seeing as how you never get to wear one. Thought you'd appreciate it."

Beyond them, Reuben saw Squire Prefect Ellison coming from the castle and taking a seat on the edge of the well to watch.

"It's fun. We've all taken turns." Dills shoved the helm

against Reuben's chest again. "With the pads and helm you can't get hurt."

Willard scowled. "Look, we're trying to be nice here—don't be a git."

As bizarre as it all was, Reuben didn't see any malice in their eyes. They all smiled like he'd seen them look at one another—sloppy, unguarded grins. The whole thing made a kind of sense in Reuben's head. After three years the novelty of bullying him had finally worn off. Being the only one their age who wasn't noble had made him a natural target, but times had changed and everyone grew up. This was a peace offering, and given that Reuben hadn't made a single friend since his arrival, he couldn't afford to be picky.

He lifted the helm, which was stuffed with rags, and slipped it on. Despite the wads of cloth, the helmet was too big, hung loose. He suspected something wasn't right but didn't know for sure. He had never worn armor of any kind. Since Reuben was destined to be a castle soldier, his father had been expected to train him but never had time. That deficiency was part of the allure of the squires' offer; the enticement outweighed his suspicions. This was his chance to learn about fighting and swordplay. His birthday was only a week away, and once he turned sixteen he would enter the ranks of the castle guard. With little combat training he'd be relegated to the worst posts. If the squires were serious, he might learn something—anything.

The trio trussed him up in the heavy layers of padding that restricted his movement; then Horace handed him the extra wooden sword.

That's when the beating began.

Without warning, all three squires' swords struck Reuben in the head. The metal and wadding of the helmet absorbed most, but not all, of the blows. The inside of the helmet had rough, exposed metal edges that jabbed, piercing his fore-head, cheek, and ear. He raised his sword in a feeble attempt to defend but could see little through the narrow visor. His ears packed with linen, he could just barely make out muffled laughter. One blow knocked the sword from his hands and an-other struck his back, collapsing him to his knees. After that, the strikes came in earnest. They rained on his metal-caged head as he cowered in a ball.

Finally the blows slowed, then stopped. Reuben heard heavy breathing, panting, and more laughter.

"You were right, Dills," Willard said. "The Muckraker is a much better training dummy."

"For a while—but the dummy doesn't curl up in a ball like a girl." The old disdain was back in Dills's voice.

"But there *is* the added bonus of him squealing when hit."

"Anyone else thirsty?" Horace asked, still panting.

Hearing them move away, Reuben allowed himself to breathe and his muscles to relax. His jaw was stiff from clench-ing his teeth, and everything else ached from the pounding. He lay for a moment longer, waiting, listening. With the helmet on, the world was shut out, muted, but he feared taking it off. After several minutes, even the muffled laughter and insults faded. Peering up through the slit, all he could see was the canopy of orange and yellow leaves waving in the afternoon breeze. Reuben tilted his head and spotted the Three Cruelties in the center of the courtyard filling cups from the well as they took seats on the apple cart. One was rubbing his sword arm, swinging it in wide circles.

It must be exhausting beating me senseless.

Reuben pulled the helmet off and felt the cool air kiss the sweat on his brow. He realized now that it wasn't Dills's helm at all. They must have found it discarded somewhere. He should have known Dills would never let him wear anything of his. Reuben wiped his face and was not surprised when his hand came away with blood.

Hearing someone's approach, he raised his arms to protect his head.

"That was pathetic." Ellison stood over Reuben, eating an apple that he had stolen from the merchant's cart. No one would say a word against him—certainly not the merchant. Ellison was the prefect of squires, the senior boy with the most influential father. He should have been the one to prevent such a beating.

Reuben didn't reply.

"Wadding wasn't tight enough," Ellison went on. "Of course, the idea is not to get hit in the first place." He took another bite of apple, chewing with his mouth open. Bits of dribble fell to his chest, staining his squire's tunic. He and the Cruelties all wore the same uniform, blue with the burgundy and gold falcon of House Essendon. With the stain of apple juice, it looked like the falcon was crying.

"It's hard to see in that helm." Reuben noticed the wadded cloth that had fallen on the grass was bright with his blood.

"You think knights can see better?" Ellison asked around a mouthful of apple. "They ride horses while fighting. You just had a helm and a touch of padding. Knights wear fifty pounds of steel, so don't give me your excuses. That's the problem with your kind—you always have excuses. Bad enough we have to suffer the indignity of working alongside you as pages, but we also have to listen to you complain about everything too." Ellison raised the pitch of his voice to mimic a girl. "*I need shoes to haul water in the winter. I can't split all the wood by myself.*" Returning to his normal tone, he continued, "Why they still insist on forcing young men of breeding to endure the humiliation of cleaning stables before becoming proper squires is beyond me, but having the added insult of being forced to labor alongside someone like you, a peasant and a bastard, was just—"

"I'm no bastard," Reuben said. "I have a father. I have a last name."

Ellison laughed and some of the apple flew out. "You have *two*—his *and* hers. *Reuben Hilfred*, the son of Rose Reuben and Richard Hilfred. Your parents never married. That makes you a bastard. And who knows how many soldiers your mother entertained before she died. Chambermaids do a lot of that, you know. Whores every one. Your father was just dumb enough to believe her when she said you were his. That right there shows you the man's stupidity. So assuming she wasn't lying, you're the son of an idiot and a—"

Reuben slammed into Ellison with every ounce of his body, driving the older boy to his back. He sat up swinging, hitting Ellison in the chest and face. When Ellison got an arm free, Reuben felt pain burst across his cheek. Now he was on his back and the world spun. Ellison kicked him in the side hard enough to break a rib, but Reuben barely felt it. He still wore his padding.

Ellison's face was red, flushed with anger. Reuben had never fought any of them before, certainly not Ellison. His father was a baron of East March; even the others didn't touch him.

Ellison drew his sword. The metal left the sheath with a heavy ring. Reuben just barely grabbed the practice wood, which had been left lying in the grass. He brought it up in time to prevent losing his head, but Ellison's steel cut it in half.

Reuben ran.

That was the one advantage he had over them. He did more work and ran everywhere while they did little. Even weighed down by the padding, he was faster and had the stamina of a pack of hounds. He could run for days if needed. Even so, he wasn't fast enough, and Ellison got one last blow across

Reuben's back. The slice only served to drive him forward, but when he was safely away, he discovered a deep cut through all four layers of padding, his tunic, and a bit of skin.

Ellison had tried to kill him.

༅

Reuben hid in the stables the rest of the day. Ellison and the others never went there. Horse Master Hubert had a tendency to put any castle boy to work, failing to notice the difference between the son of an earl, a baron, or a sergeant at arms. One day they might be lords, but right now they were pages and squires, and as far as Hubert was concerned, they were all just backs and hands to lift shovels. As expected, Reuben was put to mucking out the stalls, which was better than confronting Ellison's blade. His back hurt, as did his face and head, but the bleeding had stopped. Given that he could have died, he wasn't about to complain.

Ellison was just angry. Once he calmed down, the prefect would find another way to demonstrate his displeasure. He and the squires would trap and beat him—with the woods most likely, but without the padding or helmet.

Reuben paused after dumping a shovelful of manure into the wagon and sniffed the air. Wood smoke. Kitchens burned wood all year, but it smelled different in the fall—sweeter. Planting the shovel's head, he stretched, looking up at the castle. Decorations for the autumn gala were almost complete. Celebration flags and streamers flew from poles, and colored lanterns hung from trees. Though the gala was held every year, this time would be a double celebration in honor of the new chancellor. That meant it had to be bigger and better, so they adorned the castle inside and out with pumpkins, gourds, and tied stalks of corn. When the question of too few chairs arose, bundles of straw were hauled in to line every room. For the last week, farmers had been dropping off wagons full. The place did look festive, and even if Reuben wasn't invited, he knew it would be a wonderful party.

His sight drifted to the high tower, which had lately become his obsession. The royal family resided in the upper floors of the castle, where few were allowed without invitation. The tallest point of the castle held its title by only a few feet, but it soared in Reuben's imagination. He squinted, thinking he might see movement, someone passing by the window. He didn't, but then nothing ever happened in the daylight.

With a sigh, he returned to the dimness of the stable. Reuben actually enjoyed shoveling for the horses. In the cooler weather there were few flies and most of the manure was dry, mixed with straw to the consistency of stale bread or cake, and it barely smelled. The simple, mindless work granted him a sense of accomplishment. He also enjoyed being with the horses. They didn't care who he was, the color of his blood, or if his mother had married his father. They always greeted him with a nicker and rubbed their noses against his chest when he came near. He couldn't think of anyone he'd rather spend the autumn afternoon with, except one. Then, as if thoughts could grant wishes, he caught the flash of a burgundy gown.

Seeing the princess through the stable's door, Reuben found it hard to breathe. He froze up whenever he saw her, and when he could move, he was clumsy—his fingers turned stupid, unable to perform the simplest of tasks. Luckily he'd never been called on to speak in her presence. He could only imagine how his tongue would make his fingers appear deft. He'd watched her for years, catching a glimpse as she climbed into a carriage or greeted visitors. Reuben had liked her from first sight. There was something about the way she smiled, the laughter in her voice, and the often serious look on her face, as if she were older than her years. He imagined she wasn't human but some fairy—a spirit of natural grace and beauty. Spotting her was rare and that made it special, a moment of excitement, like seeing a fawn on a still morning. When she appeared, he couldn't take his eyes off her. Nearly thirteen, she was as tall as her mother. But there was something in the way she walked and how her hips shifted when she stood too long in one place that showed she was more lady than girl now. Still thin, still small, but different. Reuben fantasized of being at the well one day when she appeared in the courtyard alone and thirsty. He pictured himself drawing water to fill her cup. She would smile and perhaps thank him. As she brought the empty cup back, their fingers would meet briefly and for that one moment he would feel the warmth of her skin, and for the first time in his life know joy.

"Reuben!" Ian, the groom, struck him on the shoulder with a riding crop. It stung enough to leave a mark. "Quit your daydreaming—get to work."

Reuben resumed shoveling the manure, saying nothing. He had learned his lesson for the day and kept his head down while scooping the strata of dirt cakes. She could not see him in the stalls, but with each toss of manure he caught a glimpse of her through the door. The princess wore a burgundy dress, the new one of Calian silk that she had received for her birthday along with the horse. To Reuben, Calis was just a mythical place, somewhere far away to the south filled with jungles, goblins, and pirates. It had to be a magical land because the material of the dress shimmered as she walked, the color complementing her hair. Being the newest, it fit well. More than that, the other dresses were for a girl—this was a woman's gown.

"You'll be wanting Tamarisk, Your Highness?" Ian asked from somewhere in the stable's main entry.

"Of course. It's a beautiful day for a ride, isn't it? Tamarisk likes the cooler weather. He can run."

"Your mother has asked you not to run Tamarisk."

"Trotting is uncomfortable."

Ian gave her a dubious look. "Tamarisk is a Maranon palfrey, Your Highness. He doesn't trot—he ambles."

"I like the wind in my hair." There was a certain flair in her voice, a willfulness that made Reuben smile.

"Your mother would prefer—"

"Are you the royal groom or a nursemaid? Because I should tell Nora that her services are no longer needed."

"Forgive me, Your Highness, but your mother would—"

She pushed past the groom and entered the barn. "You there—boy!" the princess called.

Reuben paused in his scraping. She was looking right at him.

"Can you saddle a horse?"

He managed a nod.

"Saddle Tamarisk for me. Use the sidesaddle with the suede seat. You know the one?"

Reuben nodded again and jumped to the task. His hands shook as he lifted the saddle from the rack.

Tamarisk was a beautiful chestnut, imported from the kingdom of Maranon. These horses were famed for their breeding and exquisite training, which made for exceptionally smooth rides. Reuben imagined this was how the king explained the gift to his wife. Maranon mounts were also known for their speed, which was likely how the king explained the gift to his daughter.

"Where will you be going?" Ian asked.

"I thought I would ride to the Gateway Bridge."

"You can't ride so far alone."

"My father got me that horse to ride, and not just in the courtyard."

"Then I will escort you," the groom insisted.

"No! Your place is here. Besides, who will raise the alarm if I don't return?"

"If you won't have me, then Reuben will ride with you."

"Who?"

Reuben froze.

"Reuben. The boy saddling your horse."

"I don't want anyone with me."

"It's me or him or no horse is saddled, and I'll go to your mother right now."

"Fine. I'll take ... what did you say his name was?"

"Reuben."

"Really? Does he have a last name?"

"Hilfred."

She sighed. "I'll take Hilfred."

∽

Reuben had never sat a horse before, but he wasn't about to tell either of them that. He was not afraid, except of making a fool of himself in front of her. He knew all the horses well and chose Melancholy, an older black mare with a white diamond on her face. Her name matched her temperament—an attitude that reflected her age. This was the horse they saddled for the children who wanted to ride a "real" horse or for grandmothers and matronly aunts. Still, his heart was pounding as Melancholy followed behind Tamarisk, something she would do even if Reuben wasn't on her back.

They passed out of the castle gates into the city of Medford, the capital of the kingdom of Melengar. Reuben hadn't had much education, but he was a great listener and knew Melengar was one of the smallest of the eight kingdoms of Avryn—the greatest of four nations of mankind. All four countries—Trent, Avryn, Delgos, and Calis—had at one time been part of a single empire, but that was long ago and of no importance to anyone but scribes and historians. What was important was that Medford was well respected, well-to-do, and at peace, and had been for a generation or more.

The king's castle formed the central hub of the city, and around it cart vendors lay siege, circling the moat and selling all manner of autumn fruits and vegetables, breads, smoked meats, leather goods, and cider—both hot and cold, hard and soft. Three fiddlers played a lively tune next to an upturned hat placed on a nearby stump. Lesser nobles in cloaks or capes wandered the brick streets, fingering crafted baubles. Those of greater means rolled along in carriages.

The two rode straight down the wide brick avenue, past the statue of Tolin Essendon. Sculpted larger than life, the first king of Melengar was made to look like a god on his warhorse, though rumor had it he was not a big man. The artist might have aimed at capturing the full reality of Tolin rather than just his appearance, for surely the man who defeated Lothomad, Lord of Trent, and carved Melengar out of the ruins of a civil war had to have been nearly as great as Novron himself.

No one stopped or questioned Reuben and Arista as they rode by, but many bowed or curtsied. Several loud conversations actually halted when they approached, everyone staring. Reuben felt uncomfortable, but the princess appeared oblivious, and he admired her for it.

Once they were out of the city and on the open road, Arista increased their pace to a trot. At least *his* horse trotted, which was an unpleasant bouncing gait that caused the sword Ian had given him to clap against his thigh. Just as Ian had mentioned, the princess's horse did not trot. The animal pranced as if Tamarisk wished to avoid soiling his hooves.

They continued along the road, and as Reuben's comfort with the horse grew, so did a smile on his lips. He was alone with *her*, far away from Ellison and the Three Cruelties, riding a horse and wearing a sword. This was what a man's life should be, what his life might have been if he'd been born noble.

Reuben's fate was to join his father, Richard, in the service of the king as a man-at-arms. He would start on the wall or at the gate, and if lucky would work his way up to a more prestigious position like his father had. Richard Hilfred was a sergeant in the royal guard and one of those responsible for the personal protection of the king and his family. Such a title had benefits, such as securing a position for an untrained son. Reuben knew he should be thankful for the opportunity. Soldiers in a peaceful kingdom led comfortable lives, but so far life in Essendon Castle had been anything but comfortable.

In a week, on his birthday, he would don the burgundy and gold. Reuben would still be the youngest and weakest, but he would no longer be a misfit. He would have a place. That place would just never be on the back of a horse riding free on the open road with a real sword strapped to his belt. Reuben imagined the life of an errant knight, roaming the roads as he wished, seeking adventures, and gaining fame. That was the future of squires—their reward for stealing apples and beating him.

This ride might be the highpoint of his life. The weather was perfect, a late afternoon in fall. The sky a color of blue usually only seen in the crisp of winter, and the trees—many of which still had their leaves—were brilliant, as if the forests were ablaze but frozen in time. Scarecrows with pumpkin heads stood guard over the brown stalks of corn and late season gardens.

He breathed in the air; it smelled sweeter somehow.

Once they were down the road, the princess looked behind her. "Hilfred? Do you suppose they can see us from here?"

"Who, Your Highness?" he asked, amazed and grateful his voice didn't crack.

"Oh, I don't know. Anyone who might be watching...the guards on the walls or someone who may have put her needle-work down in order to climb the east tower to look out the window?"

Reuben looked back. The city was obscured by the hill and the trees. "No, Your Highness."

The princess smiled. "Wonderful." She crouched low over Tamarisk's back and made a clicking noise. The horse broke into a run, racing down the road.

Reuben had no choice but to follow, holding on to the saddle with both hands as Melancholy made a valiant effort, but the nineteen-year-old pasture mare was no match for the seven-year-old Maranon palfrey. The princess and her horse were soon out of sight and Melancholy settled to a trot, then slowed to a walk. Her sides were heaving, and nothing Reuben tried urged her to move any faster. He finally gave up and sighed in frustration.

He looked down the road, helpless. He considered abandoning Melancholy and running, for at that moment he could travel faster than the horse he was on. He didn't know what to do. What if she had fallen? If only Melancholy could gallop as fast as his heart.

Plodding to the top of the next rise, he saw the princess. Arista was on her horse, standing at the Gateway Bridge, which marked the divide between the kingdom of Melengar and their neighboring kingdom of Warric. She spotted him but made no move to flee.

At the sight of her his panic vanished. She was safe. Looking at her mounted near the riverbank, Reuben decided the ride there was not the best time of his life—*this was*.

She was beautiful, and never more so than at that moment. Sitting tall in the saddle, the wind splaying the luxurious gown across the back and side of her horse. Her long shadow reached toward him as the setting sun bathed both, playing with Tamarisk's mane and the silk of the dress the same way it played with the surface of the river. This moment was a gift, a wonder beyond words, beyond thought. Being alone with Arista Essendon in the setting sun—her in that womanly dress and he on horseback armed with a sword like a man, like a knight—was a perfect dream.

The thunder of hooves shattered the moment.

A group of horsemen burst out of the trees to Reuben's left. Three riders raced down on him. He thought they would collide with his horse, but at the last moment they veered and raced by, cloaks flying behind them. Melancholy was startled by the near miss and bolted off the road. Even if Reuben had been an expert rider, he would've had trouble staying in the saddle. Caught off guard, and unfamiliar with the motions of horses, he fell, landing on the flat of his back.

He crawled to his feet as the riders made straight for the princess and circled her, laughing and hooting. Reuben was not yet a castle guard, but Ian had given him the sword for a reason. That there were three didn't matter. That his ability with a sword could best be described, even in his own mind, as embarrassing, did not give him the slightest pause.

He drew the blade, sprinted down the hill, and when he reached them shouted, "Leave her alone!"

The laughter died.

Two of the three dismounted and drew swords together. The polished steel flashed in the low sun. As soon as they hit the ground, Reuben realized they were no more than boys, three or perhaps four years younger than himself. Their features were so similar they must have been brothers. Their swords were unlike the thick falchions of the castle guard or the short swords of the squires. They held thin, delicate weapons with adorned handguards.

"He's mine," the largest said, and Reuben could hardly believe his luck that the other two stayed back.

To defend the princess from ruffians, even if only children—to have her watch me fight for her honor, to be the one to save her. Please, Lord Maribor, I can't fail...not at this!

The boy approached all too casually, puzzling Reuben. Shorter by a good five inches, thin as a cornstalk, and with the wind at his back, he struggled to keep his wild black hair from his eyes as he strode toward him, a huge grin on his face.

When he came within a sword's length, he stopped and, to Reuben's amazement, bowed. Then he rose, sweeping his sword back and forth, such that it sang in the air. Finally, he took a stance with bent knees, his free arm behind his back.

Then the boy lunged.

His speed was alarming. The tip of the little sword slashed across Reuben's chest, failing to cut skin but leaving a gash in his smock. Reuben staggered backward. The boy advanced, shuffling his feet in a strange manner that Reuben had never seen before. The movements were fluid and graceful, as if he were dancing.

Reuben swung his sword.

The boy did not move. He did not raise his blade to parry. He only laughed as the attack missed by an inch. "I think I could just stand here trussed to a pole and you still couldn't hit me. The lady should have found a more able protector."

"That's not *a lady*. That's the Princess of Melengar!" Reuben shouted. "I won't let you harm her."

"Is she really?" He glanced over his shoulder. "Did you hear that? We've captured a princess."

I'm an idiot. Reuben felt like stabbing himself.

"Well, we aren't going to *harm* her. My fellow highwaymen and I are going to *ravage* her, *slit her throat*, and then dump the wench in the river!"

"Stop it!" Arista shouted. "You're being cruel!"

"No, he's not," the one who hadn't dismounted said. He wore a hooded cloak, and with the setting sun at his back, Reuben couldn't see his face. "He's being stupid. I say we hold her for ransom and demand our weight in gold!"

"Excellent idea," the younger of the two brothers declared. He had already sheathed his sword, pulled a wedge of cheese from his pack, and offered it to the mounted one, who took a bite.

"You'll have to kill me first," Reuben declared, and the laughter returned.

Reuben swung again. His opponent deflected the attack, his eyes locked on Reuben's face. "That was a *little* better. At least that *might* have hit me."

"Mauvin, don't!" the princess shouted. "He doesn't know who you are."

"I know!" the boy with the wild hair yelled back, and laughed. "That's what makes this so precious."

"I said stop it!" the princess demanded, riding forward.

The boy laughed again and swung his sword low toward Reuben's feet. Reuben had no idea how to counter. He thrust his blade down and in fear pulled his feet back. Off balance, he fell forward, driving his blade into the dirt. Rolling to his back and scrambling to his feet, he discovered the boy held both swords. Again laughter erupted from them all—except Arista.

"Stop it!" she shouted again. "Can't you see he doesn't know how to use a sword? He doesn't even know how to ride a horse. He's a servant. All he's ever done is split wood and carry water."

"I was only having some fun."

"Fun to you maybe." She pointed at Reuben. "He really thinks you're going to hurt me. He isn't *playing*."

"Really? Because if that's true, then he's pathetic. Honestly, if that's the best he's got, why in Maribor's name did Lawrence send this sod as your escort? A real highwayman would have killed him with the first swing, and you'd be tied to his horse while a ransom note was sent to the castle."

She scowled. "If you were real highwaymen, Tamarisk and I would have left you in the dust. You'd be coughing and spitting as we raced away."

"Not likely," the mounted one said.

"No?" The princess leaned in close, and with a whisper in Tamarisk's ear, the horse lunged as fleet as a deer and ran back up the South Road toward the city.

"Get her!" the mounted one ordered. Kicking his own horse, he chased after.

The boy with wild hair tossed Reuben's sword to him. Then he and his brother climbed atop their horses and rode after the fleeing princess, who, just as she'd said, left them all in a rising cloud of dust.

In an instant, Reuben was alone. His only consolation was that the princess wasn't in danger. Arista obviously knew the three, which furthered his humiliation. The only thing worse than being beaten by a younger boy and having them laugh at him in front of the princess was that *she* had defended *him*.

Can't you see he doesn't know how to use a sword? He doesn't even know how to ride a horse. He's a servant. All he's ever done is split wood and carry water.

Reuben stood there, staring up at the fading light and watching black clouds roll in like curtains across a stage. Tears slipped down his cheeks. He never cried, though he'd been beaten many times. He'd become used to pain, to revilements, but this was different. Reuben had always suspected he was useless; now all doubt had been removed. Whoever they were, he wished they would have killed him—at least then he wouldn't have to live with the shame.

He wiped his face with dirty hands and looked around. As night approached, mists formed near the river, and lights flickered in the windows of distant farmhouses. Melancholy was gone. She had either chased after the rest or just knew it was time to head for the stable.

Reuben Hilfred dropped the borrowed sword back into its sheath and walked home.

❧

He was tired by the time he returned. Checking in at the stable, he found Melancholy and Tamarisk safely in their stalls. Having his heart broken, taking a beating, putting in a hard day's work in the stables, then walking miles in the growing dark had left Reuben with little strength. Still, he paused partway across the courtyard to look up at the castle—and the tower.

The beautiful autumn day had turned into a dreadful fall night. A wind had risen along with a full moon, but it was masked by dark clouds. Black witch fingers of tree branches waved against the murky sky, and leaves torn from their limbs fluttered across the yard. The night turned cold, and torches whipped with the gusts. The night had a quality about it at harvest time that Reuben found disturbing. A sense of death pervaded every corner, and soon the snows would come like a blanket to drape over the dead. With that thought on Reuben's mind, he looked for any telltale sign from the tower's window. Still no light.

He was struck with the familiar mix of emotion—relief certainly, but also disappointment.

Slipping into the barracks, Reuben was met by a dozen snoring men. Boots worn during the day aired out, their scent joining company with the odor of sweat and stale beer. Reuben and his father shared their own room, but the space wasn't luxurious. Previously a storage closet, it barely fit their two

cots and a table. Before Reuben had arrived, it was a better
perk, a reward his father had received in service to the king.

A lamp still burned when he entered.

"Get supper?" his father asked.

Not a word about where he had been. His father never
asked such things, and it was only recently that Reuben began
to find that odd. The old man was on his cot, his boots off,
sword belt, chain-link, and tunic neatly stored on the hooks
and shelf. His waist belt and the three leather pouches he
always looped through it lay neatly beside his bed—always
within arm's reach. Reuben knew that one pouch held coin
and another a whetstone, but he didn't know what was in the
third pouch. Richard Hilfred lay with one arm hooked over his
face, covering his eyes. The same way he slept every night. His
father had not shaved in the last few days and dark stubble,
thick as bristled fur, shadowed his cheeks and chin. His hair,
originally black as charcoal, contained a dash of gray frosting.
Reuben's was dirty blond, which got him thinking about what
Ellison had said about his mother.

"I'm not hungry."

His father's arm came down and the old man squinted at
him. "What happened?"

A question? Since when?

"Nothing," Reuben said. He took a seat on his cot, aware
of the irony that the one time his father showed an interest,
Reuben didn't want to share.

"Where'd you get that sword?"

"Huh?" He had forgotten all about it. "Oh—Ian made me
take it."

"Take it where?"

*Four questions in a row. Is this interest, concern, or just
because my birthday is coming up?*

His father's temper was always short this time of year.

Reuben's birthday was the only day Richard had ever visited him during the years he lived with his aunt—once a year, every year without fail. Never a hug, his father usually yelled at him, with liquor on his breath. When his aunt died and his father brought him to the castle to live, Reuben had cried. He had been eleven going on twelve, and Richard Hilfred thought that was too old for tears. His father beat him. Reuben never cried again—until that evening when he watched the princess ride away, taking his hopes with her.

"The princess insisted on going for a ride," Reuben explained. "And Ian made me escort her."

His father sat up, the wood of the cot creaking. He didn't say anything for a long time, just staring until Reuben felt uncomfortable. "You stay away from her, you hear?"

"I didn't have a choice. She—"

"I don't want excuses. You just keep clear, understand?"

Reuben nodded. He learned long ago not to argue with his father. Sergeant Richard Hilfred was used to dealing with unruly men. He gave an order and it was obeyed or teeth were knocked out. That was how discipline was maintained in the ranks, in the barracks, and in their tiny room.

"Nobles are dangerous," his father went on. "They're like wild animals and will turn on you. There's no trusting them. We're nothing more to them than bugs. Sometimes they might play with us, but when they get bored, they'll crush us."

"Why are you one of the king's bodyguards, then? You're with them all day."

His father looked at him oddly, and Reuben wondered if a beating was coming. But his father's face was twisted in thought, not anger. "'Cause I was like you once, I guess. I believed in them, trusted them. Besides, there's no better job in this castle, except maybe to be assigned as *the* personal guard to a member of the royal family. Then you get access to everything, and you're treated with respect. But I'll never get the nod, so I've become a snake charmer. I know how to handle them, how to hold the blue-born behind the head so I can't be bit."

"How do you do that?"

"By never giving them a reason to notice me. I'm a shadow. As invisible and silent as a chair or a door. I'm there to guard them, but when there's no threat, my job is not to exist. You, on the other hand, got noticed, and by the princess no less. Was it fun riding with her? Everyone in the city watching you bounce in the saddle with a man's weapon on your hip and a beautiful girl at your side? Did you feel like you were one of *them*?"

Reuben said nothing, just stared at the floor.

"I see the way you look at her. She's pretty, and she'll get prettier, but you'd be smarter to cut your own eyes out now. She'll be married off in another year or two. Amrath won't wait long. He needs alliances, and he'll trade her while she's young and most valuable. She'll be sent to Alburn or Maranon. Maybe that's why he got her the horse, to give her good feelings about her new home. Doesn't matter. She's not a person—she's a commodity, like gold or silver, and the king will spend her to buy more power or protect a border. Remember that next time you look at her. Wanting to be with her is like stealing from one of his coffers. They kill people—even nobles—for that."

Reuben didn't like the conversation and opted for a new topic. "There's no light in the tower tonight."

His father stared at him for a moment to reinforce that he was serious before breaking his glare. "So?" he said, lying back down and moving slowly as if he were sore. He moved that way more and more often. His father was getting old and it showed.

"Nothing. I was just thinking that's a good thing, right?"

"It's just a room in a tower, Rue. People sometimes take candles into them."

"But it's always been dark before, except on those two nights—the night Lady Clare was burned to death and again when the chancellor died. I saw it."

"So?"

"So they say deaths come in threes."

"Who says?"

"People." Reuben unhooked the sword from his side and hung it next to his father's. It gave him no sense of pride, to do so at last. "I was just wondering, you know, what went on up there on the nights when I've seen the light." He bent down to pull off his boots, and when he looked back, his father was staring again.

"Don't be going near that tower, you understand?"

"Yes, sir."

"I mean it, Rue. If I hear you've been anywhere near there, I'll give you a worse beating than the squires did."

Reuben stared at his feet. "You know about that?"

"Your face is all marked up, you've got a line of blood staining the back of your tunic, and there's a slice in your smock. Who else? Don't worry," he said, blowing out the lamp. "Next week you'll be a castle guard."

"How will that help?"

"They'll give you chain to replace that cloth."

CHAPTER 2

ALBERT WINSLOW

A woman wielding a broom charged at them, looking as much like a witch as anyone Hadrian had ever seen. Matted black hair spilled down in brittle locks, leaving only one eye and the tip of her nose visible. The peasant skirt she wore hindered her escape from the thickets and had so many rips and muddy stains that Hadrian was certain she had tripped on it more than once.

"Stop! I need help!" she cried in desperation as if he and Royce were racing down the road. In truth the two were riding their horses at a pace just slightly faster than a man might walk. Hadrian pulled on his reins, halting while Royce continued for a bit before turning around with a curious look. Over the past year Hadrian had seen the expression often enough. He knew from experience that the puzzlement would turn to irritation as soon as his partner realized Hadrian was stopping to hear what the old woman wanted. Then would come the scowl. Hadrian was not certain what that meant—disappointment perhaps? Next, Royce's eyes would roll with open contempt and then frustration would display itself in the form of folded arms. Finally anger would rise along with his cloak's hood. Royce pulling up his hood was always a bad sign, like fur bristling on a wolf's back. A warning—and usually the only one anyone ever received.

"You must help me," the old woman shouted as she plunged through the brush, climbing out of the ditch at the side of the road. "There's a strange man in my barn, and I'm scared for my life."

"Your barn?" Hadrian asked, looking over the woman's head but not seeing a barn.

Royce and Hadrian had been traveling north on the Steward's Road near the city of Colnora. All morning they had passed numerous farms and cottages, but they had not seen either for some time.

"My husband and I have a farm 'round this bend." She pointed up the road.

"If you have a husband, why doesn't he take care of the man?"

"Dear old Danny's away. Went to Vernes to sell our lamb's wool. Won't be back for a month at least. The man in my barn is a drunken lunatic. He's naked—violent and cursing. Probably been bit by a sick dog and has *the madness*. I'm afraid to go near the barn, but I need to feed our livestock. I just don't know what to do. I'm certain he'll kill me if I set foot inside."

"You've never seen him before?"

The woman shook her head. "If you help me, if you run him off my land, I'll see that you get a fine meal for both you and your horses. I'll even wrap up some extras to take with you. I'm a fine cook, I am."

Hadrian dismounted and glanced at his friend.

"What are you doing?" Royce asked.

"It will only take a minute," Hadrian replied.

Royce sighed. The sigh was new. "You don't know this woman. This isn't your problem."

"I know that."

"So why are you helping her?"

"Because that's what people do. They help each other. If you saw a man lying in the road with an arrow in him, you'd stop, wouldn't you?"

"Of course," Royce replied, "anyone would. A wounded man is easy pickings, unless you could see from your saddle that someone else has already taken his purse."

"What? No! No one would rob a wounded man and leave him to die."

Royce nodded. "Well, no. You're right. If he has a purse and you take it, it's best to slit his throat afterward. Too many people live through arrow wounds. You taught me that. No sense risking that he might come after you."

The old woman looked at Royce aghast.

Now it was Hadrian's turn to sigh. "Don't mind him. He was raised by wolves."

Royce sat with his arms folded and a glare in his eyes. "I should never have told you about that."

"Look, it's a beautiful afternoon and we're in no hurry. Besides, you're always complaining about my cooking. I'm sure you'll be happier with her meal. I'm just going to have a quick talk with this guy." Hadrian added in a whisper, "He's probably just some poor fella desperate for shelter. I'll bet that if I can get the two of them to talk, we can work this all out. I can probably get her to pay the guy to help while her husband is away. The woman will get a hired hand, and he'll get some food and a place to sleep. What's more, we'll get a hot meal, so everybody wins."

"And when this good deed ends in disaster, will you listen to me next time and let people take care of their own problems?"

"Sure, but it'll be fine. He's just one guy. Even if he's completely unreasonable, I think we can handle a drunken squatter."

The fall had been a wet one, and the road was a muddy mess. Dead leaves hid puddles, trees were becoming black skeletons, and the songs of birds were few. Hadrian always missed them as the leaves fell and was surprised in spring at their return, having forgotten their whistling music.

Just as foretold, around the next bend was a farmhouse, if it could be called that. All of the homesteads they previously passed had been neat whitewashed cottages with thatch roofs that stood out brightly against reds and oranges. Each had fields full of golden wheat or barley ready for harvest. The woman's farm was a dilapidated shack of withered boards and tilting fences. Rising in his stirrups, Hadrian couldn't see a planted field anywhere.

"The barn is just down the hill that way." She pointed. "You can see the roof. If you like, I'll set your horses to some grain and water and start making your meal."

"You say it is just the one man?" Hadrian asked as he slipped off his horse and let the woman take the lead.

She nodded.

Hadrian, who already wore two swords hanging from his belt, unstrapped a long spadone from the side of his horse. Slipping the baldric over his shoulder, he let the massive weapon hang across his back. It was the only way the sword could be carried. The spadone was a knight's weapon, intended to be used on horseback. If he wore it on his side, the tip dragged.

"That's a lot of steel for one drunken fool," the woman said.

"Force of habit," Hadrian replied.

Royce dismounted alongside him, touching down with his right foot, then more gingerly with his left. He opened his pack and rummaged around for a bit. The woman waited until he finished; then with a final round of gratitude, she took both horses up to the house, leaving Royce and Hadrian in the farmyard.

A fieldstone well formed the centerpiece of the open space between the house and the outbuildings, and down a slope stood the barn. The whole place was badly overgrown with knee-high grass and dandelions gone to seed. Royce paused a moment and sat on the foundation of what looked to have been a small building—a chicken coop most likely, as it was too little for much else. He lifted his left foot and examined it. Hadrian could see a row of puncture marks in the soft leather.

"How's your foot?" Hadrian asked.

"It hurts."

"He had a good hold."

"Bit right through my boot."

"Yeah, that looked painful."

"So why exactly didn't you help?"

Hadrian shrugged. "It was a dog, Royce. A cute little dog. What did you want me to do, kill an innocent animal?"

Royce tilted his head, squinting into the light of the late evening sun to focus on his friend. "Is that a joke?"

"It was a puppy."

"It was not a puppy, and it was eating my foot."

"Yeah, but you were invading his home."

Royce frowned and let his foot drop. "Let's go see about this barn-invading ogre of yours."

The two headed down the grassy slope that was graced with a bounty of white and yellow wildflowers that swayed in the gentle breeze. Honeybees were still out working, droning between the daisies, bishop's lace, and wild carrots. Hadrian smiled. At least someone was hard at work farming the land here. As they approached the barn, they found it in no better shape than the house.

"You know, you didn't have to throw it out the window," Hadrian said as they walked.

Royce, who was still preoccupied with his foot, looked up.

"What did you want me to do with it? Scratch behind the little monster's ears as it gnawed my toes off? What if it started barking? That would have been a fine mess."

"It's a good thing there was a moat right under the window."

Royce stopped. "There was?"

Now was Hadrian's turn to scowl. At times like this he could never be certain whether Royce was serious or not. They had worked together for almost a year, but he was still trying to understand his new partner. One thing was certain—Royce Melborn was by far the most interesting person he had ever met but also the hardest to know.

They reached the barn, which was made of wood and field-stone and supported a straw roof. The whole structure lurched to the side, its eaves leaning against the trunk of an old maple. Several of the clapboards were gone, and the thatch roof was missing in places. The double doors hung open, but all Hadrian could see inside was darkness.

"Hello?" Hadrian called. He pushed the doors wide and peered in. "Anyone here?"

Royce was no longer behind him. He often disappeared at times like this. Being more adept at stealth, Royce enjoyed using Hadrian for the noisy distraction he was.

There was no answer.

Hadrian drew a sword and stepped inside.

The interior of the barn was much like any other except that this one showed signs of serious neglect and recent occupancy—an odd combination. The sagging loft was filled with old rotting hay. The few visible tools were rusted and wrapped in webs.

Enough light pierced the gaps in the roof and walls to reveal a man lying asleep in a pile of hay. Thin and incredibly filthy, he wore nothing but a nightshirt. Grass littered his hair, and his face was nearly lost in the unruly wreath of a wild beard.

He was curled in a ball, an old sack acting as his blanket. With his mouth hanging agape, he snored loudly.

Hadrian sheathed his weapon and then gently kicked the man's bare foot. The only response was a grumble as he resituated himself. Another prod produced a flicker of eyelids. Spotting Hadrian, he abruptly drew himself to a sitting position and squinted. "Who are you?"

"Name's Hadrian Blackwater."

"And what is it that you wish, kind sir?" His elocution was more sophisticated than his appearance suggested.

"I was sent by the lady who owns this farm to inquire why you're in her barn."

"I'm afraid I don't understand." He squinted even more.

Well spoken, but no genius. "Let's start with your name. Who are you?"

The man got to his feet, brushing hay from his shirt. "I am Viscount Albert Tyris Winslow, son of Armeter."

"Viscount?" Hadrian laughed. "Have you been drinking?"

The man looked decidedly sad as if Hadrian had inquired about a dead wife. "If only I had the coin." A realization dawned and Albert's expression turned hopeful. He got to his feet and brushed the hay from his nightshirt. "This is really all I have left, but it's made from the finest linen. I would sell it to you for a fraction of its worth. Just a single silver tenent. One simple coin. Do you have one to spend?"

"I don't need a nightshirt."

"Ah, but my good man, you could sell it." Albert spit on a dirty smudge and scrubbed the material between his fingers. "If given a good wash, this garment would be beautiful. You could easily make two silvers—perhaps three. You'd double your money most certainly."

"He's alone." Royce jumped down from the loft, hitting the ground beside them, making only the whisper of a sound.

Albert gasped and staggered backward, staring fearfully at Hadrian's partner. His reaction was not unusual—most people were frightened of Royce. Shorter than Hadrian and bearing no visible weapons, he still put people on edge. The layers of blacks and grays along with the hood did not help. But the real source of menace that caused all but the bravest to step back was simply that Royce was genuinely dangerous. People sensed it, smelling death on him the same way they smelled salt on a sailor or incense on a priest.

"So now I see...you're here to rob me, is that it?" Albert shouted. "Well, the joke is on you." He looked down at his feet and made a noise—a pathetic laugh. "I have nothing...nothing at all." Just then he dropped to his knees, put his hands to his face, and began to cry. "I have no place else to go," he whimpered. "While it provides little more shelter than the maple tree it leans on, this barn is at least a roof over my head and provides a soft place to sleep."

Royce and Hadrian stared down at him.

"So this is the great ogre, then?" Royce asked with a smirk.

"If all you needed was a place to rest, why did you threaten the farmer's wife?"

Albert wiped his face and looked up with a puzzled expression. "Who?"

"The woman who owns this farm. Why didn't you just ask her permission to sleep here?"

"I don't know what you're talking about."

"Old witchy-looking woman? She lives in the house just up the hill. She says you threatened her."

Albert looked first at Hadrian, then at Royce as if trying to decipher a riddle. "No one lives there. Have you seen it? I sleep here because the house is a disaster. The floorboards are all rotted and there's a giant wasp nest in the rafters. This farm has been abandoned for years. Any fool can tell that."

Royce looked to Hadrian, who quickly left the barn and ran up the slope.

The sun had slipped behind the tree line, casting long shadows across the fields and the house. Just as Albert had described, the building was a wreck. A good-sized sapling grew out of the kitchen floor. Even more distressing, their horses were nowhere to be seen. With slumped shoulders, he returned to the barn where Royce was gathering wood for a fire.

"See?" Royce said. "Told you this wouldn't go well. She's gone, right? The nice lady you wanted to help has fled, taking our horses and all our belongings with her."

Hadrian allowed himself to collapse on a fallen oak beam and muttered a curse about the woman.

"Don't blame her. This was all your doing. You practically begged her to rob us. Now will you listen to me next time?"

"I just can't believe someone would do such a thing." Hadrian was staring at the dirt and shaking his head.

"I know. That's why I had to show you."

Hadrian looked up. "You knew?"

"Of course I knew." Royce pointed at Albert. "Like he said, any fool could see this farm hasn't been lived in for years. And didn't you wonder why she was hiding along the road like that?"

"So why didn't you say something?"

"Because you had to learn a lesson."

"This is one costly lesson, don't you think? Our payment, our gear, not to mention the horses themselves."

"Well, that's what you get for helping people," Royce replied. "Didn't they teach you anything in Hintindar? If you had been raised properly, you'd know better." Royce turned to Albert. "Isn't that right? I bet no one has ever helped you, have they?"

"No," Albert replied with his eyes downcast.

"How long have you been here?"

Albert shrugged. "A week maybe."

"What have you been living on?"

He plucked the material of his nightshirt out from his chest. "I didn't come here in just this, you know."

"You've been selling your clothes?"

He nodded. "The road has a good flow of traffic. I had some very nice pieces. My doublet fetched enough for an entire cask of rum, but that only lasted a few days. I was serious about the nightshirt. You'd be doing me a favor if you bought it."

"That's all you have. What are you going to do, walk around naked?"

Again he shrugged. "No sense leaving anything behind. My father taught me that."

"See, this poor bastard is going to die here—penniless and miserable. He'll starve. The world is a cold, ruthless place." Royce paused to study Albert. "Probably in less than a month, and no one is going to lift a finger in his favor. That's the way the world is, cold and indifferent, even on its best days."

Hadrian sighed. "I was just trying to help."

"Yes, you can see how much she needed you. She needed to be saved from this scoundrel. Look at him. He's a monster if ever I saw one."

"You've made your point, Royce."

"I hope so. I hope we won't have to go through this again. I'll clear those stars from your eyes yet."

Royce built a pleasant fire near the door to allow the smoke to escape, and by the time he had it strong enough to put on a good-sized log, the sun had set and night arrived.

"Here," Royce said, handing Hadrian a strip of salted pork.

"So that's why you were rummaging in your pack."

"I should let you go hungry," Royce replied.

Albert stared at the bit of meat, his eyes following it.

"How long has it been since you've eaten?" Hadrian asked.

"Days. I had a bit of bread someone threw at me. That was...three days back. Yesterday I chewed some bark, which was awful, but it helped settle my stomach a bit."

Hadrian held out the strip to him, which brought a groan and an eye-roll from Royce. "Didn't we just go over this?"

"You gave it to me, didn't you? Besides, you just said that I should go hungry, and yet you gave it to me anyway. Why was that?"

"Because..." Royce scowled. "Oh, do what you want. I don't care."

Hadrian watched as Albert bit off the end and chewed, then asked, "So what's your story? Why are you here like this?"

"I know I'm a complete disgrace to the aristocracy, but—"

"Seriously? You really *are* noble?"

"I told you, I'm Viscount Albert Winslow."

"I thought that was just some line you were giving me."

"Yes. Granddad Harlan Winslow lost the family fief in a bet to the king of Warric. My father didn't do any better. He squandered what was left of the family fortune on women, gambling, and drink. Neither of them gave any thought to me and how I would survive with nothing but a title that serves as a noose around my throat."

"How's that?" Hadrian asked.

Albert took another bite. "Do you think anyone hires a noble for mucking out a stable or laying cobblestones?" He held up his hands. "I don't have a single callus. Even if I decided to leave title and pride behind, I lack any useful skills. I'm like a milk cow slapped on the backside and turned out of the barn to make her way in the forest. A chicken, returned to the wilds to fend for myself."

"I don't think chickens have ever been wild," Hadrian said.

"Exactly." Albert paused to stare at the remainder of the salt pork strip. "Your friend is right. This is just prolonging the inevitable. It's a waste. Here." He held out the meat.

"Keep it," Hadrian said, tilting his head at Royce. "I'm supposed to be learning a lesson."

"Oh, shut up, the both of you. I have more." Royce pulled another strip of pork from his vest and handed it to Hadrian.

"So that's my miserable story," Albert said. "How about you two?" He looked at Hadrian. "I'm guessing you're his apprentice?"

Hadrian laughed. "No. We're... business partners."

"What line?"

"Procurement," Royce said.

"What kind?"

"Any kind," Royce answered.

Albert stared at them for a moment; then his eyes widened. "You *are* thieves."

"He is." Hadrian pointed to Royce. "I'm new to this."

"Really? What did you used to do?"

Hadrian thought a moment. "Kill people."

"Assassin?" Albert sounded impressed.

"Soldier."

"Oh. Guess that explains the three swords. How's business? Clearly you've been making out better than I. What do you do? Pick pockets? No, with three swords here you're probably highwaymen, right? Hold up merchants? Or do you kidnap and ransom?"

Royce chuckled.

"What's funny?"

"We don't do those things," Hadrian explained.

"No?"

"No. Stealing like that, it's... wrong," Hadrian declared.

"But you're thieves, right? You *are* thieves?"

"Like I said, he is."

"Oh, I see. You're the honorable soldier—but wait. Why are you working with him, then?"

"Same reason you're trying to sell your nightshirt," Royce replied.

"For rum?"

"Rum?" Hadrian said. "Not food?"

Albert shrugged. "That's what I do with all my money. It helps take my mind off the fact that I spent all my money on rum." He quickly added, "So what do you do, if you don't rob people?"

"Contracts, mostly," Hadrian replied. "People who need help come to us and we—"

Royce grumbled. "You see how he thinks? We don't help people. We use them. Let's say...oh I don't know..." Royce whirled his fingers in the air as if trying to conjure a thought. "Let's say—purely as an example—a merchant sets up shop across the street from an established one. The established merchant, let's call him Bernie, doesn't like it, so he tells the new guy—we'll call him Andrew—to leave. Let's say Andrew doesn't. The next thing you know, some thugs tear Andrew's place apart and break his wife's arm. Then Bernie tells Andrew that he needs to leave or the next time he'll be dead."

"So you're the thugs?" Albert asked.

"No, we"—he looked at Hadrian—"we help the new merchant."

"How so?"

"I'm a creative problem solver."

"You bust up Bernie's store?"

"No, that would get Andrew killed."

"What, then?"

"I hire the same thugs to trash the store of the wealthiest merchant in town—and tell them Bernie supplied the gold.

Next day someone starts an ugly rumor that ol' Bernie is causing trouble for his competition. The story is easily confirmed because of the first incident. The wealthy merchant, we can call him Sebastian, has connections—they always do. The next day a fire burns Bernie's shop to the ground. Unfortunately for him, Bernie's caught in the fire, having accidentally fallen asleep in his shop—tied to his bed. The money we paid the thugs is only half of what Andrew paid us. We pocket the rest. Once I get Hadrian schooled in the art of intimidation, we'll make more."

"They shouldn't have killed him," Hadrian said.

"See what I have to deal with? Problem is, you don't get too many jobs like that. But what you said about ransom is true. There can be good money in that if you grab the right target. Even he can't complain too much about that kind of work."

"Well, in return for the meal, let me offer you a bit of advice," Albert said. "We're just outside the city of Colnora, and if I were you, I wouldn't pull any kind of job around here, or the Black Diamond will be after you."

"Black Diamond?" Hadrian asked. "Is that the city patrol?"

Albert chuckled, and Royce shook his head, looking at Hadrian as if he had dropped his pants in public.

"You're not from around here?" Albert asked.

"From Hintindar, a tiny manorial village south on the Bernum River."

"And you've never heard of the Black Diamond?"

"I haven't been in the area much. I've been away in the east for quite a few years. Only returned about a year ago, when I met him." Hadrian gestured at Royce. "Since then we've roamed around, but"—he looked curiously at Royce—"we've never come near Colnora until today."

"Oh," Albert said. "Well, the Black Diamond is a thieves' guild. Some would say *the* thieves' guild. The most powerful and extensive one in the world. Their headquarters is just down that road in Colnora. And like any thieves' guild, they don't like interlopers. If they find out you're practicing your trade around here, they'll track you down and slit your throats. And trust me, they'll know. The Black Diamond is not an organization to toy with. Kings have been known to bow to them rather than face their wrath."

"Well, I hope they catch up with that woman who stole our horses, then," Hadrian said.

"They already know about her." Royce threw a strand of yellow grass into the fire where it blackened and curled. "She was Black Diamond."

"What do you—" Hadrian shook his head. "I can't believe you let her take our horses and gear."

"What part of 'you need to learn a lesson' didn't you understand?"

"You're insane, do you know that?"

"Yeah, well, you're not the first to bring it up. But there's nothing more to be done tonight. I suggest we settle in and get some sleep."

Royce scrambled up to the loft and bedded down there. Hadrian continued to stare after him in shock for a minute before giving up and mounding a pile of hay near the fire. "I honestly can't believe him sometimes."

༞

The nights had turned chilly and by morning there was a damp fog hanging in the air. Royce was the first one up. He got the fire going again, which surprised Hadrian, as they had nothing to cook. He likely built it out of boredom while he waited for Albert and Hadrian to wake. Most people would have done it to stave off the cold, but Hadrian had never seen Royce affected by the temperature, cold or hot.

"Morning," Albert said as Hadrian sat up, shivered, and moved to the fire with the rest of them.

He scrubbed his face with his hands and wiped his eyes clear. The day was cloudy and the valley filled with a thick mist. Hadrian enjoyed mornings like this, quiet and serene, like a drowsy pause a lazy world was taking. He crouched to catch the warmth of the fire while dodging the smoke.

"So where were you two headed before misfortune dropped you here with me?" Albert asked. He lay sprawled next to Hadrian like a dog before a hearth.

"Up north. A place called Medford," Hadrian replied, and began brushing hay off his shirt. "Royce and I have some friends up there we want to visit. Ever hear of it?"

Albert nodded. "Capital of Melengar, royal seat of King Amrath and Queen Ann. They have two children, a boy and girl. What's their names…begin with A's. All the Essendons' names begin with A's—Alric and Arista. Yes, that's them. Close friends of the Pickerings. Have you ever seen Belinda Pickering?"

Both Hadrian and Royce shook their heads.

"She's a fine beauty, but her husband has a bit of a temper. He's very protective of her and good with a sword. But if you ever get a chance to see her, it's worth chancing a look."

"You know a lot about these people," Royce said.

Albert shrugged. "I'm noble. We all know each other. There are many parties, balls, and feasts. Not to mention the holidays and weddings. Most of us are actually related."

Royce tapped his fingers to his lips. "Nobles have a lot more money than merchants."

"Well, not all, clearly." Albert made a wry smile; then the smile dropped and his eyes lit up. "Yes…yes, they do. And they also have problems—problems that could use creative solutions. Court is a very interesting place, a bloodless battlefield where rumors can ruin lives and embarrassments can be worse than death. Many would pay great sums to avoid—or cause—such humiliations. The trick is discovering who needs what done and arranging for meetings."

Royce nodded. "I suspect nobles won't speak to the likes of us."

"Of course not. They would never stoop so low as to confer with a commoner, much less a dubious one. They prefer to do business with their own kind. You would need a go-between, a representative, but he'd have to be noble."

"Too bad we don't know anyone like that," Royce said.

"Well...with a haircut, shave, some new clothes—"

"And no more rum," Royce said.

Albert grimaced. "But—"

"No buts. You can stay here and die or work for us, and if you work for us, you work sober."

Albert rubbed his bristly chin. "That really should be an easy choice, shouldn't it?"

Hadrian spoke up. "Exactly how are we going to provide all this? Have you forgotten that we've lost everything? At the moment we're not much better off than he is."

Royce smiled and stood up. "Details, details. Are you two ready to go?"

"I suppose you'll want to hunt down that witch of a woman and kill her?" Hadrian inquired with a tone of distaste as they all began to walk up the slope of wildflowers.

"You know," Albert said, "for a soldier you don't seem to care much for killing."

"I've seen enough of that to last three lifetimes. And I don't relish the thought of hunting a woman or like knowing what he'll do when we find her."

"We aren't going after the witch," Royce said.

"Really?" Hadrian asked. "But what about our horses and gear?"

"Look." Royce pointed up the remainder of the hill at the house. There, standing tethered to what was left of the porch, were their horses.

"I don't understand." Hadrian trotted the rest of the way and checked their packs and saddles. "Everything's here."

"They've been brushed and I expect fed and watered too," Royce said. "Oh, and look." He reached down and bent one of the horse's legs to reveal a bright shoe underneath. "Freshly shod."

"I don't get it. Why would she return them?"

"I suspect she, or someone she reports to, read the note I left in my pack."

"You left a note for the thieves' guild? What did it say?"

"Just that these horses are my animals and that they might want to reconsider taking them."

Albert and Hadrian exchanged looks of bewilderment.

"They know me. We have an arrangement. They leave me alone...and I leave them alone."

"You leave them alone?" Albert said in a mocking tone.

Royce smiled at him—not a friendly smile. Then he searched his pack and pulled out a small bit of parchment.

"What does it say?" Albert asked.

"Please accept our apologies for this inconvenience," Royce recited, then chuckled before finishing. "The bitch didn't know."

Royce held up the parchment and in a loud voice said, "Accepted."

Albert nervously looked at the trees around them. "They're here?"

"They're watching to see what I'll do."

"And what will you do?" Hadrian asked.

Royce looked at Albert. "I think I'll try fishing in a bigger pond, now that I have better bait. Shall we ride to Medford?"

The viscount looked back in the direction of the barn and then down at his filth-covered nightshirt. He nodded.

"You can ride with me," Hadrian said as he swung his leg over the saddle. Then addressing his friend he said, "Well, I hope you learned your lesson."

Royce raised an eyebrow. "Me?" He untied his horse and climbed on.

"You said the world is a cold, ruthless place."

"It is."

"You also said Albert would die from starvation in that barn—that no one would help him." He smiled broadly and reached out to the viscount. "Care for a hand up, Albert?"

"I'm only helping him for the profit he can—"

"Doesn't matter. You were wrong."

"I was not. I—"

"Even if you're doing it for selfish reasons, you're still helping to save his life. It just goes to show that good can come from helping a stranger, and it proves that the world isn't so bad after all."

Royce scowled. He opened his mouth to speak, then stopped and scowled again. Finally he just raised his hood and kicked his horse into a trot.

"I'll make a human being out of him yet," Hadrian said to Albert as they trotted off.

CHAPTER 3

THE COUNCIL OF AMRATH

The chair was a problem. Amrath Essendon could sit a horse for two days straight and feel fine, but five minutes in a chair left him miserable. He was unaccustomed to being still. The best days of his life had been spent with a sword in his hand and blood on his face. As king of a peaceful realm, he had few good days. Most were like this one. Locked in a gray room, trapped in a stiff chair, and surrounded by powerful men—men he couldn't trust.

Percy Braga was speaking again. Amrath could tell as much by the movement of his lace cuffs as by the drone of his voice. The new chancellor had a habit of gesturing too much and using too many words. Bad upbringing and excessive education ruined the brain for thinking. Pity, as he was an exceptional fighter. Even his conversational gestures betrayed his training with a blade. His balanced steps and wrist movements reminded Amrath of his best friend, Leo Pickering. While both were accomplished swordsmen, the king did not care for their fighting style—too much finesse. Such delicacy might look impressive in a Wintertide contest, but on a blood-soaked battlefield, Amrath would rather have an axe.

"As a result, we could see another flare-up in the trade war with Warric," Braga was saying. "We have reason to believe that Chadwick will most certainly raise their import tax. Glouston might follow—they have been known to. If that happens, we will lose one hundred tenents for every two we make."

"And all this is because of the church?" King Amrath lay more than sat in his chair, drooping like so much wax facing heat.

"It is because of the pressure they are applying in retaliation for you not adopting many of their policies here in Melengar. The church feels that—"

"Don't talk to me about the bloody church," Amrath growled. "That's all I hear now. I'm tired of it."

"Maybe you should take a nap, Your Majesty," Simon Exeter said, "and leave the task of running the kingdom to those of us with a mind to do so."

Amrath focused his glare on Lord Exeter. If there was an image for *trouble*, he was looking at it. Even his choice of insisting on wearing the black and white colors of a sheriff's uniform was designed to provoke—to remind everyone of his office as high constable. What bothered the king the most was that Simon was his cousin and their families' resemblance was strong. But Simon was not an axe, nor a rapier like Leo and Braga. Simon was a broadsword, and a sharp one at that.

The king had expected an outburst from him. This was the first formal meeting since the appointment of the new chancellor, and Amrath was surprised it took Simon this long. All the Lords of Exeter had been hard men. It was in their blood and the reason why they had always been chosen to defend East March. They made for ruthless guard dogs, but such an animal needed a firm hand lest it turn on its master. Amrath leaned forward so that his bushy beard brushed the table. "You want to try and put me to bed, Simon? Think you're man enough, do you?"

Simon allowed himself a smile before saying, "My point, Your Majesty, is that you need to be more concerned than you are of an Imperialist church turning your friendly neighbors into our enemies. Today it is an escalating trade war. Tomorrow there will be troops marching over the Gateway Bridge—very pious, very faithful troops no doubt, but just as intent on melting that crown of yours."

"I'm well aware of the possible dangers the church poses," the king said.

"All evidence to the contrary." Simon glared not at the king but at the chancellor.

Braga stiffened. "I can't say I care for your implication."

"And I can't say I care for *you*, Lord Chancellor."

"That's enough, Simon," Count Pickering snapped.

Good old Leo. Amrath found himself smiling at his friend.

Leo Pickering was the only face in the room Amrath trusted. The only one he could drink with and not worry how drunk he got. They had been friends since boyhood. In their youth they had nearly started a war with Glouston but in the end had won the hand of the fair Lady Belinda Lanaklin for Leo. Those were the days. Amrath had a knack for getting them in trouble, and it always fell to Leo to get them out. Even in the council room his friend was still watching Amrath's back, still his king's ever-ready sword.

Simon turned to Leo with an expression of surprise that may have been authentic. "You of all people should side with me. The chain of chancellor should have gone to one of us—to me by virtue of lineage or to you by the king's favoritism."

Leo rose to his feet, but Simon gestured for him to sit down. "No need to take offense. I'm not insulting you—not this time. Granted, I would have objected had His Majesty appointed you to the chancery rather than me, and I would have used your friendship with the king against you. But I would kiss your boots and personally place the chain of state on your shoulders rather than accept this import from southern Maranon—this third son of a wanting earl—as our chancellor."

"Lord Exeter!" Lord Valin exclaimed. The old revered warrior slammed his fist on the table before him.

This did nothing to deter Simon. "The man was a Seret Knight."

"We know that, Simon," Amrath said. His voice tired of repeating. "We knew that before he arrived. We knew it last week when you complained then."

"But did you also know he applied to be a sentinel? My recent investigations uncovered that little secret just yesterday."

Serets were the martial branch of the Nyphron Church, generally disliked by all except the most devout, as their claimed jurisdiction had no boundaries. Kings suffered their intrusion and tribunal judgments of their citizenry or faced sanctions imposed by the church. Sentinels, on the other hand, were despised, hated, and feared by everyone, including monarchs and even ranking church officials. They were the high officers of the seret army— only a handful ever appointed—and all known to be fanatics. Legend held that a sentinel once charged a king with heresy. No one dared to interfere when the sentinel carried out the death sentence by burning the king in the center of his own city. Likely it was only a fable, but the church never denied it.

"It that true?" Amrath asked Braga.

Heads turned toward the chancellor.

"As Lord Exeter has so clearly pointed out," Braga replied, "I am the third son of an earl. The church is the preferred refuge when you have no part to play in extending your family's lineage, and my skills did not match those required for the priesthood. Being a knight of the Nyphron Church was one of the few options that suited my abilities. Seeking to be chief among them is merely the result of my desire to excel."

"But a sentinel is more than just a senior position," Simon explained. "The sentinel's sworn duty—besides keeping the faith pure—is to locate the descendant of the old imperial empire and return him to power. Such an event would require all the kings—including His Majesty—to be stripped of their crowns." Simon turned to Amrath. "And yet this is the man you chose to put in the kingdom's highest office. A man who actively sought the job of destroying your throne."

"Are you accusing me of treason?" Braga asked.

Simon sneered, an expression complemented by his goat's beard and the way he wore his hair pulled back.

"Careful, Simon," Leo warned. "You're about to be challenged to a duel you can't win."

Braga glared at Lord Exeter. "I will not stand here and—"

"You will do as you're commanded by your king—*both of you*." Amrath stood up, as did everyone else. He let his voice drop to a growl, which along with his size, beard, and prowess at wrestling had earned him the nickname of *the Bear*. He wanted the argument to end. After a day of debate, his head was hurting. He paused a moment to see if any fight remained in either. In their silence, he resumed his seat. "I think I've had enough for one day. Braga and Leo remain. The rest of you… I'll see you at the party."

༄

"I was right about Exeter," Amrath said.

He was out of his chair now that there was only Braga and Leo. As monarch, whenever he rose so did everyone else, which was one of the reasons he felt trapped by the chair. But Leo ignored formality when the rest were gone, and Braga never sat. He was a strange man, darker skinned than most and possessing the thick black hair common to a southern native from Maranon. They were almost as dark as Calians down that way, especially along the coast. Braga was swarthy, handsome, and always moving. Just watching him tired the king. By contrast Leo was relaxed and comfortable. He rocked back in his seat and put his feet on the table, boots clicking to a tune in his head. Dear Maribor, how he loved Leo. Amrath would have gone insane by now if not for that man.

"Are you speaking to me or Percy?" Leo asked.

"Both of you."

"He wants my job," Braga said.

"If only that were the case," Amrath replied. "The problem is that he wants *my* job. He just can't figure a way to get it. You're just this season's target."

"Should I resign? It's not like I have been in this position long. I've hardly—"

"No!" Amrath and Leo responded together.

"But Lord Exeter made a good point." Braga motioned toward Leo. "Count Pickering holds your confidence. He should be chancellor."

Amrath gazed out the window. He often wandered the room without thought or pattern but always found himself at the window, drawn by the fresh air and open sky. "That's not possible. You see, that's the problem with Simon—though he can be a piss pot, he's also usually right. It's what makes him such a problem." Outside, the king spotted the apple merchant, wheeling his cart out the main gate and returning to Gentry Square. *What must life be like for such a man? A man with no worries or concerns. A man whose cousins don't conspire against him?* "So, yes, I would love to make Leo chancellor, but I can't because, as Simon pointed out, there is the little issue of favoritism. Everyone knows we're close. Leo holds the wealthiest province in Melengar, and we aren't related, not even by marriage. If I gave him an office, the nobles would—" Amrath threw his hands up in a frustration that he lacked words to express. Being king was supposed to mean—should mean—that he could do as he wished. The truth of the matter was that his life was just a little short of imprisoned servitude to power-hungry nobles. The emperor of the ancient Novronian Empire had it easy—he was a god and ruled without reproach. "Why, I can't even name him treasurer or keeper of the privy seal, much less chancellor!"

"So why didn't you name Lord Exeter as chancellor? He is your cousin and, unless I'm wrong, next in line to the throne after your own children, yes?"

Leo chuckled. "You're absolutely right."

"Two reasons," Amrath said, turning and bending back a finger. "First is his obsessive hatred of Imperialists. The man thinks that anyone who believes in the Heir of Novron or supports the Nyphron Church is his mortal enemy. Being a reigning king, I'd like to see this fantasy of a restored empire fade away, too, and a man with Exeter's views is good to have around. My forefathers waged wars to make Melengar a free and independent kingdom. My crown was won by spilling rivers of blood, and the idea that the Imperialists will one day find the lost heir and everyone will just take a knee to him is… well, it's offensive, damn it! The church continues to promote this poisonous myth. Now it appears Warric is slipping into their twisted mentality. And if the most powerful kingdom in Avryn can succumb to this insanity, anyone can. Fact is, I agree with Simon. I just can't afford to make enemies of Clovis or his son."

"And the other?" Braga asked.

"The other what?" The king looked back and forth between the two.

"The other reason you can't appoint Simon as chancellor," Leo reminded him.

"Oh." The king presented Braga with a wry smile. "Because

I hate him. That's why he's such a pain. He really can't get in any worse with his king. So he needles me and revels in his position of being one of the most powerful and disliked nobles in the realm. Worst thing about it is," Amrath grumbled as he looked back out the window, "if I were to get into a scuffle with Warric, there are no two men I'd rather have at my side than Leo and Simon. It's true that he hates me. Nothing personal—he just hates everyone, really. I've never met a more disagreeable codpiece. But he loves the kingdom. And while he may be misguided, arrogant, and ambitious beyond reason, he's also tireless in his efforts to keep Melengar safe. That is why I appointed him lord high constable. I imagine there was a mass exodus of thieves and cutthroats the day of that announcement. But don't worry, once you get to know Simon better, you'll learn to truly despise him the way Leo and I do."

"I'm just not certain I'm right for this job," Braga said. "I'm not native to the kingdom, and as he said, I was a knight of the Church of Nyphron."

"Which, if you take politics out of it, is a true achievement," Leo pointed out. "The seret's reputation for excellence is well known."

"Still, I've only been here a year—"

"Percy," the king said in a gentle voice. "When you married Clare, you became family."

"Blood is thicker than paper," Braga challenged.

"You're assuming Simon has blood. We haven't yet determined if he even has a heart," Leo said. "But you're right, and while I find you more appealing than Lord Exeter, it is because of his lineage that I, and the rest of the nobles, would back him should something happen to the Bear and his family." Leo made a show of shivering. "Stay healthy, Your Majesty."

The king smirked. "Yeah, that's why I won't die, because I don't wish to inconvenience you."

"I'll take that as a promise."

Braga looked down at the chain as if it had gained weight.

"If Clare had lived, at least…" Braga began. An awkward pause followed.

Clare had been Amrath's sister-in-law, the aging second daughter of Llewellyn Ethelred, Duke of Rise. The duke had taken too long finding her a proper husband and at the death of her father she asked to live with her sister Queen Ann in Melengar. Amrath could only guess at the state of the court in Aquesta that a granddaughter of the reigning king would choose to flee her own home for a neighboring kingdom. Amrath and Ann were happy to take her in, as she was a gentle soul. A bit bookish, living in exile, and over the age of thirty, they all expected her to remain unwed. Everyone thought she would grow old as the kindly spinster aunt to the royal children, but then Bishop Saldur introduced her to Percy Braga and everything changed. Clare found the dashing young swordsman charming. For months he and Ann commented at Clare's brimming smile.

"She loved you very much, and I never saw her happier than the day you took the oath of office. She believed in you, and so do I." Amrath left the window and clapped his big hand on Braga's shoulder, giving it a squeeze. "You're the only one for the job, Percy. I wouldn't dare give Simon any more power. And I can't give it to Leo. Being from Maranon actually has its benefits. Singling out any other noble would cause divisions and launch rumors that could lead to bigger problems than just a bruised ego. You have no ties, no known bias. You'll be called to pass judgment over all of them in the chancery, to make laws and keep the rolls. And only a man with no affiliation can successfully do that."

"Yes," Leo put in, "only a man as equally despised as you can hope to be effective as chancellor of our unruly mob of nobles. In that way you're Simon's equal. Being a source of universal hatred, you are free to act as your conscience dictates."

"Wonderful," Braga said, but managed a smile.

Amrath clapped him soundly on the back, staggering the smaller man forward a step.

"Is it really true?" Leo asked. "Did you actually apply to be a sentinel?"

Braga nodded.

"Becoming a sentinel is no easy feat."

"Clearly I failed." He folded his hands behind his back. "I didn't have a lot of prospects, you understand. And the church is more dominant in Maranon than here. I felt that since I had won the Silver Shield, the Golden Laurel, as well as the Grand Circuit Tournament of Swords at Wintertide that I would be considered. After all, I had no problem with my induction into the Seret Knights, but…"

"What happened?"

"The Patriarch explained that I did not exhibit the necessary level of devotion to be a sentinel."

Amrath laughed. "That just means you're not a lunatic. All of them are insane, you know." Braga smiled at the king, but it was the same polite look Amrath often got from those unable to disagree because of his position.

"Having failed, having been judged as inferior, I no longer felt comfortable in the black and red. After resigning from the order, I really didn't know what to do. That's when Bishop Saldur approached me about coming here. I think he felt I might be of some use to him at Mares Cathedral."

"Sauly means well," Amrath said, "but anyone can tell you're not deacon material."

"I just hope I'm chancellor material."

"Don't worry about that," the king said. "If I were you, I'd be more concerned about how you'll fare against Leo here in this year's Wintertide fencing match. I'm going to be in for a treat, aren't I? I'll get to see two men dance in public."

Leo scowled. "Just ignore him."

Braga raised his eyebrows. "But he's the king."

"All the more reason."

CHAPTER 4

THE GHOST OF THE HIGH TOWER

Reuben placed another log up on its end and, with a single stroke, split it. The trick was to cut the wood clean in one swing but not plant the head of the axe in the chopping block. Sinking the blade added work and chewed up the block. Sometimes the grain and knots made it impossible; then he was stuck with using wedges and the blunt face of the axe. While just brute work, he'd developed a skill that made his swing more likely to succeed on the first try, and he liked to think he was good at something. As if to prove him wrong, his last stroke had too much force and the axe went firmly into the block. He left it there and tossed the splits aside. When done, he reached out once more for the old worn handle and paused. This was the last day he would ever split wood. The thought surprised him. Looking at the chopping block and knowing he would never again swing that axe was the first bit of reality to invade his routine.

Being a soldier would be a step up. Now he would receive a wage that he could spend as he saw fit. Although most of that salary he would never see, as it would go toward paying for his food, uniform, weapons, and living space—something his father's pay had covered so far. He should have been excited at the impending promotion, at the recognition that he was a man at last, only he didn't feel like one. The squires had beaten, and a child had bested, him both in the same day. He didn't feel worthy to take the burgundy and gold. He was only fit to open doors, haul water, and split wood. These were the tasks he was good at, what he was comfortable with, and what was being taken from him.

Hidden from the castle doors, Reuben was splitting wood under the oak on the far side of the woodpile when he heard them. He'd thought the stormy sky would have been enough to keep the squires indoors learning table manners, helping to dress their lords, or listening to the tales of the knights. The sound of the approaching laughter proved him wrong.

"What do we have here?" Ellison rounded the woodpile with the Three Cruelties in tow. "Muckraker, how wonderful. I was looking for you." Ellison stepped in front of Reuben while the others circled around.

There was no chance to run. The best he could do was yank the axe from the block, but a heavy splitting axe was a slow weapon, and each of the squires wore their swords—metal this time.

"Word has it that you're to be sworn in as a guard of the castle tomorrow. There are complications with beating a soldier in the king's service, so this will be my last chance to pay you back for the bruise."

Reuben only then noticed a small purple mark on Ellison's cheek.

"The bad news is that you'll spend your first day of service in the infirmary."

Ellison punched him in the jaw. The blow stunned him and Reuben staggered back into Horace, who shoved him to the ground. Reuben crouched, dazed for a moment before jumping up and breaking the axe free of the block by slapping the handle. He held it with both hands. Horace seized Reuben from behind in a bear hug. While not skilled with a sword, Reuben knew his way around an axe. He thrust backward with the handle, jamming it hard into Horace's broad gut. The big arms let go and the squire dropped to his knees. Ellison rushed forward, but Reuben expected that and dodged behind Horace, who was still doubled over. Ellison and Horace both fell.

That's when Willard and Dills drew their swords. Once he got to his feet, so did Ellison.

Reuben had at least managed to put his back to the woodpile. Now all four were out in front.

"Get his arms and legs. I don't want him to ever forget us," Ellison said. "We'll each carve our initials into him."

"My name's short enough to write the whole thing," Dills declared.

They closed in, jabbing, leering, and grinning.

"Is this a private party or can anyone play?" a familiar voice asked.

Looking over Ellison's shoulder, Reuben spotted the wild-haired boy who had bested him at the bridge, the one the princess had called Mauvin.

"No one wants you here, Pickering, so go catch your stupid frogs."

"Hey, Fanen," the boy shouted over his shoulder and toward the castle keep. "It's the hero from yesterday, the one who risked himself to save Arista." He looked at Reuben. "What kind of trouble have you gotten yourself into now?"

"None of your business, boy," Dills snapped.

At the sound of the word *boy*, Reuben saw Mauvin grin.

His younger brother came around the woodpile a moment

later. When he did, Mauvin pointed. "No one at the castle can see a thing."

This was exactly what Reuben guessed Ellison had realized, only now Ellison and the Three Cruelties looked less pleased.

"Muckraker and I have a score to settle," Ellison explained. "This has nothing to do with you two."

"Muckraker? Oh, you're mistaken. His name is Hilfred and he's a friend of ours," Mauvin said, surprising all, but none more than Reuben. "We had great fun sparring a few days ago. Hilfred didn't do so well, but he *was* fighting a Pickering." The boy winked at him. "I'm sure he'll fare much better against you, even though he only has an axe and all four of you have swords."

"But still, that's not very sporting," Fanen said.

"Downright rude if you ask me." Mauvin continued to grin. "Hilfred, how dare you hog all of these squires to yourself. I demand that Fanen and I get to play too."

The Pickering boys drew their swords in unison with elegant ease. As they did, Dills and Willard spun to face them. "Didn't one of you say something about carving initials?" Mauvin asked. Looking at Dills, he added, "That will be fun. And just to jog your dim-witted memory, I'm the son of Count Leopold Pickering of Galilin, one of the five Lords of the Charter—no one calls me *boy*."

"Mauvin? Fanen?" Shouts came from the direction of the castle.

"Here, Alric—we're on the other side of the woodpile," Mauvin shouted back, a touch of regret in his voice.

Alric? Reuben thought. *It can't be.* A moment later none other than the Prince of Melengar rounded the pile. He was dressed in a lavish three-quarter-length white satin tunic with extensive embroidery, heavy gold piping, and full sleeves and broad triple-folded cuffs. His suede belt, while lacking even a dagger, was ornamented with metallic studs and a buckle that Reuben guessed to be worth more than he and his father could ever hope to earn if both of them lived to be a hundred.

The squires all dropped to one knee. Reuben followed suit an instant later. Neither of the Pickerings so much as bowed.

"What's going on?" the prince asked.

Mauvin was frowning at him. "Fanen, Hilfred, and I were about to have some fun...then you ruined it. You always ruin it."

The prince looked at the kneeling squires, puzzled, until he spotted the drawn swords. "Hilfred?" he asked; then, turning, he made eye contact with Reuben. "Oh, the hero from the Battle of Gateway Bridge!" He looked back at the squires and added, "He risked his life to defend my sister against a band of highwaymen. Don't tell me this pool of pond scum was thinking of taking advantage of our friend?"

Reuben could hardly believe his ears. *The prince had been the third horseman who'd chased the princess?*

"We were just leaving, Your Highness," Ellison said, slipping his sword into its sheath and standing up. He took one step away when the prince stepped in front of him.

"You haven't answered my question, Ellison." Alric moved uncomfortably close.

"No, Your Highness, we would never think of harming a friend of *yours*."

Alric looked at Reuben. "Is he telling the truth? I can have him ripped apart by dogs, you know. I love dogs. We use them to hunt, but they aren't allowed to actually take down or eat their quarry. Always thought that was a shame, you know? I think they would appreciate the opportunity. It could be fun too. We could just let these fools run and bet on how far they can get before the dogs catch them."

"I bet Horace doesn't make it to the gate," Mauvin said; then all heads turned to Reuben.

Ellison looked at him, too, his face frozen in a tense, wide-eyed stare.

"I wasn't aware of any threat from Squire Ellison, Your Highness," Reuben replied.

"Are you sure?" Alric pressed, and flicked a small yellow leaf off Ellison's shoulder. "We don't have to use the dogs." He smiled and tilted his head toward the Pickerings. "They'd love to teach them a lesson, you know. In a way they're a lot like hunting dogs—they never get the chance to kill anyone either. Ever since they reached their tenth birthday, no one has been stupid enough to challenge them."

"I was, Your Highness," Reuben said.

That got a laugh from the Pickerings and the prince, although Reuben didn't know why. "Yes, you did, didn't you?"

"That's why you're our friend," Mauvin explained.

"He didn't know who we were," Fanen pointed out. "He had no idea about the skill of a Pickering blade."

"It wouldn't have mattered," Reuben said. His blood was still up from the fight, and his mouth ran away with him. "If I thought you were there to harm the princess, I would still have fought you."

A moment of silence followed this and Reuben watched as Alric smiled; then he glanced at Mauvin and they laughed again. "Tell me, Hilfred, how are you at catching frogs?"

ॐ

"Did you see Ellison-Jellison piss himself when I said I could have dogs tear him apart?" the prince asked as they trotted along the road.

"Ha! Yeah," Mauvin replied. "Thought he might faint like a girl."

"Can you really do that?" Fanen asked.

The two brothers were only separated by a year, but they were very different. Fanen kept his hair neat, his thoughts to himself, and when he did speak it was in a soft voice, which was difficult to hear above the clapping of the hooves and the rising wind.

Alric laughed. "*Sure*, Fanen. I'll just go to my dad and say, 'Hey, do you mind if I have Lord Trevail's son torn apart by dogs?' "

Mauvin chuckled as if he alone understood some joke. Although Reuben also thought the boy just enjoyed laughing. He did a lot of it. "What do you think your dad would say?"

Alric shrugged. "I wouldn't want to be there to find out."

Alric insisted Reuben accompany them to a swamp for a bit of frog hunting, and there was no refusing the son of the king. Not that he wanted to. Despite the humiliation of the previous day, he found he liked the trio. And after saving him from a severe beating, he was more than happy to join them frog hunting—or even dragon hunting if that had been the prince's preference. Reuben learned they each had a small collection of frogs at the castle. Mauvin in the lead with eight, but Fanen, with five, had the most diverse assortment. Alric had the least with only four. Being the prince, Alric probably did not like being outdone. He told Ian to fetch their mounts and bring one for his new pal, Hilfred. They all grabbed cloaks, and for the second time in less than a week, Reuben rode out of the city in the presence of royalty.

They traveled north past the King's Road toward East March. The late afternoon sun dipped low in the west, and farms in the shadows of hills already had their lamps lit. Cows were making the trip back to the barns, and smoke was rising from chimneys as the temperature turned colder. They were a good hour from the city walls, where the farms were thin and the hills forested. When they veered off the road, it was toward what looked to be a good-sized pond surrounded by thickets, forests, and mist. The boys called it Edgar's Swamp because Edgar the Carpenter had told them about it. The best place in the world to catch frogs, he had declared.

They dismounted and walked their horses the last bit to the water's edge.

"Isn't it a bit late to be going all the way out here...ah... Your Highness?" Reuben asked.

"Best time to catch them is right after the sun sets," Alric replied.

"I'm surprised your father allows you to go all this way at night without an escort."

The prince chuckled. "He wouldn't. I had to assure him I had a guard."

"Who?"

"You."

"But I'm not a guard yet!"

"Really? That's strange, because when I told my father that Hilfred had agreed to ride out with us, he was fine with that."

Reuben was stunned. "He thought you were talking about *my father*!"

"Really? You think so?" Alric was having a hard time keeping a straight face. "You know...you may be right."

The three broke out in laughter again and continued to do so even as they tied their reins to a fallen tree on the edge of the pond, giving their horses a chance to drink. "It's not my fault, you know," the prince said. "Arista never told us your first name."

"If my father thinks I was trying to impersonate him, he'll kill me," Reuben said.

"It's not your fault either." Fanen pulled his frogging sack off the saddle. "You didn't know."

"My father doesn't like the idea of me associating with nobility, period."

"Why not?"

"He thinks it will get me in trouble."

"And so it has!" Mauvin shouted, and they all laughed again. "You have a wise father."

"No sense worrying about it now," Alric said, throwing his own frogging sack over his shoulder. "We're here. Let's get some frogs."

"What am I to do?" Reuben asked.

Alric shrugged. "Guard us. So don't forget to bring your sword."

They laughed again.

The four of them slogged into the tall grass, using fallen logs as bridges and leaping from tufts of grass to rocks as they made their way deep into the misty bog.

"You really *are* awful at sword fighting," Mauvin told Reuben. "And is it true what Ellison said? That you're to be sworn into service tomorrow?"

Reuben nodded.

"So this is the quality of arms at Essendon, is it, Alric?"

"I'll take it up with Captain Lawrence in the morning," the prince said so seriously it worried Reuben.

"You're not really going to, are you, Your Highness?"

Alric looked back at him and rolled his eyes. "We need to keep him around. This guy is hilarious."

"Oh feathers!" Fanen exclaimed right after Reuben heard a liquid plunk. Glancing back, he saw the boy's left foot was ankle-deep in water. "Foot slipped," he said with a grimace.

"You need better balance, Fanen," Mauvin said. "A mistake like that in battle could get you killed."

Fanen pulled his foot out and shook it.

"Say, Hilfred." Mauvin turned to him. "Your father is pretty fair with a blade."

"My father is excellent," Reuben corrected. "He's known to be the best sword in the royal guard next to the lieutenant and the captain."

"You're talking to a Pickering, Hilfred," the prince reminded him. "That's like speaking to a family of Thorough-bred racehorses and saying your father is the fastest plow horse in the county. *Their* father"—Alric waved at the brothers—"is the greatest living sword master...anywhere."

Mauvin ducked a branch. "My father started training all of us before we could even lift a blade. Even my sister Lenare, who I think can still best Fanen, although she no longer thinks sword fighting is ladylike."

"You don't have to tell everyone about that, you know," Fanen said, his left foot making a slopping sound each time he stepped with it.

"Yeah I do—it's funny."

"Not so much, no."

"So, okay, your father is better than my father," Reuben grumbled.

"That's not my point at all. I meant it as a compliment... that your father is fair with a blade—"

"That's a huge compliment coming from him, trust me," the prince said.

"So what are you getting at?"

"Well"—Mauvin paused a moment as he checked the sup-port of a partially submerged log—"if your father knows how to use a sword, how come you don't?"

Reuben shrugged. "He's too busy, I guess."

"*I* could teach you." Mauvin steadied himself by grabbing hold of a fistful of cattails, then jogged up the log to a small patch of grass that formed an island near the center of the pond. "That is assuming you don't mind learning from someone younger."

"I'd accept," the prince said. "When he turned ten, Mauvin bested our Captain Lawrence in a Wintertide exhibition."

"That was two years ago," Mauvin reminded him. "Father says I'll master the first tier of the Tek'chin this month."

"Nice."

They each kneeled down, and Fanen lit a small lantern. The sun was well behind the forest now, leaving them in shadow. All around were the chirps and peeps of frogs.

"I see one!" Fanen whispered, pointing toward the water. "Go ahead, Alric."

"Thanks, Fanen. Most noble of you."

The prince left his bag and walked carefully with hands out like the claws of an attacking bear. He crept into the pond and in a fast grab scooped at the water, making a great splash. "Got him!"

Alric rushed back, cupping something, his tunic soaked. Fanen held the prince's bag open for him and Alric deposited his prize. "Now we are even, my friend," he said to Fanen. "One more and I will pass you. Then I'll be setting my sights at replacing Mad Mauvin as the Frog King."

This was obviously some great honor that Reuben had never heard of. Perhaps no one other than the three boys had.

"What kind is it?" Mauvin asked.

"A horned."

"I have two of them." Mauvin grinned.

Alric frowned, then turned to Reuben. "Let him teach you to fight—just don't ever listen to him."

Reuben sat on the mossy turf surrounded by the forest of cattails and floating lily pads, watching them hunt. He offered to help but was told that was against the rules. Reuben had no idea frog hunting had rules, but apparently it did. Being late in the season, most of the harvests were already in, and snow would be falling soon. But there, in Edgar's Swamp, the place was alive with sounds—the swish of treetops, the brush of grass, and the deafening chirps and peeps of frogs. The carpenter knew his ponds.

Reuben marveled at his strange turn of fortune. Only a bit over an hour before, he had faced the certainty of a pounding— likely worse. Ellison might not have been kidding about cutting their initials into him. To them he was barely human and not worthy of sympathy. Yet now he was here, safe and surrounded by nobility, catching frogs with the prince of the realm. Just then Reuben was struck by the unique opportunity he had. "Hey, have any of you been to the room at the top of the high tower?"

"The haunted tower?" Alric asked without looking up from the surface of the water where he was stalking another elusive toad.

"Haunted?"

"Sure," Alric said, creeping through the tufts, trying not to fall. "Nora tells the story every year about this time. I guess because it happened in the late fall."

"What happened?"

"Nora said it was years ago, before I was born. A girl who used to work in the castle, a chambermaid, jumped to her death. She climbed the tower in just her nightgown. She set a lantern on the window ledge, then jumped. On windy nights you can hear the scream she let out as she fell...and the *splat* when she landed. They found her body, or what was left of it, on the cobblestones before the main doors."

"Ewwww." Fanen looked up from his bag of frogs and grimaced.

"Why'd she do it?"

"She loved a man who didn't love her back. Just had his baby too. Only the guy said she was lying. She couldn't keep her job as a chambermaid with a child, didn't have any family, no way to take care of the baby, so as the legend goes she placed the infant on the father's bunk, then climbed the tower and jumped to her death. They say her ghost haunts that tower and in the fall, when it's cold but not yet snowed, she puts her lantern on the window ledge whenever someone in the castle is going to die. They also say that if you go up there when she's there, she thinks you're the lover who betrayed her and will push you out of the window to get her revenge."

"What happened to the baby?"

Mauvin laughed. "It's just a story."

"Although a woman did fall from that tower once," Alric said.

"Who?"

"Nora always called her Rose."

ॐ

They got back late because Alric had tied Mauvin's number of frogs, and the prince wanted to beat his friend. They only gave up after both he and Mauvin fell into the pond while making desperate attempts to catch a rare red-spotted frog. As they were completely soaked, the call of a warm fire was more alluring than the title of Frog King.

Overhead the clouds raced across the face of the full moon as if it were a light underwater and the surface was gliding past. A storm was coming, and as with all storms, Reuben felt uneasy. Guards had been looking for the prince, and the gates were opened before they reached them. Wet, cold, and tired, the three boys left Reuben without a parting good night. They disappeared into the castle keep, leaving Reuben the task of putting all four horses to bed.

The wind shook the boards of the stable and spooked the animals as he pulled the saddles off and brushed them down. Reuben, who had only soaked his feet, was not terribly tired. He was used to harder days than frog hunting. More importantly he wanted to put off seeing his father. Richard Hilfred knew everything that went on at the castle and would have learned of his son going off with the prince and the young Pickering lords. If Reuben came back late enough, his father might be asleep. To this end, Reuben took his time brushing and feeding the horses before stepping back out into the empty courtyard.

The wind had blown out several torches around the ward. The one at the well was out, as were the two near the front doors to the keep. The others were being whipped viciously. A distinct howling could be heard on the wind as it blew between the buildings, kicking up whirlwinds of leaves. The branches of the old oak, now nearly bare, were clacking against each other. The door to the woodshed alternated between creaking and slapping, and the chains on the well's windlass were jingling as the bucket rocked.

Looking up, Reuben saw it—a light in the top window of the high tower.

He stared. Over the course of the last month, he'd seen a light in that tower twice, and each time someone had died. First old Chancellor Wainwright, then Clare Braga, who died in a horrible fire at the estate the king had just awarded to her husband. Reuben shuddered just thinking about it. Burning must be the worst way to die. Cuts and bruises didn't bother him, but he touched a hot kettle once and the pain was unbearable for days. His father had slapped him just to stop his complaining.

And then there was that story the prince had told. A chambermaid, a woman named Rose, who had killed herself. *Could she be...?* According to his father, his mother had died in childbirth. But the prince's story explained so much, like why his father rarely spoke of his mother and his ill temper around Reuben's birthday. But he wondered if he just wanted it to be true. Then his mother's death wouldn't be his fault and the light might be his mother returning to tell him he was innocent of a crime he had blamed himself for all those years.

Reuben took three steps toward the castle, his neck craned, his eyes focused on the window, wondering if he could catch sight of his mother's ghostly image. The light flickered as a shape moved between it and the window. Reuben held his breath, waiting, watching as the wind blew his hair.

The light went out.

He continued to stand before the front doors of the castle, looking up, but nothing happened. Did this mean there had been another death? Who could it be? Was it someone in the castle or far away? Having waited for more than two weeks for the light to reappear, now that it had, the moment felt empty. There was no bloodcurdling scream or a body falling to the courtyard. The night was like any other. Then, just as he was about to turn and head for the barracks, a shadow slipped out the window.

If not for the moonlight bathing that side of the tower, and the fact that he was staring, he would not have seen her—a woman in a wind-whipped dress.

Reuben held his breath, staring in shock. *Is that her?*

The woman's hands clung to the ledge while her feet felt for a toehold. She found it and dropped carefully to the decorative cornice below. There she cowered.

She set the lantern on the window ledge, then jumped. On

windy nights you can hear the scream she let out as she fell...
and the splat when she landed.

Reuben heard only the sound of crying.

Who is it and what is she doing? Is this the ghost? Is it
my...

Slowly the woman inched around the side of the tower,
toward where a small dormer roof extended. Hanging once
more, she reached out with her feet and touched the spine of
the dormer below and inched down farther. Then she slipped.

Reuben gasped in horror as he watched her fall.

She slid down the side of the peak and with a scream
dropped onto the spire of the Winsome Tower. She clawed at
the clay tiles as she continued to skid.

Reuben took a step closer as if to help, but there was nothing he could do.

As she reached the edge, her toes caught the lip. The woman
lay on her stomach, pressed against the spire, crying in terror.

Reuben stared, one of his hands covering his mouth. He
waited to see what she would do next, but the woman didn't
move. She lay there, panting and whimpering.

"There's a wide balcony beneath you," Reuben called up, not
certain if he was speaking to a woman or a ghost. Her surviving
the fall and catching hold of the roofline made her seem more
than human. The hard part was done—assuming she wasn't
intent on suicide. Reuben saw how it was possible to make the
rest of the trip. He waited, but the woman did not move.

"You're safe—well, sort of. Just drop and you'll be okay, as
long as you don't land badly."

"I can't!" the woman cried, though most of her voice was
stolen by the wind. "I don't want to die."

What is she talking about? She just climbed out a tower
window!

"Trust me. Just scoot off the roof you are on and lower yourself as best you can. Even if you fall, you'll be okay. There's a terrace right below you."

It took several minutes before he saw her move. She inched down, not daring to look. Her legs dangled, searching for something to support herself but finding only air. The strength of her arms gave out and she fell again, screaming once more.

While not how he would have tried getting down, it worked nonetheless. The drop was longer than it looked from where Reuben stood and she disappeared behind the balcony's wall. He feared she might have hurt herself until he saw her head appear.

"Are you all right?"

The head nodded.

"Follow the wall to your left. You'll find stairs."

She vanished from his view.

A light returned to the tower window and Reuben looked up with anticipation, but no one else came out.

He waited in the courtyard, trying to determine what had just happened. If it was the ghost, why hadn't she jumped to her death again? Wasn't that what ghosts did—repeat the past by reliving the moment of their death in eternal torment or something? If she wasn't the ghost, who was she? And why would anyone climb out of the high tower window if they weren't intent on suicide?

I don't want to die.

It didn't make any sense.

One of the double doors to the keep opened. All he saw was a pale hand at first; then the face of a young woman peeked out.

He had never seen her before. She was about his age, but her face was painted and she wore a dress the likes of which he had never seen. With a tight bodice and a plunging, shoulder-baring neckline, it might not be a dress at all but rather what women wore underneath them. She was still crying. He could see the tears on her face as they glistened and left dark streaks in her makeup.

She shrank from him when he approached. "Please don't kill me. Please...please..."

"You're all right. You're safe. I won't hurt you."

She stared at him with frightened eyes, her hands shaking. "I didn't do anything wrong, I swear."

"It's okay. Just tell me what happened. Why did you climb out the window?"

"They would've...they would've killed me if they discovered I was there. If they knew I heard what they said."

"Who? What are you talking about?"

The girl's eyes were locked on the light in the high tower.

"Please," she pleaded. "You have to hide me. I didn't do anything wrong."

༄

The castle was alive with activity. Every window was alight, and guards, roused from their beds, strode across the courtyard to the keep. Reuben ducked back into the woodshed where he had hidden the girl. The shed was his sanctuary, the place he always went to be alone. Although tonight he was uncertain how long his little refuge would be safe. Outside, Reuben heard shouts for the gate to be sealed.

What is going on? They say deaths always come in threes, and the light was in the tower...

Since bringing her there, the girl had sat balled up on the cord of maple he had split the month before. All he could see clearly was a slice of her face illuminated by the moonlight that slipped through the crack of the door. Her cheeks were puffed and wet, her eyes red and glassy.

"Do you hear that? The alarm has been sounded. If you want my help, you have to talk to me. Now tell me what's going on," Reuben said.

She nodded and managed to swallow and take a breath. "I came for a party—a surprise party for someone."

"For who?"

"I don't know. I didn't ask."

"You were invited to a party, but you don't know who it was for?"

"I wasn't *invited*. I came to work."

Reuben was confused. That didn't make sense. The castle had more than enough waitstaff. "What kind of—"

"I was hired to *pleasure* the guest of honor."

"Huh?"

The girl gave him a smirk. "How old are you?"

"Almost sixteen, but I don't see—Oh!" Reuben took a half step back as if the girl were a dangerous animal. "You're a—"

"Yes."

"Oh." He couldn't think of anything else to say. Reuben had spoken to only a few girls. Occasionally he talked about the weather with Alice, the washwoman. She was a little older and never seemed interested in his conversations. And he was certain Grace, who polished the candlesticks and carried water from the well, made a habit of avoiding him. Girls made Reuben uncomfortable, and this one wasn't just a girl. This was a...He had trouble even thinking it.

"The party was in the tower, but like I said, it was supposed to be a surprise. So I was put in the wardrobe and when they told the guest of honor to look in the closet for his present, I was supposed to jump out. While I was there, two men came in and started talking. I figured any minute the door would be flung open, but they just kept talking. At first I didn't really listen. I didn't understand most of what was said anyway, a bunch of stuff about Imperialists and Monarchists and how Melengar would be one of the first."

"First what?"

"I have no idea. But then I heard one say, 'After we kill the king, we'll begin making the changes.' "

"Someone said what?" Reuben asked, even though he had heard her just fine.

"He said they were going to kill the royal family. And I couldn't figure out why they would say something like that with me in the room. Then I realized these two weren't the ones who had put me in the wardrobe and neither of them knew I was there. When I heard them leave, I knew I had to get away. If either of them came to the party, they'd know I'd over-heard what they'd said. I had to get out. I had to disappear."

"Why didn't you just come down the stairs?"

"I heard voices outside the door. It might have been them. The only other way out was the window. I thought I could climb down. I thought... but I slipped..." She started to cry again.

"Do you have any idea who they were? Did they use any names?"

She shook her head. "No, I didn't hear anything like that. Please, I just want to go home."

"You can't leave—the gate has been sealed."

The question was why? Maybe it had already happened. Maybe there had been an assassination. The girl might have been part of it. Looking at her, it seemed impossible, but he never would have thought she'd have climbed out of that window either.

"Something bad has happened," Reuben told her. "That's why they've rung the alarm. If what you say is true, someone might have just tried to kill the king."

The girl closed her eyes and shook her head. "They'll think

I was part of it now—because I ran, because I climbed out the window. I wasn't. I didn't do anything. You have to believe me."

"Listen, just try and relax, okay?" Reuben wasn't sure which of them he was talking to. His heart was still racing from seeing what he had thought was a ghost but what turned out to be a girl—a girl in trouble, one he'd found like a stray dog. He was thankful they had made it to the shed before the alarm was called. The smell of maple wood, like the smells of the stable, were familiar to him. He could think there. "I'll just go and tell them what happened."

"No!" She grabbed him. "Don't, please."

"But if you're innocent, you'll be fine."

"What if you tell the wrong person?"

"What do you mean?"

"What if you tell one of the men who planned to kill the king? Even if you don't, if the king is dead and they think I did it...they won't listen to me. They won't believe me. I just want to go home."

He couldn't let her leave.

Reuben ran a hand through his hair. He needed a better place to keep her, somewhere safe, hidden, and where she couldn't get away—just in case she was lying.

"Okay, this is what I'll do. I know another place I can hide you. You'll stay there and I'll go see what's happening. Then I'll go to my father. He's a sergeant at arms with the royal guard and it's his job to protect the royal family. He'll know what to do. Don't worry—I won't let anything happen to you. You just have to trust me."

"I trust you, I do. You didn't have to hide me or help me when I was climbing down. But I don't even know your name."

"Oh, yeah...sorry. I'm Reuben, Reuben Hilfred. What's yours?"

"Rose."

Reuben just stared for a moment. "Really?"

She nodded. "Why?"

"Ah...nothing. It's just..." He reached out and took her hand. She may have thought it was to comfort her, but Reuben just wanted to make sure she was real. "Rose was my mother's name."

CHAPTER 5

AFTER THE PARTY

Sergeant Richard Hilfred climbed the high tower's steps two at a time, and in between wishing he was in better shape and concentrating on breathing, he imagined ways to kill Lieutenant Wylin.

Why do things like this have to happen on my watch, when I'm responsible?

He should have been notified of anything happening at the castle. How else could he be expected to provide protection for the royal family? Wylin—the little git that he was—had never said a word about a party for Captain Lawrence. Something had happened, and the entire castle was now on alert and Richard knew that somehow he would be blamed for the night's fiasco.

"Barnes!" Richard shouted. "Where is he? Where's Wylin?"

Sergeant Barnes was in the room at the top. The one that his son had become so fascinated with and the same one that made Richard so uncomfortable. There wasn't much to it, just a round room of stone, long abandoned because it was out of the way, up too many stairs, hot in summer and freezing in winter. A harsh wind ripped through the open window, blowing curtains that were frayed and tattered. The chamber's light came from a lantern on the table in the center. Littered with

mugs and a picked-over tray of meats and cheese, it complemented the barrel of ale in the corner. The only other furniture
was an old wardrobe and a dusty bed.

"I don't know where the lieutenant is," Barnes replied.
He stood at attention, making Richard think he was being
mocked. "Captain Lawrence ordered him to seal the gate."

Richard's mouth was already forming his next words when
he noticed why Barnes was so formal. They were not alone.
Outside the immediate glow of the lantern light stood Lord
Simon Exeter. His Lordship was near the window, in his
floor-length white cape. Underneath he wore a black leather
tunic with buckles down the front that looked like sutures, as
if someone had sliced his chest open and then strapped him
closed again. His thumbs were hooked in his sword belt as he
stared at Richard with an amused scowl.

"Your Lordship." Richard snapped to attention.

Richard didn't like being around nobles any more than
he liked being around bees. He knew that if he didn't bother
them, they wouldn't bother him, but Exeter was like a wasp—
he was known to sting for little or no reason.

"I'm pleased to have you join us. I hope the alarm didn't
interrupt a pleasant dream. We wouldn't want your duties to
your king to get in the way of a good night's sleep."

Richard chose his reply carefully. "I wasn't asleep, Your
Lordship. I'm the senior royal guard on duty this evening.
It's my responsibility to investigate any possible threats to the
king."

"I see. You'll forgive me if I conduct my own investigation."

"Of course, Your Lordship. I welcome any and all assis-
tance."

Richard would have preferred to speak to Barnes alone, but
as high constable, Exeter was the chief enforcer of the king's
law throughout Melengar. Every county or quarter sheriff, as

well as each city constable, took their orders from him. He generally concerned himself with incidents beyond the castle's walls, but Richard wasn't about to challenge him over jurisdiction. Besides, Exeter was the Marquis of East March and the third most powerful man in the kingdom after the king and Chancellor Braga.

"Let's bring Sergeant Hilfred up-to-date so we can hear what he thinks, shall we, Barnes?" Exeter said. "Repeat what you just told me."

Barnes hesitated. He refused to look at either of them, his sight shifting to the barrel as he licked his lips. Barnes was one of the old guard, what Richard called the King's Men, and one of those who took part in suppressing the Asper Uprising the year before Richard joined the guard. Having missed the event was something they never let him forget. Lawrence had been lieutenant then and Wylin the senior sergeant. Richard felt left out when they drank and reminisced about the campaign. According to them, the king had led the charge, but Richard guessed it was a lie. Nobles didn't lead in battle. They waited safely in the rear until the tide had turned. Then they trotted around the dead, smiling at their victory.

The King's Men were a tight and loyal group. They would say or do anything to protect each other, which was probably the reason why Barnes hesitated. Still, the presence of Lord Exeter was hard to withstand.

"Lieutenant Wylin planned a surprise birthday party for the captain. A few of us pooled our coin to buy him a present—a lady of pleasure."

"You brought a *whore* into the royal residence?" Richard asked, stunned. "Did Wylin or Captain Lawrence know?"

"No, it was all very quiet-like. No one knew."

"Obviously, as you kept the information from both the royal guard and the high constable," Exeter said. "I won't even bother mentioning the trouble that puts you in. Please continue."

"Well...she disappeared."

"What do you mean, disappeared?" Richard asked.

"The girl—Rose—she vanished. We had her hiding in that wardrobe." Barnes pointed. "The plan was to get the captain here by telling him the princess was scared after seeing the ghost of—" Barnes coughed unconvincingly. He glanced at Richard, then looked at his feet. "Anyway, everything was going fine, but when the captain went to get his present, she wasn't there."

"Where'd she go?" Richard asked.

"Where indeed?" Exeter asked. "So let me get this straight, Sergeant Barnes. You secretly smuggled someone into the personal residence of the royal family—someone who I am guessing you knew nothing about—then left her alone to roam the castle wherever she pleased? What good are moats, gates, and walls if the king's own men circumvent the castle's defenses?"

"She's just a young girl, a local whore. She's not going to cause any trouble."

Exeter's eyebrows rose. "And yet here the three of us are. Do you think the entire castle goes on alert for no reason? Do we often search through every cellar and woodshed because we've nothing better to do? Oh, I think she's caused quite a bit of trouble."

A puzzled look crossed the high constable's face. "Hmm... you do raise an interesting point, though. If this is a mere protocol blunder on the part of a dim-witted, ill-disciplined guard staff, why was the alarm sounded? I'm sure this isn't the first time rules have been bent. Bringing her here demonstrated poor judgment on your part, and losing her is proof of your incompetence. But it hardly justifies sealing the castle and calling for a full-scale search. So why did Captain Lawrence empty the rest of the barracks?"

"I honestly don't think he planned to. He was mad, all right—you know how the captain is. But at first he just told us to go find her and get her out of the castle. But then Bishop Saldur piped up and—"

Exeter raised a hand to stop him. He tilted his head down and peered up at Barnes. This was a peculiar habit of the high constable that Richard always felt was threatening, for no reason he could articulate. "Bishop Saldur was here?"

Barnes nodded.

"Was he invited to the party?"

Barnes almost laughed, which would have been a first. Richard had never seen anyone laugh in front of Exeter—not even the king. "No, Your Lordship. We don't exactly run in the same *social circles*, if you get my meaning. We bumped into the bishop on the stairs when we were carrying up the refreshments and he just kinda joined us."

"And you didn't find that strange?"

"I think he might have just been curious, seeing all of us heading up the tower in the middle of the night. I would have been. And it's not like we can tell the bishop he can't share a drink. To be honest, I wasn't looking forward to the sermon he would give us when Rose jumped out, but I figured that was Wylin's problem, not mine."

"And what did Bishop Saldur have to do with Captain Lawrence raising the alarm?"

"Oh, right. So when the captain opens the wardrobe and there's nothing there, he knew something was going on. We finally told him about Rose, and he said we should go find her and take her home. But Saldur started going on and on about what a big deal it was. He kept referring to Rose as an *intruder* and squawking about how she could be a spy or assassin or whatever. He told Captain Lawrence that if he didn't raise the alarm, he'd go to Percy Braga himself and tell the chancellor that the captain was putting the king's life in danger. He was making a big fuss over nothing, but Saldur's not a soldier and doesn't understand these things. I think part of the reason Captain Lawrence agreed was just to get the bishop to calm down. Well, that and he didn't want to get on the wrong side of his new boss."

"And you are *absolutely* sure that the bishop is wrong? That this girl isn't a danger? Where did you find her?" Exeter resumed his tilt-headed glare.

"A brothel in the Lower Quarter."

"You got the captain a *Lower Quarter* whore?" Richard was too shocked to keep quiet.

"Oh no, it's not like that." Barnes shook his head. "It's new. They call it Medford House. Even though it's on Wayward Street, it's a real nice place, clean, classy even. And Rose is a real sweet girl. She'd never do anything—"

"Oh really? Then tell me, Sergeant, why isn't she here? Why didn't this *sweet girl* do her job, collect her money, and go back to the Lower Quarter?"

Barnes remained silent.

Exeter started to pace, deep in thought. He tugged on his lower lip, and his cape flared dramatically each time he turned and walked in the other direction. Richard, and presumably Barnes, thought it best to leave him to his thoughts. They stood silently at attention. After several minutes Exeter stopped and addressed them.

"Rose's disappearance is indeed cause for concern, and finding her should be the realm's highest priority, but not for the reasons stated by our *esteemed* bishop. To think that the girl is a spy or assassin is ludicrous. You selected the girl to come here, not the other way around. Am I correct?"

Barnes nodded his agreement.

"Melengar has many enemies, and I suspect spies do indeed

lurk in many places, but the likelihood of you picking one at random from a local brothel is absurd, as is the possibility of someone finding out about her coming to the palace and bribing her to open a door or lure a guard away from a post."

"She wouldn't have any time to do that anyway. We walked in, picked her out, and brought her right back. She didn't talk to no one."

Exeter walked until he was nearly nose-to-nose with Barnes, fixing him squarely in his gaze. "If the girl is part of a conspiracy, the most likely explanation would be that Barnes here is a traitor."

"Oh no, Your Lordship! I swear I'm not." He looked as if he might faint.

After studying his face, Exeter said, "I'm inclined to believe you. If that was your plan, there would be no reason to make up a story about her being a gift for Captain Lawrence. You would have just hidden her in the castle and none of us would be here.

"Perhaps we are making too much of this. Could it simply be that you were taking too long to fetch Captain Lawrence, and she just got bored, walked down the stairs, and is home right now?"

Barnes shook his head. "We had Grisham watching the hallway downstairs. You know, keeping an eye out for the captain? If she came down, he would have seen her."

Lord Exeter went to the window, leaned over, and looked down. "So that leaves only one remaining possibility."

"You think she went out the window?" Richard asked.

"Unless Sergeant Barnes is mistaken or lying, I see no other alternative. And since we found no body from a fall, she must have climbed down."

"No one in their right mind would climb down from here," Barnes said, and this time he did let out a little chuckle.

Richard cringed for him.

"No?" Exeter asked. He crossed the room and closed the door. "I think someone who is highly motivated might give it a try. But you're right. It's not a task one tries without good reason, and it may not even be possible no matter how hard one tries."

He turned his attention to Richard. "Sergeant Hilfred, draw your weapon."

Richard did as ordered while His Lordship did likewise. Exeter pointed the tip of his broadsword at Barnes, motioned to the window with a nod of his head, and simply said, "Give it a try."

Barnes glanced at the window, then smiled uncomfortably. "You're not...you're not serious, Your Lordship."

"I assure you I am. I have to determine if it is possible, and I'm providing you compelling motivation."

"But, Your Lordship!"

"Do as ordered or Sergeant Hilfred and I will kill you where you stand. You could draw as well. It's your choice, but I've seen you use your blade and you're not very good. You stand a better chance of survival out the window." Exeter sidestepped to his left, placing Barnes between them. "But if you draw, be sure you can kill me. Anything less and I'll have the king quarter you. I am, after all, his cousin."

Exeter rushed forward and slashed. Barnes shuffled backward toward the window with a slice in his tunic. He winced and clutched his chest, suggesting Exeter cut more than just cloth. His eyes were wide as he watched Exeter's blade, but he never touched his own.

If Barnes had drawn, Richard would have fought him. He had to—it was his job to defend the castle nobility, no matter the situation. He also never cared much for Barnes. He and the other King's Men had always looked down on him with expressions that said, *Even after all these years you still aren't one of us, and you don't deserve to guard the king.*

Maybe that's why Barnes did it. He had no choice—neither of them did.

Barnes grabbed hold of the stone and climbed up so that he was standing on the sill, framed in the window. He looked down and Richard could see him shaking.

"Relax, Sergeant," Exeter said. "I'm fairly certain the young girl—that *local whore* as you put it—successfully climbed down."

Lord Exeter's observation didn't appear to help. Panting with tension, Barnes turned around, crouched, and taking a firm hold, slid his legs out the window until his stomach rested on the sill.

"There's a ledge here," Barnes said with sudden delight.

Richard suspected anything positive would be joyous to Barnes at that moment.

The sergeant continued to slip out, dropping until only his fingers were visible and then he let go. "I did it."

Exeter leaned out the window. They both did. Barnes was just an arm's length below, standing on a tiny decorative ledge no more than a foot wide.

"Keep going," Exeter ordered.

In the moonlight, Richard could see the peak of a dormer below and to the right. Barnes saw it, too, and began to inch along the ledge until he found a handhold in the stone letting him crouch. He struggled to lower his feet again, only he didn't have a window to lean through this time. The wind gusted and nearly blew Barnes off balance. Richard wondered if the sergeant would just stay where he was all night. He was beyond the reach of Exeter's sword, although His Lordship might decide to order Richard out after him. If he did, Richard wasn't sure what he'd do. Unlike Barnes, he guessed he was a better swordsman than Exeter. Luckily—at least for Richard—the wind seemed to have scared Barnes and that's when he made a desperate attempt to reach out with his feet. Without enough room on the ledge to balance, he fell.

Barnes landed on the dormer and slid down the steep slope. He cried out when he ran out of roof and dropped on the spire of the Winsome Tower. The roof there was not as steep, but it was angled enough to make him slide. Barnes clawed at the clay tiles trying to stop himself. He failed to grasp anything and Richard and Exeter watched as Barnes slipped off like a raindrop and fell to the courtyard. At that height the sound was slight, only a faint thump, hardly the noise anyone would associate with the death of a man.

"Well, there you have it," Exeter said. "Conclusive proof that someone *would* indeed climb out this window." Exeter focused on Richard's sword. "You can put that away now."

Richard wasn't certain that was such good advice, but under His Lordship's watchful glare, he sheathed the metal just the same.

"So now that we know the how, all that remains is the why. The only reason anyone would go out that window is if they felt they had *absolutely* no other choice." He paused, staring at Richard. "But then I shouldn't have to tell you that, should I?"

Richard felt his face flush with anger, the only outward expression he allowed.

"Still, in the case of this girl—this new Rose—amusing that they have the same name, isn't it?"

Richard didn't find it amusing at all.

"I think we can conclude that she, like Sergeant Barnes, was in fear of her life. But from whom and why?"

Exeter looked out the window again. Below, a handful of figures gathered around the dead body of Barnes. "He almost made it, didn't he? If he could have caught the ledge, then he could easily have dropped to the terrace. She's still alive, I think." His Lordship looked toward the gate. "Probably got out of the castle before anyone knew she was missing. Probably already back at the Medford House."

"We can ask Kells about a girl. He was on the gate," Richard said. "But I did check in with him before coming here, and he reported no one has left the keep since sundown."

Exeter smirked. "No one saw her leave this room either." The high constable headed for the stairs.

"What should I say in my report about what happened to Barnes?" Richard stopped him.

Exeter spun, his cape whirling. "Exactly what happened. Barnes was demonstrating how the girl escaped and in the process, he slipped, fell, and died." Exeter tilted his head down again, peering up. "Did you know that I opposed your appointment to the royal guard? Your sword skills are good, but you lack loyalty. If Wylin or Lawrence had been here with Barnes, they would have protested. They would have told him to draw and risked their careers by standing against me to save one of their own. Two against one—I would've had to back down. Each of you would have received a harsh reprimand because the king can't have open displays of insubordination, but he would have secretly agreed with you. Everything would have resolved itself in the end. Instead, Barnes is lying in the courtyard like a shattered bag of glass. So I have to wonder, with such a keen sense of loyalty, when the time comes to defend your king—will you?"

Richard's jaw stiffened. "I already have."

"Oh yes, the attack in Pilin."

"I saved His Majesty when everyone else ran. I stayed and nearly died."

"But that was long ago, and I have to wonder...would you do so now? Perhaps if the king had shown more gratitude.

Active soldiers can't have wives, can they? I suspect you asked for an exception because Rose Reuben carried your son in her belly. That's what happened, isn't it?"

It was a question Exeter already knew the answer to, and Richard didn't bother answering.

"It seems like such a small price to pay, especially after exhibiting such bravery, but your request was denied. The king needs his soldiers in their barracks and ready at all times, and if he makes an exception for one...I'm certain he made all this clear when he turned you down."

Richard stood straight, doing his best not to show emotion, something he'd developed a skill for over the last sixteen years.

"And when he refused, your loyalty to Rose was tested. You could have resigned your commission and taken her, and your soon-to-be son, somewhere to start a new life. But you cared more about your promotion to sergeant at arms than for Rose and your bastard child. You turned her away." Exeter adjusted his cape, which had slipped off one shoulder after his abrupt turn. "Of course, what did that leave her? Now that her condition was known, she was released from her position, and with no man to provide for her, what was she to do? I suppose she could have found an old midwife with a twisted twig to relieve her from the burden you planted. But she didn't do that. Now that's loyalty. I would've advocated Rose Reuben for a position in the royal guard without hesitation. What did you tell her when she returned with the child and pleaded once more for your help? Did you even offer her coin? I suspect you turned her away with nothing. I might have granted you some concession for at least sending the child to your sister after Rose's death, but then that was more out of guilt and embarrassment, wasn't it? Pity you didn't offer that option sooner.

"I judge a man by the decisions he makes, and you proved once again that you value your job over all else. Siding against me would have jeopardized your position—and Barnes paid the price, just like Rose did. So why don't you attend to your job, and I'll do the same. Go protect the king and I'll find the missing Rose from Medford House."

Exeter left the room, his footfalls fading.

Left alone, Richard stepped to the window and laid a hand on the sill. This room was indeed haunted. He let his fingers slide across the stone and felt the tears come again. Grabbing a cup, Richard walked to the ale barrel and drank.

CHAPTER 6

THE HOUSE AND THE TAVERN

Buckets were kicked from under the feet of the three men tied by their necks to the scaffolding. The whole structure lurched with the jerk and the crossbeam bowed with their weight.

Royce had seen many hangings and was always surprised by the silence. The cheering and insults stopped. No one spoke—certainly not the dangling men. The only sound they made was the soft flutter of their feet, which could be heard in the sudden quiet. Royce guessed it wasn't reverence for the passing of life, and certainly not out of respect for the men. The crowd had been throwing rotted vegetables at them moments before. He could not prove it, but he suspected the silence came from the jolting thought that it would happen to them one day. Viewing death, this passage from breathing, thinking people into corpses, struck them dumb. They saw themselves hanging in their place and for the duration of those kicking feet, shuddered.

"Scary little town," Hadrian whispered across saddles as the three rode on through the rest of the Gentry Quarter.

It had been a year since their first visit to the city of Medford. Arriving as fugitives in the back of a cart, they had wallowed in their own blood. Returning put Royce on edge, like visiting his own grave that bore the epitaph ROYCE MELBORN...ANY MINUTE NOW. But he had to come back. He'd left something important behind.

They avoided the crowd in the square with its fountain, which had a stone statue of a king rearing on his horse. Veering to the left of the castle, they aimed for the Tradesmen's Arch and the artisan section beyond. A family of ducks splashed among cattails in the moat that ringed the gray walls of Essendon Castle. The water was a murky green with lily pads dotting the surface. Royce took note of the pair of guards who stood at the gate dressed in tabards of burgundy with the stylized image of a gold falcon on them. Two more stood on the far side of the bridge. A dozen more walked the battlements, their metal helms glinting in the morning sun. Just riding by, Royce noticed two blind spots on the walls where they could be scaled out of sight of the guards. Maybe there were more guards at night.

"Have you been here before, Albert?" Hadrian asked the viscount, who still rode behind him.

"Oh yes, many times. I have a good friend, Lord Daref, who used to live down that street." He pointed. "He invited me to his niece's wedding just four years ago—when I still had clothes—and to a spring social the following year, which I had to skip because I was poor and growing poorer by the day. The nobility are always having parties, and it looks like another is approaching." He pointed at banners out in front of the castle gates that proclaimed CHANCELLOR'S GALA. "Sometimes I think they publically announce these things just to remind those who aren't invited how miserable their lives are."

The wide brick boulevards with their flower boxes and fountains turned into simple streets as they passed under the Tradesmen's Arch. The sound of cart wheels on cobblestone and the bang of hammers on wood or steel came from all directions. Doors to workshops stood open as people passed in and out, carrying lumber, heavy buckets, and sacks. Unlike the Merchant Quarter, which was on the other side of the castle, there were no shop signs. Most of the buildings in the artisan district were anonymous. They didn't need to hang signboards, as each workshop spilled their wares out onto porches and into the street. Wagon wheels, five deep, listed against posts, and stacked barrels formed small forests. A cobbler enjoyed the autumn sun, having dragged his table outside where he pounded the heel of a boot. Nearby he displayed a rack of the finished product. Down at the docks, a river barge had arrived and pulleys were hoisting up crates while net-covered boats dodged their way to the fishery. People moved quickly here. Workers walked fast, some even jogged. Merchants breezed through the throng of laborers. They were usually big men in brightly colored clothes. They did not jog but rather sauntered, pausing to study a barrel or bend a boot.

"This *is* the way, isn't it?" Hadrian asked as they turned right onto Artisan Row.

Royce looked around, unsure.

"I thought you knew the way?" Albert asked.

"We know the way *out* better," Hadrian said. "On the way in we didn't see much. In fact, I was unconscious."

"I'm guessing the two of you were caught stealing something?"

"Not really—that is, we were never caught. Stabbed and shot with an arrow, but not caught. And the job wasn't here. It's just where we ended up. What we're looking for is a section of town they call the Lower Quarter."

Albert shrugged. "As you might guess, I spent most of my time in Gentry Square, with the occasional foray to the Merchant Quarter. I never had occasion to come down this way."

"I remember that carpenter's shop." Royce pointed. "That's the one she did most of her business with."

Each of the quarters had its own entrance gate, but vines suggested they had never been closed. By process of elimination they finally found the Lower Quarter and the streets narrowed dramatically once they entered it. Buildings rose to either side like canyon walls. Three-story shops with living quarters on the top floors jutted out over the street, casting the dirt lane in shadow. The buildings were stained and cracked, and instead of workers plying their trade on the street, the poor clustered in makeshift hovels. There were no sewers here, so the streets sufficed, giving the neighborhood a pungent odor.

The farther they went, the worse the conditions became. When they finally turned onto Wayward Street, they knew they had reached the bottom. The buildings were poorly built and leaned to one side or the other. Four rats enjoyed a feast of apple rinds, bones, and waste dumped from a window above. Three stories up, clothes hung on lines to dry, none without a patch, tear, or permanent stain. At the end of the street were two businesses that couldn't have been more different. On the right was The Hideous Head Tavern and Alehouse. Without the badly painted sign that misspelled the word *hideous*, it would easily be mistaken for an abandoned shack. Across from it stood a beautiful building—as nice as any in the Artisan Quarter and as well cared for as any in Gentry Square. It looked like a quaint home with a broad porch complete with a bench swing and flowerbeds. The sign above the door simply read MEDFORD HOUSE.

"You came all this way for a whore?" Albert asked, and Royce shot him a harsh look.

"Don't call her that if you want to live a long and happy life," Hadrian said as they dismounted.

"But this *is* a whorehouse—a brothel, right? And you're here to see a woman, so—"

"So keep talking, Albert." Hadrian tied his horse to the post. "Just let me get farther away."

"Gwen saved our lives," Royce said, looking up at the porch. "I beat on doors. I even yelled for help." He looked at Albert, letting that image sink in. *Yes, I yelled for help.* "No one cared." Royce gestured toward Hadrian. "He was dying in a pool of blood, and I was about to pass out. Broken leg, my side sliced open, the world spinning. Then she was there saying, 'I've got you. You'll be all right now.' We would have died in the mud and the rain, but she took us in, nursed us back to health. People were after us—*lots of people*...lots of *powerful* people—but she kept us hidden for weeks, and she never asked for payment or explanation. She never asked for anything." Royce turned back to Albert. "So if you call her a whore again, I'll cut your tongue out and nail it to your chest."

Albert nodded. "Point taken."

Royce climbed the steps to the House and rapped once.

Albert leaned over to Hadrian and whispered, "He knocks at a—"

"Royce can still hear you." Hadrian stopped him.

"Really?"

"Pretty sure. You have no idea how much trouble I got into before I learned that. Now I never say anything I don't want him to know."

The door opened and a young woman greeted them with a smile. Royce didn't recognize her. Maybe she was new. "Welcome, please come in, gentlemen."

"Wow, this is really nice and so genteel," the viscount marveled as he entered the parlor. "It's like I'm in the Duchess of Rochelle's salon again. I've never seen a"—he paused and smiled at Royce—"a house of comfort that was so clean and...pretty."

"Gwen's wonderful," Hadrian stated as he stood awkwardly, looking at the dirt on his boots.

A moment later, another girl joined them in the parlor. "Hello, gentlemen, I'm called Jasmine. How may I help you?"

"I'm here to see Gwen," Royce told the girl, who he was certain had been called Jollin the last time they were there.

"Gwen?" she replied cautiously. "Ah...Gwen isn't taking visitors."

"I didn't mean *that*. Ah...I'm Royce Melborn. You might remember us. She—well, all of you—helped my friend and I last year. I just wanted to thank her again, maybe buy her dinner."

"Oh...ah...wait here just a minute."

Jasmine scurried up the stairs.

"Jasmine?" Hadrian said, watching her leave. "Didn't she used to call herself Julie?"

"I thought it was Jollin," Royce corrected.

"It smells like apples and cinnamon in here." Albert sat down on one of the elaborately embroidered couches. Hadrian had loaned Albert his thick woolen winter trousers and his cloak, which he had wrapped about him. Underneath he still wore his filthy nightshirt.

"The girls smell even better," Hadrian said.

"I can only imagine. And it's quiet. Usually you can hear the creaking of the bed frames overhead. This place is great. Must be expensive, and popular, and yet I never heard of it. Is it new?"

Hadrian shrugged. "We were only here the one time."

"We need to get you cleaned up," Royce told the viscount, realizing just how unpleasant the noble looked. He didn't want to meet her with him like that, but he didn't have a choice now. "Hadrian, while I take Gwen to dinner, do you think you could maybe—"

Hadrian laughed.

"What?"

"Do you really think you're fooling me?"

"I just thought that—"

"You just want time alone with Gwen."

Royce made to protest, but Hadrian held up his hand. "Relax. I'll deal with Count Nightshirt."

"Viscount."

"What's the difference?"

"A whole lot of money."

Jasmine came back down the stairs, moving much slower than she had gone up. "Um...Gwen asked me to tell you that...she doesn't want to see you."

Royce wasn't certain he'd heard her correctly. "I don't understand. She doesn't want...but why? Did you tell her I just wanted to take her to dinner? Did you tell her Hadrian is with me? We'll all go together if she prefers. It won't be just the two of us, if that's the problem."

"So much for my shave and new clothes," Albert said.

"I'm sorry, she really made herself quite clear," the girl replied. "She won't see you under any circumstances. I really am sorry."

～∽～

Hadrian placed his elbows on the table and frowned when it rocked. "I hate when they wobble like this."

They were in The Hideous Head Tavern and Alehouse across Wayward Street. The place had looked destitute from the outside, similar to the barn in which they'd found Albert, and Hadrian had thought it couldn't be any worse inside. He was wrong.

Thin planks of uneven widths formed the walls, leaving gaps between warped boards that granted ample passage to both sunlight and cold air. The shoddy carpentry turned out to be a benefit, as the place had few windows—none that opened—and the fireplace was poorly ventilated. The gaps helped provide an escape for the smoke and an exit for the rats that appeared to frequent the storeroom.

"We passed, what, four carpenters on the way here?" Hadrian was looking under the table and rocking it. "I mean, how hard can it be to level a table?" He pulled his short sword and, drawing it along his chair's leg, planed off a small wedge-shaped sliver, which he tucked under the table. He tested it and smiled.

"I don't understand," Royce said for the third time. "Why wouldn't she even come out?"

"Perhaps she didn't recall your name," Albert suggested. "Also she might have been *busy*."

Royce shook his head. "The girl said she wasn't accepting guests. I'm not even sure she does *that*—not anymore at least. She never entertained when we were there. I think she just manages the place. And if she was busy, we would've been told to wait, not, 'She won't see you *under any circumstances*.'"

Hadrian knew that it was those three words at the end that irked Royce the most. He almost never saw his partner caught off guard. Royce expected the worst of people and, unfortunately, they rarely proved him wrong. But this was different. He had seen Royce's face when Jasmine, Julie—or was it Jollin?—had said those words. Royce had been visibly stunned. To be honest, Hadrian had also been surprised.

After catching an arrow in the back and passing out in Tom the Feather's barnyard, Hadrian had woken up on a comfortable bed surrounded by lovely women. He thought he'd died and regretted every time he'd ever cursed Maribor's name. Gwen had spent most of her time with Royce but had ordered the girls around like a seasoned marshal and she saw to it his every need was met. Not knowing how they had arrived there, Hadrian assumed Medford House was a refuge Royce had used in the past and that he and Gwen were old friends. But as the days passed, he learned that they had never met before the night they showed up on her doorstep.

Hadrian wasn't sure how many days he had lost, drifting in and out of consciousness while the Nyphron Church had continued to search for them. Patrols entered the Lower Quarter. Questions were asked. Gwen had made preparations to hide them at a moment's notice, but no one ever attempted to search the house. After the first week, things had calmed down. By the end of the first month it appeared they had been forgotten. Still, he and Royce rarely set foot outside.

It was Royce who had finally announced that they would be leaving. He hadn't heard of any disagreement between the two and Gwen gave them both a tight hug, and Royce received a kiss when they left. That kiss had shocked Royce too. Maybe she did it because she liked spooking him. Royce often reminded Hadrian of a cat, a bit too self-assured and sure-footed. It was entertaining to see him knocked off balance. They had left on good terms and that's why her refusal to see them made no sense. She had seemed genuinely sad when they had gone away.

Albert sat with his back to the bar, his hands folded on the table, looking over his shoulder longingly.

"We're here for a meal," Hadrian reminded the viscount. "The nonliquid kind."

Albert turned back, licking his lips. "Right...of course."

Hadrian stared at the viscount. The man was the very picture of poverty, his face little more than a pair of eyes peering out of a wreath of grimy hair. "You know, it's hard to imagine what you'd look like without that beard. Is there really a face under there?"

Albert sat up straight. "Of course, and a handsome one at that. I was a looker when I could afford it."

"I just don't understand," Royce mumbled again.

"Understand what?" A man approached the table, wiping dirty hands on a dirtier rag.

The moment he saw him, Hadrian thought of the scarecrows that had dotted the farms along the country roads. There had been one in particular, with a pumpkin for a head and a straw-stuffed hat, that could have been this man's twin. The main differences being that the man was far older and less attractive than the pumpkin.

"Why there is such a shortage of fetching barmaids," Hadrian answered for him. Hadrian had meant it as a joke, but the man scowled back, causing Hadrian to rethink whether he had anything in common with a pumpkin at all.

"They're all across the street," he replied with a sour look at the wall, which if it had a window would look out on Medford House. His stare was so intense and sustained that all three followed his line of sight. "Had a whole passel working a year ago, but *she* made them all leave."

"She?" Royce asked.

"Yeah," the barman said with a sneer and a dismissive wave of his hand at the wall. "That Calian whore that runs the joint. She used to work here. Then the bitch betrayed me. She left and took the rest with her. Now look at the place. A man can hardly make a decent living with them across the street."

"How about we get a round of ale?" Hadrian said quickly, causing Albert to brighten.

"I'd prefer rum," Albert declared.

"No rum," Hadrian said. "Oh yeah, and no ale for him either—just bring a small beer for him and a pint for me. How about some wine, Royce?"

"No."

"Well, think on it while I get the others. Only got two hands anyway," the man said. "Name's Grue, by the way...Raynor Grue. I own this place."

"Royce?" Hadrian asked after Grue left. "Whatcha thinking?"

He only smiled back.

For most people smiling was a good thing, but Hadrian couldn't recall if he'd ever seen Royce smile from pleasure. Or maybe what gave Royce pleasure was different from most people. In any case, he'd learned that it was rarely a good sign, especially if accompanied by a raised hood and an eerie silence.

"Are you sure you want to eat here?" Albert asked. "I'll bet it's cheap, but we'll need to check our pork chops for tails."

"Maybe they have a good soup," Hadrian suggested.

"Still gonna have to check for tails...and whiskers."

Royce ignored them both and never took his eyes off Grue, who soon returned as promised.

"Make a decision yet?" Grue asked, dropping off the drinks, which made a healthy thud on the table.

"Still thinking," Royce replied, wearing the same smile. "Why don't you tell me more about the woman who runs that place across the street."

"Gwen DeLancy? Not much to tell. She's an ungrateful whore."

Albert shot Hadrian a look of alarm.

"When she came to Medford, no one would hire her. Being the tolerant, understanding man I am, I looked past her being from Calis. Heck, I thought it might even be a benefit...you know, exotic and all. So I took her in, but she just wanted to serve drinks." He gave a little snort that actually made Hadrian want to punch him. "I set her straight quick enough. A good thick belt will do that, you know?"

"You beat her?" Royce asked.

"Had to—she refused to make my customers happy.

'Course, nothing like what that other fella did last night. Right now I bet she was wishing she hadn't run out on me. She has a hired man, but he didn't do much. People around here respect me. They know there's a high price to pay for damaging the merchandise, and I've not had much of that kind of trouble."

Royce's smile vanished as his eyes narrowed. "Gwen's hurt? What happened?"

"I told you, she got the piss beat out of her last night by one of her *customers*. Rumor has it she can't even walk. Might be true—I ain't seen her today. I don't think anyone has. From what I heard he messed her up bad. Maybe he cut her up and she's too embarrassed to show her face—now that it ain't so pretty no more."

Royce began squeezing his hands into fists. "Who did it?"

Grue shrugged. "No idea. I was sleeping one off last night. Just heard about it from Willard, who said she was dragged out into the street by some fella he didn't recognize—but Willard ain't the shiniest pot on the shelf."

"Did she tell the sheriff?" Hadrian asked.

Grue chuckled. "Ethan don't care what happens to no stupid whore—less she dies. Then he's required to see the body is removed from the city and make sure restitution is paid. I had that happen once. There's this guy named Stane, a real ugly sort who works the docks and always smells of fish. He killed one of my girls." Grue made a face like he tasted something awful. "It was bad. But there was nothing that could be done about it. Well Gwen, being crazy like she is, she went and got Ethan. I told him Stane's a good customer and that he had agreed on a price for damages, pretty generous, I might add. And that should have been the end of it. But Gwen got mad and that's when she left for good. She thought Stane might get her, too, but he and I had a real good talk and he wasn't gonna do it again. Didn't matter, though. Turns out she had money saved and leased the shack across the street."

"You're sitting *here* and call *that* a shack?" Albert asked.

"Oh yeah, it was a dump. They fixed it up some. Not sure how. She couldn't have had *that* much coin. I'm guessing she serviced a whole lot of people along Artisan Row. All I know is she's made it impossible to run a decent business anymore. I tried getting more girls, but they all go over there. I used to make a quarter of my coin from prostitution. Now I'm left with only the ale and gambling."

"What about food?"

"I don't sell no food."

Hadrian glanced at Albert, who offered a smile.

"I guess I could've beat her again—probably should've, but I don't suspect it would've done much good. She's too willful, that one. She'll end up dead because of it, believe me." He turned to Royce. "Say, have you decided what ya want yet? There isn't a lot of choices, to be honest."

"You're right about that. Right now all I want is to find out who hurt Gwen."

Grue chuckled. "That sort of thing can get an idiot killed."

Royce offered that cold smile of his again and said, "I'm thinking more than one."

❧

They stepped out of The Hideous Head, and Royce made a quick left, heading up Wayward Street in the direction of Artisan Row.

"You're moving like you've got a purpose," Hadrian said as he and Albert struggled to keep up.

"Heading to a tailor now I hope," Albert mentioned. "For living in a barn this nightshirt is ample, but out in the wind it's not up to the task."

"And you're aware that our horses are still back at the House, right?"

Without a word Royce paused at a fence that blocked the entrance to the alley running behind The Hideous Head. He kicked it hard, breaking two slats. He kicked again, popping off the crossbeam.

"Easy, Royce," Hadrian said, stunned. In all the time they'd been together he'd never seen Royce lose control like that.

Royce picked up the crossbeam and entered the alley.

"Does this mean no tailor?" Albert asked as they chased after him.

Grabbing Albert by the chest of his nightshirt, Royce shoved him behind a stack of crates set against the side of a storage barn.

"Sorry!" the viscount said. "I was just asking."

"Shut up," Royce ordered. He wasn't looking at Albert. He peered back toward the street.

Royce tilted his head slightly toward the mouth of the alley and then ducked in alongside Albert. Seeing this, Hadrian did the same. No one moved or said a word.

A minute later a man walked past. He was thin, dressed in a beat-up jacket with the collar raised, and his hands were stuffed in his sleeves. He could have been anyone, a weaver, a messenger, a dyer, or a baker. Startled upon seeing them, the man tried to hurry past. Royce walked out and hit him hard from behind with the board.

"Royce!" Hadrian yelled.

The man collapsed with a grunt and before he could recover his wind, Royce leapt on his back and used the crossbeam under the man's neck for a choke hold.

"What are you doing?" Albert asked, shocked.

"He's been watching us since we tried to see Gwen." Royce

slammed the man's head against the stones, hard enough for it to bounce. Grabbing him by the hair, he pulled his head back and placed his white dagger against the prone man's throat. "I'm not a patient person in general, and today is a bad one. You're only going to get one shot at this. Tell me why you're following us to my satisfaction or I'm going to open your neck and let your blood drain. You're leaning downhill, so I won't even get my boots wet. Got it?"

The man gasped out a yes.

"Okay, go ahead."

"I'm supposed to check out anyone who visits the brothel."

"Why?"

"To see where they go, who they talk to."

"Why?"

"We're trying to find a girl."

"Gwen?"

"No. Her name is Rose." The man coughed.

Royce ignored it and kept the pressure tight. "She's a girl from the House?"

"Yes. Disappeared last night."

"And who is this *we* that's looking for her?"

The man hesitated and Royce began to cut.

"The Crimson Hand," he blurted out.

"Thieves' guild?"

"Yes."

"And why are you looking for Rose?"

"I don't know—honest I don't. I just know everyone's looking for her. I'm only supposed to watch and follow. That's all I can tell you."

Royce nodded. "Then you're no longer of value."

Hadrian saw the man's muscles stiffen and assumed Royce had slit his throat. It would not have been the first time. When

Royce said he had little patience, he meant it, and Hadrian was already wondering what to do with the body when a second later he noticed the man was still breathing.

"You can still save yourself by performing a service," Royce explained.

"Why? You'll just kill me afterward."

"Don't jump to conclusions before you hear what I have to say."

"I should warn you, if you kill me the Hand will find you."

"That's just the thing. I'm going to save them the trouble. I want you to take me to your guild."

CHAPTER 7

THE LADY OF FLOWERS

Gwen sat rocking on the edge of the bed, her face in her hand, crying.

Why now? Why did he have to come back now?

It hurt to cry. It hurt to do anything, but the shuddering was especially painful. Two of her ribs were cracked, and they ached whenever she took a breath. Closing her eyes brought images of Avon—her hair dyed crimson, eyes open but not seeing as they stared at the rafters of The Hideous Head. That was the last thing her friend ever saw—that and Stane's ugly face.

For Gwen, she had been convinced that the porch steps and the beautiful balustrades would be her last sight. They were painted white just like the fancy house in the Gentry Quarter. Just like she had always wanted. She had lain in the street, staring at the porch railings while he kicked her. She couldn't scream anymore—he had kicked out all the air. She expected to die. A whole year after leaving the Head, after thinking she might have escaped Avon's fate, it had happened again.

It would always happen.

The girls had done so well. Better than Gwen had ever thought possible. Medford House was the reality she dreamed of, a sanctuary for women like her. They had grown strong over the past year. Medford House had a prized reputation and men came from as far away as Westfield and East March. Over the last few months the clientele had shifted. While they still drew dockworkers and merchants, new faces—men with swords or those dressed in silks and fur—had recently visited. The nobility had discovered Medford House and had liked it enough to return. Names were never given—not real ones. They called themselves Todd the Tinker or Bill the Baker, except the baker arrived in a coach and wore a fur mantle...and the tinker dressed in velvet and silk. Patrons using false monikers is what gave Gwen the idea of changing the girls' names.

She'd always hoped that the women who worked the House would eventually leave it. That they would find new, better lives, but how could they if their names followed them? How could Jollin, Mae, or even Etta settle down somewhere if everyone knew what they had been? All the girls had picked pretty, exotic, or cute names. Jasmine, Daisy, Olive—Mae had wanted to be called Lily-of-the-Valley, but they had talked her into going with just Lily. The only two who had kept their real names were Rose and Gwen. It just seemed silly to Rose to change her name to a different flower, and Gwen could never imagine leaving Medford House.

"They've left the Head," Abby, now known as Tulip, said. "All three went around to the alley. Royce looked awfully mad. He beat up the fence."

Gwen brought her good hand to her lips, trying to hold in a sob.

"Do you need anything?" Tulip asked.

With her head down so that the scarf hid her eyes, Gwen shook her head. Tulip lingered, and Gwen heard the faint close of her door and the creak of the steps.

Why now?

Every day since Royce and Hadrian had left, Gwen had

looked for their return. In the evening she sat on the porch swing, staring down the length of Wayward Street, imagining she could see Royce riding up or perhaps just walking with that cloak of his rippling in the breeze. She had always known there was no guarantee he would return.

In all the time he had lain on her bed, she never once looked at his palm. The idea felt deceitful, indecent. She was there to help, not rifle his pockets.

Gwen's entire life had been leading to that single event. Her mother had known. She had dragged her daughter on the road west, then died along the way, but she had made Gwen promise to finish the trip and make Medford her home. She never said why. Gwen might have never completed the journey if not for the mysterious man, in whose eyes she had seen so much and yet understood so little. All she knew was that she needed to save a man who would come in the night, dressed in his own blood. After so many years of waiting, of not knowing if it was true or if the choices she had made had changed her future, Royce had arrived. She had saved him just as foretold. After so long, she finally had the key to the riddle, but she refused to open his palm to look for answers.

After the men had been cleaned and the doctor had finished his work, Royce had lain unconscious, wrapped in white linens. He had looked so serene. She had touched his hand, soft and so unlike other men. Royce Melborn was, in a word, *elegant*. Her only hint to his identity was the brand on his shoulder, a dark M.

"How is Hadrian?" Those were the first words out of his mouth when Royce finally woke. He had no concern for himself. This, she knew, was a good man.

"He's fine." She could tell from the look in his eyes that such a simple answer wouldn't do. She added, "A doctor tended to his wounds and he's sleeping quietly."

"It was you on the street." His expression shifted from recognition to confusion. "Who are you? Why did you help us?"

In all of her imaginings of that moment, she had always expected him to know who she was and why he was there—he was supposed to be the one with all the answers, filling in the blanks for her. In that instant she realized this man hadn't a clue, and Gwen smiled at the thought of actually telling him, *I'm the daughter of a fortune-teller, and I've traveled across four nations to make Medford my home just to be here when you arrived so that I could save your life.* But that wasn't the time; the man was barely alive.

"My name is Gwen DeLancy. I run this brothel. I helped because you needed me."

This didn't alleviate his confusion, but he didn't inquire further. He was still exhausted, still in pain.

"Who are you?" She had to ask. After waiting so long for this foretold meeting, she needed to know. He didn't answer for a long time, only stared at her.

"Royce," he finally said. The word had come out reluctantly, grudgingly, handed over only out of obligation.

She let him sleep again after that—she had enough; she had his name.

He was quiet after that first exchange. In the following few days, he asked only about Hadrian, and it wasn't until she finally helped him walk into the other room to see his friend that he had started to relax.

"You don't look like you should be walking yet," Hadrian had said from his bed as Gwen helped Royce stagger into Etta's room.

"He shouldn't be," Gwen replied.

"You all right?" Royce asked, his voice harsh and demanding.

Hadrian offered a lopsided smile. "Last thing I remember,

you were knee-deep in a bloody puddle and I was trying to dig you out from under a dead horse in the pouring rain. And oh yes—I had just been shot with an arrow." He looked around at Etta's bedroom, which had an excess of lace and an abundance of flowers. "Yeah…I'd say I'm doing better."

"Okay," Royce said, and with Gwen's help had turned to leave.

"You got up and came in here just for that?" Hadrian asked.

"I was bored," Royce replied.

"He's been worried to the point of not sleeping," Gwen said.

Royce scowled. "I wanted to make certain these people weren't…you know."

"By Mar, Royce." Hadrian shook his head, amazed. "They saved our lives. You can trust them."

By the time Gwen had Royce back in bed, he was bleeding again, and she had to redress the wound in his side. Before they arrived, someone had done such a terrible job of stitching him that the doctor was forced to fix it. When she was done, he caught her hand.

"If you…if you're up to something…if you're trying to…" Royce hesitated, holding her, his arms weak and shaking. She could see him struggling. "Why did you really do it? Why'd you help us?"

"I told you."

His expression didn't change. He didn't believe her.

Gwen smiled.

Royce smirked. "I don't get it. Something's not right, and trust me, I'm not the kind you want to cross. Understand?"

She nodded, still smiling.

"Well…good." He let go of her. "And you should probably be careful, because just about the entire world is looking for us."

Royce had never provided details, but Gwen understood the two were wanted and on the run. She was housing criminals, a hanging offense if she was caught.

Looking back on those months, Gwen saw them as the most intensely lived of her life. She was never more frightened and never so euphoric. She spent her days tracking gossip and trying to squelch any rumors about a man who had cried for help on Wayward Street the week of the big storm. Her nights had been spent feeding, cleaning, and dressing Royce, during which they held short—often cryptic—conversations she never fully understood. Weak as a kitten, he needed her for everything, and she could see it pained him more than his wounds.

At first he was quiet, but as the days passed they began to discuss such serious things as cooking, sewing, the snow that soon fell, and Wintertide.

"You probably celebrate the holiday with a feast and decorations," Royce said. By then he was able to sit up and the two spoke in the light of the single candle. "Lots of family and friends, dancing and songs."

Gwen noticed a twinge of sadness, even spite in his voice. She shook her head. "I've never celebrated Wintertide. My mother and I were always traveling, usually alone, and we never had money for any feasts. Since she died"—Gwen shrugged—"I've been struggling just to survive. It's hard to celebrate when your choices are starving or being a slave."

She remembered he appeared surprised, even suspicious. "You don't look like you're hurting for food."

"No, not now. I finally decided I didn't want to be a victim anymore. I got to the point where I was just tired of being afraid."

He reached out then and for the first time touched her for no reason. He placed his hand on hers and gave a soft squeeze. The hint of malice she'd seen in his face had been replaced by sympathy—not pity, but understanding, a shared appreciation that nearly made her cry.

Until then she had always been the loyal daughter, the detested Calian immigrant, the whore. Even the girls, who knew most of her story, viewed her as either some sort of hero or opportunist, depending on their mood. In Royce's eyes she could see the pain of struggling to survive reflected back. They were the same, two pieces of wood from different worlds but whose grain lined up, and it was then she knew she was falling in love.

That was the closest either had come to discussing themselves. Gwen had hoped he would volunteer more about himself, but he never did. From his and Hadrian's comments she guessed the two were bandits, highwaymen perhaps—but who was she to judge after so many had judged her.

She never did tell him about her gift to tell the future by reading palms or how her saving Royce had been foretold years before. With the touch of his hand and that gentle squeeze, such things became trivial—part of a past that she preferred to let go. She had him finally, and it didn't matter who he was or what he had done.

Snow fell outside while inside Royce and Hadrian convalesced. As they grew stronger, they came downstairs to sit with the rest around the fire. They had sung songs and told stories—at least Hadrian had. Royce made a habit of sitting quietly beside her—always beside her. And she couldn't help noticing the glares he had given Dixon.

Dixon was quite literally the man of the House, a local carter with a strong back and a soft spot for Gwen. She had employed him to do the heavy lifting in the days when they built Medford House. Since then, Dixon remained as the unofficial guardian of the girls.

"Listen," Royce told her, and then hesitated. He did that

a lot, as if every sentence suffered a debate in his head. It had been two months after they had arrived and Royce and Gwen were in the bedroom. Outside, snow was falling again as Wintertide neared. "I...ah..." He faltered once more. "You didn't have to help us. Shouldn't have, really. Makes no sense. Dangerous and nothing in it for you. You spent money paying that doctor and more feeding us, not to mention all the time you... you...well, you know what you did. So anyway..." He sighed and shook his head. "This doesn't come easy to me, but...I want to thank you, okay?"

She waited. Gwen thought he might kiss her then. She hoped he would—hoped he'd throw his arms around her, say he was in love and that he'd stay with her always, but he didn't. Instead he announced he and Hadrian would be leaving at dawn.

It felt as if he were taking her heart with him that chilly morning when he and Hadrian had set out. She had kept her teeth tight together for fear she would say more than she should, or worse, start to cry. The prophecy had never promised anything for her. The fantasy of him being her destiny, of them living happily ever after was all Gwen's doing, but still she had hoped, and she continued to hope as she watched them ride away, leaving two lines of tracks in the newly fallen snow.

She prayed he would be back.

But why now? Why now, when I can't even see him?

She refused to let Royce see her battered. Maybe it wouldn't matter. Maybe he didn't really care, but if he did, then he would want to know who did it and like a fool he would want revenge. Men always wanted revenge. Royce would get himself killed trying to protect her, and she wouldn't let that happen. Better that he thought she didn't care about him. Better that he never found out the truth. Better that she kept him out of it or he would end up like Dixon—or worse.

Why now? And where is Rose?

༄

Gwen heard the front door bang open and her heart fluttered. Loud voices came up though the floorboards but were too muffled to understand. She pushed to her feet. She was unsteady and groped for the bedpost and then the wall as she shuffled toward the door. Keeping herself upright with only one arm was a challenge; seeing clearly was another. Both eyes were swollen, her right entirely closed, and the crying hadn't helped.

Reaching the hallway, she could hear better.

"...we don't know. That's all he said." William the Carpenter's voice.

"What about Rose?" Mae asked.

"Thought she might have returned." A pause, then William continued. "The high constable has all his sheriffs out looking for her. Even hired on a whole bunch of new deputies."

Jollin came up the steps, shocked to see Gwen in the hallway. "It's okay—just Will."

Gwen nodded and Jollin took her arm. Together they shuffled back to the bedroom.

"You're supposed to be sleeping." Jollin pretended to be cross. "Doctor's orders. Remember?"

"I should have never let her go," Gwen said as Jollin laid her back on the mattress.

"How could you know? It was the castle. Were you going to say no to *them*? And it was just a surprise party." Jollin pulled the blanket up, covering Gwen. "Rose is young and stupid. She's probably whooping it up with some squire who bought her too much wine. Or maybe some baron took her away in a fancy carriage to his country estate for a few days. She's probably making bags of money while we worry."

"I should have realized. I just didn't think it would be this soon, because Rose hadn't..."

"Hadn't what?"

"Fallen in love."

Jollin clamped her palm over Gwen's forehead. "You're a little warm. I'm going to ask the doctor to come back."

"I'm—" Gwen was going to say *fine* but realized how stupid that sounded. "I don't have a fever. I'm not out of my head." Gwen thought how she might explain that she had seen a glimpse of Rose's future in her palm but didn't think that would help. "I'm just worried."

"We all are. And I'll go across the street and borrow Grue's strap to beat her senseless for doing this to us. I can't believe she can be so insensitive. She has to know we'd be sick to death by now." She reached up and fluffed Gwen's pillow with a little too much effort.

"I think she's in trouble," Gwen said. "Serious trouble."

Jollin nodded. "I think so too." She paused. "Maybe we all are. And we don't even have Dixon to protect us anymore."

"Have you checked in on him?"

"I was about to head over to the doctor's when I found you dancing in the hallway."

"You call that dancing?"

"I didn't say you were any good at it."

This brought a reluctant smile to Gwen's lips. "Thank you."

Jollin gave her a kiss. "Dixon will be fine. He's not nearly as bad as Royce and Hadrian were. No stitches even, just a few broken bones—like you—only he's an ox. Just needs time to rest and when he wakes he'll eat us into poverty he will."

"I just wish I knew what happened to Rose."

CHAPTER 8

THE NEW SWORD

"Try it now."

Reuben ducked and pulled the heavy chain mail over his head. The steel ring shirt dropped with a jingle. Heavier than he expected. He had watched the king's soldiers run, jump, and fight as if it weighed nothing. Now he wondered how they did it.

"Walk around, see how it feels." The smith watched him carefully. Bastion—sometimes called the *Old Bastard* by many of the castle guards—always reminded Reuben of a dwarf, like in the fairy tales his aunt used to tell. Short, stocky, and hairy, he had a graying beard and eight stubby fingers. He lost two once upon a time and jested that as long as he still had one finger and a thumb on each hand, he would still be the best smith in Melengar.

Reuben strode around the yard, circling the anvil. All the weight was on his shoulders, as if he were carrying two sacks of barley. When he turned, the shirt dragged, slowing him down, then the momentum would catch up and push him farther than he wanted to go.

"What do you think, boy?"

He thought it was terrible that he was expected to wear something so limiting, but he guessed he would think differently when a sword hit him. He also did not have time to discuss it. Reuben had been on his way to the castle when the smith dragged him over to do the fitting. He couldn't refuse; he needed the mail that night, and putting him off would have been suspicious.

"Hard to move."

"You'll get used to it. Everyone does. Soon you'll feel naked without it. And here's your sword." The smith handed him the long blade, encased in a sheath complete with belt. Reuben had expected a secondhand falchion, something beat-up and rusted. This one looked new.

"Wow," he muttered as he drew the blade. Old Bastion knew how to make swords but this... "It's beautiful. I didn't know you—"

"I didn't. That's Delgos steel." The smith took one of his big gloves off and wiped his forehead with it. "We get most of our metal, and a lot of our swords, from Trent. Lousy chunks of mountain turds. Mostly iron. Ruddy things can't hold any kind of an edge and will notch if you tap them. Trent smiths don't care. They're just meeting quotas. They get paid the same no matter what the quality. But down in Delgos, sword makers can sell to the open market. So it's worth the extra effort. That blade you're holding was folded maybe half a dozen times. Harder and sharper than anything I can make. You'll be able to shave with that when you get enough hair on your face. This here blade was bought special."

"Why are you giving it to me?"

"On account I was told to."

"By who?"

"Prince Alric."

"The prince? Did he say why?"

"Nope."

"Did you ask?"

Bastion looked at him funny. "You don't ask a prince nothing, boy. He says give you this sword and I give it. And I wouldn't say nothing about it to anyone, neither. Best to keep such favor with the great ones to yourself—otherwise people can get jealous, and a sound beating is no way to start your new career. Now be careful with that. When I said it was sharp as a bloody razor, I meant it."

Reuben sheathed his sword, appreciating the sound it made. *Sharp as a razor.* He slipped his burgundy and gold tabard on and, grabbing his cloak and equally new helm, jogged to the castle, jingling as he went. Running was harder than walking. His balance was off, something he'd need to get used to. He entered the great doors to the northern foyer, a wide gallery of polished stone pillars, displayed suits of armor, and hallways that led to sweeping staircases. Reuben never spent much time in the castle. He didn't feel comfortable there. The only place he really felt comfortable, besides the woodshed, was the stables. No one looked down on him there except the horses. The castle was filled with eyes, judgmental, cruel eyes. It was the den of the squires and their like. Here had been where they learned the kindnesses that they had shown him time and again. Everything was cold stone.

Almost everything.

As he made a quick right turn to avoid the large halls, he nearly ran into Arista Essendon. She let out a noise of surprise and staggered backward, her hand to her chest and eyes wide. Reuben's new outfit had made his ability to stop or veer awkward. It wasn't much, just a half second off, but enough to make him look, or at least feel, stupid.

"We keep running into each other, don't we?" she said, her voice soft and beautiful as bird song.

"I'm sorry." He bowed to her and then hastily added, "Your Highness."

She glanced at the helm in his arms. "Lunch?"

He looked down at the apple, cheese, and meat he had stuffed inside. "Ah...yes, sort of."

"Have a good day," she said, but stood still.

It took a second for Reuben to realize he was blocking her passage, and he stepped aside.

He felt like a fool as he watched her walk past. Why did he do everything wrong in front of her? His stomach sank and his shoulders drooped as he faced the reality that his clumsiness didn't matter. She was the princess, and what he wanted could never be. She would marry a prince, duke, or king and then he would watch her leave. She would ride out the gate waving from the carriage window, never to be seen again—at least not by him. He had always known she was beyond his reach. In all his daydreams, he had never once envisioned touching her, except that one moment when their fingers might collide as he handed her the cup of water at the well. The idea of kissing her lips was too absurd even for dreams. All he longed for was to do something right, to have her notice him, to see him as brave, or smart, or good. He wanted her to look back over her shoulder as they parted with an impressed expression that said, *If only he were noble.* He didn't think that was too much to ask of the world, a simple moment of acknowledgment, an instant to turn her head and know that for one brief breath of time she saw him the way he saw her. He could suffer in silence the rest of his life knowing she had truly seen him and that maybe she felt the same way toward him that he did toward her.

Feeling as though he had been stabbed in the heart yet again, he followed the servant corridors the rest of the way. Grabbing a lantern, he went down the stairs and entered the castle dungeons. They were empty. The dungeons rarely housed prisoners, or when they did, it wasn't for long. Justice was dispensed quickly in Medford. Thieves had any number of fingers or hands cut off. Debtors were beaten. Killers were hanged. Saboteurs were torn limb from limb and traitors quartered. The dungeon was merely the waiting place for hangings, and recently the lord high constable was being swift with those. Which made it the perfect place for isolation.

Reuben walked to the last cell on the last row, which being L-shaped was the perfect choice. In there a prisoner couldn't be seen from the window. He unlocked the door with the key that normally hung from the peg at the top of the stairs, which he now kept. He had locked the door not to imprison her but to prevent anyone else from entering. As far as he knew, that was the only key. She was still there, huddled in a ball against the far wall, wrapped in the blanket he'd brought her.

"Morning, Rose, how are you?"

She opened her eyes and peered up, blinking against the light. This was the first time he had had a good look. She was cute, downright pretty, and he imagined she would be prettier without all the paint, especially since a good deal of it had been smeared by tears. She had a bruise on her cheek and ugly scrapes on her arms and legs from the climb the night before.

"It's morning?"

"Yes." He knelt down before her. "Are you hungry? I brought food."

She sat up to look and took the block of cheese, biting into it. "Thank you," she said, her words muffled.

He handed her the little skin of weak wine. She swallowed, then asked, "What's going on? Is the king alive?"

"The king is fine. As far as I can tell, nothing at all happened last night. Well, except that everyone is looking for you."

"Why? I didn't do anything."

"I don't know."

"What did your father say?"

"I haven't seen him yet. He was on duty all night and hasn't returned."

"You didn't tell anyone else, did you?"

"No." Reuben shook his head. "I've been thinking about what you said. How not just anyone can get in that tower. That's part of the royal residence wing. Only the castle guards and nobles are allowed above the third floor. Whoever you heard either had to be part of the castle's security or someone important, and I'm afraid of telling the wrong person."

"So now what? I just sit here?"

"I'm sorry. I'm sure it must be awful, but I think this is the safest thing. I don't know what else to do."

She nodded but he could tell she was disappointed. "I owe you my life. Thank you."

A silly thing to say, but he could see she was sincere. He felt awkward. He wasn't used to anyone being grateful for anything he did. "Most people would say I really haven't done much."

She gave him a sad, twisted smile. "I think most people would say my life really isn't worth much."

Reuben thought again about just how pretty she was—big trusting eyes, tiny nose, and round face. It felt like a crime locking her in such a horrible place.

"If my father can discover the traitor, it will be the king who will owe you his life. Who knows, maybe he will reward you with your own estate."

"I'd settle for being back home and sharing a room at Medford House."

He smiled at her. She smiled back.

He honestly hoped she would be rewarded, taken care of so she could live a different life. But Reuben had already seen enough of the world to know dreams almost never came true.

❧

"Hilfred!" Alric called out as Reuben was walking back to
the barracks in the hope of finding his father. Turning, he saw
the prince flanked by the Pickerings. All of them in tunics he
hadn't seen them wear before. Reuben wondered just how
much fine clothing the nobility could afford.

"Your Highness." He bowed. "Your Lordships." He
repeated the gesture.

"Got your new sword, I see."

"Yes, Your Highness, and thank you."

Alric waved with nonchalance. "It's one of my practice
blades."

Mauvin stared at his new sword. "May I?"

Reuben drew it and presented the pommel.

The elder Pickering took it and sliced the air, weaving the
blade back and forth in figure eights. Then he released the
grip, let the sword roll over the back of his hand, and grabbed
it again. He tossed the sword up and caught it on his forearm
where the hilt met the blade. He watched the balance for a
moment before tossing it again and taking it by the grip once
more. He looked down the length of the blade, turning it in the
light, then glanced at the prince. "This has never been used."

Alric shrugged. "I don't do as much practicing as I should.
But that's why I need men like Hilfred to be well armed, yes?"

"A bit too heavy, and the balance is off about an eighth of
an inch, but not bad," Mauvin declared. "And I'd wrap that
grip with a good rough hide or it will slip as soon as your hand
starts to sweat, which will be exactly when you don't want
your grip to slip."

Mauvin spun the blade expertly and presented the sword
back to Reuben.

The prince pulled an apple from the small purse that hung

from his belt and began tossing it up in the air and catching it. "How much trouble did you get in last night?" Alric asked him.

"My father was on duty all night, so I don't know yet."

"Oh right, I heard they had run some security drill or something. Luckily I slept through it." The prince threw the apple up through the branches of the oak tree, where it cut through the leaves. On the way back, it glanced off a branch and bounced wide of his catch. Fanen was there to make the save and held the fruit up in silent victory.

Alric smiled. "Say, we're thinking of doing some more hunting tonight. Interested?"

"I'm sorry, Your Highness, but I can't. Tonight will be my first shift as a *real* guard. I'll be standing the front gate. And the big party for the new chancellor is tonight. Aren't you expected to be there?"

They glanced at each other with sinister smiles. "These galas are boring. Our parents are always introducing us to people we don't know and don't want to know—like old women in jewels who like to kiss and smell of cheese. We thought we'd sneak out. Since everyone will be busy and the castle filled with people, no one will even know we're gone."

"Except the gate guard," Mauvin mentioned, and raising an incriminating finger, he added, "Who would be you."

"Oh...I see. You want me to pretend I never saw you leave."

"Just if anyone asks, which I doubt."

Fanen tossed the apple back to the prince, who threw it once more. It went up higher, sending a cloud of yellow leaves cascading down and making it difficult to tell where the apple had gone. This time the fruit bounced off several branches, and Fanen made a valiant grab before the apple hit the grass.

"These parties are hectic and go on all night," Alric

explained. "No one wants us around anyway, so you'll be fine. What do you say?"

"What *can* I say? You're the prince."

Alric smiled. "What'd I tell you—I love this guy." He turned to the Pickerings. "I've got to do a fitting for a new doublet. Wanna come watch me annoy the tailor?"

"Tempting," Mauvin said sarcastically, "but I think I'll stay here and give our new guard some tips. Who knows, maybe we'll take him to Percepliquis with us."

"Suit yourself." Alric trotted back up the hill, forgetting his apple.

Mauvin circled Reuben, studying him. "Care to try out the new equipment?" He had a mischievous glint in his eye. "I did promise to train you, remember?"

Reuben felt as if a bumblebee hummed around him, unsure if it might sting. Until recently, Reuben's experience with nobles hadn't been good. "I thought you were joking. And I do have to—"

"Pickerings don't joke about sword fighting. Now draw your weapon."

Certain he was about to be humiliated by a boy three years younger, Reuben nevertheless drew his blade. It sang in a way no sword he had ever touched before had. A high ring that sounded deadly.

"Guard up."

Reuben raised the blade. So much lighter than the others he had practiced with.

"Is that your stance? Good Maribor, what have they been teaching you? Fanen!"

His brother walked behind Reuben and repositioned him like he was a doll. Dropping on his knees, the boy grabbed Reuben's ankles and shifted his feet. "Left foot back and turned out," Fanen muttered. "Right foot forward."

When he was done, Reuben was standing sideways and feeling a bit awkward.

"Okay, now bend your knees—just a little—and get up on the balls of your feet. Okay, good. Now attack me."

Sharp as a razor.

Reuben made a weak effort, and Mauvin raised his eyebrows. "Are you joking?"

"This sword is sharp. I'd rather not hurt a nobleman in—"

Mauvin rolled his eyes and shook his head. "You stand about as much chance of touching me with that blade as you do of marrying the princess. Now c'mon."

Reuben knew Mauvin hadn't meant it—well, he did, but he couldn't have known his words had cut deeper than his sword was ever likely to. Still, it made attacking Mauvin easier.

Reuben stepped forward and made two attempts to swing before Mauvin stopped him. "It's not a bloody *axe*, Hilfred. Think of it more like a knife. You wouldn't hammer at a loaf of bread the way you split logs, would you? This is a blade. Slice, stab, use your wrist as well as your arm."

"He's not even holding the grip right." Fanen pointed at his hand.

Mauvin and Fanen taught him together, starting with his grip, then his feet. He learned to shuffle instead of step. Then it was thrusts and finally parries. Fanen eventually got bored, snatched up the apple, and sat down on the stone bench next to the rosebushes. He bit into the fruit and, holding it clutched in his teeth, began jotting something down with a bit of graphite into a small book of parchment.

Mauvin rolled his eyes at his brother. "More poetry?"

Fanen ignored him.

"Okay, Hilfred, try that move again, only this time—"

"Sorry," Reuben said. "I really do appreciate this, but I have something very important I must do."

Mauvin's shoulders slumped.

"I'm sorry. I really have to go."

Mauvin sighed. "We didn't get far, but Alric ought to sleep a little better knowing at least one of his guards understands the basics. Well...good luck tonight."

Reuben didn't know if he should bow or what. He opted for a polite head bob and then jogged down the hill toward the barracks. His father had to be back by now. As he ran, he felt his new sword clap his thigh and a small smile pulled at his lips. The prince had given him a sword. *The prince!* And the Pickerings had taught him fencing—actually taught him, instead of pummeling him senseless. His elation was tempered when he concluded they were only using him to sneak out. The three were buying his silence with pretend friendship. Nobles didn't make friends with common soldiers. Still, the sword was nice—he might even get to keep it—and he had to admit he did feel a bit more confident using it, now that Mauvin had explained things better. When going through basic training, he had failed to learn much. The instructors spent all their time with the noble boys, while he was left to watch over their shoulders. His practice was against fence posts, as the others had refused to pair off with him. His two sparrings with Mauvin were the first real practices he had ever experienced.

ༀ

"Where you been, boy?" Richard Hilfred barked as soon as Reuben entered.

Reuben knew the tone—a harsh accusation, with the snap of military authority. His father sat at the little table. His shirt was off, his feet bare, everything else cast on the floor. His father's uniform had never touched the ground before, and Reuben stared at the crumpled tunic as if it were a dead body.

"I was getting my chain and—"

His father stood and struck Reuben with his left fist. He swung backhand but had put his weight into the blow. Reuben fell, hitting the door with his head on the way down. There was a loud hollow *thunk*, but he couldn't tell if the sound came from the door or his skull.

"What'd I tell you about getting noticed? What'd I tell you about the greats? Stupid kid."

Only then did he notice his father had a dark bottle in his right hand. Reuben wondered if that was why he used his left hand. When struck, he had thought maybe his father was softening the blow, but now he wondered if he just didn't want to bother putting down the drink. His father lifted the bottle to his lips. He had to tilt the bottom high.

"You have no idea what these bastards are like," he growled. "The moment you get mixed up with them you're..." His father kicked the cot so that it hopped up, knocking the pillow to the floor. He sniffled, wiped his nose with his arm, and sat back down while taking another swig from the dark bottle. Reuben wondered where he got it. Bottles with labels were expensive, too expensive for soldiers, even members of the royal guard. "There's no such thing as honor, Rue. Chivalry is a joke, an idea some rotter poet made up. A snowball in midsummer, that's what it is. A chicken that can lay golden eggs. The great ones pretend to keep it for themselves so that fools like us will think it's real, but it's all lies. Remember that, boy."

Reuben got up. His face stung and he could taste blood from where his teeth cut the inside of his mouth. He stood on the far side of the room, his back pressed against the closed door. The distance afforded no real protection. The room was little more than twelve feet and his father need only take a step or two to hit him again.

"Take what you can get. Steal what you can get away with.

And trust no one. Love no one. That's the worst. Love is an awful thing. You let it in and it eats you from the inside. Turns your head around. You find yourself doing things, betraying yourself—and for what? For what! He could have done something. I...I risk my life every day for him, but what does he do for me? Where is he when I needed him?" He smacked his lips and sighed. "Everyone's out for themselves. And you had better be too—we all have to be or we'll be swallowed up."

Reuben felt the rough wood of the door with his fingers as his tongue played with the cut in his cheek. He didn't dare move or speak, but he knew he had to. Even if that meant another blow. Even if it brought the right hand. Even if his father forgot he still held the bottle. He had to tell his father the king was in danger. Maybe the news would snap him out of it. Looking back at the uniform, he doubted that.

His father sat down hard on the chair. Reuben took that as a good sign. He might not want to bother getting up just to kill his son.

"And you...what were you thinking? Raised by a woman, fussed over until you're good for nothing but merchant work. That's all boys raised by women are good for. Soft, pink things that think too much. Beware of thinking too much, boy. That, too, will get you in trouble."

As he spoke, the scar on the left side of his face moved with the pinching of his wrinkles, the stiff skin lagging a hair behind the rest, wiggling like a snake. The way his father had told the story, a big, crazy drunk had come at the king, killing three men on his way. The remaining two of the king's guards ran. Richard Hilfred had been the last to stand in the way. He got the scar, and before it had healed, he said it was possible to whistle a tune through the slit in his cheek. But the king had been saved.

"Dad?" Reuben said.

His father did not look up. He stared at the bottle, holding it slightly tilted as if he were judging the remainder.

"Someone is plotting to kill the king."

"Someone is *always* plotting to kill the king. That's why I have a job."

"I think it's someone in the castle."

Richard Hilfred cocked his head and squinted at him, his mouth slightly open, showing the gap of a missing lower tooth.

"What got this into your head?"

"I met someone who overheard a conversation between two men."

"What, at some tavern while you were out gallivanting with the prince? I warned you—"

"No, sir, right here in the castle."

His father's squint tightened, his mouth opening a hair wider. "One of them squires?" He shook his head and waved the bottle at him. "Don't listen to those silver-plated codpieces. They just want to start trouble. You should know that by now."

"Wasn't them."

"Whoever it is he's lying." His father finished the last of his bottle.

"It was a girl named Rose, the one everyone is looking for. She's a prostitute and was here for a party. She was hiding in a wardrobe in the high tower and overheard two men say they were going to kill the king. I hid her until I could talk to you. I didn't know who to trust."

His father stared at his son for a long time. He reached out to place the bottle on the table, but because he wasn't looking, he missed and it fell. It didn't shatter. The good heavy glass clinked and, being too empty to spill, just rolled under the bunk. His father got up slowly. Reuben was just as tall but felt infinitely smaller. Dozens of white lines cut across his father's chest, shoulders, and arms—more scars. Shadows of pain, framed with stretched tissue, some with rows of dots along them—sewing holes. They rode up and down with his breath.

"You know where this girl is?" His father's tone was clear, cold.

Reuben nodded.

"Where did you hide her?"

"She doesn't know any more than what I told you already. She didn't hear any names."

"Where?" He took a step, cutting the length of the room.

"The dungeon."

His father thought a moment, then nodded. "Keep her there. Keep her locked in."

"But she didn't do—"

"Don't *but* me, boy! Keep her there until I sort this out. That's the best place. And don't tell anyone else—you haven't, have you?"

He shook his head.

"Good. Now let me think."

His father bent down and picked up his tunic, then paused and glanced at Reuben. "It looks better on you."

CHAPTER 9

THE CRIMSON HAND

Hadrian walked behind the Crimson Hand thief. He had refused to give them his name, so Hadrian declared it to be Puzzle. Puzzle was not a trusting man and looked about as relaxed as a well-wound spring. Hadrian hadn't known many professional thieves. Until that walk from the Lower Quarter into Merchant Square, Royce had been the only one. He saw similarities, but differences too. Puzzle dressed like a thug. His short-waisted coat, with big cuffs and high collar, along with the woolen pants had the hardness of a dockworker, but he was too small and thin to pull the look off. His jacket swallowed him. He didn't walk like Royce either. There was none of the grace of his partner in the loping strides of the Hand's thief. Puzzle had all the body language of a rat or ferret, while Royce was a hawk, which explained why Puzzle was so eager to get back to his den.

Royce was out in front and Hadrian shadowed them. There was no need to bind Puzzle, who walked between them calling directions. Hadrian gauged the thief's chances of escape at somewhere between nonexistent and impossible. If the man bolted, Royce would swoop. Puzzle might get five steps before the talons sunk in. Hadrian had seen Royce play with victims before. His partner would turn his back, wander away, or leave a door open. Those were the nights Hadrian drank more than usual. The nights when he had woke drenched in sweat after dreaming about his father. The nights he questioned everything, including the point of his own birth.

They had dropped Albert off at a barber, with enough coin to get him cleaned up and buy a decent set of clothes. They were planning to rendezvous back at The Hideous Head. Judging from the lack of business, everyone had a similar opinion of the alehouse, which made it ideal. Albert was all smiles when Royce handed over the coins, as if he'd thought such a thing would never really happen. Hadrian had doubts they would see the viscount again but agreed with Royce that they had bigger issues to deal with.

If someone had hurt Gwen, Royce wasn't the only one who wanted to find him.

The sun was rising high as they pressed their way through the Merchant Quarter. The streets were clean, the shops adorned with numerous windows, and above each door were painted signboards carved into clever advertisements. A tailor sported a giant thimble and needle with a line of thread whipping above it. A barrister's advertisement displayed a wig that looked real until closer inspection revealed that it was made of wood. The thoroughfares—the maze of lanes and aisles—were as colorful as the wealthy shoppers who wandered by dressed in clothes of dyed cloth. Yellows, oranges, greens, and reds were the most predominate, and the brighter the better. Hadrian wondered if it was just a coincidence or if they were all consciously trying to mimic the color of the autumn trees. A few wore noble furs, imports from the Gentry Quarter. No one could ignore the lure of Merchant Square. It was a thrill of sights, sounds, and smells.

Merchant pitchmen walked with elaborate tree-poles, whose branches displayed hats, shoes, cheap jewelry, and purses. Fetching girls carried baskets of glass baubles, medicines, and cloth. Minstrels played while jugglers tossed gourds, dancers performed acrobatics, storytellers on boxes captivated crowds of listeners, and games of chance were everywhere. The smell of cinnamon and apples fought with the smoky aroma of roasting pig.

It didn't seem likely that thieves would have a home in such an environment. Hadrian imagined cutpurses would live in abandoned hovels in a neighborhood much like the Lower Quarter, or in a sewer, or perhaps above some dockside bar. On the other hand, mice were more likely to take up residence in a full cupboard than an empty barn.

"What game is this?" Puzzle asked, having not needed to direct Royce for several turns. "Your friend knows where he's going."

Hadrian was certain that was not true. Royce said he had never been to Medford before their last visit, and despite everything, as far as Hadrian knew, Royce had never lied to him. He always thought that was odd given the man was a thief with no more ethics than a shrub, but it wasn't the only thing strange about Royce Melborn, and his ability to find his way was one of those.

Royce came to a halt at the end of Paper Street in front of a large iron gate between Faringham's Bookbindery and Virgil and Harrington's Engravings. On the far side was a small graveyard. The gate was sealed with a massive and hopelessly rusted lock.

Royce faced Puzzle. He motioned toward the cemetery. "In there, right? But you have another way in. Something quick and simple."

Puzzle stared at him with suspicion.

"It doesn't take a genius," Royce explained. "In the heart

of everything but isolated. No one has touched that chain in a decade. How do you get in?"

The thief glanced over each shoulder, then with a specific sequence of slaps, popped one of the iron bars out of place and slipped through the gap.

"You don't have too many fat members, do you?" Hadrian said, but the thief was running now, sprinting between the graves. Royce didn't follow. They had arrived. The thief was just distancing himself from the bloodshed that was sure to follow.

Hadrian wondered if trees in graveyards were different from others. The few that grew among the headstones were like premature balding men, having already shed all their leaves. Their bark was black, their trunks twisted and bent. A blanket of recently deceased leaves hung in the crooks of statues and covered the mounds and mortuaries. Sculptures of women in flowing robes revealed faces streaked with the tarnish left by rain. They appeared at best to be weeping and at worst to be bleeding from their eyes. It was quiet there. Behind them, the bustle of the Merchant Quarter was a faint echo, a lonely sound that marked their isolation. Graveyards were supposed to be peaceful, serene resting places, but this one was infested with two-legged rats. Rats who did not like visitors, especially those who barged in unannounced.

Standing in the middle of the graveyard, they lingered like kids who had just whacked a beehive and were waiting to see what would emerge. Hadrian didn't consider this the most reckless, or even the most peculiar, thing he had done recently. Life with Royce was like that. A year earlier, if anyone had suggested they would still be working together, Hadrian would have laughed. Well, maybe not laughed—he didn't do a lot of laughing back then. He had suffered from a kind of despondency that made even the stupidest ideas seem sensible. This was how he ended up agreeing to team with Royce Melborn, a brooding, vicious sort of criminal, and only Maribor knew all the things he'd done. After a year, all Hadrian had managed to learn was that he needed to tread carefully when Royce raised his hood, that his friend disliked any beverage except an obscure and expensive wine, that his dagger had a name but his horse did not, that he was abandoned at a young age, and that he was indeed very good at stealing. He also knew Royce placed little value on human life. He had a habit of seeing murder as the easiest solution to life's many problems. Normally this was an issue between them—but not that day.

Deep within the shadows, faces appeared. No one said a word. They gathered slowly, circling, threading between the headstones. In a few minutes Puzzle reappeared, coming out of a gargoyle-decorated crypt. Five others came with him. They fanned out, creeping closer. Hadrian guessed the odds at maybe five-to-one.

"This pinky finger says you asked to be brought here." The speaker was surprisingly short and wore a high-topped black hat with the red imprint of a hand stamped on it. He had a nasty bruise on the left side of his face and a deep cut along his cheekbone that appeared to be recently stitched. It didn't appear to bother him much, as he was in the process of eating a drumstick and licking his fingers as he spoke. "We have this sort of rule, though. It says that no one sees where we live and keeps living unless they is willing to join."

"Yeah, I can see your need for secrecy," Royce said. "I'm sure no one knows you're here."

"We got ourselves a smart one, boys. Maybe you ought to tell me why it is you decided to kill yourself today—while you still have the privilege."

"You're looking for a girl named Rose from Medford House. I want to know why."

This brought a few chuckles from the circle of onlookers, laughter that made Hadrian think of crows on a fence. Each member of the Crimson Hand looked like patchworks of people. One wore a hunting vest over a sailor shirt; another had a painter's smock, a jester's hat, and knee-high waders. One fella even sported a riding boot on one foot and a satin slipper on the other. Stray dogs living in an alley—thin, vicious, dirty, and very likely diseased.

"Mighty demanding, aren't you?" Top Hat asked. "What makes you think we'd tell you anything?"

"Honor among thieves."

Top Hat narrowed his eyes. "You a thief, then? Do you know what we do to thieves who practice in our city?"

"No, and I don't really care—besides, I haven't stolen anything. Your man there can vouch for me. He's followed us ever since we arrived."

Top Hat turned. Puzzle nodded.

Top Hat hummed as he took another rip from the drumstick, sucking in a long strand of meat. He chewed a bit. "Who are you, then? Fellas don't walk into a den demanding information, lest you're touched or..." He paused, took a step forward, and squinted at Royce. Motioning with the chicken leg like it was a pointer, he asked, "Who you working for?"

"Nobody."

"They were with another fella earlier," Puzzle put in. "Left him at a barber with a bag of coins to buy new clothes."

"Fancy fella? Rich?"

Puzzle shook his head. "More like Roy the Sewer."

Top Hat threw away his chicken bone and began to circle them, sucking his fingers and wiping them on his pants. He carried a naked saber at his side. From the single-edge, slightly curved blade and the brass-plated handguard, Hadrian guessed it was a sea dog cleaver—standard issue for sailors on western vessels. He also wore a long bladed dirk, another naval weapon. While it was possible, Hadrian couldn't imagine Top Hat had ever been on a ship, but his steel was a matched set. "What's your name?"

"Royce Melborn."

"Royce…Royce…" He paused. "Why is that name familiar? You come up from the south, didn't you? Colnora maybe?"

Royce didn't answer.

"You're working for the BD, ain't you?"

"BD have designs on Medford?" one of the others asked, the one with the mismatched footwear.

Top Hat scowled and slapped his arm against his sides in disgust. "Ah…'course they do. Bloody BD have designs on every ruddy thing in the world, don't they? Can't stand not having a pinch of every honest copper. Miserable piss pots. Ain't it enough the Jewel runs half the world? I should kill the both of you right now."

"I'm not a member of the Black Diamond."

"Says you." Top Hat took off his headgear and scrubbed his thinning hair. "Bugger me."

"We can't afford trouble with the BD," the dramatically tall thief wearing the waders said.

Top Hat looked up as if he might hit him. "Figure that out by yourself, did you?" He popped his lid back on and faced Royce. "But maybe you're right—maybe you ain't BD." Top Hat wiped his nose and straightened up. "I'll tell you what, being as how we is so honorable here, I'm gonna send a rider to Colnora to look you up. If he says you're Black Diamond, we'll talk. Sure, why not. I'll hear the Jewel's proposal." His expression indicated it wasn't going to be a fun conversation. "If you're a nobody, like you say, you have your choice of joining up or getting added to our courtyard here." He spread out his hands and turned around slowly as if showing off a grand estate. "Or"—he took another step closer and let his hand caress the handle of his dirk—"you can leave the same way you came. Given that it will take a while for the rider, you've got some time to disappear."

"How kind." Royce's voice was flat and he took his own step forward. "But I don't care what you think, and you can waste all the time you like sending messengers—this isn't a social call. Why are you looking for Rose?"

For the first time, Top Hat seemed uncomfortable and retreated a step. Looking into Royce's eyes from that distance took more nerve than a little man with stolen weapons could muster, even surrounded by an army.

"What business is it of yours?"

"I want to know if it has anything to do with Gwen DeLancy being attacked last night."

"Again, what business is it of yours?"

"DeLancy is a friend, and I'd like to *thank* the man who hurt her."

Top Hat's caustic demeanor slipped and Hadrian thought he saw a flash of sympathy. "Sorry to hear that. If you're telling the truth, then you have all the more reason to leave, and before you get in real trouble. You don't want anything to do with that mess."

"Why not?"

Top Hat took a deep breath and looked at the faces around him. He lighted on Hadrian's for a moment before turning back to Royce. "Reason we're looking for Rose is on account of the quarter sheriffs are looking, and they're looking because the high constable wants her. He and a few of his feather-heads paid a personal visit here asking questions about Rose. They want her—bad. Suggested we look *real* hard. They were very…*insistent*." He rubbed his scarred cheek. "To show he wasn't joking, His Lordship took three of my boys and hung them in Gentry Square. Never accused them of nothing, just gave them a swing." He pulled the brim of his hat down and sighed. "No, sir, the greats are serious about this one, and you'd be smart to steer clear."

"Do you know who beat Gwen?"

" 'Course I do."

"Who is he?"

"No one to play with. Trust me, this is one party you don't want an invitation to. The gods are warring and the best we mortals can do is try not to get noticed."

"I wasn't planning on being noticed," Royce said, his eyes fixed on the small man with the big hat before him. Hadrian didn't think he'd even blinked during the whole conversation.

"Out of your league, cutthroat."

"How do you know?"

"You sound tough." Top Hat nodded. "You walked into my den, we have you circled—no way out—but I ain't smelled fear. You get marks for that. I'm not joking about letting you join. Him too." He pointed at Hadrian. "I like a man who knows how to stay quiet. Besides, I just lost three boys. With my luck it'll be four before the cock crows. So, sure, maybe you're a killer. Maybe you're even one of the BD's fabled bucket men. The Jewel's ghosts-with-a-blade, but this guy..." He let the comment linger, then shook his head. "Uh-uh. This guy is beyond *anyone*."

"Everyone has to die."

Top Hat rubbed his chin. "Have to admit I wouldn't mind seeing him pay after what he done to my boys. We have a history that goes back a long way. But no one can touch him."

"Who is he?"

"Same bastard who beat me bloody the same night and who hung my boys for no more reason than to make a point— the Marquis of East March, Lord Simon Exeter, High Constable of Melengar." Top Hat shook his head. "Have to admit I was flattered His Lordship made a personal appearance down here, but I'd rather he hadn't. If you're smart, you'll forget all about this, before you learn what real trouble is."

※

"So where are we going?" Hadrian asked as they dodged a lumber cart and walked back up Paper Street.

"To talk to Gwen."

"But she refused to see us."

"And I respected her privacy, but that was before I knew why."

"And why is that?"

"You really need to walk faster." For such a large man, it often surprised Royce how slow Hadrian's long legs could be. They turned right at the portrait painter's shop and veered toward the Lower Quarter once more.

"Why doesn't she want to see us?"

"She's trying to save our lives again."

※

The man on the porch of Medford House laughed and Royce took an instant dislike to him. Royce took an instant dislike to most people, but as he and Hadrian approached, Royce had the feeling that this time was justified. Two guys stood on the porch. Big field hand types, with deep tans and calloused hands. One was holding Jasmine against the doorframe by her throat. The other, the one who had laughed, was shoving another girl—Royce remembered her name was Abby—off the porch to the ground.

Hadrian no longer had any trouble keeping up, and Royce felt a hand on his shoulder as the bigger man passed him. "You might want to just take a few breaths and let me talk to them first."

Royce didn't slow down. "I'm not going to talk—"

"Afternoon, gentlemen." Hadrian helped Abby to her feet. "What seems to be the problem here?"

"They're stealing our wort!" Abby shouted.

"Your *what*?" Royce asked.

"It's used to make ale," Hadrian explained, climbing the steps of the porch.

"They're taking the whole tun!" Jasmine croaked out, causing the man to slap her.

Royce started for the steps.

Hadrian whirled with his hand up. "No! Just relax. Let me deal with this."

Royce hesitated, more because Hadrian was blocking the way than because he agreed.

Everyone turned to look at Hadrian as he began kicking at one of the pretty lathed spindles that decorated the porch railing. He snapped one off and wrenched it free.

"Hey!" Abby said.

"Sorry, I'll fix it later, but I need something blunt to hit them with."

This got the men's attention and the one let go of Jasmine, who escaped into the house.

"All I can say is you'd better do a good job," Royce threatened. "If either of them leaves that porch, they're *mine*."

"Royce, they're not even armed."

"They have arms—but I'll remedy that."

Royce thought the men looked decidedly less confident but no more intelligent, which was proven when the one who had held Jasmine took a swing at Hadrian.

What bothered Royce the most was that the moment the fool attacked, he knew his chances of killing the two ploughboys had passed. He heard the crack as Hadrian broke the first one's arm with the spindle. Then he doubled him over before laying him out with a blow across the back of his head. And all before the second had taken more than two steps.

To his great pleasure those two steps were away from Hadrian. Royce reached under his cloak, his fingers following the line of his belt to the handle of Alverstone. He was torn between actually cutting the man's hands off or just slitting his throat. There was no real reason to torture the poor sap; he was just a thug. Still, he did not like how people felt it was safe to push their way into Medford House. An example might deter that, and a pair of hands nailed to either side of the porch steps might just do the trick.

Unfortunately, Hadrian ended Royce's mental debate when he slammed the man in the lower back, dropping him to his knees. His forward momentum drove his head into the porch railing and cracked another spindle, thereby saving Hadrian the need to do any more.

Royce frowned.

"There," Hadrian said. "Problem solved, and you aren't wanted for murder. Isn't that nice?"

"It's only nice not being wanted for murder if you've actually killed someone. Otherwise, what's the point? Besides, what makes you think I'm not wanted for murder?"

They entered the parlor and found two more men hauling a large metal tub up the stairs from the cellar, while a flock of women beat on them. They set their burden down long enough to growl and shove a few away.

"That's enough!" one of the men shouted while drawing a hunting knife. "Next one comes close will get cut!"

Again Hadrian was quick to step forward.

Where was all this speed when we were walking here?

"Who the prince's peter are you?" the guy with the dagger asked as he watched Hadrian advance.

"I'm fairly certain that tun doesn't belong to you."

"It's ours!" one of the girls shouted. "They're stealing it for The Hideous Head."

"I'll carve you up, too, if you don't get out of our way." The man brandished the knife menacingly.

Hadrian reached behind his head and drew his big spadone. Royce had only seen him draw it once before. Usually Hadrian made do with his short and bastard swords. This time it was just for effect.

Hadrian extended the tip of the massive blade. He was a good eight feet away, but the sword crossed most of the distance. "Maybe you'd rather just leave?"

The man shoved his knife back into his belt and turned toward the door.

"Make them put it back where they found it," Royce said, "or I'll be nailing hands to the porch posts."

The two looked at him, then at their hands, and finally back to Hadrian's sword. "Ah..." the one said, and glanced at the other, who shrugged. "Sure, why not. No need to get crazy. Just a job." They hoisted the tun and carried it back down the steps.

That's when Royce saw her. Gwen was at the top of the broad staircase leaning over the rail. One arm in a sling and she wore a scarf wrapped around her head and face so that only her eyes shone. While one was swollen completely closed, Royce recognized the other. It belonged to the woman who had held him when he thought he was dying. The one who promised he would be safe and who had kept that promise. No one had ever done that before. His parents had abandoned him, his friends betrayed him, but she, this stranger with emerald eyes, took care of him when no one else would. If there really was such a thing in the world as a good person, he was looking at her. And seeing the bruises and cuts that the wrap did not quite cover, he also knew he was going to kill the man who had done it, and he was going to take his time.

Royce was up the stairs before the girls had a chance to stop him, before she could get away.

"Thank you," she said, her voice muffled by the wrap. She started back up the steps. "Now please leave."

"I know about Rose," Royce told her. "And I know it was the high constable—the marquis, something, something Exeter."

She stopped but didn't look at him. Her hand tightened on the banister.

He waited, and slowly she turned, holding up the edges of the scarf around her face. "I...I wanted you to return." There was a strangeness in her voice. A quaver. "Ever since you left, I looked and thought...maybe...but I never believed, not really. You're not the type to be sentimental, the kind that looks back. But I wanted you to, only...only not like this...not now."

She began to cry and, turning away, she climbed the stairs. She moved slowly, pulling hard on the railing, inching up, dragging a weak leg. He followed.

Reaching her room, Gwen crawled onto her bed—the bed Royce had occupied for weeks. The place was sacred to him— something he didn't realize until that moment. The room was a sanctuary of kindness and comfort. He'd stayed there only a couple months, but coming back he wondered if what he was feeling could be what others felt about places they called home.

Gwen lay facedown, muffling her tears. "Go away."

He sat alongside her and placed his palm on her back. She was wearing a simple linen dress. He felt the rough material beneath his fingers, letting his thumb slide back and forth, gently rubbing. He felt stupid. He wanted to help her, but he had no experience at comfort. He felt her body as she quivered, and while his left hand gently caressed her back, his right made a fist so tight it ached.

"I'm sorry," she told him, her voice sluggish with tears. "I didn't want you to see me like this."

"Maybe," he said. "But that's not the real reason you don't want me here."

She turned over and looked up at him with a wet, puzzled eye.

"You're protecting me again. You're afraid I'll do something stupid and get myself killed."

"Am I wrong?"

"Yes. I have no intention of getting killed."

"But you're going to do something."

"Tell me what happened."

Gwen wiped her face with her good hand. "There must have been ten at least. Sheriffs and castle guards, too, I think. I don't know all the uniforms. They wanted to know where Rose was. I told them she went to the castle—that she was invited for a party. His Lordship seemed to think she'd come back, only she hadn't. None of us had seen her all night. We still haven't. Lord Exeter didn't believe me, I guess."

Gwen paused. She touched her fingertips to her lips. "Dixon tried to stop them. They...He's still unconscious. I don't know if he'll live." She rolled over again, burying her face in the pillow. "You need to leave. You need to get out of the city, away from Melengar. Go back to where you came from and forget all about me. I don't want anything to happen to you. I'm the one who's supposed to keep *you* safe. I'm supposed to...If you stay, you'll be killed and I'd rather die than have that happen."

Royce's stomach tightened, breathing became harder, and a prickly heat made him begin to sweat. *She barely knows me.* He squeezed his fist tighter. The hand he touched her with began to quiver and he pulled it away. "Don't worry about me."

She turned to face him. Her eyes, though always dark, were now blackened, swollen. It didn't look like Gwen peering out from under the scarf, but it was her voice, the same one he had heard out in the dark, the voice that once saved him.

"No, Royce. You don't understand. He's too powerful."

"You underestimate me."

"He's the high constable. He has an army of sheriffs and deputies and he's cousin to the king, who has a real army. I don't want you beaten like Dixon. I don't want you to die."

"Gwen, I'm not used to trusting people. It's not in my nature. You found us bleeding and near death on the street but never asked me anything but my name. Most people would have posed a question or twenty-five. And I never offered to explain. I never told you anything about me, about my past."

"Are you going to tell me now?"

"No. I'm going to show you."

CHAPTER 10

THE DANDY AND THE TROLL

The Hideous Head hadn't changed from earlier that day, except that Hadrian thought there might be even less customers at the bar and even more dead leaves scattered across the floor. As he expected, Albert was nowhere to be found, but at the same table they had shared the day before sat a dandy gent wiping his nose with a lace handkerchief and sipping a glass of cider. Until he stood up and waved, neither Royce nor Hadrian had any idea he was the same man they had saved from the barn near Colnora.

Viscount Albert Winslow had been transformed.

The beard was gone and his long hair had been cleaned, combed, powdered, pulled back, and tied with a black velvet bow. They could see his face for the first time. It was pink and lean with sharp cheekbones and a handsome chin. Hadrian had no idea why, but he only then noticed that Albert had startling blue eyes. He had traded his filthy nightshirt for a doublet of gold with a high starched neck and shimmering silk accents. The new lace shirt underneath peeked out in ruffles and embroidered cuffs. On his legs were opaque hose and he wore brass-buckle shoes, and on the table beside him was a luxuriant wide-brimmed hat with one side pinned up by a plumed feather.

"Welcome, gentlemen," he said, adjusting his cuffs.

"I didn't give you *that* much money." Royce glared.

"No. What you gave me was ill suited to the task. You obviously have no idea the costs of being noble."

"Then how'd you manage this?"

"Credit."

"Credit?"

"Yes. That's where I promise to pay later for things I want now."

Royce rolled his eyes. "I know what credit is. I just can't believe they agreed."

"The first barber certainly wouldn't. I went to a cheap one and got nicked a few times for my effort."

"The *first* barber?"

"Oh yes. And the first clothier. I went to a secondhand shop in the Merchant Quarter and bought a ghastly used doublet. The thing smelled of fish. I also bought worn shoes, a torn and stained shirt—the offensive parts blessedly hidden by the doublet—and a pair of hose. Dressing myself thusly, and cleaned up as well as your coin would allow, I then went to the most expensive shops in Gentry Square. There I introduced myself as the road-weary Viscount Winslow who was in town for the celebration tonight at the castle and in desperate need of a new look. I then proceeded to buy all new clothes and visited a coiffeur, all on credit."

"And they just let you?"

"Nobility has its perks."

"How many *perks* did you spend?" Royce's tone shifted between amazed and angry but finally settled on a nice restrained tempest.

Albert hummed for a moment. "Only about thirteen gold tenents."

"Thirteen!" Royce hit the table with his fist, making Albert and the candle jump.

Albert leaned back with his palms up in defense. "The clothes were very cheap. I know several barons who spend twenty-five, even thirty on just a jacket, and I really couldn't quibble and still convincingly play the part of a wealthy noble who they could trust to pay later."

Royce huffed and dropped back in his chair hard enough to rock it. "You might be surprised to discover we don't have thirteen gold."

Albert straightened up at this and a confident grin filled his face. "Shouldn't be a problem. I have a month to pay."

"A month—a whole month? Are you crazy? I think the largest haul Hadrian and I've scored was only five gold coins, and those were local stamps, not tenents. Usually we bring in twenty or thirty bits of silver."

"Which is good money," Hadrian added.

"Yes... yes it is. But thirteen gold!" Royce grabbed the glass of cider and smelled it.

"Not fermented." Albert grinned at him.

Royce leaned over to sniff Albert's breath. "I hope you enjoy those clothes, because you'll hang in them, or go to debtor's prison, or have your thumbs cut off, or whatever they do to nobles who don't pay their bills. Don't expect us to help you out."

"Tut-tut. We'll be fine. After dressing myself properly, I paid an unexpected visit to an old friend, Lord Daref. I asked if he was free this evening and offered to treat him to a night of decadence and debauchery—"

"You did *what*? Are you out of your mind?" Royce turned to Hadrian. "He's nuts. Maybe drying out his brain was too much too soon."

Hadrian had to agree. The viscount was happily running headlong off a cliff and didn't appear to have a care.

Albert reached out to console Royce, who snapped his hand back.

"Relax. I'm not an idiot. I knew full well he would refuse. He, like every other noble in the city, is attending the autumn gala. It's an annual harvest soirée, only this year there is the added attraction of celebrating the appointment of a new chancellor. It would be a black mark not to be in attendance. When he asked why *I* was not going, I feigned ignorance, saying I only just arrived in the city and had no idea."

"He invited you as his guest?" Royce asked.

Albert smiled. "He did indeed. So tonight I will be dining on venison and pheasant until I am stuffed as a bird. While I am, I will see about finding the hidden foibles and prying those dark sinister secrets out into the sacred and inebriated light of candles. Then, as we discussed, I will nonchalantly suggest a possible, and decidedly irresistible, option. I will dangle the chance for them to get even with any rival at no risk whatsoever, just for the cost of, say, twenty or fifty golden tenents."

"Fifty gold? You are crazy."

"Trust me. I know these people. Gold means little when balanced against a single moment of humiliation to an enemy, or sometimes even a friend. If you can do the jobs, we'll all be wealthy soon."

Royce's line of sight veered off toward the bar. Hadrian glanced over his shoulder to see the same man he had drawn his sword on in Medford House leaning over the bar speaking to Grue and looking in their direction.

"I notice you didn't include a blade with your new attire," Royce said. "Not even a little jeweled dagger."

"Lords no." Albert looked appalled. "I don't fight."

"I thought all nobles learned sword fighting." Royce looked to Hadrian.

"I thought so too."

"Nobles with competent fathers perhaps. I spent my formative years at my aunt's at Huffington Manor. She held a daily salon, where a dozen noble ladies came to discuss all manner of philosophical topics, like how much they hated their husbands. I've never actually held a sword, but I can tie a mean corset and apply face paint like a gold-coin whore."

This caused Royce and Hadrian to chuckle. When Royce stopped abruptly, Hadrian didn't need to turn this time. He could hear the footfalls on the wooden floor.

"Having a good time, are you?" Grue asked. He was as greasy-looking as ever. "So it turns out you two are friends with that harlot. Willard says you stopped him from taking their tun. Says you busted up Gitty and Brock. Gitty's still laid up and bemoaning the loss of his front tooth."

"That was an accident. He hit the banister badly," Hadrian said. "Still, they shouldn't have been stealing the ladies' tun."

"*Ladies!*" Grue laughed. "That's a good one, mister. Never heard no whores called *ladies* before. Those boys were there on my orders. I told you earlier how they've been cutting in on my business, making it impossible to turn any profit by stealing all my customers. The only reason I survive is because I'm the only place down here on Wayward with the royal writ to sell ale. But now it turns out they're starting to make their own, and she's in tight with the administrators. Cast some sort of witchy spell on them so they agree to whatever she asks. She'll get her writ—then I'll be out of business. A man would be stupid to drink here when he can go across the street and have his ale with a pretty wench sitting on his knee. With that much business, she could give drinks for free and I'd have to close my doors. I ain't gonna let that happen. That's why I sent the boys over to take her cask of wort and shut her down before she can hatch her plans."

"So *you* sent them over." Royce stated the obvious, which was not like him, but his voice had a tone like a tumbler clicking into place.

"Of course I did, only you two had to interfere. I can't say I'm happy with that."

Hadrian marveled at how every time Grue spoke, he tied a noose tighter around his neck. "Are you asking us to leave, or is this where you and your friends teach us a lesson?"

"Neither. Gitty's awful mad, but Gitty's also an idiot. I was thinking just the opposite. You boys handled yourselves well. Maybe I could hire you to work for me."

"Hire us?" Hadrian asked.

"I could use a couple of toughs to keep things orderly. You know, stop the bricklayers from smashing the cups and glasses and keep fellas like Stane from killing girls. That sort of thing. Despite what *she* likely told you, I learned from that mistake. It's really bad for business when anyone gets killed in your alehouse—even a whore."

"Thought you didn't have any girls," Royce said. He was crouching more than sitting now, leaning forward, his eyes focused and wide. Hadrian had seen cats like that just before they pounced.

"Well, I might just be getting me some. I'll even do you a favor and tell you who beat her, if you're still interested."

"You told us you didn't know," Royce said.

"I'm a businessman. I don't give stuff away for free." He grinned.

"Too late, we already learned it was Lord Exeter."

"Too bad. I bet I can give you details she didn't. I seen the whole thing out my window—him dragging her down off the porch, down those pretty steps she built. He had her by the hair. Just slapped her at first, but he didn't like how she kept quiet I guess, 'cause he closed his fist then. Bet you could hear her screams all the way in Artisan Row. By the time Dixon ran out, she was on her knees and they were starting to kick her." Grue paused. He had a little smile on his face, and Hadrian wondered what was restraining Royce. Even he wanted to send Grue's face into a wall.

"Lord Exeter runs this city—him and his sheriffs. Lives in the castle proper. Untouchable. Fact is, that Calian whore got herself on the wrong side of things now. Never know what a noble might do. Might come back. Might kill her the next time if he thinks she's hiding something. You see, in all honesty, I sent the boys over to get the tun because folks will ransack the place after she's dead. I figured getting it ahead of the rush was the smart move. Actually, Rose did me a big favor—I just want to hug that girl."

"Might want to be careful," Royce said, smiling. "Roses have thorns."

～

"I'm from a small village," Hadrian said. He leaned out into the fountain and, after catching some water in his hands, wiped his face. "But lord high constable, that's like a big sheriff, right?"

"Yes," Albert replied as the three stood in the shadow of the rearing king statue. The sun was warm and he, too, dipped his hands in the Gentry Square's fountain, flicking droplets on his face in a dainty manner befitting a man with lace cuffs.

Hadrian sighed.

"What?" Royce asked.

"Maybe it's this city, or the north in general. It doesn't like us. You know my leg only recently stopped hurting." He looked at Albert. "Last time we were up here—almost a year ago—I was stabbed, and my thigh ached every time it rained. Just a few weeks ago, I realized it was raining and it didn't hurt. First time…and now."

"Now what?" Albert asked, looking lost, but Hadrian didn't offer any more insight.

Royce was staring at the castle. Spearhead towers rose above the wall, casting late afternoon shadows across the square. The quaint moat was a tranquil pond with its lily pads, dragonflies, cattails, and bright green scum. The gate stood open, the bridge down, a gaping mouth with a tongue sticking out. Two guards stood to either side just across the bridge, challenging anyone who crossed. A few did. All who stopped showed a scroll. A summons? Invitation? Identification? Maybe all three.

"Albert, what do you know about Lord Exeter?" Royce asked.

"Simon Exeter is the son of Vincent Exeter and Marie Essendon—King Amrath's aunt. The Exeters, like the Essendons, Pickerings, Reds, Valins, and Jerls, are all descendants of the signers of the charter that created the kingdom in…ah…" Albert paused, thinking.

"I don't need dates."

"Good, I'm lousy with them. Let's just say it was a long time ago. Anyway, these six form the houses of nobility in Melengar. Exeter rules over the East March. A very important fief, as it's the gateway to the kingdom and the bulwark against any invasion from the east. Really any invasion at all, as it controls the great north–south roadway."

"Get to the man himself," Royce said, taking his eyes off the castle to survey the rest of the square.

All around it were three-story homes of the gentry, crowded shoulder to shoulder forming a high wall, mostly of stone with gates of their own that led to small courtyards. Each different, each with a personality of pretty windows and painted facades that vied with the others for dominance. Velvet-clad men, sipping from goblets, looked down on everyone from balconies.

"Simon is…intense," Albert explained. "I've never cared for him personally. I suppose few do. Arrogant certainly, but also self-assured to the point of being a royal ass. His way is always the right way, you understand. If you disagree, then he insults and belittles you. In short, he's a bully. He doesn't like Imperialists, hates Warric—hates most of the south really, maybe the whole world, who knows. Rumor has it that he doesn't get along well with the king."

"How does that work?"

Albert shrugged.

"When you talked to your gentry pal, did he mention any recent events?"

"The gala, of course. The sorry news that the price of brocade has risen to insane levels. There's a trade war going on with Warric, and as always, fashion is the first casualty. He also mentioned the impossibility of finding a good manservant. Daref has a taste for young men and he rotates them out on a regular schedule. He says it keeps life from growing stale. Ah..." Albert raised a finger as he thought of something. "Old Chancellor Wainwright died and was replaced by Percy Braga, some foreigner from the south. According to Daref, the appointment had Lord Exeter in a *tizzy* as he put it. Not only did he want the office, but also it went to a stranger with strong ties to the church. I can only imagine the storm that must have started."

Albert tapped his lips. "What else...Oh, the princess was gifted a Maranon horse for her birthday, which she rides through the square just about every day. They had a hanging— but we saw that on our way in. There was something else..." He shook his head in frustration.

"How did Wainwright die?"

"Actually there is some mystery to that. The official story is that he died from a fever."

"And the unofficial?"

"Apparently the fever was abrupt."

"Poisoned?"

"Possibly."

"How long ago?"

"Sometime this month I believe. The gala is to honor his successor, Chancellor Braga, who just took up the vacancy."

Bells rang a complex melody and Royce looked up at the twin spires of the cathedral jabbing a brilliant blue sky. The castle and church faced each other across the square, rival giants at opposite ends of an arena where ants labored. He noted the shadow lengths. Time was running short.

"Know anything about this new guy, this Braga?"

Albert shook his head. "Just what Daref told me. He's from the south, has some connections to the church as I said, and was married to the queen's sister Clare—Oh yes! That was it. Lady Clare also died recently."

"A lot of deaths."

"It would seem so." Albert squinted at Royce. "Why all the questions? What are you trying to figure out?"

"A prostitute went to the castle and disappeared. No one seems to know where, and the lord high constable is searching desperately for her. Why?"

"Because he's the constable?" Albert offered. "That's his job."

"Do you think a bigwig lord high constable personally roughs up people in the middle of the night in search of a missing prostitute?"

Albert looked decidedly less certain. "Not when you put it that way."

"Why do you think he did it?" Hadrian asked.

"No idea." Royce looked at the castle, at the guards and the towers. "And the girl is likely dead. All that's important is that Exeter wants her, and that makes him vulnerable."

"Vulnerable to what?" the viscount asked. "What's all this about?"

"You'll have two jobs to do tonight, Albert," Royce told him. "First you have to find us a job that will pay for those clothes. Second, you need to help me kill Lord Exeter."

Chapter 11

The New Guard

Reuben walked through the castle feeling conspicuous. He wore his new tunic, chain, helm, and sword. He grimaced when it came time to put the helmet on. The cuts still hurt from the last one he had worn. But his new helm felt nothing like that. He had no wadding, no need to stuff rags around his head. It fit snug, felt good, and lacked the narrow visor that had left him nearly blind. His new uniform gave him confidence. So did the sword, now that he knew at least enough not to look stupid whenever he drew it. He was not about to win any Wintertide ribbons, but he might make someone think twice before taking a swing. And he suspected that was the majority of a guard's job—intimidation. He wondered if he could get Mauvin to show him more. He liked to think the Pickerings, if not the prince himself, genuinely liked him, but Reuben liked to think a lot of things.

He wanted to think there was nothing strange going on and that his father had a perfectly reasonable explanation for being drunk in the middle of the day—the day of a major castle event, when all guards were expected to be at their finest. He wanted to think that Rose was no longer in danger, that his father had picked his uniform off the floor and was, at that very minute, taking action to apprehend the assassins plotting to kill the king. He also liked to believe the squires would no longer bother him, now that he was a full-fledged Essendon castle guard, or if that wasn't the case, that his new training, and new friends, would help keep him safe. He liked to think he would now command respect from everyone, including his father. And he liked to think—

He saw a flash of burgundy gown and paused at the stairs next to the fancy suits of armor. Turning, he saw it was only Lady Drundiline, the queen's secretary. He should have realized. The princess would be in her chambers, still dressing up the way she always did for celebrations. Her hair piled, showing her long neck, and she would have a new gown he guessed. She almost always did, and recently the queen had allowed her to wear lower necklines. Nothing like what Rose came dressed in, but less childlike than she used to wear. The king and queen were starting to show off their daughter, positioning her for the eventual marriage that would be arranged.

Reuben liked to pretend that Arista wouldn't be forced to wed. That she wasn't going to leave Medford for some far-off castle where he would never see her again, but she was almost thirteen. It wouldn't be long now. Just thinking of it hurt, and that one thought stole all the happiness that his uniform and new prince-gifted sword had granted. All the dread he had unloaded when he told his father about Rose was replaced with what felt like a pending execution date. Vague and hazy, it loomed in front of him. Except death was far too indefinable to truly fear. Reuben couldn't imagine being dead, but he could imagine walking those halls knowing there was no chance at all of seeing a glimpse of her. When they sent Arista away, they would banish his dream as well. He had foolish dreams, insane thoughts, but as long as she was there, as long as she had not married, there was always hope. And with so little to sustain him, that thin strand of promise was how he convinced himself that breathing was still a good thing.

Reuben liked to think that one day he would hold Arista in his arms and that he would feel her trembling stop because he was there. That one day, when they were both older, he would know what it was like to kiss her lips.

Reuben sighed.

He liked to think a lot of things, just nothing useful.

He waited until no one was watching and slipped down the steps into the lower corridors that led to the dungeon. Panic seized him as he noticed the bales of straw. The party decorations were all over the castle: bales of straw, bundles of corn stalks, pumpkins, and squash.

But why would someone put them down here? Maybe they had too much? More importantly, had they found Rose?

He raced to the last cell and, pulling a lantern from the ceiling, yanked open the door and peered in. He held his breath and his heart raced until he saw movement in the corner. He stepped in, raising the lantern higher. Two big brown eyes blinked at him.

"Reuben?" Rose said anxiously. "Is it time? Can I go now?"

He relaxed and breathed again. "No, not yet. How are you?"

"Scared." She was kneeling on the stone, her arms pulled in tight. One side of her hair was out of place, pushed up with bits of straw in it. "Did you tell your father yet?"

"Yes, and he's going to take care of everything. He said it was actually good you stayed here." Reuben paused. "Anyway, my dad will clear it all up."

"Are you sure?" Her eyes were red and deep with shadows. She had been crying.

"I told you—my father is a member of the king's bodyguard. It's his job to protect the royal family. Trust me, he'll take care of this."

"I don't like it in here. It's cold and the floor is hard and I haven't done anything." She looked at the floor. "I was just here for a party. Just doing what I was asked." She glanced toward the exit and gestured with her hand. "Earlier someone came down. I saw a light outside the door and heard some men. I was terrified."

"I know." Reuben smiled, then hung the lantern from the claw in the ceiling and went back into the corridor. He grabbed a couple bales of straw and hauled them in. "There, you can sit on these or spread them out and lie down. Straw is plenty soft and it will make you warmer by keeping you off the stone. I'm about to go on duty, so I can't stay long. You'll probably only have to spend one more night." He said this as gently as he could.

She moved to sit on the straw bale and nodded. What else could she do? Cry, he supposed, maybe scream. He was glad she didn't. "I wish I had a light at least. It's frightening not to see anything. I try to sleep, but you can only sleep so much, you know?"

"I could get you a candle, but it really would be best if you stayed in the dark. No one is supposed to be down here, and if you'd had a light earlier, those men who brought the straw bales would have seen it. I know this must be awful for you, but it's just another day—just a night really, and it's better to be safe, don't you think?"

She sucked in her lower lip and nodded, looking defeated.

He felt terrible.

"Hey, what do you think of my new uniform? Handsome, aren't I?" He meant it as a joke—anything to lighten the mood, to cheer her up. Anyone else would have picked up on his insincerity. Reuben's humor was almost always self-deprecating.

"You look nice," she said. "Even more dashing than usual."

Reuben was stunned. She thought he was serious. The urge to correct her flared—no one had ever called Reuben dashing before, and he had certainly never felt that way. He straightened his back a tad. As he did, he noticed again the extremely tight waist of her bodice and her breasts shining bright and smooth in the flicker of the lantern light.

"I just took my oath to serve the king a few minutes ago."

"Congratulations."

"Thanks." Reuben realized she was the first person to tell him that—ever. Imagining the path his life would likely take, he guessed she would be the only one. "Well, I should get going. I just wanted to stop in before my shift and let you know I talked to my father."

"Do you have to leave?" she asked. "Or can you sit and keep me company awhile? You'd be surprised how unexciting it is to sit in a dark cell. All I do is listen to myself breathe."

He smiled, thinking she was making a joke, then felt self-conscious after realizing it wasn't. He cringed, but she smiled back. She had such big eyes—large and dark. They reminded him of the horses in the stable—friendly eyes.

He sat down and she immediately moved next to him, shifting her hips until she pressed against his side. "Cold," she said.

"Maybe I should see if I can get you another blanket. I could—"

"Don't go." She grabbed hold of his arm and hugged.

"What's wrong?"

"I just don't want to be alone anymore." He felt her rubbing his arm, petting it. "Tell me what it's like to live in a castle?"

Reuben laughed. "I don't know. I live in a tiny room in the barracks with my father and a bunch of other grumpy men. I'm only in the castle when delivering wood or buckets of water or hauling out ash. I spend most of my time in the courtyard."

"You're not out there when it rains, are you?"

"I go in the stables then. Especially if it's cold. The horses keep the stables toasty. And if it's really cold, I stand between them and watch as they make these huge clouds with their breath. I brush and talk to them. They seem to like having me there."

"If they are anything like me, they do." She gave his arm a light squeeze and stared at him with those big eyes.

"Maybe I should bring a brush when I come back."

He meant it as a joke—another poor attempt at being funny. Not until he heard the words did he realize he'd just compared her to a horse. Now he expected her to push him away and take offense. Instead she laid her head against his shoulder.

"I'd love to have you brush my hair." She nuzzled him. He guessed she was pretending to be a horse now, just being playful, making a joke out of his joke perhaps. But it didn't feel that way. It felt nice. Really nice. Warm, comforting, and exciting. Girls were never so kind, so...friendly. "You're not like other men I know."

His mind caught on the word *men*. Most people referred to him as a boy or worse. Even the princess, who was only twelve, called him a boy. Hearing Rose say it made him feel better than he would have imagined—better than putting on a new uniform, better than wearing a fine sword. "How would you know? We only just met."

She laughed. It was a sad laugh. "I've known you longer than I've known most men."

"Oh, right," he muttered. He'd forgotten. With the exception of her dress, nothing about Rose made him think she was anything other than a pretty girl. Now that most of the makeup was gone, he found a cuteness about her, an open quality he liked. Reuben didn't feel he had to be on guard around her the way he was with everyone else. When he made mistakes, she didn't mock him. She had yet to laugh or ridicule him. He could be himself—relaxed—the way he had previously only felt in the company of chopped wood or horses. Rose was incredibly nice, and it was hard to think of her as a—"So what's life like for you?"

She smiled up at him. "See, right there. You're very odd."

If anyone else had said this, Reuben would have cringed, but he could tell by the tone of her voice and the look on her face that Rose meant it as a compliment.

"I am?" he asked.

"Yes. It's as if you actually want to know."

"I do. I want to know what it's like being... well... *you*."

She looked at him, and he stared back. Her smile faded then and a sadness filled her face.

He'd done something wrong, said an awful thing. He just couldn't figure out... "What?" he asked.

"Nothing."

"No, tell me. What is it?"

She looked away, letting her hair cover her face. "You didn't say *whore*."

He sat not knowing how to respond, not knowing if he should say anything.

"Why not? Why didn't you?"

He shrugged. "It didn't seem... I don't know... nice, I guess."

Her face came up again, and her cheeks were wet so that some of the strands of her hair stuck to them. "See!" she said a bit too loudly, her voice cracking so that she paused to cough. "Other men never have a problem saying it, and very few have ever been concerned about being nice to *me*. It's always been my job to be *nice* to them. You don't have to be *nice* when you pay. You don't have to be thoughtful, or even gentle. And no one wants to talk, and if they do, they want to talk at you. They don't want to hear you say anything, or if they do, they want you to say awful things, and they *absolutely* don't want to hear the sob story of some poor girl." She laughed again, a nervous, miserable laugh that sounded and looked more like crying.

"I do."

"No, you don't. *I* don't even want to hear it. It's depressing."

She bent over and covered her face with her hands. Her body shook with sobs. Reuben didn't know what to do. He reached out and thought to pat her shoulder, but that didn't feel right. Instead, he just laid a hand on her arm, giving a light—and what he hoped was a comforting—squeeze. She responded by turning in to him and pressing her face to his chest. He let his arms circle and hug her. They sat under the flickering lantern for several minutes. He wanted her to feel better, but part of him didn't—holding her was wonderful, and if she felt better, she would pull away.

"Thank you," she said in a voice muffled by his tabard.

"For what?"

"For being different. For listening to me. For keeping me safe."

"You don't have to thank people for that. Anyone would—"

She was shaking her head. "No man I've ever known would, or has. I honestly didn't think you existed."

"Me?"

Rose pulled away then, breathing deep and wiping her eyes clear. "Well, a man like you. Strong, handsome, all dressed up and shining like one of those knights I hear about in fairy tales."

"I'm a lowborn guard. I can't ever be a knight."

"I think you're a knight. At least what a knight should be. I've actually known several real knights. They all look the same without their armor. None of them have ever been noble."

She took his face in her hands, leaned in, and kissed him. She was gentle. A light touch. Her lips the softest thing he'd ever felt. Her fingers drifted down from his cheek along the length of his neck. Pulling away just enough to speak, still so close he felt her words, she said, "If you don't want to dirty your new uniform, we can fold it up and set it on the other straw bale."

"Rose," he said, not certain where the air to speak came from, as she had just stolen every bit he had. He gained a moment by taking hold of her hands. "I can't."

"It's your first day. How upset will they be if you're a little late?"

"It's not that. It's . . . not right."

She smiled, trying not to laugh. "No, it's okay. Honestly. This is the first time I've ever really wanted to. And I'll be able to sleep afterward—it will help. Really."

She kissed him again, and he pulled back.

"What's wrong?"

"I really can't."

"If you're afraid—if it's your first time—that's okay. I like that. I'll get to feel special."

"That's just it. This *would* be special, and that's why I can't."

She stared at him, confused; then slowly she pulled back, letting her hands fall to her sides, an understanding dawning on her face. "She must be an amazing woman."

"She is."

"How long have you been in love with her?"

"All my life, although I only met her three years ago," he said, realizing he'd never told that to another living soul.

Rose looked down and he thought she might start crying

again. Instead she sucked in a breath and forced a stiff smile. "You're a good kisser. Did she teach you that?"

"No, but thank you."

Rose reached out and let her fingers brush along his cheek. She had a sad, wistful look in her eyes. "I hope she knows how lucky she is."

Reuben looked away, closed his eyes, and bit the inside of his mouth.

ॐ

How much of a fool am I?

Reuben came out of the dungeons into the whirl of celebration. Like surfacing after a dive, reality felt too bright, too loud. Lights were everywhere—illuminated pumpkins carved with faces, lanterns, torches, and candles that sat on shelves, hung from the ceiling, or were mounted on poles. The sound of flutes and fiddles rang through the stone corridors, being muffled by the patter of shoes as hosts rushed, guests arrived, and servants trotted.

Such a marvelous world. Such sights and sounds. Such beauty that they kept locked away, hidden from those who chummed with horses on cold winter nights. Reuben paused at the entrance for a moment, looking through the sweep and majesty of gowns and cloaks, wondering if he would see her. What would she be wearing for such a grand event? What might she think of his new uniform? Would he be suddenly dashing in her eyes too?

He knew the truth of it. If the princess saw him now, she wouldn't notice. Her sight would glance off him as if he were the surface of a still pond. He was just another guard—as interesting as a table or pillar.

He turned and walked toward the big doors. He didn't want to see her. He didn't want to prove himself right—not after speaking with Rose. What would she have thought if he had told her? What might she have said? How could he explain? No one could ever understand; even he struggled at times.

There was almost as much commotion out in the courtyard as inside. Servants with buckets and bundles ran with their deliveries. For years Reuben had watched the parties from the roof of the woodshed, or in winter from the windows of the stable. In the shadows he would sit for hours marveling at the capes, hats, walking sticks, feathers, and furs. All the parties started like a parade, a traveling show put on just for him. That day, however, he was working the parade.

"You're late!" Lieutenant Wylin was at the front gate along with Grisham and Bale. Bale looked irritated and gave him a reproachful stare. "You can take your leave now, Bale."

"Yes, sir," Bale said, still glaring at Reuben. " 'Bout bloody time."

"When you fail to do your job properly, Hilfred," Wylin spoke sternly, "your fellows suffer. Remember that. You're part of a team now. Trust me, you don't want to be the weak link in this chain. The castle guard has a way of solving its own problems."

Reuben found it strange that Wylin called him by his surname. He never had before, and it sounded odd, as if he were speaking to his father.

"Grisham here will show you what's to be done. Do as he says, and I'll be back later." He paused and then almost as if reading his mind added, "Your father spent many years attaching respect and dignity to the name of Hilfred. Watch yourself, do your duty with honor and courage, fulfill your vow to protect His Majesty and his family, and you'll make your father proud. Then perhaps one day you'll find yourself as a sergeant at arms like him."

Wylin nodded briskly at Grisham and then marched off.

"So what do I do?" Reuben asked.

"Nothing," Grisham replied. "Think you can handle that?"

"Then why was it so important that I get here on time?"

" 'Cause Bale's feet hurt, and he was hungry. You're gonna stand in that spot for six hours. You'll see."

"I really just stand here?"

"That's the outgoing side," Grisham said, then pointed across the bridge at the central square of the Gentry Quarter, where a long line of coaches waited, wrapping in a circle around the statue of Tolin Essendon. "See the carriages? They come up on my side. I check their invitations and wave them through. Then they roll to the front door, drop off the guests, and the driver goes back out on your side. The king don't care about empty coaches leaving his castle. So you just stand there and wave them through. Even you ought to be able to handle that, right?"

"What if they don't have an invitation?"

"Then we tell them to leave."

"What if they don't?"

Grisham smiled. "We never get that lucky. The only fun we ever have is watching the drunks at night. Sometimes they get surly and if they're merchants, you can give them a kick to the backside. But be sure you aren't kicking a noble. If they're really drunk, they might not remember, but if they do, you'll lose that foot."

A pair of trumpets played a fanfare from the battlements and the lead carriage rolled forward. On top was the typical driver in heavy black robes and the traditional soft hat. He pulled the pair of mismatched black and white horses to a stop.

"Invitation, please." He heard Grisham's voice on the far side.

A boy in a high-collared doublet and fur hat looked out the window at Reuben with an expression of disdain. He rotated a silver dagger with a handle shaped like a dragon through his fingers like a coin trick.

"Welcome to Essendon Castle," Grisham announced a minute or two later, and the carriage rolled in.

As it did, another pulled up in its place. Across the bridge, Reuben watched the line move and more carriages appeared in Gentry Square from various side streets. Most were open coaches, many of which looked identical to one another. These each had candle-lanterns mounted on the four corners hanging from ornamental iron arms that curled like vines near the top. He wondered if all the identical carriages were hired from the city liveries, as all of those were pulled by a single horse and came equipped with the same retractable top, which could be unfurled like a lady's fan. That night, being clear and not yet cold, few had them up. Reuben guessed it was just as important to be seen visiting the castle as it was to get invited in the first place. Some of the carriages were drawn by pairs of horses. The more horses the more money, Reuben guessed. The truly rich had no need for hired carriages, and each of theirs was unique, larger, and well decorated. Reuben noticed that Grisham passed these through the gate faster and with more formality.

After the bulk of the parade had passed, as gaps began to form and the flood slowed to a drip, Grisham called him over.

"You take the next one. I may need to piss at some point."

They switched sides and Reuben waited as the next carriage rolled up. It was one of the open-tops, pulled by a single horse. Riding in back were two men dressed in high-collared cloaks—one heavy, one thin.

The carriage halted at the gate. "Invitation, please," Reuben asked in the same monotone voice he had heard Grisham use.

The heavy man handed over a folded parchment with white-gloved hands.

Reuben opened it and glanced at the contents. He had no idea what it said—he couldn't read. He was fairly certain Grisham couldn't either. Still, it was the same-looking document that all the others had, and the royal seal was all he was really looking for. This was the first time he saw the writing, however, and he marveled at the beautiful lines.

He handed the invitation back. "And your invitation, sir?" He reached out to the thin man.

"This is Viscount Albert Winslow," the heavy man said. "He is my guest this evening."

Dozens of carriages had passed the gate and none ever said this. Reuben began to sweat as he wondered what he should do. Feeling foolish, knowing he failed, Reuben took a step to the side to make eye contact with Grisham.

The older guard nodded.

"Ah...thank you. Welcome to Essendon Castle," Reuben said, then waved them through.

Grisham chuckled as they switched sides again but didn't say anything.

Soon the carriages stopped coming and Grisham had him close the little gates, swinging the iron bars around and locking them in place with the big crank. This gave them something to lean on, but Grisham warned not to get caught doing so. The sergeants might let it slide, but Wylin and Lawrence didn't like it, and after the unexpected death of Sergeant Barnes, who used to supervise the guards at the front gate, Wylin would be by more likely to check on them.

"The easy work is done," Grisham told him. "Now comes the long hours of boredom. We just stand here and open the gate when people leave."

"Won't the carriages return?"

"Yeah, but they have to park out on the street for now. There's no room for all of them in the yard." Grisham looked up at the castle and then back out at the city. "Okay, I've got to hit the privy. It might take me a while—things been backed up, if you know what I mean. You all right to just stand here and not get both of us in trouble?"

Reuben nodded.

"Nothing should happen for the next few hours anyhow. Not out here. Just try not to stab anyone or let an enemy army in, okay?"

"I'll do my best."

"Good boy." Grisham walked off toward the barracks.

Reuben stared out of the gate across the bridge at the city, but he wasn't seeing it. Instead he was remembering the feel of Rose's hands on his arm, the shift of her hips as she moved against him, and the look of her face. No one had ever looked at him like that before. There was admiration, even awe in those wide eyes, as if he were someone important. It felt dishonest to let her look at him that way, to allow her to think he was something other than what he was. Reuben wondered what it was like for her. How awful must it be to sleep with men for money? Part of him was angry. He wanted to protect her. To save her from what he imagined was a horror. She should not be doing that. Whores were supposed to be ugly, dirty, vile women with no morals, no kindness—they were not Rose. This got him thinking that maybe he had no idea about anything. She was a whore, and he was a new castle guard, but in the broader scope of things, Rose was more worthy of respect. She had seen the world and survived on her own. She was free to do what she wanted and as such he imagined she had experienced much more. He admired her and supposed she would be surprised to learn that.

Still, it was nice to be looked at that way—to be noticed, to be seen as something more than a tree, or a door, or a pair of hands. It was outright thrilling to be thought of as a man.

That title he was certain was premature, but it sounded wonderful coming from those soft lips. There was more to it than that, more than simple recognition. When she had congratulated him on his success, he felt both happy and empty. Never having known such admiration, or even the support of a real friend, it was as if he'd only realized he was hungry after smelling food.

He liked Rose. Yes, he did.

The idea settled in his head as if it had been flying around the corners of his sight. When he actually bothered to *really* look, the idea gained substance and became unmistakably solid. He liked Rose a lot. She felt like a friend. Having never had one before, he wasn't completely sure, but he couldn't imagine her giving him a helmet and then beating him with wooden swords or getting drunk and punching his face. She was better than that—better than *them*. When he first spotted her coming out of that window, he thought she was a ghost, but now he thought that perhaps he was the ghost—a ghost that only she could see.

Rose. Is it just a coincidence that she has my mother's name? That she climbed out of that same window?

"Hilfred!"

Reuben looked up to see the prince and the Pickerings riding horses toward him.

"Hurry. Get the gate open."

Reuben did not bother with the bow. He grabbed the hand crank and lifted the catch until he could swing the gate back out of the way.

The prince was dressed in heavy wool, a thick cloak with his hood up. Mauvin and Fanen followed suit, each appearing as night riders or mounted monks. They had packs that bulged—a picnic stolen from the castle kitchens or the party tables, perhaps? Reuben wondered how long they planned to stay out and hoped they wouldn't be as long as their bags suggested. If anything did happen to them, how could he excuse it? And if the sun came up and they weren't back, what then?

"Back to Edgar's Swamp?" he asked. Best to be certain he knew where to send the search party before they dragged him to the gallows.

"Yeah, it's getting cold. Tonight might be my last chance to beat Mauvin and become the new frog-hunting champ so we plan to spend the whole night. When snows set in, we'll be able to hold races in the castle. Maybe sucker the squires into doing a little betting. Now remember, don't tell anyone we left. Even if they beat you with whips or set hot tongs to your feet."

"Yeah, with all that's going on, they'll think we're just off in some remote part of the castle doing something stupid," Mauvin said.

"Not like chasing frogs in a wet pond in the middle of a cold autumn night," Fanen said with a smirk.

"Right!" Mauvin grinned.

"Wish you could come, Hilfred," the prince said.

"Thank you, Your Highness."

"C'mon, slowpokes!" Alric jabbed his heels into the sides of his horse and raced out into the Gentry Quarter followed by the two brothers, their horses' hooves clattering on the brick.

Reuben closed the gate once more and watched them go, wishing he were with them, disappearing into the night with frog bags flapping.

CHAPTER 12

THE AUTUMN GALA

W hat is taking so long, woman?" the king roared at the
queen.

"I'm brushing your daughter's hair."

Amrath entered the bedroom.

Arista sat on a stool facing Ann's swan mirror, while his
wife stood behind peering over her shoulder. They both stared
into the mirror's depths as if watching a riveting battle through
a window. The two were dressed in gala finery. Ann had on
her infamous silver silk gown. He should never have allowed
her that dress; he had lost too many arguments on its account.
The delicate silk that so perfectly, and strategically, adorned
her body turned out to be more formidable than any armor.

The king leaned against the doorframe and folded his big arms
across his chest.

The queen looked up. "Why the rush?"

"I'm thirsty."

"Oh, you aren't going to get drunk tonight, are you?"

"It's a party, isn't it?"

"But you don't have to..." She sighed. "Do whatever you
want."

The king frowned. He'd been looking forward to a night
of revelry, to getting soaked with Leo and possibly introducing

the new chancellor to the wonderful world of hard cider. Everyone should make a fool of themselves once in a while, and he wanted to see the proper young gentleman from Maranon fall on his ass. But with that one sigh, his plans were foiled.

"What?" Ann asked.

"Nothing."

She was still as lovely as the day they had wed, which was also the day they met. He had lucked out there. Leo had had the luxury of meeting Belinda Lanaklin ahead of time. His friend knew what he was getting into. Amrath's future had been dictated by his father, Eric, and Ann's father, Llewellyn. Or was it old Clovis who had decided who his granddaughter would marry? Who she would love.

Does she love me? He had asked himself that question dozens of times over the years, never certain why it was so hard to believe. A lot had to do with being an arrangement. She never had the chance to say no. Anyone would make the best of a situation they couldn't escape by pretending happiness and hoping that one day it would be true.

When his father informed Amrath of the agreement he had reached with Clovis Ethelred for his granddaughter Ann to marry him, the first thing Amrath had asked was what she looked like.

"Look like?" His father squinted at him, puzzled.

"Is she pretty?"

"Ahhh..." He appeared pained. "Hard to say. I don't remember."

"You...don't remember?"

"The last time I saw her was years ago. She was only a child."

His heart had stopped at that admission. He recalled standing before his father, running all the ghastly girls he'd ever seen through his mind and, yes, he was fairly certain his heart *had* stopped, if only for a second. He didn't even know how old she was. Clovis was ancient, so his granddaughter might have been some old maid of thirty or more. This sent new images through Amrath's head of the rat-haired witch who made the bread, and his great-aunt Margaret who had a face that sprouted warts that had then grown hair. "She could be monstrous. Some vicious badger-like thing."

"I'm sure she doesn't have a snout."

"You don't know. How could you know? You've never seen her. And she's an Ethelred! By Mar! She's bound to be hideous! How could you do this to me?"

"I didn't do anything to you!" The old man's tone had switched from sympathetic to sharp—his ruling voice. "I strengthened the kingdom. I saved that throne in the great hall so you could sit in it one day. So that when you did, it would be more than just an ugly chair. This marriage had nothing to do with you and nothing to do with her. Its value is in coin and security. That's what matters. Not your petty concerns about having a beautiful girl. You're a prince! You'll be king! You'll have everything the kingdom can give. How spoiled *are* you?"

"Easy for you to say. You don't have to sleep with it."

"If you do the job right the first time, you only have to sleep with her once. Then you can wash away the memory with a hundred girls. You can have them lined up outside your door."

That was true, he realized. He would be king. He could do whatever he wanted and have as many women as he wished. At the time that thought consoled him; then he thought of his mother and how he was an only child. The woman rarely smiled; perhaps he'd just discovered why. His father's advice did not seem so wise then.

He dreaded the countdown to the wedding and contemplated running off. He would flee on horseback in the starlit night and live by his sword, become a hero. But he didn't and a funny thing happened. From the day he met Ann Ethelred, from the moment he took her as his wife, he had never wanted anyone else. He discovered that he measured all other women on how similar they were to Ann. Only none could ever compete with her, and watching his wife brush their daughter's hair in the lovely gown of shimmering silver, he knew that would never change.

"What?" Ann asked.

"I didn't say anything."

"I know. You're just standing there staring. What are you thinking?"

"I was wondering if you loved me."

She smiled at the mirror, the magical world between the two swans. Amrath imagined it was a beautiful place, a pretty country where troubles never found entry.

"I bore you two wonderful children." She kissed the crown of Arista's head.

"That was your duty as queen, but do—"

"Really?" She paused with the brush still holding on to a few strands of Arista's hair to look at him. "A duty? Is that how *you* found it?"

"Not for my part—of course not."

She returned to the mirror and the brushing. "Then why would you think I saw it that way? Did I appear to be suffering? Do I now? It's such a hardship being your wife. Perhaps you should summon the guard to whip me, lest I stop brushing my daughter's hair."

Arista laughed and covered her face with her hands.

Amrath scowled at her. "I could have sworn we had a dozen servants whose job it is to see to Arista's grooming."

"There, you see? What more proof do you need? I do this because I want to."

"That just proves you love your children."

"Actually it just proves you love *me*," Arista whispered.

Ann gave her a gentle slap on the head that caused her to giggle again. "Quiet, you."

"It doesn't speak to the question of your love for me." Amrath unfolded his arms and took Ann by the shoulders, turning her to face him. "Do you?"

She stood defiantly stone-faced, holding up the brush like a weapon before her—a tiny maiden warding off a giant bear. "Of course! How else could I live with such a hairy brute?" He held her still, his eyes searching hers, pleading. She melted. "How could any woman not love you?"

Amrath raised an eyebrow. "Because I'm king?"

"Well, there is that." She grinned and wrapped her arms as far around his waist as she could. "But I meant because there is nothing so attractive, so romantic, so wonderful as a man who is so clearly in love with me."

"Hold on," Amrath said. "*I* never admitted to anything here. You're the one who—"

She tilted her head so that her chin rested on his chest as she gazed up at his face, her arms squeezing.

"A man could get lost in those eyes, you know."

"Really? But I thought you didn't love me."

"Well…maybe."

"Maybe?"

"It depends."

"On what?"

"On whether you're ready to go down to the party yet. You remember the party, right? We have this new chancellor that I appointed to the job because you insisted I give Clare's husband a position."

"That's not why you did it."

"It was one of them."

"For being such a bear, you're awfully soft." She rubbed his belly.

"Winter is coming. I'm putting on fat for the cold season."

Ann smirked, then set the brush on the dresser. "Come along, Arista, Daddy wants to show us off to his friends."

"I like making them jealous," the king said. "Where's Alric?"

"He went down already with Mauvin and Fanen. I've never seen him so anxious to get to a party before. Maybe he's seen someone, or maybe he's taken a fancy to Lenare."

"Eww." Arista made a face as she stood up.

"Lenare is becoming a lovely young lady," Ann said. "Very respectable. You would do well to emulate her."

Arista rolled her eyes.

"Arista!" The moment Amrath barked at her, he recognized his own father's voice—the ruling voice—and winced inside.

"Sorry," she said.

The apology sounded sincere, but not weak, not hurt. There was fiber there. She might bend, but there was no breaking his daughter. She was tough, that one; took after him in that way. Smart too—she took after Ann in that fashion. A shame she was a girl.

ॐ

As usual, the musicians played "Falcon's Flight" as Amrath and Ann descended the stairs. All heads turned and lifted to see the royal family's entrance. No one said a word, and not even the old sat while they came down. Like a pipe and drum corps on a battlefield, the musicians played while standing. Amrath was dying for a drink. Bad enough that he had to wait until the last guest arrived, but he also had to take his time creeping down the steps with all the speed of a change in seasons. He had to time his footfalls so that the anthem concluded with the end of their procession. The whole thing was theatrics, but expected. This was part of his job, part of being king, and he reminded himself it was one of the easier tasks.

Only Wintertide was more festive than the autumn gala, but the king always thought there was a kind of coercion in the celebration of Wintertide—a party to divert the attention of people facing the longest, often coldest, night of the year. The harvest gala was different and truly festive as long as there was a good harvest. There was nothing worse than trying to make merry after an early frost or torrential rains that wiped out the coming winter's food. Luckily, he didn't have to be concerned with either since the harvest had been plentiful. They would have a surplus, and aside from the unpleasant death of Ann's sister and Chancellor Wainwright, the future looked worthy of a fine celebration.

The party planners had outdone themselves this year. He had never seen so many pumpkin lanterns. They must have bought every candle in the city. The Artisan Quarter would be dark but happy that night. At least the candlemakers would be smiling, not to mention the pumpkin farmers. He chuckled and shook his head at all the bales of hay and straw. Only the privileged would dream of making a castle appear like a barn. Already several bales had broken, the floor scattered with brittle straw and dry clover. They would be cleaning up for weeks.

Kegs of beer and trays of sweetmeats graced every room, accompanied by casks of cider. Barrels had ladles hanging off the sides and slices of apples floating—fruit that would be prized by the end of the night, having absorbed the fermented cider. Streamers that mimicked the color of falling leaves spilled down from the rafters and looped the banisters. A number of the real ones lay scattered across the floor, escapees from the large pile of leaves mounded in the center of the reception hall that the younger attendees had been diving into.

When at last he reached the main floor, the music stopped and everyone took a knee.

"Welcome, my friends, to my humble home," he said with a loud voice that boomed and bounced. "Please rise."

The room rumbled with movement. "Tonight we celebrate the bounty that Maribor and Novron granted us this year, and they were generous indeed. All of our provinces report a surplus, and not just in the fields, for the year was good to the forests as well, and game is plentiful. The coming winter will indeed be a merry and safe one. But our joy is doubled as we also celebrate the appointment of our new chancellor. The son of the Earl of Swanwick, who married my wife's recently passed sister, making him Duke of Quarters, the same man who just three years previously had distinguished himself by winning the Silver Shield and Golden Laurel, not to mention taking the Grand Circuit Tournament of Swords Master title at the Highcourt Games. A man whom my own wife has declared possesses the Valin tongue, the Pickering physique, and the bold determination of the Exeters!"

This brought a round of laughter.

He called for a glass of wine and looked over the crowd. "Where is my brother-in-law anyway?" Heads turned, looking around.

"Here, Your Majesty."

Amrath spotted the new chancellor's hand rising out of the sea of heads, and those who hadn't realized turned to face him. Amrath lifted his glass. Those who had drink followed suit. "To the new Lord High Chancellor, His Excellency, Percy Braga."

"To Percy Braga," the room echoed back. They clinked, drank, and applauded.

The musicians in the gallery began playing once more and he and Ann waded through the room. Always like fording a river, the king thought. Everyone was seeking his attention for a word, which always started with flattery and was followed by a request. Luckily the gala was a local affair. To his knowledge only Melengarian nobles were in attendance. Little solace, as they were just as annoying, but at least he wouldn't have to weather Imperialist rhetoric. If he had to sit through one more debate over the need of a central authority or how kingdoms like Melengar were an abomination in the eyes of Novron, he'd likely strangle someone. That was one of the benefits of these events—no swords. In a room of unarmed men, he wasn't just the king; he was *the Bear*.

Amrath and Ann joined Leo near the hearth. Pickering sat on a table, legs stretched out and his boots resting on a nearby cider barrel. Between his teeth he puffed from a long-stemmed clay pipe.

"Just make yourself at home," Amrath growled playfully, swatting at his boots.

"Already have, Bear."

"Where is Belinda? I thought she would be here."

Leo got to his feet to speak to the queen. "She and Lenare are visiting her mother in Glouston. She's not well." His expression suggested it was more than a simple cold.

Voices erupted behind them.

"The shield belonged to Cornick," Conrad the Red told Heft Jerl. His voice was loud and getting louder.

Not again, thought the king.

The two neighbors, the Earl of West March and the Earl of Longbow, faced each other over a cider barrel. Both were in their forties, grizzled old roosters cleaned up for the day. They each wore fancy doublets, and their combed hair didn't suit either. These were men at home sitting on dirt with their bare feet resting on the backs of hunting dogs. He imagined their wives had had a say in how they arrived at court.

"It belonged to Hinge," Heft Jerl, the Earl of Longbow, replied. He was matching volume with Conrad and sloshing the cider in his cup, as he was another of those men who couldn't speak without moving his hands.

"It has a mountain on it," Conrad insisted as he ladled a cup of cider, struggling to scoop up an apple slice.

"No one knows what it has on it."

"Open the tomb and you'll see." Conrad caught the apple and grinned.

"No one is digging up the sacred grave of my ancestor!"

"Sacred? It's just old bones…and a shield—a shield with a mountain crest—Cornick the Red's shield!"

"Just because you keep saying that doesn't make it true. Besides, the mountain wasn't even your family crest until…?" Heft looked to Amrath.

"You two aren't seriously debating that again, are you?" the king asked.

"They're on their eighth cup," Leo said. "What did you expect?"

"Eight already?"

"They arrived early."

Amrath sighed, not because two of his earls were well down the happy cider path but because waiting on his wife had left him seriously behind in the cup race. "You two need to find something else to bicker about, if for no other reason than to provide a little variety for the rest of us forced to listen. What about the Ribbon River?"

Heft looked at him, wiping dribble from the front of his doublet with the sort of concern that came from having been warned not to muss his clothes. *What have we become?* Amrath felt the old depression coming on. *We used to be men. Now we're dress-up dolls for women.*

"What about it?" Heft asked.

"It's changed course over the centuries. One of you has gained land while the other has lost some. That sounds far more sensible than this old argument."

"That's just land," Conrad said. "This is the honor of my fathers. It wasn't Cornick the Red who failed to hold the flank. It was Hinge Jerl."

"Every story tells of the red mountain shield being driven from the battle," Heft declared.

"Go to Drondil Fields," Conrad said. "Look at the painting next to the charter. It's Hinge Jerl holding Cornick's shield! Cornick lent it when Hinge's broke. If you'd just stop being so damn stubborn, admit your whole family have been cowards for centuries, and open your bloody tomb, my forefathers could be vindicated."

"You're drunk," Heft said, which made Amrath smile given Heft's own wobbling stance.

"Hinge's arms were the hammer." Conrad clapped his hand on the hammer symbol embroidered on the front of Jerl's now hopelessly stained doublet. He struck harder than necessary to make the point. Eight cups of hard cider had that effect on him.

Jerl shoved Conrad back and didn't see what everyone else—who hadn't had eight cups—saw, which was that Jerl was too tipsy to judge distances fairly and that he didn't mean anything by it. Jerl's shove was badly timed, catching Conrad off balance. He staggered back, caught the barrel with his heel, and fell on his backside, spilling a full cup of cider and losing his coveted apple slice in the process. This brought laughter from everyone in the hall, except Conrad.

Conrad the Red had always been hot-tempered—all Reds were—and he never needed to be drunk to take offense at being made a fool. When he came up from the floor, he had his dagger in hand. While swords were not allowed, daggers were considered ornamental. Conrad thought differently. His glassy eyes were focused as best they could be on Heft Jerl.

Amrath heard Ann gasp. That did it. The king stepped between the two.

Amrath was like a mountain—Conrad could not get to Heft; he could not even see him. The king's massive hand took hold of Conrad's wrist. "It's a party, Conrad." Amrath spoke softly but deeply—a warning growl.

Conrad glanced at his immobilized hand, then up at the bearded face. There was a moment of hesitancy. Then he nodded with a murky expression as if he had just woken up.

"Keep an eye on these two," the king whispered to Leo as they watched Conrad struggle to return his dagger to its sheath.

"I'll watch, but my growl is not as effective as yours. And I don't have my sword."

Amrath felt a small hand slip into his, and Ann gave a pleasant squeeze that said, *Thank you.*

The king surveyed the crowd. Being a head above helped. The throng had spread out since the toast, spilling into the dining hall, the ballroom, even the throne room. White-gloved stewards navigated the mob with silver trays over their heads. Percy Braga was in a corner speaking to Lord Valin and Sir Ecton.

"I think Percy is working at his own party," Amrath told Ann.

"That's good, isn't it? Shows he's dedicated."

"Or ambitious."

"Sounds like Simon," Ann said.

"Simon's an ass, but he's smart. Smarter than I am."

"Percy is smart too."

"I know…that's what worries me. I'm surrounded by geniuses."

"Does that include me?"

"Especially you." He eyed her with feigned suspicion and gave her hand a squeeze. "You're more dangerous than the lot of them."

Looking around the room, he couldn't spot his son Alric, but Arista was seated near the fireplace, alone, reading.

She's going to be another Clare if I don't do something.

"Your Majesty!"

Amrath turned to see Bishop Saldur rushing at him in his dress robes of black and red. He had not seen the cleric in several months, but the old man never changed. Amrath would swear he looked exactly the same as he had when the king was a boy, only shorter. The bishop grew old, then just stopped changing. The elderly were like that. Children matured quickly, then hovered briefly in that sweet period of perfectly ripe youth. Soon after, the scourge of age set in like a disease. Hair lines slipped, bald spots revealed themselves, dark hair turned gray, stomachs grew, and skin sagged, but at some point there was nothing else to erode.

"Sauly, how are you? How was your trip to Ervanon? Is the Patriarch still alive?"

"Thank you for asking. His holiness is fine and the carriage ride exhausting. I only returned two days ago, and rushed all the way. I didn't want to disappoint our new chancellor. What was going on with..." Saldur tilted his head toward Conrad. Leo had taken him by the arm and was leading him away with promises of better sources of drink than cider.

"Nothing, just too much celebration and not enough to eat."

Saldur looked over his shoulder. "The shield again?"

Amrath smiled. "It wouldn't be a party without at least one brawl."

"That's the kind of brawl that sparks a civil war."

"House Jerl and House Red have been sparking for five hundred years. I won't lose any sleep."

Saldur straightened the wrinkles on his sleeves. "Your Majesty, I need to speak with you privately."

"Something wrong?"

The old bishop lowered his voice to a whisper. "I'm afraid so, and it concerns you and your family."

"My family? What about them?"

"Perhaps we should continue this conversation in the upstairs chapel where I will be able to speak freely."

"You act like we are among enemies."

The bishop leaned close and in a low voice said, "If I am right, we most certainly are, and they are bent on royal blood."

❧

Bishop Saldur had always made Amrath uncomfortable—most religious people did. Amrath's mother and father had been devoted members of the Nyphron Church. Given his contentious relationship with his parents, it wasn't hard to understand why Amrath entered Mares Cathedral only on high holy days, marriages, and funerals. He'd skip the holy days, too, if he wasn't required to participate as head of state. His rejection of the church was not entirely funded by his paternal feud; church people had a strange way about them. They smiled too much, were quick to compliment and support, but behind the stretched lips and soft words was a judgment. No one was ever good enough—at least not until they were dead. The dead were exemplary.

Saldur looked like he should be dead. *How old is he?* That was something else about members of the church—they grew old. Most men never lived long enough to have many gray hairs, but Saldur looked like a snowcapped mountain. Amrath didn't think it was natural that all these bishops and priests lingered decade after decade. Amrath's father and mother were gone, but Saldur was still calling him into the chapel for lessons. There was nowhere worse to speak to a bishop than in their church or in a castle chapel, especially a bishop who used to instruct him as a boy. They had spent long hours in the room exploring the mysteries of Novron. Mysteries that, for Amrath, were never made clear. As a boy, he had a list of issues with various church doctrines, but he couldn't remember much of it anymore. He stopped worrying about the questions when he stopped suffering the lessons. If Maribor existed, how come no one ever saw him? Supposedly they used to—at least one woman saw an awful lot of him and gave birth to his son, Novron. And whatever happened to Novron? The teachings were always a bit sketchy. Did he die? And if he could die, why did people pray to him? Amrath never prayed to his own dead father. Of course, his father wouldn't lift a corporeal finger to aid his son, much less an ethereal one. Amrath's father felt it was more practical that his son learn how to cleave a man's head off than to accurately recall the seven trials of Novron. To that day whenever he saw Sauly, Amrath felt like a boy who had skipped his chores.

Entering the chapel, Amrath wasn't about to resume his childhood role. He was king now and was going to make damn sure the bishop respected that. The moment the chapel door closed, he demanded, "So what's this all about?" His voice boomed. Intimidation was key to most meetings, and he couldn't imagine how anyone could control a kingdom without it.

"I have been reluctant to say anything," the bishop replied, folding his hands before him as if he were about to pray. He didn't appear the least bit intimidated. "But my conscience refuses to let me wait any longer. You see, the problem is I have no conclusive proof, and yet if something were to happen and I hadn't said anything, then..."

Rambling. He used to do this when Amrath was a boy. A simple question could never have a simple answer. "What are you talking about?"

"Please bear in mind that I could very easily be wrong. Most of what I'm about to say is mere supposition."

"Most of what? Spit it out."

Saldur began nodding, his old head bouncing as if his neck no longer worked right. Maybe it didn't; maybe the old muscles were nothing more than dead strings now. "I have reason to believe that Lord Exeter may be planning to—well, there's really no other way to say it than to say it—seize control of the kingdom."

Amrath should have been shocked, and he might have been if the bishop accused Leo or even the feuding Conrad and Heft, but he was pointing a finger at Simon, and not a day went by that someone didn't accuse *him* of treason. But the bishop had mentioned the welfare of his family, and that was the only thing he was concerned with.

"Simon is many things, but he's no traitor. He loves this kingdom. Yes, he can be ruthless but do you really expect me to believe that he would resort to regicide?"

"That is *exactly* what I'm saying. It's because of his devotion to the realm that he feels a duty to replace you as king—to save Melengar from destruction."

Sauly offered a friendly smile, but Amrath wasn't buying. No one accused a loyal marquis of the realm of treason and smiled about it. "I'm afraid you'll have to do better than that. What makes you think that he's planning anything?"

"I don't believe Chancellor Wainwright's death was an accident. I'm convinced Lord Exeter killed him. He expected to be given the position of chancellor—then you and Alric would have suffered similar fates. With your appointment of Percy Braga, he'll have to work quickly. Before our new chancellor develops loyalties that could challenge him for the throne. Is there any question that with you and Alric in the grave that he would rule?"

"That's your accusation? That Simon doesn't like me or how I run the kingdom? Are you just now learning this, Bishop?" He used his title rather than his name intentionally. He wanted the old man to understand that he was speaking to the king, not an old student.

The bishop looked disappointed but shook it off and spoke his next words with solid confidence. "Are you aware Exeter murdered the castle guard Barnes?"

"There was no murder. The man fell during some investigation regarding a party for Captain Lawrence."

"But did you know that Exeter forced Sergeant Barnes out that window? And can you explain why the high constable has every man at his disposal looking for a girl who had been hiding in a wardrobe in the high tower? Could it be that the girl can implicate Lord Exeter in a plot on your life?"

"Seriously? That's the conclusion you came to? That some party favor the guards smuggled in for Lawrence's birthday has to be a threat to my life because she ran away? It couldn't just be that Simon is trying to find the girl because, one, it's his job, and two, he sees conspiracies everywhere? Always has. As to Barnes, Lawrence's report *did* mention that Exeter ordered Barnes to attempt the climb. He was just trying to prove a hypothesis. Was it extreme? Certainly—but we're talking about Simon Exeter here. Do you have *any* real proof that he is planning my death? Any at all?"

"I am merely informing you of the possibility based on what seems to me to be some very suspicious events."

"I'm sure Simon's zeal might seem nefarious to you, but let me shatter your innocence, Bishop. Simon Exeter has done far worse than throw a castle guard out a tower window, and surprisingly, I'm still the king."

"I told you at the beginning that my thoughts were nothing more than speculation. I'm only thinking about your welfare."

The bishop knew he had overextended himself and was retreating. If it had been Simon standing there accusing Saldur of treason, there would be no such withdraw. But then again, Simon wouldn't have made an accusation without any proof. He'd be able to stand by his words. Simon was a man of steel and Saldur was a man of cloth.

"...and my conscience required me to make you aware of the possibilities. I could never forgive myself should something happen while I stood by in silence. All I ask is that you keep a wary eye on Simon Exeter."

Amrath looked toward the door, where footsteps and voices approached. Guards, by the sound of their boots. There was a knock. "Your Majesty?"

"Enter," the king replied.

Richard Hilfred and one of his men opened the door and bowed. "Count Pickering urgently requests your presence in the great hall."

"What is it?"

"The Earl of West March and the Earl of Longbow are at it again, sire."

CHAPTER 13

THE COACHMAN, THE LADY, AND THE DRUNKS

The carriage stopped in front of The Hallowed Sword Tavern on Merchant Square. With the closing of the shops, Hadrian had seen jugglers and pitchmen call it a day and join the musicians who had all moved inside to one of the three largest taverns. The Hallowed Sword was the nicest and the loudest, with shouts and song. The only people still on the street were the sheriff's patrols. They had passed four of them just traveling from the Lower Quarter.

"That will be a silver, if you please," the driver said, holding out his hand.

"We're going to need a ride home as well," Royce said. "So you'll need to wait."

"I'm afraid I can't do that. Not tonight."

"No?"

The driver shook his head, causing the long pheasant-tail feather in his hat to snap like a buggy whip. "There's a big ta-do at the castle. Every driver has his rig in Gentry Square. Nobles pay handsomely."

"That would explain why it took so long to find you." This was a lie. They had passed on five drivers perfectly willing to take their business. They were just too big or too small. Number six was just right.

"And why I should be going. A silver tenent, please." He leaned down farther from his perch on the carriage's high bench, as if getting his palm closer would aid Royce in opening his purse.

Royce stared at him a moment. "Listen. It's my birthday and I happened into a lot of money just this morning—a small fortune—and I want to celebrate. I plan to drink heavily and I'll need a secure means of getting back to my friend's house. Still, I can see that it would be unpleasant to sit out here for hours, so I'll tell you what... why don't you come inside as my guest. I'll pay you the silver for the trip here and another for the trip home in advance, and I'll buy you drinks while you wait. How does that sound?"

The man looked at him suspiciously.

"Or you can go sit in the cold all night in Gentry Square hoping to catch a couple of good fares."

"Gonna be a cold night too," Hadrian mentioned, pulling at his cloak and shivering.

The driver took his hat off and scratched his head.

"It's my birthday," Royce said forlornly, as if someone had just killed his dog and the driver was refusing to lend him a shovel for the burial. "I want to celebrate, but I don't know anyone in town except Mr. Baldwin here." Royce clapped Hadrian on the back. "You'd be doing me a favor. What do you say?"

The driver squinted his eyes and pursed his lips tightly, shifting them around in serious thought. "How many drinks?"

Royce smiled. "More than you can handle."

"Ha. I wouldn't count on that. It takes a lot to reach my fill. I'm a bottomless hole—that's what my wife used to say."

"I'm sorry. Has she passed?"

"Ran back to her family years ago, on account of my drinking."

"Sounds like you could use a friend as well."

The driver nodded, pulling the collar of his long carriage coat tighter. "I think you're right. And it is getting bleeding cold out."

The inside of The Hallowed Sword was as festive as the windows promised. A quartet comprised of two fiddlers, a pipe, and a drum stationed themselves on a balcony above the bar, working up a sweat. Below, folks danced and hammered the wooden floor with their heels. Tables circled the revelers, piled high with the empty mugs and cups the patrons were stacking in a contest. Two teams competed for the tallest tower and one daring lad was standing on his table, where he drained his cup and then gingerly placed it atop the swaying pillar. The moment he let go, the tavern burst out in cheers. Even those at the rival table applauded, then started drinking faster.

Royce found them a table not far from the fireplace and near the window. He offered the driver the chair that afforded him a view of the street so he could watch his rig. The man smiled at the thoughtfulness.

"I'm Pensive Stevens," Royce said. He was absolutely charming, and Hadrian was amazed at the transformation. His hood was thrown back and the brooding specter had become a fun-loving, charitable man. "And this is my close friend, Edward Baldwin. What's your name, good sir?"

"Dunwoodie, they call me." The driver looked different in the light of the tavern. Out in the night, he appeared as a pale face lost in a bundle of dark clothes. Inside, the man's cheeks and round nose were flushed red, his skin dry and creased from a life in the wind.

Royce held out his hand. The driver again seemed surprised.

A smile came to his face and he shook with an approving nod of his head.

"Well, Mr. Dunwoodie, I'd—"

"No *mister*, just Dunwoodie."

"Tonight you're my guest, so tonight you're *Mr. Dunwoodie*— the noble Mr. Dunwoodie of the Carriage." Royce winked at him. And Hadrian had a hard time keeping a straight face. Royce could be just plain eerie sometimes. "Now, you said this was the best place in the city for drink, right? So how about I fetch a round."

"They have maids that will come by and serve—"

"We can't wait, not tonight! Tonight is special. And *Mr.* Dunwoodie shouldn't have to wait for anything."

Royce jumped up and headed off to the bar.

"Your friend is a very generous man," Dunwoodie said.

"A heart of gold, that one." Hadrian couldn't help smiling.

"Nice place, this."

"One of the best in the city. See that blade above the bar? That's the Hallowed Sword. Legend goes that there is the weapon of Novron the Great, the one he done defeated the elves with."

"Really?"

"'Course not, but that doesn't stop everyone from toasting it every night. Just one more reason to drink. And who knows, maybe it *is* Novron's sword."

Royce returned with three cups of cider and handed them out. "To Mr. Dunwoodie of the Wheels!" he declared, and raised his cup.

Hadrian drank, not surprised to discover his was soft cider.

"To Mr. Stevens and his birthday!" Dunwoodie raised his cup again.

"To the Hallowed Sword!" Hadrian raised his cup to the blade above the bar, and it wasn't long before Royce was off fetching another round.

They toasted the sword eight times that night as well as the musicians, Diamond—the mare that pulled Dunwoodie's carriage—and every tier that went on the cup-stacking pile at the nearby tables. At last Dunwoodie looked at the two of them, struggling to focus.

"You are wonderful people," he slurred. "I love you, I really do. I just met you, but I love you. And damn do you know how to drink."

Ten minutes later Dunwoodie's head was down.

The tower nearest the rafters fell with a clatter, and the room erupted in a resounding cheer, but Dunwoodie noticed none of it.

"What now?" Hadrian asked.

"Let's get him a room. Mr. Dunwoodie of the Carriage deserves a soft bed to sleep this one off."

Royce paid the innkeeper and Hadrian carried Dunwoodie upstairs, where they stripped him of clothes. Just as planned, they fit Hadrian well enough, driver's jackets and pants being notoriously loose. Hadrian pulled the blanket up over Dunwoodie and was surprised to see Royce place a stack of silver coins on the nightstand.

They hurried back down and out the front door only to be met by five now-familiar lads waiting on the street.

"Still here, I see." Top Hat had his thumbs hooked in his belt, exposing a dagger, and his hat tilted up, revealing an unhappy face. Puzzle was with them too. None looked pleased. Hadrian guessed that with each passing hour, their continued presence in the city made it appear all the more likely that he and Royce were members of the rival thieves' guild, and that was a possibility Top Hat and the others weren't happy about.

"You really ought to leave. Even if you are Black Diamond. This city is an empty pocket. It ain't like Colnora with all the fancy merchants warring with each other to see who can build the biggest fortune. Down south, coins spill. Here, purses are tight. You can see we ain't living like no kings. You tell the Jewel, Melengar is a desert and Medford an empty sewer. There ain't enough to share." He took a step forward and his face grew hard. "But since this is all we got, we'll fight for it. You tell the Jewel that."

He made to shove Royce, who moved out of the way. Top Hat missed, stumbling forward a step.

"I told you," Royce said. "I don't work for the Black Diamond. I don't work for anyone."

Top Hat regained his balance and turned, frustrated and flushed. "I hope you're right. That way when my messenger returns with the truth of it, I get to kill you."

"Then shouldn't you be off sharpening something?"

Top Hat and the others watched as Hadrian and Royce climbed onto the carriage. Hadrian took the driver's bench and Royce sat in the back like a noble lord.

"You have a bleedin' carriage?" Top Hat asked.

"Beats walking," Hadrian replied.

The five stared in wonder as Hadrian snapped the reins, waking up Dunwoodie's old ink-black mare. He called, "Let's go, Diamond." This brought alarmed looks from the members of the Crimson Hand and took a moment for Hadrian to understand why. Afterward he couldn't stop laughing.

❦

This beats the straw out of living in a barn.

Albert Winslow stood in the great hall and took a deep breath, savoring the luscious scents of an autumn gala. Cinnamon, wood smoke, apples, and the burning caps of pumpkin lanterns. He even imagined he could smell the crisp chill of the coming winter, one he narrowly avoided dying in. The seasons all had scents that added to their personalities, just like the women he'd known. And just like the seasons, they fell into the same categories: fresh, hot, ripe, and cold as the grave. Sweet music rose over the crowd, buoyed up by the warmth of gaiety. It drifted above the laughter and measured steps of the dance that dominated the chamber. The lush sweep of luxurious gowns twirled from the delicate waists of ladies, and the click of the men's shoe heels kept perfect time with the music.

He had missed it all so.

He glanced at the cider barrel. There was one at every door and several in every room in the castle. Cups hooked to the rims by their handles along with pewter ladles. And the slices of apple floated like smiles. His mouth watered at the memories. He hadn't had a drink in two weeks, or was it longer? The days in the barn blurred. He'd tried to sleep through most of them. His strategy had been to die in his sleep, but he found it was not as pleasant or easy as it sounded. The pains in his stomach kept waking him. If he could have afforded it, Albert would have drank himself to death. He couldn't think of a better way to die—blissful and oblivious. And if there was agony as he took his final breaths, he'd never know it. The best part—the true genius of the plan—was that no matter how much drink he consumed, he'd have zero chance of waking with a hangover. Pleasure without consequence or without payment—surely there could be no better exit.

What shocked Albert was that he was back standing in the castle's drawing room amidst the familiar revelry—the barn already no more than a nightmare, no longer real. One moment he was near naked and casting himself into the lonely straw, begging for a quick death and the next he was in Essendon Castle, his feet sore from dancing in new shoes. He marveled at the shifting of the world, at fortunes shuffled by the whims of gods who were clearly insane.

*Am I the only one to see the truth of it? Or is everyone
thinking the same and keeping their mouths shut?*

Lord Daref had been a perfect host. To the blind, deaf, and
dumb, associating with Viscount Winslow would be seen as a
source of bolstered status for a mere lord. Walking in with a
viscount beside him, Daref hoped to increase his standing at
court. Albert would have preferred a blonde with a big chest,
wide hips, and a great laugh.

While Daref was jealous of the viscount's rank, Albert, on
the other hand, was envious of the extra layer of fat Lord Daref
had put on since the last time they'd met. He literally jiggled
when he walked. After Daref inquired about his lean frame,
the viscount had lied, saying he was taking a vow of absti-
nence for the love of a lady. She had refused to speak to him,
he had explained, but his heart had been so chained that he
fasted until she granted him an audience. Turned out she was
a stubborn wench. When at last she had relented, he found her
a bore beyond suffering. After denying himself for so long, he
had wanted to cast his dice and ride the wind. His first thought,
naturally, had been to visit his good friend Lord Daref.

Albert chewed on an almond sweetmeat as he watched the
crowd. He had two tasks to perform that night and was ever
thoughtful of the consequences of both. Success in one would
result in a man's death; failure in the other would result in his
own. He needed to line up a job worth paying for his expenses,
and he needed to deliver a message to Lord Simon Exeter.
The second had been impossible, since the high constable was
nowhere to be seen.

"Albert, is that really you?" Lady Constance approached,
waving a fan at the top of her breasts.

"Of course not. Albert Winslow is a much more considerate
man than I, for he would never have waited so long to greet

so magnificent a creature as yourself." He bowed, took her offered hand, and kissed its back with barely a touch.

Constance was the quintessential lady-in-waiting—gorgeous, but proper to a fault. She spoke with perfect diction, which gave a hard edge to her words, as if she were biting celery. Many men wanted to take her to bed, and dozens claimed they had, but they were all liars. Albert knew only three who had ever succeeded in this endeavor, and none of those ever boasted. He knew this because he was a member of the lucky trio.

"You're so thin." She let her eyes linger, her sight roaming up and down his person with a whimsically wicked smile. "Have you been ill?"

"Utterly sick with my longing to see you again."

She giggled. She did a lot of that. It was her most annoying trait, especially when she did it in bed. There were few things that could kill a romantic mood more than a woman giggling—unless it was her apologizing afterward.

"How have you been?" Albert deftly shifted the course of the conversation. He did not want to spend all night parrying inquiries into how he had spent the last two years, and he had learned long ago that women preferred to talk about themselves whenever possible, even more about other women. "What mischief have you caused since the last time we spoke?"

Another giggle, this one followed by a half-turn and a sultry over-her-bare-shoulder gaze. "You know I would never do anything unseemly." She batted her eyes.

"Of course not. You are a paragon of virtue."

"You jest, but as of late it's unfortunately true. I'm forced into a corner of boredom by a dull landscape."

"So *you* haven't done anything, but surely you know of some decadent gossip."

"Let's see... Baroness Quipple is rumored to have had Lady

Brendon's poodle killed for tearing up her roses. Word has it she drowned the poor thing in the same crystal punch bowl that the baroness had gifted to her this past Wintertide."

"Is it true?"

"I haven't seen the dog yet." She offered a wicked smile.

Albert couldn't share her humor. A dead dog offered few possibilities of employment and he'd been working the party for hours without any luck. "As wonderful a tale as that is—"

"Actually it didn't have much of a tail!" Constance burst out, and giggled, covering her mouth with her free hand. "I'm absolutely awful, aren't I?" She caught his eyes and frowned. "What's wrong?"

"I had been hoping you were only joking when you spoke of a tired landscape."

"I think I actually described it as *dull*."

Always so miserably precise. He wondered if she made a point to giggle an exact number of times. That might be why he found it so annoying. Her laughter wasn't only excessive, it was repetitious.

"So disappointed."

"In me?"

"Well...you used to have your ear to the door of every noble, and I could always count on you for something... well...really entertaining."

"First of all, it's not my ear to the doors—I have servants for that." Another uniform giggle. "Second, well..." She hesitated.

"Oh, please, you must indulge me. I am so dying for a good story."

"Actually..." she began, and then stopped. Her eyes focused on his hands. "Oh dear, where is your drink?"

"Ah, uh, well, that is to say, I was out late last night—if you understand me. My head is still a bit thick."

"All the more reason, right?" She stood with her hands clasped in front of her, smiling expectantly.

"Oh! Of course, forgive me. Shall I bring you a cider as well?"

"Oh, would you? That would be so kind."

Albert felt rusty as he wormed his way to the nearest cider barrel. He used to be better at this. He should have offered first. In the past he often had extra cups around him that he offered up without needing to leave.

"Because it is ridiculous!" the Earl of Longbow shouted. "The man has been dead for five hundred years!"

"You're a coward!" the Earl of West March shouted back.

"You're a fool!"

The two were near the big oak table, spilling drinks on each other and on Count Pickering, who stood between them like a fence between two bulls. Albert got the drink quickly, making certain to scoop an apple slice into the cup, and returned to Lady Constance.

"The shield argument?" she asked, not noticing or caring that he had no beverage for himself.

"Good to see nothing has changed."

"They seem more adamant this time."

"More drunk, I think. Now, you were saying?"

"Oh yes." Lady Constance pointed across the room. "Do you remember Lady Lillian?"

Albert searched the far side of the hall, seeing a pretty woman who was in a ball gown of pale blue but who looked decidedly stiff. She stared more than watched as if she were in another world. He nodded in her direction. "Lillian Traval of Oaktonshire?"

"Yes, that's her husband, Hurbert, beside her, the one with the lucrative fleet of trade ships that he runs out of Roe. Well, it seems she got herself in a fine state."

"She's not…"

"Oh no, worse—I think. Oh, I really shouldn't be telling you any of this."

"How many cups have *you* had?"

Constance paused, her eyes shifting. "Just since I got here?"

"Never mind, have another sip and go on."

She followed his instructions, except it was more of a gulp than a sip. "Well, as you may know, she has been suspected of having a fling with Lord Edmund of Sansbury. Which, of course, is true, but she stopped seeing him well over a year ago. As there was never any proof, her husband agreed with her that it was just cruel gossip. But… recently Hurbert asked about her earrings, the ones he gave for their anniversary. He wanted to see them and was oddly demanding. She explained that they must have been stolen, but her husband accused her of leaving them in Edmund's bedroom."

"Coincidence?"

"Not likely. And it was then that a chambermaid came to her defense and said that Her Ladyship had lent them to Lady Gertrude just a few days before."

"Had she?"

"Of course not."

"Then why did the maid lie?"

"Because she knew where the earrings really were. She knew because she had stolen them. The maid snatched the pair from her lady's table and handed them over to Baron McMannis, who, as it happens, is in heated negotiations concerning Lord Hurbert's shipping fleet. McMannis would dearly love to get a peek at Hurbert's trade manifests."

"So he put the maid up to it?"

"Absolutely. Planned the whole thing. The maid will come to work at McMannis's estate where she will no doubt receive several promised perks. Now, in order to avoid appearing to have betrayed her husband, poor Lillian needs to *actually* betray him and hand over the manifests to get the earrings back. The only problem is that she really does love old Hurbert, and it will break her heart to do it. So as you can see, poor Lillian is beside herself tonight and, sadly, not at all enjoying this wonderful party. Clearly this is not mischief of my making, but I do so enjoy spreading the tale."

"Gossip becomes you, milady."

"I know." The fan beat faster.

"Lady Constance," Albert said. "I wonder if Lady Lillian would prefer to part with coin to get her earrings back, rather than turn over her husband's manifests."

"Well, of course she would, but McMannis will make far more money from the manifests than Lillian could ever offer him. Besides, there is the embarrassment…McMannis isn't doing this only for the money."

"Paying McMannis isn't what I meant. As it happens, I know some individuals who I'm sure would be willing to retrieve the lady's stolen property—for a reasonable price. What do you think?"

"I would say it's not possible. McMannis has those earrings well secured. I wouldn't be surprised if he wore the things in his own ears when he went to bed at night. There is simply no way to get them from him."

"I'm not so sure. The individuals I speak of are very talented."

Lady Constance smiled at him. "Really? What sorts of talents are we speaking of?"

"The sort that shouldn't be discussed with a respectable lady such as yourself."

Her eyes narrowed. "Well, Albert Winslow, this is a side of you that I've never seen."

"I, too, am a man of many talents."

"And how much would such talents cost?"

"Fifty golden royal-stamped tenents would do it."

"Really?"

"I think so. I would need only to know what the earrings looked like and a small advance on the payment, say twenty? Perhaps she could demand that McMannis provide one of the earrings to prove he had them. I could pass the earring on to my associates, and in no time the pair would be returned."

"And you can *really* arrange for such a thing? That would be perfect. Not only will it help out poor Lady Lillian, but she also would then owe me a favor, and we all know how valuable favors can be." Lady Constance giggled again. Her darting eyes indicated a racing mind. "It is so nice having you back again, Albert. Things were so terribly dull."

"It's nice to be back."

A crash of glass and the ping of pewter caught their attention. Across the room, the Earl of Longbow lay on the floor with Conrad the Red looming over him. The other men at the gala pulled their ladies back protectively, and the music stopped. A castle guard approached and Conrad grabbed the soldier's sword, pulling it from its sheath and shoving the guard away.

"You pitiful excuse for a man!" Conrad bellowed, brandishing the weapon above his head. "You're no better than your ancestors—lying cowards, the lot of you."

"That's enough!" The voice boomed in the great hall like a crack of thunder.

All heads turned to see the king striding across the room, his grand mantle of purple velvet and ermine fur wafting behind.

"Amrath, don't try and stop—" Conrad was in the midst of saying when the king slapped the sword from his hand.

"You've had too much to drink, old friend." His Majesty

looked down at Heft as Leo helped him to his feet. "You both have."

"I'm going to end this right now," Conrad declared with slurred speech. "I'm going to kill that bastard."

"You'll do nothing of the sort. He's one of your oldest friends."

"He's a blackguard and a snake."

"He's also your cousin."

"I don't care."

"Bring him," the king told Count Pickering.

Together the four left the hall with Conrad still explaining how he would smite Heft Jerl so that his great-great-great-grandfather *"smite* feel it!"

By the time the music resumed and the dancers were taking position once more, Albert discovered he was alone. Making a quick survey of the room, he spotted Lady Constance leaning into Lady Lillian's ear, their fans up, covering their faces. Then Lady Lillian's face rose above the fan, her eyes focused on Albert, and in between the wing beats of the fan, he spotted a smile.

Task one—complete.

꒰ᐦ꒱

The row of waiting carriages stretched along King's Boulevard. Horses shifted weight; tails swished; hooves stomped. Drivers chatted or napped on their high benches, cloaked in thick blankets. Each wore a hat adorned with pheasant feathers. The carriage lanterns burned, creating a pretty line of twinkling lights that when taken together appeared like a flaming arrow aimed at the castle.

"You know…they won't stay put." The voice cut through the night. "You know that."

From his perch on the driver's bench of Dunwoodie's coach, Hadrian watched a group of men in cloaks leaving the castle.

"Sure they will," a louder, deeper voice replied. "Just need to get them drunker."

"Drunker? Are you mad? They're at each other's throats as it is."

"Yes, but they can't fight if they can't stand."

The group approached the front gate. Four were gentlemen, well dressed. Two were soldiers of the king. The two guards on station at the gate snapped to attention at their approach and bowed.

"You're Reuben, right? Richard's boy?" the loud one asked.

"Yes, sire." The boy's reply was barely above a whisper, but in the still night it carried across the moat.

"Good. Now listen, the both of you." The loud one paused and sighed. "Count Pickering and I are going to take these idiots home so they don't kill each other. But"—he looked over his shoulder at the castle where every window was bright—"if anyone asks, I want you to say I never left. Tell them I retired for the evening. I've put in my time and made my appearance. The rest of the night is mine to do as I please, and it pleases me to spend some time with old friends and be free of my obligations for one blasted evening. Understand?"

"Yes, Your Majesty," both guards replied.

"I already told the queen, and she is going to go to bed. So just tell anyone looking for me that I joined her. Got it? I'll have a single night's peace, by Maribor. Have I made myself clear?"

"Yes, Your Majesty."

The two soldiers who had exited with the four men brought horses from the stables and helped the drunks onto the animals' backs.

"Come, Leo, the night is crisp, and my backside is in a saddle and not a throne. Let's go have us a *real* party."

"Here! Here!" one of the drunks said.

"Your wish is my command, Your Majesty."

The group slipped out the gate, rode across the bridge, and clip-clopped off toward the city's gate.

"King's gone," Hadrian said.

"Yeah," was all he heard from the interior of the coach.

Mr. Pensive Stevens was gone and the old Royce was back. He was in a stalking mood, hood raised.

Hadrian could see his own breath and pulled the collar of Dunwoodie's jacket up and the sides of the driver's pheasant-feathered hat down. In his years of military service, Hadrian had faced worse conditions, but he usually had something more to do than just sit around. Before a battle there were swords to sharpen and armor to don. He had a hard time imagining a lifetime of sitting on a cold bench waiting for customers.

Hadrian never sat idle in one place for very long. Most of his life was spent in motion. Over the past six years, since leaving home, Hadrian had wandered and never spent more than a few weeks in any one place. He'd seen a lot of the world, but not the details. He marveled at how much went unseen except by patient carriage drivers and their silent horses. There was just a small hint of a breeze, which, combined with the colder air, had a way of letting sounds carry. He heard the distant crack of someone splitting wood and the inevitable curse when the blade clipped. There were random bursts of laughter that echoed between the buildings and unintelligible shouts that Hadrian attributed to the wandering bands of recent alehouse visitors having trouble finding their way home or perhaps to the next alehouse. He could tell which homes were most affluent by the number of servants fetching water and wood and which public houses were the most popular by the number of times their doors opened and closed. The Broken Helm was doing considerably better business than either The Wild Barrel or The Iron Ogre. He actually had not seen a single person enter The Iron Ogre and was not certain if it was even an alehouse. Places

in the Gentry Quarter were so neat and ordered that The Iron
Ogre might actually have been the nicest-looking smithy he'd
ever seen, or judging by the name, perhaps it was a money-
lender. He watched individuals walk briskly to alehouses only
to leave hours later in packs that meandered aimlessly. Sheriff
patrols also wandered in packs. He guessed quite a few were deputies, as they lacked uniforms. He had seen five such patrols pass
by, usually three or four to a bunch.

All things considered, there weren't that many people
around. Maybe they were all at the castle for the party, and the
sudden invasion of colder weather was keeping the uninvited
inside. Or it could be that they were frightened off by the sheriff patrols, who seemed to be accosting everyone they passed.

The later it got, the quieter the street grew, which suited
Hadrian just fine. The work that lay ahead would best be done
in the hours that men shunned. The closer the time came, the
more miserable Hadrian felt. He agreed with Royce that no
matter his position, the man who had beaten Gwen should
be punished, but Royce's methods never meshed well with his
own. Hadrian would prefer to meet him sword to sword on
a well-lit field—not that such a pairing would be fair, but at
least it would have the illusion of such. Certainly the high constable, a marquis, would not agree to such an arrangement,
so Royce's less-honorable techniques were necessary. He still
didn't like the idea of sneaking up and...

Hadrian hopped down and leaned against the side of the
coach. "Exactly what do you plan on doing with him when he
comes out?"

"You don't want to know."

Hadrian looked at the delicate rose whose stem was stuffed
in the latticework of the carriage lantern. There was one on each
of the four corners. Royce had purchased them from a street
vendor. He was in a poetic mood, and that was never good.

CHAPTER 14

TRAITORS

I don't care, young lady." Queen Ann argued with her daughter. Richard Hilfred stood in the corridor of the royal residence watching through the open doorway. Nora, the handmaid with the lazy eye, was helping the queen with Arista, who was straining to be free of them.

"I'm nearly thirteen!" the princess shouted. "I could be married and having my own children, and you'd still be sending me to bed before the moon has peaked."

The girl was red-faced, furious, and had fought with her mother ever since he had delivered the princess to her bedroom as per the queen's orders. *Royals.*

Hilfred never understood this nightly ritual. A man who stole an apple to stave off death would have his hand severed by the greats with hardly a thought, but they indulged their children recklessly. If Arista were his daughter, she'd never speak to him that way twice—not while keeping the same number of teeth.

The queen, with hands on hips, leaned in, her tone harsh. "See, that's where you're wrong, Arista. When you're married and have your own children, I won't tell you what to do anymore. That will be *your husband's* job. And you'll do what he says then just as you'll do what I say now."

"That's not fair."

"Like you said, you're nearly thirteen—practically a woman, right? Then it's about time you understood what it means to be a woman. And fairness doesn't play any part in *that*. You'll curtsy, obey, smile, and keep your mouth shut."

"That's not what you do. You and Father—"

"I was lucky. Your father is…well, he's very kind, but I also know to do what he says when his voice turns into that growl. You'll learn that, too, and tonight is good practice for the future."

"Then I'll never get married."

"That's really not your decision."

"It should be."

"You and all your 'should bes.' You aren't becoming a woman, Arista. You're becoming a brat. Now get to bed."

The queen whirled and stepped out in the hallway, closing the door harder than necessary. She stood rigid for a moment, her hands in fists, jaw clenched. "Stubborn, combative, never willing to accept the inevitable," the queen grumbled.

Hilfred wondered if she was speaking to him. Sometimes they just talked to themselves. He felt awkward. If she had spoken to him, he must offer a reply or risk offending her—not something he wished to do in her present state, as he was certain the queen would not offer him the same degree of leniency and patience that she extended to her daughter.

"A bit like her father," Hilfred offered.

Queen Ann nodded without looking at him. Then she turned to look at the door. "That's what I love about her."

"Would you like me to escort you back to the party, Your Majesty?"

"Hmm?" She looked up. "No. I've had enough party for one night. I'll get Arista to bed and then retire as well. I won't be needing your services for the rest of the evening, thank you."

"Then I will take my leave." He bowed formally. "Good night, Your Majesty."

"Good night, Sergeant, and thank you." The queen looked at the door to her daughter's bedchamber and sighed before going back inside.

Richard was alone in the corridor.

He'd thought the nonsense with the princess might never end. Any other time he could have stolen away, but the party was as much a help as a hindrance. If only Reuben had told him about Rose sooner.

Richard needed to speak with the bishop; he needed guidance. The king would be downstairs getting drunk with Count Pickering. Safe enough in his own castle with Bernie and Mal on duty as body men. With the queen and princess in their quarters, all he needed to be concerned about was the prince. Nora always put the boy to bed first, but he'd still have to check the kitchens. Alric, along with the Pickerings, had a habit of sneaking down and gambling with the older squires.

But where was Saldur?

He'd last seen the bishop with Amrath in the chapel. Being as it was on the way to the stair, it was worth a look. He stopped outside the chapel door, reached out to knock, but stopped when he heard two familiar voices.

"...because I was concerned," Bishop Saldur was explaining.

"But why were you there?" There was no mistaking the voice of Lord Exeter, crisp and accusatory.

"Is there a rule against a bishop fraternizing with castle guards? I will apologize to the king at once if I've inadvertently breeched some line of etiquette—but I assure you I was unaware of any restriction."

"It's not an issue of protocol. It's just strange. Sergeant Barnes said he saw you on the tower's steps. The tower is an odd place for a cleric in the middle of the night. What were you doing there?"

"Is it by the king's orders that my presence in the castle must be *accounted for* now? Or has there been a crime I am unaware of that I'm suspected of having committed?"

"Is there a reason you are refusing to answer such a simple question?"

A brief pause.

"I had just returned from my trip to Ervanon that night and was at the castle to see the king, but when I arrived he was busy and I was asked to wait. I had nothing better to do and I'd never seen the view from the high tower, so I decided to make the climb—good for me to get some exercise. At my age, I don't get nearly enough. I took a peek out the window—couldn't actually see much in the dark." He chuckled. "I suppose I should have anticipated that, but I didn't. I was heading back down when I ran into this parade of soldiers coming up the stairs. I was curious what so many men were doing in the tower. Turned out it was a birthday party for the captain of the guard. They had a barrel of ale and a tray of meat and cheese. Having not had time to eat, and still waiting for the king, I lingered."

"And after it was discovered that the girl was missing, why were you so insistent on Captain Lawrence sounding the alarm?"

"I was concerned for my king. She could have been anyone. A woman who sells her body is capable of anything. What if she had a dagger and was planning on slitting the king's throat?"

"She was just a girl—an ignorant whore from Medford House. Do you expect me to believe you were fearful she could reach the king armed with a butcher's knife? And even if she did, that she'd pose any serious threat to his life?"

"I was in the room with a dozen or so castle guards who had admitted to breaking rules and then somehow lost a girl they had smuggled in. I wasn't quite as confident as you about their competence in protecting the king. I would think that you of all people would agree with me, that you would be on my side."

"Your side?" The words were spiteful. "You know what I think, Bishop? I think *you* and your *side* would like nothing better than to see an end to monarchal rule. I also think that tower is conveniently isolated despite being part of the royal residence. The stairs are long, it's cold up there, and it's supposed to be haunted—perfectly out of the way and yet a nearby place to plot against the king. I think you were there—before the party—not to look at the view but to conspire with someone. There's a rumor that a light was seen in the tower the night before Wainwright's death. Perhaps you had a habit of meeting there, and finding the king's soldiers unexpectedly rushing up the steps gave you reason for concern. What you discovered was alarming. A woman had been hiding in the wardrobe. Was she there when you were? Had she overheard what you and your fellow conspirators said? You needed to find out. That's why you raised the alarm. You had to find and cut her throat."

"My dear boy, that is quite an elaborate tale—so inventive. But why waste it on me? Surely this speech has been concocted to make the king, or at least the chancellor, distrust me—and dare I say, to divert attention from yourself? We both know it's *you* who is plotting against the king and *you* who is so intent on finding this girl. Was it you who arranged for Barnes to smuggle her in? Is that why you killed him? To keep Barnes from telling the truth? You see, accusations are easy to throw around but account for absolutely nothing. I know, I tried to get the king to understand. He was less than receptive. He wants facts not assumptions. Now, unless you intend to arrest me, I'm going back to the cathedral. I'm too old for parties."

Richard knocked and waited. "Who's there?" Exeter shouted. "What do you want?"

"Richard Hilfred. I'm here to see the bishop."

"By all means, come in, Hilfred," Saldur said.

"Don't you ever *actually* guard the king?" Exeter asked.

"I was assigned to the queen this evening, Your Lordship, and she has just dismissed me for the evening."

"Is there anything else, Constable?" Saldur asked.

"I'll find the girl," he said to Saldur. "I'll find Rose, and then I suspect we'll have another, very different conversation." He pushed past Richard and stormed down the halls toward the stairs.

"Do come in, Richard. How can I help you this evening?"

Richard closed the door to the hall but was still concerned about being overheard. After all, he'd just overheard the previous conversation in that room.

He said softly, "I found Rose."

CHAPTER 15

ROSE

They moved swiftly down the uncomfortably narrow corridor. Richard led the way, holding a lantern high to help the bishop on what had to be his maiden visit to the dungeon. The sounds of the gala barely reached them—a muffled, muted blend of conversation, laughter, and music. When he reached the last cell, Richard used the key his son had given him.

"Reuben?" the girl called as he opened the door.

"No," Richard said, entering, raising the lantern again, this time to reveal Rose as she sat huddled against the far wall. "I'm Reuben's father. He sent me and I've brought Bishop Saldur, who wants to ask you some questions."

They entered the straw-filled cell, and the bishop appraised the girl with a dismissive shake of his head. "Were you in the high tower last night?"

Rose nodded, wrapped in a straw-covered blanket.

Richard was pleased that she looked nothing like his Rose. She was much younger, about Reuben's age, and had a round, doe-eyed face.

"Sergeant Hilfred tells me you overheard a conversation between two men. What did you hear?"

"They talked about killing the king."

"Who were they?"

"I don't know, sir."

Saldur stepped closer. "Are you certain? This is very important."

"They never said their names."

He took another step. "You're positive?"

Huddled in the straw, Rose looked terrified. "I...ah, yes... no names, but one did refer to the other as 'Your Grace' once."

"Anything else?"

She hesitated. Richard could see she was struggling to think of anything to appease the bishop, who towered over her. He saw her eyes brighten. "Yes...yes! They said the name *Clare*."

"Clare?" Saldur pressed.

"I heard..." She looked at Richard, then at the floor. Her eyes drifted in thought as she struggled to remember. "Yes! They said what a shame it was that Clare had to die. That she had discovered who murdered the chancellor." Rose was nodding rapidly, causing some bits of straw to slip free from her hair.

"Did they say who that was?"

Rose struggled again, her face revealing her frustration. "No."

"Do you think you could identify the voices if you heard them again?"

Again she paused to think. Her eyes studied both of them, and in a pitiably small voice she admitted, "I don't know."

Saldur peered at the girl for only a breath longer, then walked out. Richard followed. They moved down the empty cell-lined corridor, then the bishop stopped and spoke, barely above a whisper. "Who else knows she's here?"

"No one, just my son."

"Your son?"

"Reuben. Today is his first day as a gate guard."

"Is he on duty now?"

"Yes."

Saldur smiled. "Perfect. You need to get Rose out of the castle. Do it now, before Exeter finds her. Take care of her. Find a safe place—somewhere no one will look. Then hurry back—I'll need your help tonight. The fate of the kingdom is in our hands now."

～

Reuben was starting to understand why Bale had been upset at his tardiness. Standing in one place turned out to be harder than splitting wood and a lot harder than brushing horses. Nothing of note had happened for hours, and the night had turned cold.

"So what was the fight about this time?" Grisham asked.

His fellow defender of the front gate was a grizzled veteran who had always frightened Reuben. He had a gravelly voice, unruly eyebrows, and stubble perpetually covering his chin. Reuben found it a mystery that he had never known the man to shave, but neither had he grown a beard. "What fight?" Reuben was surprised Grisham spoke to him. He rarely did, but perhaps boredom affected everyone.

"Between you and your dad, this morning. I heard you hit the door again. Woke me up."

"Sorry." Reuben left it at that, thinking Grisham just wanted to complain.

"Well? What was it about?"

Reuben looked at the old soldier, confused. *Does he really want to know?* Maybe putting the uniform on changed his status with more than just dungeon-trapped girls. "He didn't like me being with the prince and his friends."

"Oh, yeah. I heard about that. You're lucky you got back when you did. They were about to get a patrol together to go out looking. If that had happened, you would have had more than just your father to answer to."

"What exactly was I supposed to do? When a prince asks you to ride with him, you can't really say no."

"I don't care what you did or why. I just wondered why Richard was bouncing your head against the door."

"He had been drinking," Reuben added, not knowing why. His father had beaten him plenty of times sober, and Grisham knew it.

The older guard looked out across the bridge at the line of carriages all still burning their lamps, then scratched at his stubble. He did that a lot. "He's not a bad guy, you know—your father. Just hard. World made him that way, makes us all that way eventually. He's just trying to toughen you up, build some calluses so you don't bleed to death. Understand what I'm saying? It's how you survive. The world's a miserable place, kid. Give it any chance and it will kill you and not always with a blade or a cough. You know, there's a reason men prefer to die in battle—living can sometimes be worse. You don't make a tough son by coddling him. You do it by bouncing heads against doors."

This was the most Grisham had ever said to Reuben, and with him in such a talkative mood, Reuben decided to push his luck. "Did you know my mother?"

"Sure, we all did." Grisham caught himself and quickly added, "Not like that, though. She wasn't...you know...like they say. She was a good girl, a nice girl." He paused, then added, "That's probably part of it too. He doesn't want you to be like her."

"How's that?"

"Weak."

"Because she killed herself?"

"It's like I was saying. Some folks, they don't have no armor at all. Rose Reuben was that way. You could tell what she was thinking just looking at her. She'd tell you anything—didn't know what a secret was. If she was unhappy, she cried. If happy, she smiled."

"And if her heart was broken?"

"You get the idea, I see."

The castle doors opened and a sliver of light escaped along with two figures. One was wrapped in a blanket. Even at a distance, Reuben recognized his own Rose and his father as they moved quickly across the courtyard to the gate.

"I'm taking her home," Richard Hilfred said before either had asked anything. He looked at Grisham. "This girl, Rose, overheard two men planning to murder the king. Isn't that right?"

Rose nodded.

"One of them was Lord Exeter," Reuben's father said. "Exeter is looking to kill her. So I need to get her away from him."

"Exeter?" Grisham said. "A traitor?"

"Afraid so. Obviously I would appreciate it if you forgot you ever saw her and didn't tell anyone I left the castle."

Reuben noticed Grisham glance at him with a look that said, *Again, are you kidding me?*

"You know the sheriffs are patrolling the city streets," Grisham said. "They're out looking for her."

"I'll go with you," Reuben volunteered.

"You'll stay here," his father snapped. "This is your post." He grabbed Reuben by the chain of his chest and pushed him against the castle wall. "I got you assigned to this post tonight to keep you safe." He spoke softly. "So you stay here, understand? You don't go anywhere. Not in the city and absolutely not in the castle—for any reason. Got it?"

He didn't understand but nodded just the same.

"Listen…" Richard sighed, letting go of him. "Your mother, she wanted me to take care of you. I did that. I did the best I could and paid that debt. You survived. You're a man now. I did that, so tomorrow just remember that I got you posted to this gate. Okay?"

Reuben felt like he was missing part of this conversation, like when his father drank. The words that spilled out of his mouth might make sentences, but they didn't make much sense. He nodded again, pretending to be smarter than he was.

His father reached out and grabbed Rose by the wrist, pulling her away. As she passed through the gate, Rose looked back at him with frightened eyes. He wanted to say something to her, *goodbye* maybe. Before he could find the words, she was gone.

❧

Rose would have been terrified if it were anyone but Reuben's father dragging her along. Grim-faced, he pinched her wrist as he jerked her across the moat. The man was nothing like Reuben, and until they reached the gate, she had wondered if he'd lied about his identity.

She had calmed down the moment she saw Reuben again. Just seeing his face made her feel safe. Rose had only known him a little more than a day, but he'd already done more for her than any man ever had. He wasn't like other men—men were evil. She had come to this conclusion ever since her father had abandoned Rose and her mother. Over the years that followed, she had many more examples that proved the point. But Reuben was different, unexpected—shocking. Finding him was like discovering dogs could talk. He was more than special; he was a miracle. For Rose, Reuben was a bright light and she a moth. During all those hours, alone in the darkness of the cell, he was all she thought about. What did he like? What didn't he like? Who was the girl he loved? Finding the answer to that last one was a needle in her heart. And yet, she loved him all the more because of it. He was faithful. She couldn't say the same for any of the men who came to The Hideous Head or the House. And wasn't there a moment—just a moment—when she sensed something?

He was saving himself for her. He wanted the first time to be special. How amazing was that? Rose found it both touching and silly. She had no fond memories of her first time and did her best not to remember any of the times since. Her mind had a tendency to remember the good parts of life and forget the bad, though not nearly well enough. Still, it also meant that Reuben and his lady love hadn't shared a *first time*. It didn't sound as if he'd even kissed her. And there was a pain in his voice—his eyes too. She saw it, and wondered if that was how Gwen was able to see things when she read people's palms. Maybe everyone had the power to look into the souls of others and see glimpses of truth. Gwen simply knew how to look, or maybe it was just that she took the time. Some people don't want to know—most people don't. But if a person truly cared about someone else, maybe they could search their eyes and know what troubled them—that it would be visible, if you really wanted to see. Looking into Reuben's eyes, Rose thought she understood something about him and something about the girl he was saving himself for. He'd given his heart to her, but the gift hadn't been accepted. Whoever the moronic girl was, Rose hated her. She was also grateful for her stupidity, because Rose was certain she had fallen in love with Reuben Hilfred.

A chill ran through her as Reuben's father hauled her

through the city, but it came more from the wind than the thought. The thin dress offered little protection, but that had never been its purpose. It was difficult keeping the blanket from falling off her shoulders and the wind whipped it open. Winter was knocking, and its icy fingers were everywhere.

She should thank him. He was the father of the man she loved, and this was her chance to make a good impression. Rose understood she was already off on several bad feet. She was a prostitute, wanted by the constable, and had met his son as an escaped party favor. Her only consolation was that it would make a great story to tell his grandchildren. She frowned. Maybe the story about how Mommy was a whore would best be forgotten. Still she imagined the conversation.

Thank you for helping me, Richard. Your name is Richard, isn't it? Or should I call you Father? Yes, I should—so much nicer, and I've always wanted a real father ever since mine ran off, leaving me and my mother to starve. So you won't have any contender for that title. Can't you imagine us all before the fireplace on Wintertide, Father? I'll be cooking the goose that you and Reuben brought home while little...ah...little Gwendolyn and little Richard—yes, we'll name him after you—play on the floor.

"Thank you for helping me," Rose said.

"Shut up." Richard Hilfred jerked her arm again, twisting her wrist slightly so that it hurt. He sounded angry.

Maybe he was upset because her talking might give them away. Rose forgot she was a fugitive, and it made perfect sense that he would be fearful. All he needed was a chatty girl getting them both killed. Just one more bad foot she put forth. This one into her own mouth. Winning over her future husband's father was going to take a lot of repairing, but if Gwen could make a pearl out of the ruins of that Wayward Inn, Rose could fix this. Reuben would help smooth things over and

Richard would come around once she gave him grandsons. Grandfathers were suckers for grandsons. In the meantime, she'd be quiet.

A smile invaded her face as she imagined what she would tell Gwen when she got home.

Remember what you said about me falling in love?

CHAPTER 16

THE LORD HIGH CONSTABLE

Rose was in the castle?" Hadrian asked. He had returned to the driver's seat, and even Dunwoodie's coat wasn't enough to keep out the chill.

"Didn't expect that." Royce's voice came hollow out of the dark interior of the carriage beneath him.

"We in trouble?"

"Don't think so. Sounds like we just lucked out. He said Exeter was still looking for her. The timing might be perfect."

"They'll never make it to the Lower Quarter." Hadrian watched the girl and the guard walk briskly past the line of carriages heading for the city. He remembered her from the year before. Rose was the one who had brought him soup all the time. She spilled some on him once and they had a good laugh. She used to love his stories and once, just before they left, he danced with her in front of the fire. "We should give them a ride."

"I'm here for Exeter and I need the carriage. You can go escort them if you want. I don't need you for this."

Hadrian dropped down off the driver's seat and stood next to the coach's window. The curtain was drawn, but Hadrian could see Royce's fingers holding part of it open.

He watched the pair walk into the shadows and sighed. "I'll stay."

"No. You should go."

"Royce, you're hoping to ambush a high noble and you don't think you might need help with that?"

"This is familiar ground."

"How so?" Hadrian said.

"There's a reason the Black Diamond returned our horses. A reason why people still fear men in dark hoods in Colnora. I have a lot of practice in this. I don't need your help, but that castle guard could use another sword—or three."

"I thought you didn't believe in the whole *good deed* thing?"

"Maybe Arcadius was right. Maybe you're rubbing off."

Hadrian wished he could see Royce's eyes. Not that they ever told him much, but he was certain the thief was hiding something. Normally, convincing Royce to think of someone other than himself was like trying to explain to water that it shouldn't always flow downhill. He also didn't like him bringing up that Arcadius might be right. The last time they had seen the old university professor was when he'd practically twisted their arms into teaming up. Twisting Royce's arm was never a good idea, and to hear him applaud the old man only convinced Hadrian something wasn't right.

Hadrian took off the driver's coat and hat and pulled his swords from where he'd hidden them on the driver's seat. "I might still be back in time."

"No rush," Royce said. "Either way this works out, I'll be busy all night."

All night.

The words lingered as Hadrian walked away and would return to his mind several times before it ended. He slipped his cloak back on as he walked in shadows, and once he was out of sight of the gate guards, he ran.

He sprinted past the gentry shops, then slowed when he

spotted the two. Hadrian kept a good distance. Following them wasn't hard; he already knew where they were going. The guard glanced around a few times, but not nearly as much as Hadrian thought he should. The year Hadrian had spent with Royce taught him the value of awareness, and the last few hours of sitting on the coach's bench had showed him just how active the streets were.

The pair cut through the homes and then passed under the Tradesmen's Arch into the Artisan Quarter. There the world was darker, the homes smaller. Without enough income to pay for streetlamps, illumination came from the rare candlelight leaking out of windows through thin curtains that veiled the private lives of craftsmen, their wives, and children. Overhead, the moon had risen, turning the narrow streets into patterns of black and ghostly white. The tight buildings bounced sound, allowing Hadrian to hear their steps, loud and crisp.

He wondered what had gone on in the castle that night, and what might still be going on. Normally he didn't indulge in pointless speculation about the nobility any more than he wondered what it was like to be a hawk or a fish. Meeting Albert had changed that. The viscount was...surprisingly human. He used too many big words but breathed air like everyone else. Hadrian worried about him. If there was some treachery going on, he hoped Albert had the sense to stay out of it.

The loud shuffle and clack of fast-moving heels on cobblestone filtered out of a side street. The folks of the Artisan Quarter were hardworking. Few wandered outside after dark, and none in such large groups. Hadrian ducked into the recess of a cobbler shop's doorway, hitting his head on the boot-shaped signage, just as a patrol came into view. They marched quickly toward Rose and her escort.

"Halt!"

The pair stopped, and the men closed in. Like all the other patrols, this one had only one member in the black and white sheriff uniform. The rest were dressed in simple tunics and wool trousers, but each sported a white feather in his hat.

"What are your names?" the one in the uniform demanded.

"I'm Sergeant Richard Hilfred, of the royal guard."

"You're a castle guard?" one of the deputies asked.

The quarter sheriff shook his head and frowned. "The burgundy and gold falcon tunic and the chain mail didn't give it away, huh?"

The other man shrugged, and another suppressed a laugh.

"And who is this?" the sheriff asked, nodding at Rose.

"That's none of your concern. I am on the king's business—leave us be."

"Can't do that. We've got orders to find a young girl—a whore." He paused, looking at Rose carefully, shifting around her to get a full view. "For two nights a tiny army has crawled up every alley and looked in every rat hole. But no one's seen anything close—until now."

"And yet, I'm telling you I'm on the king's business." The escort's voice didn't have a hint of fear. If anything, he sounded irritated. "You see the uniform, you know what it means. Now leave us be. I don't have time for your provincial games tonight."

"Maybe you're on king's orders, maybe not. If you are, then there'll be no trouble with you coming with us to the castle so we can ask Lord Exeter. If it checks out, we'll apologize real proper-like and provide an escort to wherever it is you're going so no other patrols interfere. How's that sound?"

"I told you I don't have time for games, boy."

The sheriff didn't like that. "I think you're gonna have to make time, Sergeant Hilfred, because I'm not a boy. I'm a

Medford quarter sheriff, this is my quarter, and the two of you are under arrest."

The moment the sheriff reached out for Rose, Richard wasted no time. He jerked Rose back hard, causing her to cry out and fall to the street behind him. At the same time, he drew his sword. Before anyone else moved, he shoved the blade in and out of the stomach of the largest deputy, who at the time wasn't even looking his way. Rose started screaming as the big guy crumpled in a little spin to the stone as if he were a dying top.

Richard swung at the uniformed sheriff, but by then all swords were out and the stroke met steel. The clang rang through the empty square as the men faced off. His focus on the sheriff gave the deputy an opening, and he slashed Richard across the back. The blow rocked him, but nothing more.

"He's wearing chain, you idiot!" the sheriff shouted. "Grab the girl. Take her to Exeter!" The sheriff advanced, swinging and driving Richard to the side with a series of chops aimed at his head.

Still screaming, Rose crawled away until the deputy grabbed her by the arm and pulled the girl to her feet. She fought, kicking him in the shin, but the man held on. In frustration, he finally just dropped his sword, lifted Rose over his shoulder, and started carrying her toward the castle.

Hadrian waited until he approached the cobbler shop. "Evening, Deputy," he said, stepping out of the doorway. "That's a heavy load you're carrying. Could you use some help?"

The man looked at him suspiciously for a moment, then said, "I dropped my sword back there. Could you get it?"

"You don't have a sword, huh?" Hadrian replied. "That's the problem with only carrying one." In a breath, Hadrian had the point of his own blade touching the throat of the deputy. "Put her down."

"I'm an appointed deputy. I'm working for Lord Exeter. Look at the hat!"

"Funny—that strategy didn't work for the sergeant either."

"You'll be hanged for interfering."

Rose did something behind the man's back that Hadrian couldn't see, and the deputy cried out, dropping her.

"Damn it! You bit me!" He reached out to grab her again and Hadrian pressed the point of his blade tighter against the man's neck.

Thirty feet away, Richard and the sheriff danced to the tune of ringing swords. The sergeant was the better of the two, and being the only one dressed in chain doubled his advantage. The sheriff kept his distance, lunging only when Richard was distracted.

"Terence!" the sheriff shouted. "Just run and get help."

The deputy took a step back, turned, and ran toward the Gentry Quarter. Hadrian let him go and sheathed his blade.

No longer distracted, the sergeant pressed the sheriff, who fell back but not fast enough. The sergeant cut him in the leg, and when he dropped, Richard thrust his blade through his side, twisting it before drawing it back out.

Hadrian grimaced. That was uncalled for. He had him the moment he slashed the thigh.

With blood dripping from his sword, Richard charged Hadrian, who raised his hands in surrender.

"Easy, I'm on your side."

The sergeant hesitated a moment, glanced at Rose, then nodded and sheathed his sword. "Thanks. Who are you?"

Hadrian looked at Rose. "I'm a friend of Gwen's."

"Who?"

"She's the lady who runs Medford House," Rose explained. "Hadrian was a guest."

"Medford House?" Richard looked confused.

"Yeah, where I live. You know, where we're going—where you're taking me."

"Oh yeah, right." The sergeant nodded several times. "And we need to get going. Thanks for the help, friend." He grabbed Rose once more and the two began to run.

They trotted through the central square past the fountain where the cobblestone formed a circle pattern. During the day, Hadrian had hardly noticed the fountain amidst the activity and the crowds, but in the silence of the chill night, it bubbled like a cauldron. Following behind them, Hadrian cringed. Rose's white skirt stood out as brightly as a surrender flag, and Richard's military boots slapped the street with enough noise to be a call to arms. Maybe it was the time he had spent with Royce, but the two appeared as deft as oxen. Ironically, after a year of being berated for his own noise and clumsiness, Hadrian could finally appreciate Royce's frustration. *Why don't they just shout, "Over here! Come find us!"?*

Richard stopped when they reached the gate to the Lower Quarter and turned, looking irritated to see Hadrian still with them. "What are you doing?"

"I thought you might need—" Shouts and the stamp of boots cut him off. Hadrian saw lanterns casting jittery shadows of running men.

"Stay here," Richard told him. "Slow them down. I've got to get her away."

Hadrian nodded. "I'll see what I can do."

The sergeant smiled, and grabbing Rose's wrist once more, they ran into the dark narrow streets of the Lower Quarter.

Hadrian turned to face the approaching noise.

"There! He's one of them!" Terence, the once-unarmed deputy, had picked up his sword on the way back and now brandished it at him. At his side were three more men wearing hats with white feathers. None of them wore a uniform but all drew their swords.

꒐

Albert waited in the reception hall listening to the muffled sounds of gaiety seeping through the corridors. He could smell the scent of meat. Dinner was at long last being served, and he hoped he was about to be finished with his obligations for the night so he could enjoy himself. He looked forward to spending the rest of the evening indulging in the luxury afforded to his class, a lifestyle he had so sorely missed.

He tapped his toes together. His shoes were too tight. New shoes always were. The leather, always stiff at first, needed time to mold to the wearer's foot and walking style. Albert could hardly recall the last time he had new shoes. Four, maybe five years ago? These were nice. He stared at his toes and realized he couldn't care less about shoes—he wanted a drink. Maybe after proving himself, Royce would lengthen his leash. In some ways he felt like he had sold his soul, given away his freedom, and yet perhaps freedom was overrated. He had never been more free than when he was living in that barn in Colnora. Any freer and he'd be dead. It was impossible to argue with Royce or Hadrian that he could drink responsibly. They knew so little about him. All they had ever seen was a filthy, penniless vagrant who would sell the shirt off his back for a cup of rum. What they couldn't see was that drink had not brought him there—drink was how he dealt with it. How else could a man accept helplessness and the inevitability of starvation? How could a man born to a world of castles, carriages, and kings accept a pauper's end, except by washing it away?

The problem was that while he had his doubts about

Hadrian, Albert was certain Royce was not above killing him if he messed up. There was something about that man that reeked of death. Albert spent many years in castle courts learning to assess people, knowing who could be pushed and who might draw a sword at a joke. These were skills courtiers either developed quickly or died in an early misty-morning duel. Albert hadn't been lying. He was terrible at fencing, but he had developed other skills. The combat skills of the court were the ability to evaluate a man's intents and purposes in an instant. This is what made Albert certain Royce was more than capable of murder; he sensed a degree of experience in him. There was also a total lack of hesitancy. Royce wouldn't give Albert a chance to explain or excuse himself. For now there could be no drinking, but maybe one day, when he had proven himself an asset—

"What's this all about? Who are you?"

Lord Exeter came at him swiftly. The man was imposing. His long dark hair pulled back, the finely trimmed goatee, and harsh eyes. When taken together, it presented a severe presence that screamed, *Threat!* In that instant, Albert could see that he, too, had killed and would kill again. Men of power—of real power—were always scary.

Exeter surprised him so much that Albert barely remembered what he was supposed to say.

"Your Lordship." Albert bowed. "I am Viscount Albert Winslow."

Exeter glared. "Who?"

"I would not expect you to have heard of me."

"What do you want?"

"I was bidden to relay a message to you from a very generous man. I honestly don't know what it means, but it sounded most disturbing. I was asked to say the following…" He had also been asked to say the previous. The preamble worked out between himself and Royce as a means of insurance to keep him safe. He was unleashing a lion after rattling his cage, and Albert felt it was important to at least have a chair. Albert took a deep breath—he wanted to get through the whole message without pause. It was important that Exeter heard it all before rushing off. "'I know your plan,'" Albert said in his reciting voice. "'I have Rose. Perhaps we can make a deal. I am waiting in a carriage out front—a carriage marked by a rose. Come alone.'"

"Who is *this person*?" Exeter asked.

"I have no idea. I only just met him tonight at the gala. He never mentioned his name. Odd, don't you think? He was very insistent that I get this message to you immediately, saying he would be waiting at the front gate."

Exeter continued to stare at Albert for a moment longer, looking both puzzled and angry, apparently undecided which to commit to. The gate was open, but the lion was in no hurry to escape. He turned to the guard with him. "Vince, keep him here." Exeter retreated back toward the interior of the castle from which he'd come.

Albert did not like the *keep him here* comment and stood uncomfortably in the shadow of the guard.

Vince was one of those men who Albert assumed was born to the job of professional soldier. He stood too close for Albert's sensibilities. He could smell the reek of stale sweat. And Albert, who was proud of his ability to read men, found looking at Vince was like peering at a blank wall. No complexity, no mystery, no color—cows had more depth. He was a full head taller than Albert, a large, balding, unpleasant head. His face was a map of scars. And even without the souvenir blemishes of his trade, Vince could never have been considered handsome. The viscount wondered what poor woman once called this her baby, and how she had managed to avoid drowning it.

Exeter returned with a lieutenant of the guard and six other soldiers. He was moving quickly.

"Keep him here until I get back," he told Vince; then facing the lieutenant, he said, "Wylin, there's an idiot sitting in a carriage out front marked by a rose. Go arrest him."

৵

Simon Exeter followed behind Wylin and his men but stopped at the keep's entryway while the rest walked to the front gate, then beyond. Across the bridge, the line of carriages waited. Each had lanterns lit. Some of the horses wore blankets as they waited for their fares or lords to return from the feast.

Simon might have suspected the gods were allied against him if not for the viscount's unexpected message. After the girl's vanishing act, he had spent last night and all that day canvassing the city, interrogating whores and thieves. He deputized two dozen men and had sheriffs working double duty searching every closet and cupboard for the girl. Now he might actually have her.

Simon didn't like the way the gate guards were acting. Both stared at him oddly.

Wylin trotted back across the bridge and up to Exeter. "Empty, sir."

"Empty?"

"Nothing inside, well, except for this." Lieutenant Wylin held out a parchment.

I said come alone. And I meant it.
You have one more chance. Get in this carriage.
Tell the driver to take you to the graveyard on Paper Street in the Merchant Quarter. When I see the carriage arrive, and that you're alone, I will contact you.

Simon crushed the note in his fist and marched across the bridge toward the carriages. The men waited, watching him.

"You there!" he shouted at the carriage driver, who sat nervously.

"I didn't do nothing, Your Lordship. Honest."

"The man who was in here. Your passenger. Where did he go?"

"He switched carriages but paid me to wait for him, sir. Said he would be back, sir."

"He switched?" Simon grinned. "Which one is he in, then?"

"Oh, the one that left, sir."

Simon's smile vanished.

"Which way did it go?"

"Ah…that way, sir." He pointed. "Made a left at the square."

"Merchant Quarter." Simon slapped the side of the carriage, making the driver jump.

"You aren't thinking of actually going, are you, Your Lordship?" Wylin asked. "I mean alone."

Simon fixed him with a withering glare. "Don't talk to me as if I were one of your idiot men."

"My apologies, Your Lordship."

"He's cagey, this one." Simon had his doubts when the viscount delivered the message, but as he looked across the dark square, he became convinced whoever it was did indeed have the girl. "Not a complete idiot."

"What's that, sir?"

"Never mind. I'll go alone, but I want you and your men to split up and walk to Paper Street. Send a dozen this time. Have them take off their colors and chain and go by different routes. When you get there, fan out around the entrance to the graveyard and wait for my arrival. When you hear me whistle, close in. Can you handle that?"

"Yes, sir, but where do you want me to pull the men from? I don't have authority to draw men away from the walls, not on a night when the king is holding a party."

"Pull them from the city guard, Gentry Square. Start with my sheriffs and fill out the ranks with their deputies. They don't need to patrol anymore. That should be more than enough. Gather them on your way, but be quick. I want you there before I arrive."

"Yes, sir. We're on our way."

"What do you want me to do, sir?" the driver asked.

"Wait here. I'll need you to drive me."

"As you wish."

When Simon returned to the reception hall, Vince was still keeping an eye on the viscount, who had a decidedly nervous look on his face.

"Vince, go to my chambers. Fetch my sword and cloak." He turned to the viscount. "This man who gave you the message. What did he look like?"

"Big man. Dark complexion. Blond hair, though, with a thin mustache that ran down around his mouth, you know." The man swirled his finger around his lips. "Slurred his words a bit I remember. I take it you didn't see him."

"No, but I will." He looked the viscount over. "Who did you say you were again?"

"Viscount Albert Winslow."

"What holding?"

He smiled sheepishly. "My grandfather lost the family fief. I'm just a landless noble."

"Worst kind of vagrant—a noble one. Do nothing, contribute nothing, but suck off of every landowner's teat like it's your god-given right. Isn't that so?"

"That's me exactly, Your Lordship."

"You've served your purpose. Go on. Go steal the meal you came for."

"Thank you, Your Lordship."

Simon left the castle, crossed the courtyard, and passed once more through the gate under the withering stare of the boy-guard. He climbed into the carriage marked with roses and yelled to the driver, "Take me to Paper Street, to the grave-yard in the Merchant Quarter."

"As you wish, my lord." The carriage pulled away from the line and entered the city streets.

Who could he be? Most likely that stupid thief I beat the other night. Thinks he can make a coin selling the girl to me. Hanging three of his cohort clearly wasn't enough to penetrate that top hat.

Simon was torn between having the thief leader killed or rewarded. He guessed it would all depend on what the girl told him. He just hoped he wasn't chasing a ghost. And who was this mysterious giant blond the viscount mentioned? This was the problem with conspiracies and coups—they were never simple.

The carriage came to a stop. Looking out the window, Simon was puzzled. They hadn't traveled far. They were only in Gentry Square.

"Keep going. I said Paper Street. That's in the Merchant Quarter."

The driver climbed down and opened the carriage door, stepping in.

"What are you doing? Get out! Are you mad?"

"Yes. Very." The man was small and thin, but there was something about his eyes, something unnerving. Even more disturbing was the prick of a blade that the driver suddenly pressed to his throat.

"I don't have many friends," the driver said. "I can actually count them all on one hand and not use all my fingers. Like anything rare, they are precious. And yes, I get very mad when one is hurt. But I'm sure you didn't mean it that way. What you were *actually* asking is if I'm insane—crazy, isn't that right?" The man's voice was cavalier without any hint of fear or respect, yet soft, words whispered as gentle as a lover. "Well, to be honest, I think you might have a point there too. Oh, and feel free to whistle. Thanks to you, all the sheriffs in Gentry Square are gone, and thanks to the gala, all the residents are away as well. No one is going to hear your signal or your screams."

Chapter 17

The Feathered Hats

Hadrian watched the approach of the four deputies whose only identifying uniforms were the simple white feathers in their hats. One had his on backward such that the feather pointed forward like a one-horned bull. These were no different than the last patrol, except they lacked a trained sheriff and were making do entirely with militia. They blundered up, brandishing swords.

"He's one of them that drew on me. And they got that Rose girl! Look out for the other one."

"Hold on now!" Hadrian called out. "Let's not be hasty. You don't want to die, and honestly I don't want to kill you."

"Put your sword...ah, swords...on the ground," Terence said. "Then lie facedown, or we'll be doing the killing."

"Listen," Hadrian tried again, "Rose didn't do anything. She's just a young girl. And—"

"Someone stab this fool."

They all drew swords.

Hadrian stepped back through the Lower Quarter Gate and, dodging out of sight, pulled his two blades. They followed. The first one through the gate ran into Hadrian's short sword. His crumpled body tripped the second one. Hadrian ignored him for the moment and caught the third with his bastard sword. The last one hesitated as Hadrian expected he might. By then the second one through—the fellow with the backward feather—was on his feet and swinging. The stroke was just a basic shoulder chop—no skill at all. Hadrian caught it high with his left sword and stabbed him with his right.

His sword thrust pierced the meat of his side. Hadrian didn't want him dead. More importantly he didn't want him to fall down. Seeing him occupied, the fourth man pressed the opportunity and took his chance. Hadrian rotated the skewered man around, and the timing was perfect. The fourth man accidentally stabbed the deputy with the backward hat. Both men let out a gasp. The one on the receiving end of the blade being much louder.

Anger replaced horror, and drawing his bloody sword free, the last deputy advanced. He screamed something, maybe words, but perhaps not—Hadrian couldn't tell. The guy had lost control. Fear and anger pumped him until he couldn't think, much less speak. This was exactly the type of insanity that military discipline was supposed to prevent. He was slightly larger than the others but no more skilled. The first swing was a sloppy, overpowered stroke meant to... Actually, Hadrian had no idea what it was meant to do, and he didn't think his opponent knew either. The deputy was just chopping away like Hadrian was a tree that needed to be cleared. A step back and a turn avoided the blow.

Hadrian considered disarming the man—letting him live. Maybe he had a wife; maybe he had kids. This was just a job for him, a way to put food on the table. He didn't go out that night expecting to die. Hadrian hated killing an innocent man. Though technically he wasn't innocent—the guy had signed on to be a deputy, a job that came with certain risks, but that hardly made a difference. Hadrian felt sick as he realized he didn't have a choice. He had let Terence go and this was the result. More men would die—best to just stop it there.

"Sorry," he offered, and finished the man with a clean stroke—a rapid stab to the heart that was in and out in a blink. So fast that the man offered only a puzzled look before his legs gave out. Then he just sat down without a sound.

Hadrian cleaned his blades. While none had touched him, he was covered in blood and felt like he'd been kicked in the gut. The familiar sensation of disgust crept up his throat, causing him to grimace as he looked down at the tangled bodies. One—the backward-hat deputy—lay staring sightlessly at the stars, his mouth gaping as if in wonder. Hadrian swallowed, forcing the feeling back down, and drew in a shuddering breath. He couldn't remember how many men's lives he'd taken in the few years since he'd left home, which he counted as a blessing, but what he didn't understand was why it never got any easier. He imagined that his father would have said that was a desirable thing, that it proved he was a good man, but Hadrian didn't feel good.

It was worth it, he reminded himself. *Rose will be safe now, and* she *is innocent.*

Hadrian turned to run the way Rose and the sergeant had gone, but stopped when he spotted the Crimson Hand thief, Puzzle, crouched on the roof of the gatehouse.

The thief held his hands up. "I didn't see anything." His voice quavered a bit. "As far as I know, it was some other guy—guys even. Five, six brutes—sons of bitches from … from Chadwick—yeah, from the south, who caught that patrol off guard." He looked down at the piled bodies. "Who'd believe me anyway? If I said one guy had … I mean, no one would. They just wouldn't."

"Fine," Hadrian said, then trotted into the Lower Quarter.

He took a side street, or an alleyway; it was hard to tell the difference in the Lower Quarter. He'd never been down it before but guessed it would get him to the central square faster. In the dark he nearly hung himself on a clothesline that appeared at the last second in a shaft of moonlight. A quick turn allowed the thin rope to graze past his ear. It hurt, but not as bad as it might have. The alley narrowed until he was climbing through garbage where he disturbed a family of rats that hurriedly retreated, squeaking their displeasure. He was regretting his shortcut when at last he squeezed through a rickety fence into the square. He got his bearings and headed for Wayward Street.

When Hadrian reached Medford House, he was out of breath. He pounded on the door, then bent over and rested his hands on his knees. His legs were wet. It wasn't sweat. *Why can't it ever just be sweat?* In the light of the House's porch lanterns he saw the dark red stains. *I should get a butcher's apron.* At least none of the blood was his this time.

Jasmine opened the door.

"Did they make it?" he asked.

The girl stared at him and took a step back. "Oh...dear Maribor. Are you okay?"

"I'm fine. Did the sergeant and Rose make it? Are they here?"

"Rose?" Her expression of fear and confusion shifted to delight. She took a step backward and in a hopeful, earnest voice asked, "You saw Rose?"

"Yes, she was coming here. Where is she?"

Jasmine shook her head. "I don't know what you're talking about. Rose isn't here."

"Hadrian?" Gwen said, coming out of the parlor. She was limping, leaning on a homemade crutch. The scarf was off. Ugly black and blue marks inflated her face. Gwen's lips were bloated, puffed, and split. The whole right side of her head was a dark bruise, one eye swollen shut. Cuts left black tracks of dried blood. Looking at her, Hadrian stopped feeling sorry for the sheriffs and wasn't embarrassed for the blood on his clothes.

"I'm looking for Rose." His voice harsher, louder.

"Everyone is," Gwen replied.

"No, she was just with me. A castle guard was escorting her back here—"

"Rose was with you?" Several of the women pushed past Hadrian, stepping onto the porch.

"They were attacked by a sheriff and some deputies, and I"—he looked down at his clothes—"I helped out a little."

"I see," Gwen said.

"Rose! Rose!" the women on the porch were shouting.

"They should have been here by now. The sergeant and Rose were ahead of me."

Gwen looked at Jasmine. "I was on the door for the last two hours and no one has come by."

"Maybe they ran into more trouble," Hadrian said. "Keep an eye out." He turned.

Gwen stopped him. "Where's Royce?"

Hadrian looked back. "He's…ah…"

"Is he okay?"

"Was when I left. He's…um…" Hadrian couldn't manage to think of a way to say it that didn't sound terrible. He had that problem with Royce a lot. Normally it didn't matter so much. Royce never cared what anyone thought of him—but Gwen was different.

"It's okay," she said. "I was just—You're covered in blood, and alone. I was just worried; that's all."

"Sorry," he offered. "I'm going to look around. Maybe they ran into others."

Hadrian went back down the steps. The ladies stopped shouting. Nothing moved on the street. Most of the thoroughfares branching off Wayward and all of the alleys were just dirt paths that sliced between narrow shacks. Only the porch lanterns of Medford House and the windows of The Hideous Head provided any light. Far away, a dog cried. Hadrian could think of few night sounds as lonely as a dog's distant howl.

He walked down the street, listening, watching. *Where'd they go?*

At the start of Wayward he passed the well, pausing to peer into alleys. Manure filled most of them, like the one he'd cut through to get there. Horses made a huge mess of roads, and in the finer quarters, street sweepers were paid to haul the droppings away. In the Lower Quarter, the road apples looked to be shoveled aside. Hadrian imagined the place reeked in the heat of summer. The odd lumps and piled shapes lost in shadow made it hard to tell anything, and if it hadn't been for a fortuitous sliver of moonlight catching the hem of her dress, Hadrian would have never found Rose.

In a narrow alley between a pawnshop and a decrepit shack, it took only two steps into the manure-packed crevice to be sure. The girl lay on her side, her skirt high on one hip exposing a pale thigh. No movement. Her eyes were closed. She might have been sleeping except for the bloody slice across her throat. No blood. The pile of manure drank it up.

Hadrian stood staring. In the shaft of moonlight he could see his breath puffing. The night was growing colder by the second. His jaw clenched tight, his hands made and unmade fists. He wanted to put a sword in his hands, to swing, swing hard, but there was no one to swing at. There was just a beautiful girl—a girl who once spilled soup on him, who he'd once danced with—lying in an alley, dumped like garbage.

He looked around for the sergeant but Rose was alone.

𝒳𝓅

Light, Hadrian thought.

Carrying Rose in his arms, she hardly weighed anything. He cradled her as best he could, taking extra effort to keep her head up. He didn't want it to drop back, not with the slice across her throat. Gwen's girls had cleared a table, but he was reluctant to lay her down. Her body was still warm, still soft. He placed her gently on the dining table that had been dressed with linen as a dozen sobbing women circled him. Hands to faces, some on their knees with their heads bobbing over their laps.

Gwen stood at the head of the table, eyes moist, wet lines on her cheeks. She just stared, her hand braced on the table. She placed a quivering palm on Rose's forehead and caressed her as if soothing a troubled child, then bent and kissed her brow.

"I'm sorry," she whispered, and more tears ran unchecked down her cheeks. "Clean her up."

Gwen led Hadrian away. She took him into the drawing room, a smaller, homey space with a glowing fire in a stone hearth. Soft chairs and delicate furniture huddled inside the hug of dark wood and the smile of bright floral wallpaper.

"I don't understand," Hadrian said. "They were safe. They were only a few blocks away from here."

"Etta," she called to one of the girls. "Bring Hadrian a basin and a cloth. He needs to clean up."

"And even if they found them, why would they have killed her like that? The others didn't seem to want to kill her. They just wanted to take her back to the castle."

"You know who killed her?"

"The sheriff pa—" He stopped. She was right. He didn't *know* who had killed her. Sure, there were a lot of sheriff patrols, but not *that* many. And what happened to the sergeant? And why would they have killed her and just left the body in an alley?

Etta entered the drawing room with a pretty blue and white porcelain basin of water and a towel over her shoulder. She was rushing. Rose's death had everyone on edge. There was a sense of urgency. A drive to do things fast even though there was nothing really to be done. Etta sat him down on a stool, kneeled, and began to wash his face and hands.

Hadrian hardly noticed her. His mind was elsewhere—running up and down Wayward Street and the alleys branching off it trying to make sense of things. *Had I missed them by taking the shortcut? If I hadn't gone that way, could I have stopped it?*

At the gate he remembered the sergeant had said that Exeter was trying to kill her, but the sheriff they had run into ordered his deputy to take her to Lord Exeter, not kill her.

I'm taking her home, the sergeant had said to the castle guards, but it didn't sound like he even knew about Medford House, and he didn't like Hadrian helping. *Why?* Maybe he wasn't taking her home. Maybe he was just looking for a dark enough alley.

Gwen took the towel from Etta. "Thank you," she said. "I'll take over."

Etta nodded. As she left, Gwen motioned for her to close the door.

"You don't need to clean me," Hadrian said, taking the towel from Gwen, who sat across from him.

"Yes, I do. I need your hands clean."

Gwen peered up at him with an expression he couldn't read—fear, perhaps, or nervousness but also a sense of eager anticipation. Looking at that once-beautiful face made him wish he had stayed with Royce, if only to watch.

"I want to ask a favor, a very personal favor," she said in a serious tone. She wet her bruised lips and wiped the hair from her face. "I need you to give me your hand. I want to read your palm."

"What? Like a fortune-teller?"

"Yes, exactly."

They did that sort of thing in Calis. There were palmists' stands all over the cities, along with crystal gazers and bone seers. Hadrian never gave it much thought. He figured they just spoke in generalities that could apply to anyone, but some people he knew swore by it. "Oh, right. You're Calian."

She nodded.

"An odd time for fortune-telling, don't you think? We—"

"Please." Gwen, who had always been calm and comforting, looked desperate. Seeing her battered face broke his heart.

He extended his hand.

Gwen caught his fingers. She looked scared. He could feel the quiver of her hand on his. She turned his hand over, spread his fingers, and stared down at his open palm.

He waited. Her face cycled through a gamut of emotions: fear, curiosity, astonishment, joy, then back to troubled. New tears welled in her eyes. She let his hand go, covered her face, and began to sob.

"What is it?" He reached out for her, and to his surprise, she threw her good arm around his neck and hugged tight.

After a few minutes Gwen relaxed and let him go.

"Are you all right?" he asked.

She nodded, wiping her eyes. He waited for a long moment, allowing plenty of time, but she remained silent.

"Anything you want to tell me?"

For one awful, selfish instant he imagined her saying something like, *Hadrian, I've wanted to confess this to you ever since we first met, but it isn't Royce I'm in love with...* And what would he say? He knew what he'd like to say. He was just as smitten with her as Royce was, but he also knew that betraying Royce wouldn't just be wrong or cruel—it would be fatal.

Gwen shook her head, and in that one small movement of swaying black hair, Hadrian felt both dejected and relieved. Whatever bothered her probably had nothing to do with him or—

Royce!

Hadrian stood up. "I need to go help Royce."

"Yes...yes, you do...and he needs to help you."

Chapter 18

Duster

Gentry Square was deserted—too late for deliveries, too early for gala revelers to return home. All lights out. Royce had stopped the carriage in the main plaza, near the fountain with the stone statue of the king on a rearing horse. The few who might have been home chose not to interfere.

Royce had the man spread out, pulled tight against the statue. He had tied one wrist to the neck of the horse; the other was anchored to its raised tail. The constable's neck was stretched by a length of rope looped around the king's head. Exeter's ankles were spread and fastened to the hooves—neither touching the ground. The whole of His Lordship's body dangled several feet above the pool and the bubbling waters of the great fountain.

Royce walked along the top of the pool's retaining wall, surveying his work. He'd abandoned the carriage driver's oversized hat and coat, returning to his cloak and hood, which swirled and flapped in the wind's tides.

"You don't know what you're doing!" Lord Exeter shouted, his voice a little choked from the rope around his neck.

"Actually, I think I've done a remarkably good job. But don't worry—I'm not done. I have more decorations." He dipped into the bag that had been on the driver's seat and pulled out a handful of candles. "I want everyone to see you on their way home."

"Who are you?"

He'd been asking that a lot and Royce found it enjoyable to deny him any information, but he was getting close to finishing and it was time he knew.

"Last night, do you remember going to a brothel in the Lower Quarter?" Royce climbed the statue and placed a lit candle on the raised knee of the horse.

"Yes—so?"

"Do you recall speaking to a young woman by the name of Gwen DeLancy—the proprietor of the place?"

"Of course."

"And do you also remember beating her when she didn't know the answer to the question you asked?"

"Is that what this is about?" Exeter let out a little laugh, which irritated Royce.

"No laughing." He halted the placement of another candle on the crown of the king and instead cut off the forefinger on Exeter's right hand.

The constable screamed as blood stained the water in the fountain.

Royce lit another candle and scaled back up the statue. "Gwen is a very special person. She's kind and good—not at all like me. But I think she's suffered her whole life. Suffered at the hands of people like you and Raynor Grue and like this sailor fellow who works as a net hauler for the *Lady Banshee*. All of you figured it was safe to batter a whore. You were wrong."

Royce set the candle and climbed back down.

"You'll be drawn and quartered for this!"

Royce grinned. "No, I won't."

"You can't assault me and expect to live."

Royce looked down at the blood still dripping from the severed stump of the constable's finger. "I don't think you've lost enough blood that you'd be suffering delusions yet. You must just be confused. I'm not assaulting you. I'm murdering you."

He took his dagger and, with no more effort than cutting through a bit of tough meat, severed the third finger of his right hand. Exeter screamed again. His struggles against the rope turned into a panicked shaking.

"As for getting caught, I'm afraid you might be disappointed." The finger wore a ring and Royce pocketed both. "You wanted to know who I am. I would have thought a smart fellow like you would have put it together already. 'Course, we are quite a few miles away from Colnora. And while I never killed a ranking noble before, you still should have heard of Duster."

At the sound of the name, he could see the last of Exeter's strength fail. His eyes were large, his mouth partially open, hooked in a terrible frown. He had heard after all. "You really shouldn't have touched Gwen."

He dragged the blade up along Exeter's thigh, opening it like the casing on a sausage. Then Royce grabbed another candle.

"You can't kill me!" Exeter cried after he stopped screaming, while Royce was busy setting the new candle on the rump of the horse.

"I think you might be wrong there. As even you can see, your blood looks just as red as mine."

"No, you don't understand. There's a conspiracy." Exeter was speaking quickly now, but some of his words were difficult to understand, as he was spitting them through gritted teeth. "I've been investigating for months and Rose can provide the proof I need to stop it. I think she can identify Saldur as a conspirator and maybe even others who are involved. If you kill me, I won't be able to stop it. Bishop Saldur and his Imperialist church are trying to take over the kingdom. Others have died, Chancellor Wainwright and the new chancellor's wife. The king will be next, and his son after that. If you kill me, the king is as good as dead and Melengar—all of Avryn—might die with me."

"And that would be bad for me...how?"

"I...you...?"

"I don't care who rules. I don't care about your petty kings and silly bishops. This is bigger than all that. You hurt Gwen—nearly killed her. You beat the woman that I...that I...you know what? Less talk, more screaming."

Royce began carving his own sculpture.

CHAPTER 19

THE FIRE

R ichard Hilfred returned, passing through the gate with a grim expression and without saying a word to either of them. He looked tired and there was a dark stain on his sleeve and a slice in the back of his tunic. They both watched as he crossed the courtyard and entered the castle. Reuben glanced over at Grisham, who offered a noncommittal shrug.

The carriages had reshuffled since Lord Exeter's departure, now that a few of the party guests had also left. But most of the guests were still inside enjoying the festivities, leaving the long line of carriages waiting in the chilly night. Reuben heard a familiar tune being played in the castle. Performed at every party, he never learned the name or even if it had one. In the three years he'd lived within the castle walls, Reuben had never been to any of the parties, never seen the orchestra for himself. He imagined guests in the big hall. All the lovely ladies spinning, their gowns whirling as they and their men moved in circles beneath chandeliers of candlelight. Arista would be among them. Whenever he heard the muffled music, he always pictured her dancing. He imagined she would be lovely, graceful, elegant. In all the pictures in his head he never saw her with another man. She was always alone, dancing by herself with a bittersweet look upon her face. She might leave the dance, go to the window, and peer out into the black night, searching for the stable and the single lantern marking the place where Reuben usually lay among the straw. Perhaps she would think of him. She might wonder if he was lonely. She would grab her cloak and—

"Have either of you seen the king?" Richard Hilfred snapped.

Reuben jumped at the sound of his father's voice. He hadn't even noticed him return from the castle.

Hilfred continued. "Vince said he saw His Majesty leave with Count Pickering, the Earl of West March, and the Earl of Longbow. Said the two were drunk and fighting again." His tone was more than harsh; it was harried.

Reuben and Grisham exchanged a glance.

"Yeah, the king and the others were in the courtyard for a while," Reuben said.

"Just walked around," Grisham added. "Trying to sober them up in the cold air, I expect."

"Yeah." Reuben nodded. "Walked in circles, and then..." He looked to Grisham, who was no help, just staring back with a dull expression. "Then the three lords got horses and left, but the king went back inside."

"I just looked. His Majesty isn't at the party, and I can't find Bernie or Mal, who were assigned to him."

"He did say he was tired. Had a headache or something, I think. Mentioned he would be going to bed."

"Were Mal and Bernie with him?"

"I...ah...I think so."

Reuben's father scowled and turned to Grisham, who nodded. Apparently his son's account needed corroboration.

His father looked puzzled and stood thinking for a moment. As he did, Reuben noticed the stain on his right sleeve was blood. Not a lot, and it didn't appear to have come from a wound; the sleeve wasn't torn or damaged. Finally his father spoke. "The queen retired early, too, along with the princess."

"There you have it," Grisham said with a grin. "Wine and that silver dress has put the king in an amorous mood. So they put the kiddies to bed and left the party to the guests."

Reuben's father nodded. "So to your knowledge no one in the royal family has left the castle, right?"

"That's right," Reuben said, and Grisham nodded.

Reuben's father looked up at the castle towers for a moment.

"Did anything happen while taking Rose home?" Reuben asked.

His father saw him staring at his sleeve. "No," he said, and abruptly turned and walked back to the castle, where he disappeared inside.

"Your old da seems a bit stressed this evening. I wonder what thistle got jammed in his codpiece? You might want to keep that helmet on when you go to the barracks tonight, just in case he decides to bounce your head off that door again, eh?"

◺

Guests began leaving. Those with young children went first, cradling sleeping bundles who raised their eyelids just long enough to give the world an insulted look. Grisham waved and a carriage would peel away from the line and roll in to pick them up. The woman would climb in and the husband would pass the child over before slipping in beside her. After the steward closed the door, the coach would circle the courtyard and ride back out, stopping just long enough for Reuben to wave them through. The process was repeated over and over, and Reuben was grateful to finally have something to do.

Later the celebrants came mostly in pairs, younger couples arm in arm and older ones barely acknowledging each other. Most talked loudly and often walked crooked even though they had walked straight going in. There was a lot more laughter and even a bit of singing. One very heavy woman broke into song on the castle steps and was joined by three men in doublets with their cloaks absently left over the crux of their arms. They refused to enter the carriage until they had completed the tune, and Reuben, who had developed a bone-deep chill, wondered how they could endure the frigid night in just their thin doublets and hose.

By the time the quartet exited the gate, the bulk of the guests were filing into the courtyard. The carriages knew the routine. They lined up at the bridge and rolled in, swallowing up their passengers and moving through with practiced efficiency, but the line could only move one at a time and a crowd of fur-lined nobles remained in the courtyard waiting for their carriages.

It was then that Reuben heard the first screams.

People did stupid things when they were drunk. They laughed louder than normal, shouted, and cried. Screams or squealing weren't unthinkable, but this carried a note of panic. Reuben and Grisham glanced toward the cries, which was in the direction of the castle, but neither gave it much thought. Then a flood of remaining partygoers rushed out the main doors into the courtyard. More yelling and some shoving. An elderly man was pushed to the ground and took his wife with him. He shouted in complaint, but few noticed him; everyone's eyes were trained on the castle. This was strange but not alarming. It wasn't until the bell began ringing that Reuben knew something was wrong.

He looked across at Grisham and saw the same concern reflected back.

A moment later they heard someone say the word *fire*.

By then even the servants were filing out and several of the guards.

"What's going on?" Grisham shouted as Vince made his way through those gathered in the courtyard to the castle gate.

"There's a"—he was having a coughing fit—"a fire in the castle. All that straw—"

"Is everyone out?" Reuben asked. "Did the princess escape?" He looked around desperately, but it was impossible to find anyone in the swirling crowd.

Vince was shaking his head as he coughed again. "We can't get up the stairs."

Up the stairs...

The queen retired early, too, along with the princess.

The crowd below squealed as a loud crash sent flames out one high window.

"Who's getting them out?" Reuben asked.

"No one," Vince replied. "The chancellor ordered everyone to the courtyard. He's organizing a bucket brigade. All that straw and hay—the place is an inferno."

"Reuben!" he heard Grisham shout as he ran for the castle. "Damn it! You can't leave your post!"

Reuben dodged the crowd and sprinted up the front steps. The open doors of the castle seethed a thick black smoke. He took a deep breath and ran in. The last few servants, holding sleeves and skirts to their faces, rushed past him on their way out. Everything was smoky, hard to see, but he saw no flames and felt no heat.

Reuben found the stairs and started up when he met his father coming down.

"Reuben! What are you doing? Why are you off your post? I told you to stay out of the castle."

"The fire...they said the royal family was trapped and I—"

"Your duty is to stand at the front gate! You're a soldier now, not a child. You'll be whipped for desertion—likely discharged. You could even be executed. And don't expect me to help you. You're a man now. You'll accept responsibility for your actions. Now get out of here."

"But the princess..."

"*The princess!* You left your post for—" He paused, too furious to finish. "You get back to the front gate right now, boy! That's an order!"

"But what's being done to—"

"Nothing. No one can get up there. The royal family is going to die."

Die?

Reuben couldn't believe it. He stood dazed, as if his father had hit him again, only this hurt worse and frightened him more.

"No," Reuben muttered at first. He looked up the steps. He saw no fire, not even much smoke. Something snapped. "No!" he shouted, and tried to get past his father.

Richard shoved him back. "I gave you an order!"

Reuben charged the steps again, only this time he ducked when his father tried to stop him and he ran by.

"Don't go up there!"

Reuben cleared the steps three at a time. Just as with the squires, years of running errands while Richard Hilfred had stood behind chairs gave him the advantage. When he reached the door to the royal residence, his father was several steps below. He yanked on the big iron rings, but it didn't open... resistance. It took a moment before noticing the chain.

Why would the doors be chained shut...from the outside?

Reuben was still trying to process that when his father caught up and shoved him across the corridor. "You stupid fool! You just couldn't listen to your father, could you. I had you posted to the gate to keep you out of this, but you're as bent on killing yourself as your mother was. That's fine. I'm done with you. I did my job. You're a man now—not my responsibility anymore."

"*You...you* did this?" Reuben looked back and forth between the door and his father. "You chained the doors. You sealed them in!" His eyes went wide as the realization dawned. "You set the fire! But it's your job to protect them...Why in Maribor's name would you do this?"

"I told you not to get attached to them. They're evil. You can sacrifice your life to protect them, but if you ask one small favor in return, they can't be bothered. I threw myself in front of swords for him. All the king needed to do was tell the chamberlain that your mother could stay on as a maid. Or he could have let me marry her and we could have lived nearby in any abandoned shack in the city. But no—Amrath couldn't make exceptions. If he did it for me, he'd have to do it for others. So I had to face your mother and tell her...tell her I had failed. The king killed her, but I had to face her."

His father sneered at him. "You don't understand. How could you? You had everything handed to you—by *me*! I started out as the son of a weapon's merchant—a merchant! I taught myself to fight. I got myself a position in this castle. I worked my way up to sergeant. You don't need to understand, boy. And this isn't the time for it. A wise man taught me that we don't have to live under their heels. I could fix things so that your mother didn't die in vain. She's the spark that lit this fire, a blaze that will burn away the kingdom and usher in a new era...one without kings. And we'll be part of that—an important part. I didn't enjoy the things I've done tonight, but justice has been served!"

"*Things?* What *else* did you do?" Reuben focused on the bloodstained sleeve and his mind flashed to the image of his father leading Rose out through the gate. "What did you do with Rose?"

"It was harder than I thought. Those big eyes, and her having the same name as your mother and all."

"What did you do to Rose?"

"I did what I had to. And so will you. A lot of people are going to die tonight." He gestured at the door. "No one will be the wiser, and a whole new world will follow. You keep your mouth shut and I'll be in a position to take care of you, of us. Now get back to your post and never tell anyone that you even came up here."

Somehow Reuben's sword got out of its scabbard and into his hand. "Get away from that door."

૪

The castle was glowing when Hadrian approached. The whole place flickered like a jack-o'-lantern with too many candles inside. A crowd had formed around the outer walls, peering up across the moat as flames spit sparks out windows that fell in red streaks, sizzling in the water. The big elm growing near the north side of the keep had caught fire about midway up, and as Hadrian watched, one of the branches broke free and crashed through an upper-story window.

He pulled his cloak tight, covering the dark bloodstains as he entered the crowd of spectators. Lots of people were on hand with more coming. Folks awakened by the light and the noise, gathered in their nightclothes to stare up at the castle, their sleepy faces illuminated by the wash of firelight.

He worked his way toward the front gate only to discover the line of carriages was gone, and there was no sign of Royce. The rose-marked coach had vanished with the rest and he had no idea where. Royce never told him the plan, but Hadrian imagined it included taking Exeter somewhere secluded, somewhere no one would think to look. But what if Exeter hadn't taken the bait or if Albert hadn't been able to find him at the party? Did Royce set the fire? Did he burn down an entire castle just to smoke out one man? Was he capable of *that*?

If a bug bites you, you don't bite it back, his friend was fond of saying. *You crush the life out of the thing so it never bothers you again. And if you do that to an insect that can't cause any serious harm, why would you do any less to an enemy who will almost certainly come back and kill you if you don't?*

The worst part about Royce and his arguments was that all too often Hadrian couldn't think of an answer to such riddles, even though he knew there should be one.

With nothing to do, and feeling both physically tired and emotionally drained, Hadrian joined the rest of the crowd watching the spectacle. It had been a few years since he had seen a castle burn. This brought his total to five, but this was the first time he wasn't at least partly responsible. He wondered how many had died—and if Albert was one of them.

He hoped there was an alehouse still open in the city. He would need to drink in order to sleep. Hadrian stood there, smelling the odor of smoke. Funny how it brought feelings of warmth and safety, like a campfire or cozy hearth—but the only thing cooking tonight were men.

᠅

"Well, look at you," Richard Hilfred said, a little smile growing on his lips as he saw the sword in Reuben's hand. "That's good. About time you stood up to me. I was wondering how long it'd take, but this isn't the time or the place. This is serious. Now get back to your post."

Reuben, who had never before raised his voice to his father, raised his sword. "I said get away."

His father must have seen something new in his son's eyes because he drew his own weapon.

Reuben swung.

He didn't want to kill his father; he just wanted him away from the door.

Richard blocked.

Reuben swung again and again. His father slapped the attacks aside.

"You've learned somewhere. That's good," his father said casually. No fear, no concern. Then, as if tiring of a game, he struck Reuben's blade hard near the hilt. The sudden vibration snapped the sword from Reuben's grip. The pretty blade that the prince had given him clattered on the stone, and his father kicked it away.

"Hilfred!" They both turned to see the chancellor running to the top of the stairs, his sword in hand. Percy Braga glanced at the door, then at father and son.

"He's sealed the royal family in!" Reuben declared. "My father is a traitor."

"I see that," Braga said, his sight taking in Richard's drawn sword and the one on the ground.

The chancellor advanced on both of them.

"Lord Braga, I—" Richard began.

"Run—get help!" Braga shouted at Reuben, and swung his blade at Richard.

Reuben's father barely had time to get his own up to save himself.

Reuben wasted no time leaping his way down, throwing himself to the bottom. He scrambled to his feet and raced for the front door. Bursting out into the courtyard, he shouted, "The royal family has been locked inside! The chancellor needs help! At the top of the steps to the residence."

The crowd outside remained huddled against the cold, staring back at the upper windows of the castle that belched smoke.

No one moved.

"The chancellor needs help!" he yelled again.

Having had time to sink in, his words caused the closest

guards, Vince and Grisham, to run forward. The rest continued to stare. Reuben gave up and ran to the woodshed. Inside he found the axe, sunk in a piece of wood, where he had left it the day before. With a slap and yank, he pulled it free.

By the time he returned to the front door of the castle, Chancellor Braga, Grisham, and Vince were coming out, coughing and reeling. "No one else go in!" Braga ordered. "The fire—" He coughed. "The fire has spread."

"The boy said it was regicide," someone from the crowd shouted.

The chancellor nodded. "Sergeant Hilfred confessed that on orders of Lord Exeter, he set the fire. Lord Exeter was working with Hilfred, of the castle guard, to kill the royal family in order to take the throne for himself. As chancellor, I judged him a traitor." The chancellor raised his blood-soaked sword. "And executed him."

Reuben stopped. *My father—dead?* He ought to feel something. He didn't.

He looked up at the castle. Smoke was rising from the windows and billowing out the front door where he could just make out a flickering glow.

"What about the king? The queen?" Vince asked.

Braga shook his head. "The doors to the residence are chained and the fire has spread. The royal chambers are a death trap. All that straw in the castle is catching. It's too late to save them. You can't even get up the stairs. It's suicide to try, and by now"—he hesitated—"by now, they're all dead."

All dead.

Rose, his father, his mother, and now—*All dead.*

NO!

Reuben ran again.

"Stop him!" Braga shouted as Reuben raced for the open door. Vince was there and tackled him to the ground. Reuben got to his feet, wrestling with Vince, who held him from behind. "There's still time! We just need to—"

"No, my boy." It was an old man, white-haired and frail, dressed in a cleric's robe who spoke. He stood with the rest watching the castle burn. His voice so fatherly—not like his own father but how Reuben always imagined a father ought to be. "It is too late. You'll just kill yourself trying."

"Let me go!" Reuben shouted.

"Can't do that, kid." Vince held him fast.

"I'm not your kid! I'm not anyone's *kid* anymore." While Reuben had gotten better with a sword, he was still an expert with an axe, and just as when Horace had grabbed him, Reuben jabbed backward hard with the butt of the axe. He caught Vince in the stomach, driving the air from the man, who folded, letting go. Before anyone else could grab him, Reuben plunged into the dragon's mouth that had once been the front door of the castle.

She can't be dead!

This was less speculation and more wishful thinking on Reuben's part. He wanted to believe it—he had to believe it. He'd lost everything else. He refused to lose her.

Fire was on the stairs. Piles of straw burned and ignited the long banners hanging from the high walls. They in turn led the flames to the wooden ceiling. He dodged around scattered piles and returned to the chained door. At the foot lay his father in a pool of blood. He looked pale, his face against the floor.

Reuben swung his axe, hitting the door. He struck it repeatedly but made little progress against the solid oak. He would never get through. He switched and struck instead at the chain—at the lock holding it. Sparks flew with each kiss of the axe, but iron didn't split like logs.

It was hopeless.

He dropped the axe and kicked the door with his foot. He looked down at his father and screamed at him, "You bastard! How could you do it?"

Do it...

Reuben spun and looked at the chain.

"You *did* do it, didn't you?"

He fell to his knees and searched his father. He knew where to look, and in the third pouch on his father's belt he found the key. Reuben slipped it into the lock and prayed to Novron as it turned. The latch clicked and the shank released. Reuben tossed the lock, ripped the chain from the rings, and pulled the doors open.

Smoke plumed out and Reuben doubled over in a fit of coughing. Bending over was good. There was better air near the floor. He could actually see the smoke moving in layers, thicker at the ceiling. He lay flat, breathing low, and looked ahead. The tapestry in the hall burned with multicolored flames.

He sucked in a solid chestful of hot air and crawled forward.

He had never been in the royal residence, the solar, as it was called. He had no idea which door led where. It hardly mattered, as he was nearly blind due to the smoke. He found the first door and shoved it open. Inside was a clean pocket of air. It was the king's private chapel. Standing, he took another breath and moved on. The next door he threw open was a bedroom.

He could see clearly because not only was there little smoke but also outside the window a tree was burning and light flooded the room. A dresser, a wardrobe, a gown carefully draped across a cushioned love seat, and on the bed, a figure wadded in a twisted pile of blankets and quilts. Arista's auburn hair spilled across the pillows. He shook her awake as he began to pull her from the bed.

She jerked away. "Stop it!"

He tried to grab her again but she kicked and scratched as he tried to catch hold.

"Please, Your Highness, you must come with me."

She blinked and coughed; then she saw the burning tree outside the window. An instant later, she screamed.

"The castle is burning. We have to get out of here," he said.

Outside, a portion of the tree snapped free and crashed through the bedroom window, throwing sparks and glowing bits of wood across the floor, across the carpets.

She still fought, still screamed, swinging at him with her little fists, but Reuben ignored her. He pulled the blanket from the bed and threw it over the princess's head. Then gathering her up in his arms, he ran from the room.

He barreled down the corridor that had become a tunnel of flame. The fire on the steps had lessened, having run out of fuel, but the wooden ceiling—the floor of the upper story— was ablaze, and the flames spread out across the entire breadth of the reception hall. He leapt to the main floor and charged out of the castle. He stumbled and fell before the mass of nobles, soldiers, and servants.

Hitting the ground and released from his grip, Princess Arista threw off the blanket and scrambled away. She looked back up at the castle and clarity finally reached her. "Mother!" she screamed. "Save my mother!"

Reuben looked around.

No one moved.

"Save her!" the princess screeched, her cheeks flushed and glistening as she knelt on the grass in her white linen nightgown.

Still no one moved.

"We can't, Your Highness. It's too late." The bishop was there again with his gentle, comforting voice, and it was then that Reuben realized he preferred the harsh barks of his father. The bishop's tone was tainted, poisoned. His willingness to concede defeat before the battle was over sickened him. *Why is everyone in such a hurry to mourn those who might still live?*

"I'm sorry," Chancellor Braga offered.

She stared at them, stunned, her mouth hanging open with the shock. Then she shifted her gaze to Reuben. "Please..." she begged in a soft voice. "My mother..."

"Reuben, no!" It might have been Braga, maybe the bishop, possibly even Grisham who yelled; he never knew. A moment later he was back in the castle charging up the stairs.

Braga had been premature when he declared that the castle had become a death trap. A lot of it was stone and the scattering of straw and hay was quickly consumed; being dry as tinder, it didn't even produce much smoke. By his second trip, however, his assessment fit. The castle timbers had finally caught and there was an unmistakable roar that boiled in the depths. The fire had grown to adulthood and found its voice. Furniture burned the brightest, causing Reuben to shield his eyes. Above him sparks rained down, and what remained of the tapestry had fallen, blanketing the steps and causing him to jump through fire.

He reached the solar again, but by now the hallway was black with smoke, which billowed and churned. Remembering what he had learned, Reuben dropped to his hands and knees. He crawled down the hall but this time could not avoid the smoke. His eyes watered, and his throat burned as he struggled to breathe in a world without air.

Soon all he could see was the floor. Panic rose as he realized he couldn't get a breath. He put his face down until his nose pressed against the wood and he sucked in. He thanked Maribor for the lungful of burnt air he found and noticed he was trembling. The floor below him was hot and he could hear the crackle of flame on the underside. He realized then that the bishop and chancellor were right. This time it was too late.

He was going to burn to death within just a few feet of his father.

No. I'll suffocate first.

He closed his eyes. He had to; they were burning from the smoke.

How many breaths do I have left?

He coughed, pushed his lips against the floor, and sucked.

At least one more.

He had saved her. He had done that much. Rose was dead. His father, too, but he had done that one good thing. And maybe it was best this way. Arista would have married and left him heartbroken and alone. This had been his moment. Perhaps this was the reason he'd been born—why Maribor had spent so little time on him. He never had to learn how to fight or ride, and what need was there for friends, or a mother, or even a father, if all he was destined for was to save the princess on a cold autumn night and then die? What point was there in providing him a full life?

He thought of Rose.

I should have done more than kiss her. If only I knew how little time I had left—how little time she had.

Overhead, a beam snapped with a crack like thunder. He waited, but nothing fell.

He took another breath, his lips pressed against the hardwood. He had never been so intimate with nor loved a floor as much as he did at that moment. He would never make it to the queen. Even if he did, she had to be dead, suffocated in her sleep. And if she was still alive, he could never get either of them to safety. He couldn't get himself out. There just wasn't enough air.

If he had been smart, he would have soaked his shirt in water from the well when he got the axe. Then he could have wrapped it around his face. Maybe that would have helped, but—

He peered out through squinting eyes. He was just in front of Arista's open bedroom. The tree that had crashed through her window was blazing. He crawled into her room, moving toward the bed. It, too, was on fire. He could feel the heat bristling, singeing his hair. He reached out and it felt like he was sticking his arm into open flame. He felt the metal container and, grabbing hold of the rim, dragged over the princess's chamber pot.

He could feel the urine slopping inside.

He stripped off his tabard, tore it in half, and wadded up a handful, then soaked it in the pot. Holding it to his face, he inhaled. The air smelled and tasted foul, but he could breathe.

He thought of the queen once more, but he would have only one chance to get out.

"I'm sorry," he whispered, his voice choked.

Dumping the remaining contents of the pot over his head and holding the soaked rag to his nose and mouth, he blindly ran, trusting his route to memory. He bounced off the walls and staggered ahead. The hallway felt too long. *What if I've gotten turned around in the smoke?* He might be running *into* the castle to die with the queen. Then he stepped on something soft. His father. He knew where he was.

He had to turn and pushed on through the darkness. The stairs were coming; he should already have found them. It was hard not to just run, hard not to panic. The urine he had poured on his hair and face had already dried. His skin tingled, sizzling like a pig on a spit. The heat was burning him. He'd catch fire soon; maybe he already had. He kept pushing forward but still couldn't find the steps. He was lost. Panic set in and he stopped. He froze, too frightened to move.

No, Reuben, my sweet boy, you're fine. Run forward. You're almost out. Run forward!

He did as he was told.

Now turn right. You're almost to the stairs! That's it. You're there, but everything is on fire. You'll have to jump. Do it! Do it now! Jump!

Reuben threw himself forward, leaping into the air, and as he fell, in that weightless instant, he couldn't help wondering who was helping him. Who else was crazy enough to be there in the burning castle with him? It didn't matter; he just hoped she was right.

✦

Hadrian was still watching the castle burn as the crowd around the castle gate thickened. The entire population of the Gentry Quarter, if not the whole city, had turned out for the show. In a society where people were distinguished by the clothes they wore, this gathering of humanity at the gates appeared oddly homogeneous. Rich and poor could hardly be distinguished, as aside from those who'd just left the gala, mostly everyone else had rushed out of homes forgetting their stockings, doublets, tunics, and gowns. They approached the moat in simple white linen, looking like an army of ghosts, the flicker of fire illuminating their faces, which stared in disbelief, as blank and sorrowful as any lost soul.

The castle had become a full blaze. What had been the moat became a bright mirror, reflecting. Somewhere metal hit metal. It might have been something as simple as a ladle striking a kettle, but that's all it took. Hadrian swore he could hear screams, the cries of men dying. Trumpets and drums, the thunder of horses rolling out across a smoldering field. Grunts and gasps.

He was covered in blood; he was always covered in blood. That's why his sword's grips were wrapped in rough leather. Blood was like oil. Hadrian had always been shocked at how much blood a body held. People were nothing more than bags of liquid that burst and sprayed. Around him, a wall of corpses piled up, dismembered and disemboweled. They circled him like sandbags—horses, too, which were just as filled with blood but took longer to die. He would find the animals afterward, their big hulks lying on their sides, heaving and still snorting clouds into frigid air. No matter how tired he was—by the end he was always exhausted—he still took the time to drive his sword into their throats. He wished he knew a prayer to say, but all he managed was to repeat the two words that kept bouncing in his head: *I'm sorry.*

Always, along with the smell of blood in his nose, there was smoke—braziers and torches, campfires and the burning of homes, forts, and castles. With the host defeated on the field, the gates thrown wide, the spoils of victory were his. The men would rush in howling and near mad, having shaken hands with death and lived. Afterward they felt like gods. They deserved everything—and who could deny them? They took what they wished and slaughtered any with a different opinion.

Hadrian's ritual afterward had been trying to drown himself. Someone would drag a barrel of something into the street, splinter the lid, and they would all dunk cups to toast themselves. Hadrian would continue to drink. Trying to make it all go away. He wanted to wash the blood off, but he could never rid himself of the stain. As he sat there, beside the barrel, they would offer him his choice of the women they ripped from their homes, because they knew he was instrumental in their victory. He picked a pretty blonde with the torn dress. She reminded him of Arbor, the girl he once loved back in Hintindar, the girl he lost to his best friend. He grabbed her. She screamed, but all he did was hug the girl to his chest. She fought against him but stopped when she realized he was crying.

When he let her go, she knelt beside him, just watching. She never said a word, just a pale perfect face looking up, highlighted by the flames.

"I'm sorry," he said.

"What's that?"

Hadrian blinked. The girl was gone and he was looking at Essendon Castle again.

"What did you say?" An elderly man stood beside him, shivering.

"Nothing," Hadrian replied.

"They say the king is dead, you know."

"Do they?" Hadrian replied, wondering how to slip away.

"Betrayed by one of his own, a guard named Hilfred."

Hilfred? Hadrian was no longer in a hurry to leave. "What happened to the guard?"

"Executed by Chancellor Percy Braga. Our new chancellor is as good as Count Pickering with a sword, you know.

"I heard one of the guards saying that Lord Exeter is to blame. He's been plotting against the king and ordered the doors to the royal residence chained and the fire set. The whole royal family is gone."

"Not the whole family." A woman clutching a child to her chest spoke just above a whisper, as if imparting a dangerous secret. "One of the children lived."

"Which one?"

"The girl, Arista."

"Lord Exeter will have the child killed, then."

"The hateful bastard," the woman cursed, covering the ears of her own child.

"Careful," the old man said. "He might be our new king."

This brought a look of horror to the woman's face. "The new chancellor won't allow that. He'll see justice is done."

"Chancellor Braga is foreign-born," another man said. This one had managed to pull a blanket with him on his way out as well as a misshapen hat that he tugged down over his reddening ears. "He's had no time to make alliances. Lord Exeter commands the guards and all the sheriffs. Given a choice between the two, even if it can be proved that Exeter killed the royal family, I don't know which way the army will side. We could be looking at civil war."

"It's a dark, dark day," the woman muttered, hugging the child tight and twisting at the waist.

With one last look up at the burning castle, Hadrian pushed out of the crowd. He slipped into the empty streets of the Gentry Quarter. Away from the castle, away from the burning heat, it was cold. A wind was picking up, a northern wind, a breath of winter.

He aimed for Gentry Square, deciding to cut through to the Merchant Quarter. He'd try poking his head into The Hallowed Sword. Maybe Royce had returned the carriage to Dunwoodie and was waiting there for him. As he entered the square, he found another crowd forming. About twenty people stood around the statue in the center, holding up lanterns and torches. As he got closer, he saw why.

The body of a man hung from the statue. Horribly mutilated, the corpse had been strung up by ropes and decorated in macabre fashion with candles. He wore the black and white uniform like the sheriffs. His eyes, ears, and several of his fingers were missing. Nailed to his chest, held there by what Hadrian assumed had been the man's own jeweled dagger, was a sign printed in large letters:

NOBLE OR NOT, THIS IS WHAT HAPPENS
TO ANYONE WHO HARMS
THE LADIES OF MEDFORD HOUSE

Royce had found Lord Exeter after all. Hadrian turned away. He'd seen enough for one night.

When he reached The Hallowed Sword, he found Dunwoodie's carriage and Diamond tied up out front, but Royce was not there. Dunwoodie himself was still sleeping, and Hadrian decided to leave him to it.

He wanted a drink but the place was deserted. Everyone who was awake was at the castle or in the square.

Hadrian left the Merchant Quarter, passing once more near the castle, which was still burning. Flames were shooting out of the rooftops, and one of the peaked cones of a lower tower had caved in, taking the falcon flag with it. A communal *Ohhh!* went up from the crowd. The bucket brigade had given up on the castle and were now hoisting water from the moat and splashing it on the courtyard's outbuildings, trying to save what they could.

Hadrian slipped back into the shadows, this time entering the Artisan Quarter. Once more he found a crowd in that quarter's central square. Only five people stood witness where another body was strung up. This one was mutilated in much the same way. The dead man was missing his eyes, ears, and fingers. The note nailed to him read simply:

He killed a lady of Medford House.

A man wearing a bright red stocking cap was trying to read it out loud for the benefit of those who couldn't. "Ka-ki-*killed*, ah laaadee…" Hadrian listened as he methodically struggled through the seven words.

"That's Stane," one of those in the small crowd said.

"I was there the night he killed that poor girl," another mentioned. He looked familiar, wearing a carpenter's hammer where a sword would be.

"What was her name?" the speaker with the red cap asked.

"It was a year ago. Don't even remember now."

"I knew he would end badly." An elderly woman wagged her finger. "Always said so."

Hadrian remembered the name Stane. He was the one Grue

had said killed Gwen's friend. The murder that caused her to leave the tavern. Hadrian looked back at the sign. Technically she was a whore from The Hideous Head at the time, but he could see Royce was keeping to a consistent message. The townsfolk didn't seem to mind him blurring the details.

Hadrian continued on through Artisan Row and the gate to the Lower Quarter. The bodies were gone, as if the fight had never happened. Dark spots remained to reassure him it had. He realized too late that he should have gone the long way around and avoided the scene, but he was too tired. It had been a long night, and he was hoping Gwen would give him a bed. He'd look for Royce again in the morning. Knowing Royce, he'd find Hadrian if he was alive.

Hadrian didn't take the shortcut this time. He took the main street through the Lower Quarter's central square. Each quarter had something. The gentry had their fancy statue, Merchant Square had pretty benches, and even the artisans had a fountain. In the Lower Quarter all they had was the old common well and a notice board. Even before he got close, Hadrian knew that a new notice had been tacked up that night.

He wasn't disappointed.

One more body hung, stretched in the now-familiar grotesque design. Blood dripped and was warm enough to raise steam off the icy street. No crowd surrounded it. The square was deserted, and Hadrian stood alone, looking up at the grisly display. Of all the men who had died that night, this was the only one he had known. Still he couldn't muster any sympathy.

Royce had indeed been busy that night, and he was thankful they had separated. Hadrian walked on, heading for Wayward Street, turning his back on the square, the well, the notice board, and the mutilated body of Raynor Grue.

CHAPTER 20

FALLOUT

Years of working for Raynor Grue had warped Gwen's internal clock to the point where she rarely slept at night. Those had been her working hours and the habit persisted. Like an owl, she couldn't fall asleep until after sunrise, which was just one of the reasons why she was dressed when the soldiers came.

The Lower Quarter never invited much activity, and there was no mistaking their arrival. Last night the ruckus had resulted in her being dragged and beaten by the lord high constable. As Gwen waited in the parlor, she noticed they were louder this time. Angry shouts and the clatter of hooves rolled in like a storm. She also heard wagon wheels—so much heavier and duller than a carriage.

Staring at the front door, expecting it to burst open, she waited stoically. Gwen told herself it would be all right. She told the others the same. No one believed her.

They didn't knock—she hadn't expected them to but had wondered just the same. Medford House, she thought, looked worthy of a little respect these days. She and the girls had done a fine job with the place. The old ruin was gone and a building finer even than the original Wayward Inn stood in its place. The House wasn't finished; Gwen didn't think it ever would be. She was always finding ways to improve. She had plans to put a pretty fence out front, some crown molding in the bedrooms, and she hadn't given up her dream of painting the whole thing blue. Still, it was the finest building in the Lower Quarter, a building that wouldn't look out of place in the Merchant Square. It didn't matter. The soldiers knew it was only a whorehouse.

They opened the door rather than breaking it down, and she was grateful for that. A dozen men entered with torches, dressed in chain mail, their dull metal helmets on. Gwen almost failed to recognize Ethan under all that steel.

"May I help you?" she asked. It was an absurd question, but so was the whole affair. A dozen men in chain barged in, only to be greeted by her standing on a crutch with a broken arm and a bandaged face and her pleasant inquiry.

"You're all under arrest for the murder of Lord Exeter, the High Constable of Melengar."

Gwen didn't recognize the man who spoke. He was old and beefy with gray in a chest-length beard. She looked instead to Ethan, the only one she knew. Ethan had been the sheriff of the Lower Quarter as long as Gwen had lived there, and while she couldn't say she liked him, she respected him. At least he tried to be fair. Ethan looked back and she could see the conflict. He was upset like the others, but not necessarily with her. There was even a little fear in his eyes, but that night, everyone was scared.

"Gwen?" Mae squeaked, rushing to her and hugging tight.

Jollin and Abby clustered close as well. Those in other rooms peeked out, asking what was happening.

Mae was ripped from Gwen. The others were taken too. Gwen was the last one seized. They dragged her out and she lost her crutch. *I should have grabbed a blanket*, she thought the moment the night air hit her. *I should have grabbed a few.*

The rear doors of the wagon were open and the girls shoved in. Gwen winced. The pressure on her bad arm and being dragged because she couldn't walk without the crutch sent stabs of pain throughout her body. She worried about getting onto the wagon. She couldn't hope to pull herself up and wondered if she would be beaten again. Some of the soldiers looked angry enough not to care why she couldn't get in. Jollin was there, trying to help her, but was shoved back. They were all being pushed around. The men were frightened and angry and had no one else to bully. In front of her Etta screamed, and Mae was crying as she scrambled up.

When Gwen reached the wagon, the bed was waist-high. Too high to get her knee up. A moment later she felt hands lifting her. They were gentle.

"You're having a really bad week, Gwen." It was Ethan. That was all he said, but she could see sympathy in his eyes, maybe even sadness. He didn't expect to see her again. A high noble had been killed. Someone had to pay. Someone had to be punished, to be executed.

Gwen sat down between Mae and Jollin, her back against the solid wood of the wagon wall.

"Are we going to die?" Abby asked in a shaky voice.

No one answered. And as the doors were closed and locked, Gwen shut her eyes and prayed that what she had seen in Hadrian's palm came true.

"Riyria," she whispered to herself like a magic spell.

~

Standing in the shadows of Wayward Street, Royce watched the wagon roll past. For a brief insane moment he considered trying to free her.

He was an idiot.

He'd made a mistake, miscalculated, and now she was paying the price. Royce wasn't used to dealing with fallout. He had never had anything to lose before. He should have gotten her away first, or maybe he shouldn't have written the notes at all. Royce didn't have a head for this sort of thing. That's what Merrick was good at.

His old partner from his Black Diamond days was a maven at planning and manipulation. Royce fought with the world, struggling against a wind that always blew in his face. Merrick floated on the wind, commanding the current as he willed. *The right word, said at the right moment, can work magic*, he was fond of saying. *You merely need to understand power, where it comes from, and the direction it flows.* He had tried to teach Royce by using analogies about water. *Spill a cup into a funnel and you don't have to wonder where the water will end up, nor the path it will take.*

Merrick had been a genius; perhaps he still was. Royce hadn't seen him in years, not since his one-time best friend had orchestrated his arrest and imprisonment. Royce had been the water that time. After Royce got out of Manzant, Merrick was no longer with the Diamond. He never bothered to look for him but wondered if he would have killed his old friend had he been there. He wanted to think he could have avoided it, but it might have been inevitable.

Merrick would never have made the mistakes Royce had that night. The question he now had to ask was, what would Merrick do to fix the situation? How could Royce make the water flow where he wanted?

He spotted Hadrian coming up the street from the square. At least he was still alive.

"Don't bother going to Medford House," Royce told him. His partner jumped at the sound of his voice.

"Royce—" He paused to take a breath. "You've got to stop doing that. You're going to kill me one of these days."

"Shut up and follow me."

Down an alley and around the back of The Hideous Head, they crossed planks used as bridges over a trough of muck and sewage. Royce popped the lock, and they slipped through the rear door of the alehouse. The place was dark and empty. Looters might visit the place in days to come, but the decoration Royce left in the Lower Square would keep even the desperate away until after dawn. Pretty much everyone would be staying in shuttered homes that night.

He moved to the windows and checked the street—deserted and dark. Not wanting to draw any attention, he kept the place dark. Not a single candle was lit. This suited him fine, but Hadrian was practically blind even in full daylight. He bumped into every piece of furniture between him and the bar.

"Think Grue would mind if I helped myself to a drink?" Hadrian asked. He was behind the bar looking like a blind man, feeling around for cups.

"Something wrong?" Royce asked.

"What? Because I want a drink?"

"No, because you're stealing one."

"The man is dead. I don't think he'll be too upset."

"Still, it's not like you."

"You're an expert on me now?"

"Getting there."

Hadrian found a large pewter mug and filled it until foam poured over the sides. He blew most of it away, then tapped off a bit more until the mug was brimming. He took a long draw, emptied the mug, and then filled it again before bumping his way back through the dark. "Well, you're right. I had a pretty crappy evening."

"What happened to Rose?"

They took seats at the table with the window, one up from their usual, so that Royce could keep an eye on the street.

Wayward Street was dark. Moonlight was all that separated objects from emptiness as the faint radiance painted edges and cast shadows in long blocky shapes. Some of the cold light spilled in the window and highlighted the planes on one half of Hadrian's face.

He had that beaten look again. If Hadrian were a child, Royce would have called it pouting. Oddly, he often slipped into one of these moods after a fight. Because the blood on him wasn't Hadrian's, Royce guessed he was better off than "the other guy." He should be happy, but Hadrian didn't always see things the same way as Royce.

"She's dead." Hadrian took another deep swallow, then wiped his mouth and rested his elbows on the table.

"Sheriff patrol?"

"No, they did get stopped but got away." He pushed back and pointed at his shirt. "I stayed behind and added another four to my list. The problem is, that didn't change a thing. She was killed anyway. I found her body in an alley."

"Another patrol?"

"No, I think it was the guy who was escorting her home. I'm pretty sure he had no intention of taking her anywhere, except away from the castle."

"Well, if it makes you feel any better, you did better than me. You only lost one of the girls. I'm pretty sure I killed the whole lot."

Hadrian stopped drinking. "Come again?"

"They've arrested everyone from Medford House."

"Because of the notes you left?"

"I'm guessing."

"Probably shouldn't have done that."

"You think?" Royce glared at him, but it lacked commitment. He sat back, folding his arms and looking off toward the bar as if hoping to catch the eye of the waitstaff.

"Don't get mad at me. You're the one who went knife happy. Nobles get cranky when you decorate their streets with one of their own." Hadrian took another swallow, then asked, "So what are you planning to do? You're not going to let them execute her, are you?"

"No."

"What, then?"

"I don't know!" he snapped.

Royce refused to look at him, his sight wandering around the tavern instead, never lighting anywhere for very long. The place was a sty, and he wondered how long Gwen had been forced to work there. Must have felt like prison. They had that in common. Now she was locked up again for something she didn't do—for something he did. How many more people did he have to kill to make this right?

Hadrian got up. "I'm getting a refill. You want one?"

"No."

"Sounds like you could use one."

"No."

Hadrian bumped his way back to the bar, while Royce struggled to think of something—anything.

He could try and break Gwen out. He had seen the fire, and everything would be in chaos. It wasn't like the high constable was around to give them orders. Security would be weak. But he knew her—Gwen wouldn't go unless the rest of the girls were safe first, and he couldn't hope to get them all out. If he did, where would he take them? He'd be on the run with a wagonload of women. If he had a month to prepare, maybe, but Royce suspected justice would be quick. He guessed he had no more than a day or two and possibly just a few hours.

There had to be a better way, and he knew what the problem was. He was still thinking like himself. He needed to think like Merrick. He needed to make things flow the way he wanted. To do that he had to understand where the power was and how to bend it.

Royce sighed. All he could think of was killing, and he couldn't kill everyone. How would Merrick handle it? Manipulation certainly, but how and who? He didn't even know who gave the order to arrest the girls. There were quarter sheriffs and probably a high sheriff, also a city constable, and finally the lord high constable of all of Melengar, whose office was presently vacant thanks to him. Which one should he put pressure on? Which one had the power to free Gwen?

"What I need is leverage. Someone I can blackmail or bribe."

"Too bad about Exeter," Hadrian said. "Could have used him, except his attempt to kill the king is pretty much common knowledge now, and of course there's the whole *dead thing*."

"What are you talking about?"

"The fire? Big old blaze in the castle? I thought you might have set it to flush Exeter out."

"No, Albert did what he was supposed to, and Exeter came out on his own."

"Yeah, well, I know that now. Actually I gathered that from all the gossip at the castle. Everyone was talking about how Exeter had it set. He was trying to take over."

"Really? That's odd. Exeter told me some bishop—Saldur, I think he said—was the one plotting for the throne."

"Was that before or after you cut his fingers off?"

"I don't remember."

"Probably would have accused his mother of killing the king after a finger or two."

Royce shook his head. "No, I've found people are pretty truthful at times like that. I think Exeter was innocent."

"You're saying you killed the wrong man?"

Royce smirked. "I meant for burning the castle and trying

to kill the king. Exeter said Rose could identify who they were. Said he wasn't looking to kill her—he wanted to *find* her. She had some kind of proof he needed."

"Hmm..." Hadrian took another long drink. Outside the wind buffeted the tavern, whistling through the many cracks.

"What?"

"When the patrol caught up to Rose, they didn't try to kill her. The sheriff wanted her taken to Exeter."

"Did you catch his name? The guard you think killed Rose?"

"Richard Hilfred, a sergeant in the royal guard."

Royce stood up. "Great! All I need to do is kill him."

"Then you're in luck. He's already dead."

"Are you sure? Are you *absolutely* sure?"

"He was the guy who started the fire. That new chancellor killed him. But what difference does that make?"

Merrick would have seen the connections. He would've seen the pieces falling into place, and for once Royce was seeing them too. He got up and started walking back and forth. Royce was on to something, and he couldn't sit still. Merrick used to pace when he planned, too, and that made him feel even more that he was on the right track.

"Hilfred was just a pawn, the inside guy. This Bishop Saldur's the one pulling the strings. And with a little convincing, he might be able to pull some for us. A friend of mine used to say 'guilt and fear are a powerful combination,' and it often only takes a small suggestion that someone else knows what you did to get the imagination running. If I plotted to kill the king, and he didn't die, I'd be a little concerned His Majesty might find out, wouldn't you?"

"Sure, but what are you gonna do? Walk into the cathedral and put a knife to the guy's throat and—"

"No," Royce found himself saying, even though he'd been

thinking the same thing. Merrick never maneuvered that way. *Too crude*, he'd say. Persuasion was an art. Too much force had unwanted consequences. Fear was good—panic unpredictable. "We need Albert."

"Albert?"

"Yeah."

Royce reached out and deliberately knocked Hadrian's mug over, spilling the ale across the end of the table and onto the floor.

Hadrian pushed away from the table and looked at Royce, surprised. "What'd you do that for?"

"You didn't get wet, did you?" He had a bemused look on his face.

"No."

Royce watched the ale drip off the end of the table for a moment. "That's because I knew where the ale would go. Besides, I need you sober, because if this fails, we might have to kill a lot of people."

CHAPTER 21

THE DAY AFTER

Rain started falling just before dawn. The soft patter on the roof of the barracks should have been soothing, a welcome relief, a gift from Maribor to finally douse the night fires, but Chancellor Percy Braga saw it as just one more thing to deal with. The barracks had become the new council chambers, with what remained of the heart and soul of the kingdom squeezed into two narrow rooms. Braga would eventually commandeer a nobleman's house in the city, possibly even move into Mares Cathedral, though Saldur might balk. For now he needed to be on the scene.

The scene was the smoldering ruin of the castle keep. The fire had burned longer than anyone would have thought. *All that straw.* Braga had heard those three words all night, but it was all that aged oak that kept the fire going. Bucket brigades did nothing but prevent the fire from spreading to the outbuildings. The keep was unassailable, as if a dragon had taken up residence, refusing to be moved. The place had burned all night, black walls with glowing eyes and a deep throaty roar.

So much had to be done and now they would do it in mud thanks to rain that had come too late. The sheer enormity of the problems aligned against him was overwhelming. He took a breath and exhaled and then took another. He shouldn't have to remind himself to breathe. The world was changing. The sun would shine again, perhaps brighter than before. He just needed to get through this.

Braga sat at the woefully small table, a size that suited the small number of attendees. Of the original twelve council members only Lord Valin, Marshall Ecton, the Chamberlain Julius, and Bishop Saldur survived to reconvene. Buried under a pile of military blankets, struggling to endure the morning chill, which was worsened by the rain, Braga sat at the head of the table feeling more exhausted and cold than he could ever recall. No one suggested starting a fire.

Braga waited on the death tally. In the chaos, no one knew who died and who might have survived, and he needed to have that list. The delay was agony, but he had to know before proceeding. At least one name wouldn't be on the list. The princess had been spared, carried to safety by that boy—Richard Hilfred's son.

Everyone had ash on them somewhere. The whole of Essendon Castle was one big lump of charcoal and everyone looked like miners recently out of the hole.

"I'd like to send scouts up the East March Road," Valin insisted with steel in his voice that Braga couldn't have imagined before. The old warrior had always struck him as a doddering steward, keeping the seat warm for the next Marquis of Asper, but the man was alive now, his eyes bright and his voice deep. "We're sitting here blind and deaf. I have known Exeter since he was a pup, and that lad was no fool. He may have commanders and an army on the march. Even though the man is dead, his forces could still pose a risk. We need to know where they are, their numbers and makeup."

"Actually, I think we have a more pressing issue directly before us," Bishop Saldur said. The elderly cleric was a mess. Wet with rain, his thin hair melted to his skull, and the soot on his face bled down from his forehead in tears of black. He looked like a corpse found floating in a river. "Before we start down any path, we need to decide who will take the helm of this kingdom. With the royal family dead, it is—"

"The princess survived," Valin pointed out a little too quickly and loudly for Braga's taste. The old man had been a mouse at all previous meetings, yet now he discovered his voice.

"Of course, of course, but she's twelve," the bishop said in his affable, warm tone while patting Valin's hand, which the marquis withdrew. No one likes to have a corpse touch them no matter how friendly he sounds. "She can't rule. Maybe someday, but not now. We need to designate a regent until she comes of age."

"Lord Valin is the ranking nobleman," Ecton spoke up. "And he's a descendant of the charter. Clearly you should be—"

"The law states that the chancellor shall act as steward until the next king is crowned," Chamberlain Julius declared. "This is indisputable. Lord Braga is a brother to the king."

"Through marriage only," Ecton replied.

"Lord Chancellor?" Wylin appeared in the doorway, where people had been coming and going all morning. Wylin was acting captain, now that Lawrence had been officially pronounced dead—found partially crushed by a fallen timber in what used to be the drawing room. Wylin was dripping wet and filthier than all of them. His hands and arms black up to his elbows.

"What is it?" Braga asked.

"We have an early tally on the dead, my lord. And, my lord"—he paused, looking at each of their faces—"things may not be as dire as we had thought. We have not found the king among the wreckage."

"Are you certain?" Saldur asked. "Surely you have—he's probably burned recognition."

"No, Your Grace. I do not believe so. We've found"—he hesitated—"the fire did little to the king's bedchamber or the chapel. Queen Ann still lies on her bed undisturbed. She likely succumbed to the smoke while sleeping, but the king was not there. Nor have we found the prince. The scribe is in the stable, writing up the official tally. He'll have it to you directly, but I thought you'd like to know about the king right away."

"Yes, yes, thank you, Lieu—ah, Captain."

"Such hopeful news," Saldur said with a beaming smile.

"What does this mean? Where could the king be?" Lord Valin asked. "Did Exeter's men abduct him?"

"Looks like we can suspend all this talk about picking a new ruler." The chancellor stood, slipping out from most of the blankets but keeping one over his shoulders. "Excuse me, as I have a chaos to order." He squeezed out of the barracks.

Wagons filled with stacked bodies were rolling through the courtyard recently turned to mud. He stood under the barracks porch eaves to survey the disaster he'd been granted.

The sound of horns drew Braga's attention.

"The king! The king!"

Horses entered the gate. King Amrath trotted in alongside Count Pickering. Behind them came the prince and the Pickering boys all sodden with rain, all eyes staring up at the blackened castle. Those in the barracks rushed out with smiles brimming on their faces.

"You're alive!" Braga shouted. "And the boys…"

"Caught them on the road this morning," Leo explained, his voice detached, his eyes unable to leave the ruins of the castle. "They slipped out to go hunting."

Amrath said nothing as he dismounted in front of the chancellor, rain dripping from his beard. "What's happened, Percy? Where's Ann and Arista?"

At that moment, given the choice, Braga would have traded

places with the Hilfred boy rather than have to be the one to answer that question.

※

Albert had spent the night at Lord Daref's Medford home in the northwest of the Gentry Quarter—a posh three-story brick and stone home outfitted with fireplaces on every floor and dainty flowerboxes under the windows. Daref also had a modest holding in Asper, but he visited it only twice a year to check on things. As his friend explained, "living in the country made it impossible to stay current and remain relevant," which Albert understood to mean it was boring. In the city, Daref lived alone but kept a staff of six servants. The lack of a wife had sparked rumors for years, rumors that were heightened by the young man with fair hair who lived with him. Daref called him Neddy and introduced him as his nephew, but Albert had been to the wedding of Daref's niece and knew she didn't have any siblings. Albert found it odd that his friend went to such lengths when most of the gentry had real secrets, but perhaps that was the point; Lord Daref felt left out of the controversy.

Daref and Albert had left the party just after the fire broke out. Neither possessed the stomach for gawking at tragedy. While others stood around in the cold all night or worked bucket brigades, they slept comfortably. It was the first decent accommodation Albert had come across in the last two years. He was grateful for it and for the savory breakfast the three of them were enjoying.

A knock at the door brought a messenger and news that the fire hadn't been an accident. The blaze was set with the intent of killing the royal family. The king and his children were spared, but the queen perished. Perhaps even more surprising, the traitor responsible, the Lord High Constable Simon Exeter, was also killed. His body found butchered in Gentry Square. The identity of his murderer remained a mystery.

The news sparked a lively conversation between Daref and Neddy about the possible implications of a conspiracy and the effect it would have on members of the court. Albert hadn't heard a word of their conversation; he was too fixated on the word *butchered*.

When Royce and Hadrian had offered him an opportunity to escape his humiliating poverty, he'd jumped at the chance. Now he wondered if that had been wise. He'd expected some good-humored embarrassments, such as what he had planned for Baron McMannis. But this—he was an accomplice in the death of a man, a high-ranking noble.

Albert couldn't finish his second helping of sausage and eggs.

Would the guards remember him? Had Vince told the chancellor or the king about the viscount who delivered an odd message to Exeter? Would he recall the name Winslow? Might they think he was part of the plot? Regicide had a way of inciting hysteria and the executioner's axe swung liberally, doling out the same sentence to the guilty as well as those unfortunate enough to be caught up in the events.

Everyone knew he had arrived with Daref. The castle guard could be on their way at that moment. He needed to disappear. Albert felt the coin in his purse. Lady Lillian had given Lady Constance twenty-five tenents to arrange for the theft of her earrings. He had clothes, gold, and as close to a full stomach as he could manage. He could walk out through the city gates and vanish. The coin would go a long way—perhaps as far as Calis, where no one would have ever heard the name Lord Simon Exeter.

"I need to be leaving," Albert interrupted Neddy, who was

speculating whether the Wintertide festival would be forgone this season.

Daref looked out at the rain and smirked. "You always were a skittish coward."

Albert's heart skipped; then he smiled. It was only a joke.

"I suspect several people will be leaving the city after last night, as if the fire and murder were the work of a plague. Like you, they will hole up in their respective country estates and wait out the next few weeks to see what matures."

"And you?" Albert asked.

"I wouldn't miss this for the world. Court will be an exciting place, and I want to be right in the center of it all."

Albert's lack of wealth made packing a matter of getting dressed. He bid farewell to Daref and set out into the rain. Walking past the square, he saw the remnants of Royce's work. Blood was everywhere. The fountain pool was dingy red, a few ropes still attached to the statue, where Exeter's body had been cut away. The display was such a horrific sight that Albert put a hand to his mouth to prevent losing the helping of the sausages and eggs he'd eaten.

How had Royce and Hadrian managed it? I still owe them money. If I run, will Royce hunt me down?

In the course of just one day, Royce had discovered Exeter's identity. He'd located, plotted against, and killed the third most powerful man in Melengar—someone with an army of sheriffs at his command—all while his victim attended a king's gala. If Royce decided to kill him, how infinitesimal were the chances of a disavowed viscount on the road to Calis?

His stomach churned. He really had no idea what kind of men they were. How could he, having just met them? Hadrian seemed affable enough, but there was something else there, something buried. He walked with a swagger that was just a little too confident for a commoner, as if he had no fear of death. Albert's father had always warned him about casual men. The Winslows were a family of gamblers, and this was likely where he gained his innate gift for reading people. Granted, his grandfather lost the fief in a game of chance, and his father lost everything else the same way, but that didn't mean he wasn't right—it was called gambling for a reason. Still, between his two new associates, Royce was the frightening one. He didn't veil his disposition in the least. That man was capable of anything.

Death as an accomplice or death in the dark?

Albert had always been a coward, but the family's gambling habit was still in his blood. If he went to Royce first and explained that he wasn't cut out for this sort of thing, then maybe he would let him go. He decided he would rather take a risk now than live in fear the rest of his life. If he gave them twenty gold tenents, that would repay the original money they had given him many times over. The two might not be pleased with him for severing their partnership, but it ought to be enough to save his life. He would still have five to live on, and he could run with that. The question was, should he tell them about the five he was keeping or just say the job had paid twenty? Five seemed fair, but they might not see it that way. Still, he needed at least five to live on. He would never be able to show his face in civilized society after taking Lady Lillian's money and not delivering on his promise, and Constance would be disgraced and vengeful. She was no Royce Melborn, but the fury of a scorned noble lady was nothing to trifle with. He could never hope to return and would be forced to vanish and start a new life. Calis was still a possibility, but he might also go to Delgos—no nobles there. Either would be nice, someplace warm for the coming winter. Someplace they sold cheap rum.

When he arrived in the Lower Quarter, Albert did so with

slow feet. He was in no hurry despite the rain that was soaking his new clothing. This was a bad day for everyone and he was not eager to receive his fair share. He headed for the tavern but paused at the common well in the square. Raynor Grue was decorating the place with his gruesome visage made uglier by the cuts, as if someone had taken pity on the crows by cutting up their meat. He'd also seen the other dead man when he came through the Artisan Quarter. The sheriffs were too preoccupied with the affairs of state to worry about removing the bodies of two peasants. How long would they hang there before someone took them down? Both scenes were gruesome, and it made Albert wonder exactly what state Exeter's body was found in. The first didn't bother him too much, but Grue was different. He had known him. He'd just talked to the man the day before. Albert's hand went absently to his own throat, his own face. He remembered how casual, how arrogant he'd been with Royce when questioned about borrowing so much for clothes. Maybe he should have been less cavalier. His feet moved even slower after that.

Sadly, no earthquake split the street to swallow him and soon he arrived at The Hideous Head Tavern and Alehouse. The door was closed and for a moment Albert wasn't certain what to do. He shouldn't just walk in, but he certainly couldn't wait for Raynor Grue to open the place. He stood at the threshold trying to determine his next move, most of which centered around, *Well, I tried to contact them. They can't fault me for that.*

The door opened.

"Winslow," Royce's voice said sharply from the darkness. "Get in here."

Albert felt his stomach rise as he compelled his legs to walk. *There's still one empty square in the city. Maybe Royce reserved it for me.*

As soon as he entered, Royce closed the door and dropped the bolt. It took a minute for his eyes to adjust to the dim light. The barroom was empty except for the three of them. Hadrian sat at the bar on one of the high stools, his big sword lying along the counter where it extended beyond three seats.

Royce gave him an exasperated look. "Where've you been? We've been waiting for hours, and I was just about to go look for you myself."

Look for him? What did that mean? Royce wasn't a heated killer. Albert had been with them only a few days but already he knew that much. Looking at the thief, he took a breath and tried to calm down. Daref was right; he was a coward.

"I...ah—"

"Never mind. Do you know the bishop here in Medford?"

"Maurice Saldur?" Albert was baffled by the question. "Oh no, you aren't planning on killing him, too, are you?"

Royce didn't bother answering and simply handed him a small purse. "Deliver this package to the bishop right now— right this minute."

"But I don't even know where he is."

Royce gripped the lapels of Albert's coat and pulled him close enough to kiss. "Get this package into the bishop's hands immediately or—"

"Not a problem," Albert said, taking the purse.

~

On the opposite side of the Gentry Quarter from Essendon Castle, Mares Cathedral brooded in its somber, dignified opulence. The two buildings dominated Medford, some said, like quarreling behemoths, but Bishop Saldur preferred to think of them as parents, looking down on a city filled with children. The castle, like a husband, provided security of the body, while the mother church nurtured the spirit. The cathedral was older than the castle, predating it and the kingdom of Melengar by centuries. A relic of the post-imperial age, it showed its years. Streaks of black stained the stone of its lofty bell tower, dark tears shed for a thousand years of mourning. The rest of the world had moved on. They had forgotten the days of imperial glory when roads were safe, water was pure, and cities such as Medford didn't need walls. The church remembered. The church waited.

For nearly a thousand years, the Nyphron Church had sought the lost heir of the last emperor who had miraculously escaped the final destruction. That one hope had kept the faith alive through turbulent times. Clinging to the dream and a memory of greatness, the church sought to steer mankind back onto the course of enlightened progress and away from selfish divisions that placed any thug with enough swords on a throne.

It had been a long journey through dark times, but the wait was nearly over.

The bishop paused long enough to look up into the pelting drops of rain at the grand facade of Mares Cathedral with its twin soaring bell spires, a masterwork so out of place in such a small city. Then he glanced over his shoulder at the still-smoldering ruins of the castle and felt the drag of wet vestments on his shoulders. He'd failed, but at least it was the castle and not him that had burned. Whoever had killed Exeter had removed a noose from the bishop's neck.

"A desperate day," Olin muttered as he held the door. Olin was always saying ridiculous things like that.

Saldur entered the church feeling instantly at peace. The dim interior of lofty marble pillars, flickering candles, and the pungent scent of salifan incense was another world, a place where the troubles of the outside were forced to wait.

The bishop stood dripping as Olin closed the door.

"What can I do?" Olin asked.

"Run to my chambers and build a fire and get a bath started. And bring me back a towel to dry off. I'm frozen to the bone."

"Of course." Olin shuffled off. The plump man never appeared to know how to lift his feet.

While his wetness hadn't bothered him before, now that he was inside it became a misery. He was reluctant to move, to feel the cling of soaked cloth against his skin. He took a forced step in the direction of his chambers and grimaced. He just needed to walk a bit farther; then he could peel the slop off. He'd dry himself, curl up in bed, and sleep. It had been a long night.

He had taken only one more step when he heard pounding at the doors.

The bishop looked around and sighed. He was alone at the front of the church. He gave the door a shove and found a blond-haired nobleman, equally sodden, waiting outside. When their eyes met, the man smiled.

"Your Grace!" He appeared delighted, not at all the sort of reaction the bishop was used to these days. "I'm so pleased to find you."

"Services won't be until—"

"I'm not here for that." The man took note of the puddle the bishop was creating in the otherwise dry vestibule. "I'm merely making a delivery."

He held out a coin purse.

"How nice of you." Saldur took the pouch, disappointed at its light weight. "I'm certain our lord Novron will bless you for your generosity."

"Oh, it's not mine, Your Grace. I actually don't know whose it is. Just now a man in a hurry stopped me on the street and asked if I would deliver it to you. He said it was important, and I always like to do the church a good turn. I could use all the help I can get in that respect, if you know what I mean."

"We all do," the bishop said.

"I'm also quite curious what's in the purse. The man told me that under no circumstances should I look inside, which of course made me want to peek."

"And did you?"

The nobleman shook his head. "Normally I would have, but..."

"But what?"

"Well, to be honest, Your Grace, I was frightened. The man was, shall I say, intimidating. I had the distinct impression that he might be watching me." The nobleman looked around.

"I see. Well, thank you, I suppose."

"Thank you, Your Grace."

The blond nobleman offered another smile and, spinning on his heels, walked back out into the downpour. Saldur peered out into the rain but couldn't spot anyone who might be watching. He closed the door.

Fueled more by the possible inconvenience that someone else might come to the door, the bishop ignored the clammy wetness of his clothes and walked down the corridor, gritting his teeth. As he did, he opened the purse and dumped the contents into his hand.

Saldur stopped.

In his palm he held a severed finger.

Saldur grimaced and dropped it. A metallic sound as it hit the floor drew his attention to a ring. The golden band was a gaudy thing, with one huge ruby and a smaller one to either side. There was no mistaking the gold and burgundy badge of Melengarian high office—this was the ring of the lord high constable.

What happened to Simon Exeter was still a mystery, but

Saldur didn't feel a need to pick at that scab. Surely Novron had killed Exeter to protect him from disaster because Saldur was working in his service. The high constable didn't have enough proof to charge him yet. But being a suspicious man, he had been putting pieces together faster than Saldur had anticipated. The bishop looked down at the finger and the ring, puzzled.

Why would anyone send me the severed finger of Lord Exeter?

Examining the bag more closely, he found a scrap of parchment still inside. Written on it in a small, tight hand, the words were few but to the point.

> *See that the ladies of Medford House are released*
> *and protected and I'll forget about you.*
> *—Rose*

Saldur read the note three times, and his hands were shaking by the third time through.

The little wide-eyed bitch did recognize my voice! And is still alive!

The bishop turned around and, retracing his steps, pushed open the doors to Gentry Square once again. The blond-haired noble was gone, and no one else could be seen. In the distance, through the curtain of rain, he could just make out the rearing stone statue of Tolin Essendon. Exeter's body had been removed and the blood washed away, but a single length of rope—too high perhaps for the soldiers to safely reach—still dangled from the neck of the king like a noose.

Why hadn't Richard killed her? Perhaps Hilfred was smarter than he thought. Only a fool would trust a man about to betray his king. Likely kept her alive to work as insurance in case something went wrong. Maybe he even planned to blackmail

him later. He should have had Richard slit her throat in the
dungeon, but he thought it was best to have her body discovered far away or not at all. Having her die in the castle would
have just provided Exeter one more piece to add to his puzzle,
and himself one more accusation to defend against.

For the first time, Saldur was forced to consider who had
killed the constable and why. They said a note had been found
on him—something about Exeter harming some women.

Could it really be as simple as the girls having hired thugs to
protect them from harm? Hadn't he heard that there were other
murders in the city just like Exeter? Each of the victims had
somehow harmed the women from this Medford House. How
ironic that the petty affairs of prostitutes from the worst quarter
of the city could hold a dagger to his throat. Saldur was always
amazed at how few people had an appreciation for seeing what
was possible. This Rose had him trapped. She could have asked
for so many things—money, power, anything really. If arranging for the release and protection of a handful of whores would
put the matter to rest, Saldur would be happy to oblige.

Forgetting the fire, his bath, and his waiting bed, Saldur
turned and headed back to the burned-out castle once more.
He needed to convince His Majesty to release the girls, before
Rose started pointing fingers.

✧

When Albert returned to The Hideous Head, Royce was waiting with the door open. Pulling him in, the thief shut the door
quickly, and Albert struggled to wipe the rain from his eyes
with his soaked sleeve.

"Well?" Royce asked.

"It went fine," Albert told them. "I got the package to
Bishop Saldur and I saw him go back to the castle. Can I ask
what was in it?"

"Leverage," Royce replied.

"So I'm involved in what now…blackmail as well as murder?"

"Gwen and the girls were arrested," Hadrian said.

"I'm sorry to hear that, but what does that have to do with Bishop Saldur?"

"Royce has come up with a plan to get them out."

Clearing his eyes, Albert could see Hadrian at one of the tables, a toppled mug of ale before him and a puddle on the floor. His big sword lay bridging the gap across the table and the chair beside him, the baldric left dangling. Royce remained on his feet, hovering uncomfortably close. Neither looked like they had slept.

"I've been thinking," the viscount said. "I'm not cut out for this nefarious sort of life. That and the fact I'm more than a little concerned that the royal guard might be looking for a certain viscount who delivered a message to Lord Exeter shortly before the fire. So perhaps it's time I left Medford."

"You're not going anywhere," Royce told him with a certainty that made Albert believe it. "I need you gathering information."

"I appreciate your confidence in me, but…here." Albert held out a coin purse. "There's twenty gold tenents for a job I secured while at the party. It's yours to do with as you please. The person who hired me will never find me where I'm going. I don't think I'll be able to show my face in Melengar, or possibly all of Avryn, ever again. I'm thinking of going south, Delgos or perhaps Calis."

"You're not going anywhere," Royce repeated, ignoring the purse.

"And what if I'm arrested?"

"Albert," Hadrian said. "You're overreacting. No one is after you. Besides, you're one of us now. We wouldn't let them hang you."

Hang me? The thought chilled him.

"You don't think they'd really—" But of course he did. Why else would he have said it? "And how could you stop it? The two of you are so cavalier about everything! I don't mean to be insulting, but please understand that you're just two men— *they have an army*. I'm sorry this is all…" Albert threw up his waterlogged hands, spraying liquid off the cuffs. He was befuddled, lost for the proper words to describe the extreme absurdity. "I'm leaving."

Royce stepped between him and the door, his face inches away, and when he spoke it was barely above a whisper. "The king's men *might* be after you. If they are, they *might* question you. If they absolutely must find a scapegoat, they *might* choose to pin a crime on you. But if you walk out that door and Gwen is executed as a result…" He licked his lips, and his eyes glared, unblinking. "Maybe you should take a tour of the city's fountains on your way out of town."

Albert didn't move. He barely breathed and Royce continued to watch him like a cat hoping the mouse would run.

"We really could use your help, Albert," Hadrian said, his voice so pleasant and casual that Albert was disoriented. These were very strange people. "I promise you, we'll have your back. If anything happens, we'll be there."

When the viscount replied, he spoke quietly, haltingly, and at a slightly higher pitch than usual as he dragged each word out with a struggle. "What is it you want me to do?"

"Good man," Hadrian said, clapping him on the back and drawing him away from Royce and the door.

"What do you want him to do, Royce?"

"Find out all you can about where Gwen and the girls are being held. If you hear anything—anything at all—about plans for their execution or release, get back here as fast as those new shoes will let you. Understand?"

He nodded. "Okay."

"If I'm right, we won't have to do anything."

"And if you're wrong?" Albert asked, not at all certain he wanted to hear the answer.

"Then Hadrian and I will have to go in and get her. I'm hoping it won't come to that."

"I agree," Hadrian said.

They planned to go *get her*—to rescue a whore imprisoned by the king of Melengar after the queen was murdered. The two of them. Common thieves nonchalantly challenging the might of an angry monarch. Albert was employed by madmen. Who did they think they were?

⁓

Except for the soot stains, the ash, and the still-rising smoke, the room was as Amrath had left it. Nothing had been burned, not the carpet, not the swan mirror, not the bed where he had found Ann beneath covers as if sleeping. If an army had breached the walls, he could comprehend her death, and he would mount his horse, lift his axe, and ride with the storm. But this. Some invisible monster had slipped into their bedroom and smothered his sweet Ann. A beast that he could still smell, whose poison he breathed as he lay holding her.

"Your Majesty?" It was Valin this time, knocking softly on their door.

"Go away! Leave us alone!" he tried to roar, but his voice, scorched by the smoke, was raspy and vicious.

"But, sire, it's not healthy—"

"Go away!"

"Just let me come in. I'll—"

"I swear I'll beat to death anyone who enters this room."

The king pulled his wife closer. If he closed his eyes hard enough, it was almost as if nothing had happened. Almost as if he hadn't left her on the one night in her whole life that she really needed him.

He couldn't see much anymore. He hadn't stopped crying since he saw her, since he entered in disbelief and rushed over to try and wake her up. He chased them all out, throwing chairs, stools, and tables. If he'd caught anyone, he would have ripped them apart. He had become a real bear, a wild bear, a wounded and dangerous bear.

Amrath was having trouble breathing. His chest ached as his heart was crushed and torn, consumed in misery. In the silence of the bedroom, even the absurd haunted him.

Why did I say it depended on if you were ready to go to the party?

"Of course I love you, Ann. I've always loved you—I'll always love you. I should have said so. I was being a fool, making a stupid joke."

The tears continued to seep out of his closed eyes and leak across his cheek into her lovely hair.

"Your Majesty." Leo this time. Then the door opened and Alric and Arista stumbled through, their cheeks wet, eyes red.

"Will you kill your own children?" Leo called out.

Before he could rise, they rushed toward the bed. "Father?" Arista was out in front, ahead of Alric, whose sight was fixed on his mother.

"You shouldn't—" He coughed again. "You shouldn't be in here. You should—" He doubled over and started to vomit.

"Get him out!" Leo ordered. "Get all of them out of this damn smoke, or we really will lose our king!"

CHAPTER 22

HOMECOMINGS

King Amrath stared out the shattered window of what had once been his council chambers. Now a gutted, scorched-black cave, it stank of smoke and death. Long black tears ran so that even the stone walls cried. The rain continued, weeping for the loss as the king looked out of his ruined home at the city below. The king had no more tears to shed.

The ache was still in his chest, a crushing sensation as if someone had punched a hole through his ribs and squeezed his heart. The rest of him was just numb. He still had trouble breathing. Leo had likely saved his life by sending his children in, but the king wasn't sure if a thank-you was appropriate, nor was he at all certain his trouble breathing had anything to do with the smoke.

But he was still king. He still had responsibilities. Leo and Braga were steering the kingdom as best they could, but they still needed him.

The meeting had begun with a tally of the dead. Remarkably only a little over a dozen people perished in the fire, mostly servants who worked the upper floors—Drundiline, his wife's favorite handmaid, and Nora, the kids' nurse. Their loss was tragic, but Amrath hardly noticed. He still puzzled at how

Ann's bedchamber was hardly touched by the fire, but Arista's room was nothing but a blackened shell.

"Your Majesty?" Leo said softly.

"What? Sorry, I..."

Leo smiled sadly. "Never mind. Go on, Chancellor."

Braga nodded. "It was Richard Hilfred who set the fire but Exeter who ordered it."

"As I tried to warn you, Your Majesty," Saldur said.

The bishop's voice irritated him. By not heeding his counsel, Saldur was blaming him for Ann's death. There was too much truth there not to hate the cleric for pointing it out.

"As far as I have been able to determine," Braga said, "Lord Exeter had long plotted to take the throne. I suspect he may have murdered Chancellor Wainwright, hoping to obtain the chancellery. When you appointed me to that position, he apparently decided to take action."

"And where is Exeter now?"

"He's dead. Butchered in Gentry Square."

"Who killed him?"

"We think he was betrayed by someone he was conspiring with."

"Yes," Saldur agreed. "That's how things look."

"Wasn't there a note? Something about a group of women taking credit?" Leo asked.

"Oh yes, some foolishness suggesting a house of prostitution was involved," Saldur said. "Obviously a poor attempt at diversion."

"I would have to agree with the bishop, Your Majesty," Braga added. "I'm continuing the investigation, but the women mentioned in the note don't appear to have had anything to do with it. Medford House is literally a handful of women struggling to survive in an alleyway. The madam of the house was recently battered by Exeter during an investigation the high constable was conducting. This appears to have been the source of the charade, but that's where it ends. The real killer was just trying to throw us off his scent."

"But the women of Medford House *were* arrested?" Leo said.

Braga raised his hands and shook his head in a show of frustration. "The sheriffs are Lord Exeter's men and some can actually read. You can hardly blame them. At the time his body was found, his treachery was not yet known. They acted in haste—without knowing the facts or about the constable's guilt. I'm just grateful they didn't kill anyone. I've already given the order for the women's release."

"I think we need to do more than that," Saldur said. "These poor girls have been treated badly, and while we know they weren't involved, rumors are already spreading. People think they were responsible for the wanton slaughter of a high-ranking nobleman and relative of the king."

"And the killer of my wife," Amrath reminded them.

"Of course, excuse me. It's just that people might be angry to think someone of their social standing might do such a thing and get away with it."

"How would it be if I knighted them?" the king said, not entirely joking.

Saldur offered an uncomfortable smile. "I think just some declaration of royal protection would suffice."

"I suppose we *could* issue an edict and instruct the sheriffs to actually enforce it," Braga said. "It's my understanding that crimes against women in that profession often have a blind eye turned by those entrusted with keeping the peace in the quarter."

"Do as you want," Amrath said to the chancellor. "I really don't care. Now what about Richard Hilfred?"

"He is dead as well, Your Majesty, by my own blade, the night of the fire," Braga said.

"Well done, Chancellor," Leo exclaimed, and it was followed by rousing applause by all in attendance.

Braga bowed his head respectfully and humbly, but his pride was evident. Amrath had been right in appointing his brother-in-law to the position. At least one member of the council had done something of value that evening.

"Richard Hilfred..." the king muttered. "He saved my life once. It's hard to believe."

"I knew Richard Hilfred well," Saldur said. "He often came to me with concerns about his life—and Richard was a very troubled man."

"Don't you dare try and excuse him." Amrath tore at his beard, pulling until it hurt.

"Absolutely not, sire. I would never—but as his bishop, I listened to him confide his many personal troubles with me and often mentioned his great sadness at the death of Rose Reuben—something he blamed you for not preventing. Still, I never suspected he would go so far."

"So Exeter and Hilfred are dead," Amrath said. "But that doesn't explain the queen's death. Why is it that no one woke her? No one thought to get her out? How is it all of you stand before me without a scratch or a burn?"

With each word the king's voice grew louder until the roar of the bear had returned and his hand had settled on the pommel of his sword.

There was a long pause.

"Your Majesty," Braga began softly. "We tried."

"How hard is it to run up a set of stairs?"

"Before setting the fire, Richard Hilfred chained the doors to the residence shut. He thought you and your family were inside. His plan was to kill all of you. I tried...please believe me, Your Majesty. After killing Richard Hilfred, I did everything I could to get the doors open, but it was useless. As the fire grew, I was pulled from the inferno by two guards. There simply was nothing that anyone could do."

He chained the doors shut?

If the conversation continued, Amrath didn't hear what was said. It was as if he were falling into a bottomless well. All he could think of was his wife and daughter, trapped as the castle burned, and all the times he had offered a kind word to a man who chained them in to die. The mention of his daughter's name pulled him out. "What was that?"

Leo spoke. "I was asking how it was that Arista survived?"

Braga said, "It was Richard Hilfred's boy. He carried the princess out."

"Hilfred's son saved my daughter?"

"But how?" Leo again. "If the doors were chained, how did a boy manage to do what none of you could?"

"Reuben Hilfred had a key," Braga said.

There was a silence as everyone paused to consider this.

"It's likely the son was in league with the father," Saldur said.

"Did he perish in the fire as well?" Amrath asked.

Braga said, "He escaped but suffered severe burns and is being cared for by a healer. It may be days until we know what really happened. He's unconscious and under guard."

"But if he was in league with his father, why did he save Arista?" Amrath asked.

"We don't know."

"I say he should be executed," Saldur said. "I've seen this many times, the poison of the father infects the son. Likely the boy's guilt drove his actions, and it was only fear of Novron's judgment that motivated his saving of the princess. Such a tragedy." Saldur shook his head. "If only you had listened to me, sire, the queen might yet live."

There it was again, the accusation that all this was his fault.

Amrath pulled the great sword of Tolin Essendon from its sheath. The huge blade came out easily and the king wanted nothing more than to sever the bishop's head from his shoulders.

He took a step forward, raising the blade and watching the bishop's eyes widen in horror as he inched backward. An instant later, Leo's shimmering blade lifted his own and forced it aside. "Amrath...he didn't mean it."

The king fumed, his chest rising and falling with his breath, which hissed through his teeth. He stared at Saldur, who fell backward, tripping on the blackened timbers, rain splattering his grandfatherly face. That fall saved his life.

"Go on, Sauly, say this is my fault one more time!" This wasn't a bear growl; this was a roar. "I'll cleave you in half and string *you* up in the square so the peasants can have a new corpse to gawk at!"

"Forgive me, Your Majesty. I only—"

"Shut up, Bishop," Leo said, still holding the massive Tolin blade with his own slender rapier. "If you want to live to draw another breath, just be quiet and leave."

Saldur got to his feet, surprisingly fast given his age, and retreated out of the ruined room.

Leo put his sword away, and the great Essendon blade lowered until the tip touched the floor. Then in a sudden burst of rage, Amrath raised it again and with a shout he cleaved through one of the more substantial oak beams, only partially chewed by the fire. The massive blade rang as it slew the wood in two. The king struck again and again in a mad fury, chipping hunks of wood, such that both Leo and Braga backed away. In a few minutes the fit ended and Amrath stood heaving in a shower of sweat and rain. He dropped his sword, fell to his knees, and covered his face. "I should have been here."

"You would have only died along with her," Leo said, his voice as soft as the patter of the rain.

"I should have. It would be better than *this*."

"The land would be without a king."

"Bugger the land! My son would rule."

"Your children are too young."

"Then Percy would rule until they came of age, but I...
I wouldn't have to feel this way." He looked up at Braga. "I
don't know how you managed. How did you find the will to
breathe after Clare died?"

"I just did."

Amrath nodded. "We have a lot in common now, you
and I."

"I'm here for you, sire. I'll help take care of everything."

⁂

The rain continued.

Royce slipped back inside The Hideous Head without
a word and went to stand at the window, soaked and dripping. He'd been going in and out all night. Hadrian had no
idea where. Maybe he visited the castle trying to find Gwen,
maybe he checked up on Albert, or maybe he just wandered
the streets in frustration.

Outside, the rain poured on Wayward Street. Hadrian
didn't know why they called it a street. Even in good weather
the dirt lane was little more than a path between shacks, and
at that moment it was on its way to being a lake.

Hadrian never left the Head. With four full kegs behind the
bar, he typically would have spent the night drinking and the
morning sleeping, but he hadn't had another drop since Royce
knocked over his cup. He never said anything, but he knew
Royce's plan wasn't going to work. Not that it wasn't worth
a try, but what were the odds that Maribor would smile on
the likes of them? In the past the gods had always demanded
blood.

It was midmorning and Royce was back to pacing, leaving a stain of rainwater on the otherwise dull floor when Hadrian spotted Albert. The viscount was in a full-out run and he suspected it wasn't because of his desire to get out of the rain.

This is it. Battles always start early.

Hadrian frowned and slipped the big sword over his shoulder as he called out, "He's coming."

Royce halted and spun, his face tense.

Albert opened the door, breathing hard and wearing a grin. "It worked!"

"Details!" Royce snapped.

"Heralds have gone out and edicts are posted. The castle announced that the women of Medford House have been cleared of all charges and are now under official protection of the crown. Chancellor Percy Braga signed the proclamation himself. I don't know how, or what you did, but whatever it was it worked!"

"Where are they?"

Albert shrugged. "In the process of being let out I suspect. You said to run right back here the moment I heard anything."

For the first time since Albert had left with Lord Exeter's finger, Royce finally sat. He ran hands over his face, and Hadrian noticed they were shaking.

Going behind the bar, Hadrian pulled out a bottle of rum, a bottle of wine, and two glasses. Adding a fresh pulled mug of ale for himself, he joined Royce and Albert at the table.

"Sorry, it's not Montemorcey," Hadrian said, pulling the wine bottle's cork. He motioned to Albert and the rum.

"Are you sure?" he asked, looking to Royce.

"To Gwen." Hadrian lifted his mug.

"Can't argue with that," Royce said, and nodded at Albert, then poured his wine.

"To Gwen," Royce and Albert echoed together as they clinked their drinks.

Royce drank and set the glass back on the table. Smiling, he said, "Wow."

"Grue had good wine? Really?"

"Huh?" Royce looked up, confused. "Oh...no. I'm amazed the plan worked. I never...I mean, it was just too easy, you know? Maybe we should try doing this sort of thing more often."

"I'm always up for anything that requires less blood."

Royce nodded and took another sip and grimaced. "Oh damn—yeah, this stuff is hideous."

"Hence the name."

Royce left the table as if needing to put distance between him and the wine and went to the window to look out at the street.

"Do you see them?" Hadrian asked.

"Not yet," Royce replied.

"I wouldn't worry. Streets are flooded, hard to walk in skirts," Albert mentioned.

Hadrian stood up. "Who's hungry?"

"Since the barn, I don't think I'll ever pass up the offer of a meal," Albert said, pouring a second glass of rum.

"Let's see what Grue has in his pantry." Hadrian searched the shelves. Grue might not have sold food, but he certainly had plenty. Hadrian found some stale bread, several bags of flour, and a kettle of something. He spotted a hunk of smoked ham on a cutting board and half a waxed round of cheese and hauled them out.

Hadrian returned to the table and set the food down.

Royce stayed by the window, his eyes glued on the street. "Albert, if you still want to leave, I won't stop you. Gwen is safe, and that's all I wanted."

"Well, I don't know now. I was searching for news in every inn and public house in the Gentry and Merchant Quarters this morning, and apparently no one remembers me from the party—or no one cares. Almost depressing if I were to really think about it. I'm rather invisible. I guess I have that sort of face or personality. Explains a lot, really. No one ever noticed me. In a world of clout and influence that's a problem, but as the liaison for a pair of thieves, can there be a better talent? Besides, I have to admit I'm impressed. No—forget that—I'm astounded. I thought I was in league with lunatics, but you did it. You took down a ranking noble, rescued all the girls from the dungeon, and no one even knows you did it."

"That *we* did it," Royce corrected.

"Right." Albert smiled. "I think I'd like to stay and see where this goes. Besides, I already lined up that job. Would seem a shame to disappoint our client."

He handed the purse of gold to Royce, who began to count the coins.

"Who's the job for?" Hadrian asked.

Albert pulled his damp hair back into a ponytail and said, "A nice lady who's being blackmailed by her servant and an evil baron to betray her husband."

"I like it."

"Twenty-five gold?" Royce looked up.

"Half now, half when you deliver."

Hadrian was concerned, but Royce was the first to ask, "What does she want us to do for *fifty tenents*?"

"Steal an earring."

"An earring?" Royce asked skeptically. "Is it guarded by demons or something?"

Albert shook his head. "I suspect it's not guarded at all. Likely just sitting in Baron McMannis's jewelry box."

"Fifty gold to return an earring?" Royce muttered incredulously. "What are these earrings worth?"

"Oh, I suspect they're actually not worth much at all. Old

Hurbert isn't known for his generosity, even to his own wife,"
Albert explained. "The money is for saving the woman's reputation, which is worth far more than any pair of earrings."

Hadrian pushed out his lower lip and nodded. "This whole
noble thing might actually work." Then turning his attention
to Royce, he added, "You owe me."

Royce scowled. "I know. I know. We'll deal with that later."

"He owes you?" Albert asked.

"When you originally went to the castle the night of
the party, Royce said you'd run. Disappear with your new
clothes." Hadrian tied up the purse. "Which once again proves
that people are basically good."

"No, it doesn't," Royce said with a gambler's confidence.
"Albert came back because he didn't want what happened to
Exeter to happen to him, right?"

Albert let his shoulders droop and nodded.

Hadrian raised a finger. "You also said he'd hold out on us
if he made any money, and he handed it right over. You didn't
even need to ask him."

Royce folded his arms across his chest. "Albert? The first
time you offered me this purse, you said it held *twenty* gold.
How do you think it magically increased to twenty-five?"

The viscount smiled awkwardly. "You remember that,
do you?"

"Albert?" Hadrian frowned and sighed.

"It was just five, and I've given you all the money this time.
Doesn't that count for something?" He had a terrified look on his
face. "I...I expected I would need them to, you know, get away."

Royce smiled. "See, you can always count on people doing
what is best for themselves."

"Like I did?" Hadrian said.

The smile left Royce's lips. "You're a freak of nature or the
world's greatest fool. I'm still trying to figure that out."

Albert watched them. "I'm sorry I lied. It *will* never happen again. Please don't kill me." He said it just above a whisper, but Royce heard everything.

The thief almost laughed. "You were only going to steal your share of our first profit—all that means is that you're officially one of us now."

"And what is that exactly?"

Royce and Hadrian exchanged glances and raised eyebrows. "I suppose we should figure that out at some point."

Albert happily turned to the food on the table. "I just discovered I'm starved. Are there any pickles?"

"Pickles?" Hadrian paused, surprised by the word and the memory it conjured.

"Yes—little things, sort of tart."

"No...I don't know. Go check for yourself."

Albert looked puzzled.

Before anything else could be said, Royce ran past both of them, punching open the front door to the tavern.

Hadrian and Albert followed the thief out into the rain, which appeared to finally be letting up. Hadrian saw the troop of ladies coming down the road. They were all there, save Rose, all clustered around Gwen, helping her walk. Then like a flock of ducks they scattered as Royce raced in. His arms wrapped around Gwen, lifting her in a hug and a gentle twirl. Scooping her up, he carried Gwen back to Medford House as the sound of rain gave way to the sound of girlish laughter.

CHAPTER 23

HILFRED

Reuben woke to dazzling sunlight streaming through a window, and his first thought was that he was dead. Something about the brilliant light, how it splintered into visible shafts as it angled across the bed, held a mystical quality. Everything was bright, so that he had to squint to focus. From the ceiling above him hung all manner of plants. Dry and brittle. Most looked like flowers, common ones that grew in the fields and even around the walls of the castle courtyard. Reuben didn't know half of them but recognized thyme, honeysuckle, and cowslip, which he found near the stables a lot, as well as ragwort and toadflax, which grew in the cracks of the castle walls. He could hear voices, lots of voices, and distant sounds like wheels and hooves. The second thing he thought was that he was not dead, because he didn't believe there would be so much pain in death, and Reuben was in agony. His throat burned as if he had swallowed molten lead, and his chest felt congested and ached as if it had a block of granite resting on it.

He tried to take a breath and instantly doubled up in a series of hacking coughs. The jerking movement brushed his skin against the linen sheet. It looked as soft as rabbit's fur, but it scratched like a million needles. His head ached, he felt nauseous, and all he could do was smell smoke. He lay back, realizing he was on a bed of some sort. He had never lain on a mattress before. He always thought they looked nice, only at that moment he could just as easily have been on a torture table, but then just breathing was torture. Even blinking hurt.

He was indeed alive; he just wasn't certain if he wanted to be.

A woman approached and peered at him. "You're awake. That's good." He'd never seen her before. With gray, almost white hair and spider lines around her eyes, she was old but friendly. "I imagine you'd prefer to keep sleeping. But I can tell you those who keep sleeping...well, they never wake up. But look at you! And I wasn't so sure. Nope, not certain at all. When they brought you in pink as a roast pig, I thought the best could be done was size you for a box. They said 'he's young and strong,' but I wasn't so sure. I've seen a lot of the young and strong nailed in boxes, and a lot looked better than you. Still, you got your hair and that's something."

She ruffled the mop on his head, but when he cringed, she stopped. "I suppose everything is sensitive. That's the way with burns, but sensitive is better than not. All that pain you feel is good. Means your flesh is still alive. If you didn't feel nothing, why, you might never feel anything again. So I know you don't think it now, but later you'll be happy for the suffering."

"Water?" he croaked, his voice broken, cracked, and thin.

She raised her eyebrows. "Water, eh? Think you're up for that? Maybe you should just stick with a weak wine."

"Water, please."

She shrugged and stepped aside to a basin to pour him a little cup. Reuben felt he could drink a lake's worth, but after two mouthfuls he began to vomit over the side of the bed.

"Now what'd I tell you?"

He was shaking. Maybe he always had been and just noticed

it then. He had never felt so horrible. He wanted to scream but was scared to, afraid it would hurt. Death would have been better. The pain was overwhelming and a panic set in as if he were drowning, submerged in suffering. Needing to endure even an hour like this was a nightmare, but the horror he knew was that the anguish would last. Reuben recalled the time he burned himself on the kettle and how long it took to heal.

What had become of him? They had a sheet draped lightly over his body. He guessed he was naked. Perhaps his clothes burned away. What was left of his flesh? He feared to look, terrified what he might see. His hands and arms were red and lacked hair, but otherwise they looked fine—just a bad sunburn, a few blisters. He gritted his teeth. It did not seem fair that even crying hurt.

Then a thought outside of himself knocked on his shuttered mind. "The princess…" he said, the words coming out as a coarse whisper. "Is she okay?"

The nurse gave him a quizzical look and then a smile broadened her face. "The princess is fine, I'm told."

He lay back down. Maybe it was his imagination, but the pain seemed to lessen somehow.

He was in a small room. The rustic wood and stone revealed he was not in the castle or any of the outbuildings. This was some place new. A small cottage perhaps, or a shop. Through the window came the sounds of traffic. He must be in the city.

"What happened?" he asked.

"I don't know. I wasn't there, but the rumor is that you ran into a burning castle yesterday."

"I carried the princess out and then went back for the queen. I couldn't reach her."

"Was that all?"

He nodded almost imperceptibly. No added pain. He was surprised.

"Most people say you had a death wish, that you wanted to die because—" She turned back to the basin and took a towel from a rack.

"Because, why?"

She looked over her shoulder at him. "I don't think it's true. I can't imagine it is, especially with you asking about the princess like that. Do you know what I think?" The nurse soaked the towel in a basin and then wrung it out and turned back to him. "I'm Dorothy, by the way. I'm a midwife. They brought you to me instead of a real doctor because I know burns. All those doctors do is leeching, and you don't need that." She paused, pursing her lips in thought, working something out. "Yes...I think you are a very brave man, Reuben Hilfred." She folded the damp towel. "I think everyone is wrong. What you just said makes so much more sense, at least to me. I think... well, it is just noble of you that lying here as you are and you ask about the princess."

"I'm not noble."

"Maybe not in name, but certainly in your heart, and if you ask me, that's where it matters most."

"If you ask everyone else, they would tell you the opposite. People kill for titles."

"Maybe, but how many would die for them? How many would throw themselves into a fire? I don't think it takes much bravery to be greedy." She laid the towel on his forehead. It stung for a moment, then felt cool, soothing. "You'll be all right. I know you have your doubts, but I have seen this before. I know it hurts, but you were lucky."

"What is everyone saying about me?"

She hesitated.

"Tell me—things certainly can't get worse than they are."

"I'm not so certain about that, Reuben. Everyone says you and your father set the fire."

꙳

Reuben hadn't realized he had fallen back asleep until he was awakened by a loud rapping on Dorothy's door. He was instantly greeted by the pain again. The solid overwhelming wall of agony jolted him awake and made him hate whoever was banging on the door.

"I'm sorry," Dorothy said as she made her way past his bed. "I'm not expecting anyone. Maybe they found some other poor soul who isn't fit for a doctor."

She slipped beyond his vision, around the brick of the chimney that came down through the center of the roof. The rough brick column vented a cooking hearth that was open on two sides and adorned with pots and blackened utensils. Pans, buckets, cups, and bowls dangled from low support beams, and above the archway dividing the rooms—where another person might display a sword or a coat of arms—Dorothy hung a well-worn broom. The home consisted of only three rooms: the kitchen, a small space behind a wooden door where he imagined she slept, and the room he lay in. Reuben noticed shelves of clay pots marked with more flower names along with other disturbing ones like *rats feet*, and *rabbits ears*.

Reuben heard the opening of the door. "Your Grace?" Dorothy sounded startled.

"Is he awake?"

"He was sleeping. The lad is sorely hurt. He needs to—"

"But has he regained consciousness since he was delivered?"

"Yes, Your Grace."

Boots scuffled on the wood floor and then the door closed. The old man, the bishop who had been at the fire, appeared through the archway, his burgundy and black robes looking as brilliant against the dull walls as a mallard duck on a gray pond.

Why is the bishop visiting me? Does he think he needs to perform last rites? No, it would be a priest, not the bishop.

"How are you feeling, son?"

"Fine," Reuben said cautiously. The pain was distracting, making it hard to think. The less he said the better.

The bishop looked puzzled. "Fine? You nearly burned to death, my boy. Are you in pain?"

"Yes."

The bishop waited, expecting more, then frowned. "We need to talk... Reuben, is it?"

"Yes."

"What do you remember from the night of the fire?"

"I saved the princess."

"Did you? What about before that? Braga said he found you and your father together. Is this true?"

"Yes, I was trying to stop him."

The bishop pursed his lips and tilted his head back to look down the length of his long nose at him. "So you say. But you could just as easily have been helping your father."

"No, I fought him."

"Again, so you say." The old man didn't look at him but stared up at the ceiling. Reuben followed his sight just the same. The bishop had that effect; if he was looking at something, Reuben felt he should too. Perhaps his next question might be about the dried plants.

The bishop dragged the spinning wheel stool over and placed it next to the bed, then sat down.

"Is there something wrong?" Dorothy asked, peeking around the chimney. Reuben guessed they were speaking too softly for her to hear from the kitchen, or she could hear and just didn't like what was said. The tone of her voice made him think it was the latter, and it was then he realized he liked Dorothy.

"Please leave us," the old bishop snapped.

Reuben, however, did not like the bishop. He had not cared for how he tried to stop him from saving the princess, and he was not winning any awards by being short with Dorothy. Still, Reuben was too miserable to generate an emotion resembling anything close to hate or anger, and the old bishop didn't look much better. His eyes were bagged with deep shadows, his face drawn and haunted as if he hadn't slept in a week.

The bishop reached out and placed his hands on his knees, leaning forward. "Reuben, I can't help you unless you tell me everything. What *exactly* did your father say to you?" He leaned even closer. His eyes focused intently, his face tense. "Did he mention anyone he was working with?"

Reuben thought. He closed his eyes. The bishop peering at him did not help his memory. He was a bit nauseous, and his skin felt as if it were still on fire, while overall he felt bizarrely chilled. His misery made focusing on even the events of the night before a challenge.

Reuben shook his head. "But I think he was promised something in return for setting the fire. I got the impression he was angry at the king. Angry about the death of my mother. He said something about someone having convinced him he could make things right again."

"And how was he going to do that?"

"I don't know."

"Are you certain? This is very important, Reuben. You must be absolutely positive."

"He never mentioned anything else."

The bishop sat back and let out a long sigh. "So you fought your own father to save the royal family?"

"Yes."

"Many will find that hard to believe. The queen died in the fire, and the king's mad with grief. He wants to punish someone.

He nearly killed me a few days ago during a council meeting after I defended you."

"Defended me?"

"Yes. I told him you were a hero for saving his daughter. I told him you ran in when all others refused."

"And?"

"He attacked me with his sword. If it had not been for Count Pickering's intervention, I would be dead. He hears the word *Hilfred* and he loses reason. Your father killed his wife, and you are guilty by relation of blood. It's an old law. Close relations are put to death for such high crimes as treason."

"Why?"

"Because it is believed that what a man will do, so will his son or brother."

"But that doesn't make sense. I *saved* her. I went back for the queen. I nearly *died*."

"I know. I believe you. I was there, and I want to help you. But you must help me do that."

"How?"

"Think very hard—are you absolutely certain your father never mentioned anyone else involved in a conspiracy to murder the royal family? *Who was it that was going to help him make things right?*"

"I honestly don't know."

"You're absolutely certain?"

"Yes."

"Very well."

"You believe me, don't you?"

"Yes, I do, but will the king? More importantly, will he want to?"

"What are you saying?"

The old man reached out and laid a hand on Reuben's,

causing him to wince. "Someone has to pay for the murder of the queen, and your name is Hilfred."

~

Reuben suffered through a span of nightmares broken by brief bouts of agonizing consciousness. He drifted in and out until he found it hard to tell what was real. The one constant was the pain. In his dreams he was always dying, slowly burning to death. In one, Ellison and the Three Cruelties had him tied like a pig on a pole being slow roasted. They jeered and laughed as his skin split and sizzled. In another he was trapped in Arista's bedchamber, unable to reach her, and together they burned— first her, then him. He would scream for the princess to wake up, to run, but his voice was so weak, so choked with smoke she never heard.

Dorothy was always there when he woke. In the tiny house she likely heard his nightmares, but he began to suspect she simply stayed at his bedside. Every time he opened his eyes, he saw her looking back with a sympathetic smile.

On the morning of the third day after his waking, he felt better. Nowhere near good, but somewhere between excruciating and terrible, which was a significant step up. He was able to drink and keep it down, and Dorothy could apply a soothing cream to his skin without having to listen to him scream.

By midday, he could smell soup or stew and found he was hungry. Before the meal came, he heard the sound of coach wheels and then shouts. The voices outside were harsh and unfriendly.

"Make way for the king!"

At this, Reuben heard Dorothy drop a pan. He hoped it wasn't the soup.

"Open in the name of His Majesty King Amrath!"

The door did not creak when opened as usual, but it practically cried as it was abruptly pulled back.

"The king has come for Reuben Hilfred." The voice was loud and powerful.

"He's done nothing wrong!" Dorothy cried.

"Out of the way, woman."

Reuben braced himself as best he could. The whole thing struck him a bit funny, which in itself was amusing. How many people could laugh about being executed for a crime they did not commit? He should have died in the castle. He had accepted his passing then but managed to gain several more days that were filled with excruciating pain. Dying now—while absurd—was not a great hardship. Given his state of agony, death was less his enemy and more a sympathetic acquaintance. His only regret was that he would not taste the soup that smelled so wonderful.

He could smell again! Reuben had only a second to revel in this accomplishment when soldiers entered the room. How would they do it? A hanging most likely, or perhaps a beheading. It would be ironic if they burned him at the stake, but he assumed everyone had enough of burning. He changed his mind an instant later, thinking the king might want an exact revenge. To do to him what his father had done to the queen.

The soldiers ducked their heads and moved out of the way as the king entered. With him came the prince and Arista. They were all dressed in black, with the princess wearing the same gown as when Lady Clare died. None looked good, their faces tired and pale, except around the eyes where the skin reddened. Still Arista looked more sullen than the rest, her stare fixed on the floor.

Reuben had never seen His Majesty this close. The man was huge, and as Reuben looked up, he seemed a giant with his rich bristling beard. He appeared as tired as the rest, but in his eyes was a storm.

"Your Majesty," one of those in the corners said. "This is Reuben Hilfred, son of Richard."

At the sound of the name, he saw the king wince. Perhaps there would be no burning after all. Maybe the king would kill him there in his bed. At least he was able to see the princess again. She was safe.

Thank you, Maribor, for that parting gift.

"Do you know the penalty for lying to your king?"

"Death?" Reuben guessed.

"Death," the king confirmed. "Did you leave your post without permission the night of the gala?"

"I did."

"That is dereliction of duty at best—desertion at worst. Do you know the penalty for desertion?"

"Death." Reuben knew that one.

"Death." The king nodded gravely.

"Were you ordered by anyone to leave your post? Told by anyone to enter the castle?"

"No." Reuben noticed a subtle change in the king's eyes but had no idea what it meant.

"Then knowing it was death to desert your post, why did you?"

"The castle was on fire. The princess and the queen were inside, and no one else was trying to save them."

"Why do you say that?"

"They were all just standing around. The chancellor gave orders—"

"It was chaos that night." Reuben heard Lord Braga's voice as he pushed into the room from the kitchen. "The darkness, the flames, all those people trying to get out."

"Finish what you were going to say, boy," the king commanded.

"The chancellor gave orders that no one was to go inside."

"Is that true?" Amrath asked Braga.

"Yes, but it was an order issued to prevent the further loss of life. The doors were sealed. There was nothing that could be done."

"Is it true you fought your own father?" the king asked.

Reuben lowered his eyes to look at his bedcovers. "Yes."

"When did you learn your father planned to murder my family?"

"I didn't. I guessed it when I found the door to the residence chained. My father told me to leave. He said he posted me at the gate for my own protection. That's when I knew he had set the fire—that he had chained the door."

"Braga asserts that he fought and killed your father—is that true?"

Reuben nodded.

"Speak up to your king," Braga demanded.

Amrath raised a hand. "He's fine. Tell me, boy, how did you get the chain off the door? After the fire, the lock was found but it hadn't been snapped or cut."

"My father had the key on his body. I took it from his belt."

"So you unlocked the door and went to Princess Arista's room?"

Reuben nodded again.

The king turned to his daughter. "Is this the boy who carried you out?"

Arista said nothing. She didn't even look up.

"I asked a question. Answer me."

"Maybe."

"Arista, look at him."

"I don't want to."

The king petted his daughter's hair. "Why?"

"I hate him."

"You hate...but he saved your life, didn't he? Carried you from the castle? Others have testified they saw him with you in his arms coming out. Are you saying that isn't true?"

"It's true."

"Then why—"

"He didn't save Mother. He let her die! *He* lived and *she* died! He's a coward, a vile, awful..." Arista broke down in tears and with a wave from the king was led out.

Reuben thought he couldn't feel worse and hated himself for his naivety. Everything could be worse. He felt tears forming and struggled to hold them back. He didn't want to cry in front of all those men.

"Everyone out," the king ordered.

"But, Father," Alric protested. Reuben noticed then that the prince had two swords, one in his hands and one on his belt. The one he held Reuben recognized as his own sword that the prince had given him, the sword he had lost in the fire. "You can't listen to her. He's innocent. He saved Arista's life. He tried—"

"I said out!" The king's voice finally boomed and everyone retreated. He waited for the door to close. It was just the two of them then. Reuben and the king. Even Dorothy was gone.

Imitating the bishop, the king sat on the spinning-wheel stool beside the bed. He didn't say anything at first and Reuben didn't dare look at him. He kept his eyes on the dried plants hanging from the ceiling.

"The castle was on fire," King Amrath began, his voice low, soft. "Leaving your post would result in severe punishment, maybe not death, not to a boy who was serving his first day, but a whipping at least. You knew that." The king paused, stroking his beard. "You were ordered not to enter the castle by the chancellor and your own father." He paused again, licked his lips, and exhaled loudly. "Even discounting everything else, you ran into an inferno when everyone else was running out. Reuben, that doesn't sound sane to me. So explain—why did you?"

"To save Arista." The words came out of his mouth, but they were born somewhere deeper, and having said them a tear slipped and fell. This time he did not notice it hurting; the pain from his burns was secondary to this new agony. He looked at the pommel of the king's sword and wished he would draw it, wished he would kill him. His life was a waste. Born unwanted by both parents, he killed his mother and drove his father to murder and treason. Now the only girl he would ever love hated him. He wanted to be dead. The fire had cheated him. How much better if he had burned to death believing in ignorance that he had finally done something right.

"I see." The king nodded. The tempest in his eyes was gone. All that remained was sadness.

"I tried to save the queen," Reuben offered. "I went back, but I couldn't see. I couldn't breathe. I thought I was going to die in there. I know I failed you. I know I'm worthless. I know you all hate me. So, please, just do it." Reuben was crying openly now. He no longer cared.

"Do what?"

"Kill me."

"Is that what you think? You think I came to execute you?"

"Didn't you?"

"Why would I punish the one man in my kingdom who did his job? The one man who risked his life for my family? Who knowingly sacrificed himself for the ones I love the most? Reuben, I am not in the habit of executing heroes."

"But your daughter..."

"She just lost her mother. She hates everyone right now, me

included. I can't blame her. I almost killed the bishop myself for speaking the truth. Maybe your father was a traitor, but you are not. I owe you a great debt. I'm not going to execute you, Reuben. I'm going to reward you. I could knight you for bravery, but I don't need another knight. As a knight, you would leave the castle, and I can't have that. The coming days will be dark ones, I fear, and I am frightened for the safety of my family. I need men to protect them. All the gold in my treasury couldn't buy a better protector for my daughter."

The king stood up. "You need to get well quickly, Reuben. I will be arranging for proper combat training, as my son tells me you are less than able with a blade, and I need you as skilled as a Pickering."

"I don't understand."

"As of this moment, you are now, Reuben Hilfred, royal sergeant at arms and the personal bodyguard of the princess. You will go where she goes, never letting her out of your sight. And as far as her protection is concerned, you act with the power of the king. That means you have my permission to kill any man who threatens her—I don't care what rank or position he holds. Do you understand?"

Reuben nodded.

"From now on, you answer only to my daughter and to me. Never let anyone tell you not to protect her again."

"But the princess hates me."

"She'll get over it." The king turned to leave, then paused. "Of course, I think we'll wait at least until you're healed and have learned how to use a sword before I break the news to her. She has a temper, that one." He walked for the door, but paused once more before opening it. "Thank you, Reuben."

"Your Majesty?"

"Yes?"

"I wasn't alone."

"What's that?"

"In the fire. When I went back for the queen, I wasn't alone. Someone else was with me. I couldn't see them. I couldn't see anything. Just a voice; she told me which way to go, how to get out, and when I finally reached the stairs, she told me to jump. Only no one else could have been in there with me, could they?"

"There was no one else. You alone braved the fire."

"I think it might have been my mother. I think she wanted to help me—see that I survived—and now she has."

The king stared at him for a long moment, then nodded. "I think everyone may have underestimated your mother's love for you. Me included."

CHAPTER 24

THE ROSE AND THE THORN

Hadrian watched as snow began to fall on the dirt. It melted faster on the newly turned soil, causing the little grave to stand out. The rough rectangle clean of any leaves, rich and dark, looked too small. It could be a child's grave. He remembered her from that night—her face so young, so frightened. She was hardly more than a child. He pictured her under all that dirt and his stomach tightened. Gwen had dressed her in a gown of white and surrounded her in the last roses the vendors had left. Then they had nailed the box shut and settled it into the hole. Gwen had paid for the plot; she never said how much. All the ladies had pitched in for the headstone. There was a place outside the city for undesirables, but after Chancellor Braga's announcement that the ladies of Medford House were under the direct protection of the king, no one protested. Not able to use her name, the headstone read GRACE FLOWERS.

If only he hadn't interfered.

Would Rose have lived? Is she in that box under all that dirt because of me?

If he hadn't helped Richard Hilfred fight off the sheriff and his deputies, if he hadn't stepped in the way and stopped Terence from taking Rose to safety, she would still be alive.

Royce hadn't said anything. What better illustration than

the cold body of a beautiful young girl to really drive home an argument. Only the thief remained silent. Previously Hadrian might have wondered why, but he was getting to know Royce now. More to the point, Royce was getting to know—if not entirely understand—him.

The majority of the mourners filed out of the graveyard. A long silent procession of bowed heads and weeping eyes. Most were women—none wore black. Hadrian imagined it was the one color that the ladies didn't own. The procession to the graveyard through town had brought stares and glares of disgust. More than a few commented on the "harlot colors," but Hadrian knew they all wore red in deference to Rose.

Royce and Gwen lingered beside the grave. For once the thief was the most appropriately dressed. Gwen cried. She stood quivering, her hands to her face. It took a moment, a few beats of delay, but then Royce awkwardly slipped an arm around her. At his touch, she buried her face in his chest and sobbed. He stiffened. Her arms circled his waist and squeezed so that his cloak tapered. For a man so adept at movement, so agile and quick, Royce moved at the pace of a watched pot. His arms inched out around her shoulders, his cloak enveloping her. They stood that way, joined as one person in the center of the graveyard at the end of Paper Street.

Watching them, Hadrian sighed and it came out as a little fog that was snatched away by the cold wind.

He doesn't deserve her. Then he shrugged. *Who does?*

First Arbor, now Gwen. Perhaps this is the way it would always be. Whenever he found the perfect woman, he would lose her to his closest friend. He breathed in a cold swallow of air that hurt.

Better to let it go.

Movement to his right caught his attention. A set of eyes

peered at them over the top of a headstone. Hadrian recognized the forehead. It was Puzzle.

Hadrian's only surprise was that it had taken this long. Since the night of the fire, they had not seen a member of the Hand. Now they were standing on their doorstep, and as inappropriate a time as it might be, they could hardly let it pass. More eyes appeared among the crypts and stones. None looked happy. They must have been aware of Royce and himself for some time, and while in the back of his mind Hadrian acknowledged the kindness that they held off, he wasn't in a good mood. With the burial of Rose, he was back in a serious drinking state of mind. He often got that way when he thought too much, when he took inventory and found his shelves bare. His mind always spiraled down to thoughts of the tiger, his father, and the emptiness—an emptiness he tried to fill with drink. It took a day or two, but eventually he always succeeded in drowning the hatred, the deep loathing of the one person he held responsible for all his failures—himself.

Of course, a good fight could help too. And it was with this eager eye that Hadrian watched the Crimson Hand rise out of the crypts and gather around them. Hadrian wondered if Royce saw them. He was unusually distracted at that moment, but then he lifted his head and drew Gwen away, positioning her between himself and Hadrian.

Top Hat approached with his trademark lid, to which he added a long wool cloak. He glanced at the grave. "My condolences," he said, tipping his hat. It even sounded sincere. He looked at Royce. "I heard back from Colnora."

"Let her go first," Hadrian ordered.

Top Hat looked at Gwen. "No need. I wouldn't dare harm a lady of Medford House. Not after the chancellor's edict. And..." Top Hat's voice lost its bravado and he looked to Royce.

"Not after what happened to Lord Exeter"—he turned to Hadrian—"and the sheriff's men. They're saying the king did it, you know? That he made an example of what happens to traitors. It was adequately gruesome, and very public to be sure, only a bit odd. Kings usually like executions done in daylight with torture and lots of screams before a cringing crowd. It also tends to happen when he's actually present, not drinking with old friends."

Top Hat paused. Maybe he expected them to say something. When they didn't, he went on.

"But I suppose it had to be the king. No one else would be crazy enough to kill Exeter, and no one would be mad enough to hang him up like that for everyone to see. I mean, if it wasn't the king, who could have done such a thing—done it and got away? Unless you're wearing a crown, you don't kill a noble and walk away whistling, now, do you?"

Hadrian watched. He began sizing them up, determining the biggest threats and their distance from him. Only the thieves didn't close in as before. They didn't circle. Top Hat stood the closest, and even he kept to the far side of the grave.

"Thing is, I heard something like this happened before. I heard it happened down south—down in Colnora. 'Bout two years ago, there was a bunch of murders there. Magistrate, lawyers, powerful folk, and nobody saw nothing. But it didn't stop there. Seems after killing the cream, this shadow began targeting members of the Black Diamond itself. Thieves were killed, butchered and strung up in the city squares—works of bleeding art like Lord Exeter. And if killing a noble is crazy, I'm not sure there's a word for declaring war on the BD, but someone did. They call it the Year of Fear. The year an assassin turned on his own. They say one guy did it all, and they say he was never caught. Some still have nightmares."

"Sounds awful." Royce still had an arm around Gwen; the other was in his cloak.

"Yeah." Top Hat glanced at both of them. "Hate to have something like that happen here."

"I heard that same story when I was down in Colnora," Royce said. "The way I heard it, the killer was provoked."

"Really?"

"A pleasant fellow otherwise."

"A regular gentleman, I suspect."

"No, not in the least, but also not the sort to bother his neighbors so long as they don't bother him."

This left Top Hat thinking for several minutes. He glanced at the grave and then back at his thieves. Finally he looked back at Royce. "You planning on staying in Medford awhile, then?"

At this Gwen tilted her head up to look at Royce.

"Hadn't really thought about it, but... what do you think, Hadrian?"

"It's a nice enough place."

Royce asked Top Hat, "You got a problem with that?"

"It's...ah...it's not customary to allow non-guild thieves to practice—"

"The Black Diamond had similar restrictions," Royce said, his voice dropping in degrees.

Top Hat licked his lips and adjusted his hat. "That so?" The guild leader looked like a bartering shopkeeper being swindled. "Well, I've never cared for the Black Diamond. And I suspect they'd think twice about pushing into this territory if they knew who was calling it home. I don't think there would be any real harm letting just the two of you pick a few pockets."

"You won't even know we're here," Royce said.

"I like that. Don't suppose you'd be willing to pay me a percentage of your take?"

"No."

"Become a member?"

"No."

"Couldn't hurt to ask." Top Hat looked to his brood and raised his voice. "From now on, these two are our guests. No one touches them. No one as much as stares at them. Got it?" Top Hat looked back at the grave and this time took his hat off, revealing a balding head. "I was serious. I liked her. Grue was an ass." He spoke these three sentences like a eulogy, then replaced his hat and took a step back. "Stay on your side and we'll stay on ours. Deal?"

"Deal."

Top Hat turned to move away, then paused. "How'd you do it?"

"Do what?" Royce asked.

"Kill Exeter."

"Never heard of him."

Top Hat smiled, nodded, and walked away.

⁓

His horse shifted a step as Royce pulled the straps tight on the saddlebags and then buckled down the blanket over the top. Baron McMannis's estate was only three days' ride, but winter doubled their gear. Inns could not be counted on, and while the season was early, storms were plentiful. They had to pack for the worst, and that meant bringing everything. No matter how much forethought he put into it, he always felt he forgot something. The feeling usually proved true, with the discovery always made ten miles down the road.

Hadrian had already packed and his mare looked like a miner's mule. He was across Wayward Street at the tavern helping the girls move the heavy stuff. Gwen had bought the certificate to Grue's tavern and together they were rolling old casks out of the way while the girls swept and scrubbed. Dixon was well enough to leave the doctor's place and had returned to the House. He sat out front wrapped in blankets, looking frustrated. The big man was thinner than Royce remembered from the previous year , but at least he was up and eating again.

Gwen stepped out of the dusty shadows of the tavern. Her dress was filthy and there were smudges on her face. With one hand leaning on her crutch and the other shielding her eyes, she peered back at the building. She, too, looked better. The bruises and cuts were fading, but the presence of the crutch made him wish he could kill Exeter twice.

"Shouldn't you leave the work to the girls?" he asked.

"There's so much to do."

"You're still healing."

"Thanks to you, I'll be fine." She wiped her hands on her apron. "We all will."

"I don't know what you're talking about." He tried to keep a straight face but couldn't resist a smile, not while she was staring. How she did that baffled him. He made a living out of lying. He was good at it, but not with her. He wanted to tell her everything—the way even a sane man who stood on the brink of a cliff might think about jumping. Knowing disaster would follow didn't change the desire; something about the view begged it. For now, the view was enough.

Hadrian came out, unrolling sleeves. "By Mar, that place was a mess, but I think you can handle the rest without me. And Royce gets grumpy when I make him wait."

"Thank you," Gwen said. "I don't suppose you'd let me pay you."

Hadrian gave her a smirk; then his eyebrows rose. "You could tell me what you saw in my palm...well, maybe not all of what you saw. Maybe just something good."

She glanced at Royce briefly and offered a weak smile, but there was a sadness that bothered him.

"What is it?" Hadrian asked. "*Did* you see my death?"

"No," she replied.

Gwen paused briefly, then smiled to herself and said, "One day you'll remember this moment. It will have faded to a mere wisp, a ghost of a long-forgotten past, but it will return to you. You'll have white hair and feeling your years. You'll be thinking about your life, about what you achieved and what you failed at and be troubled. You'll be sharpening a blade and cut yourself. You'll see the blood and it will remind you that I said this would happen. You'll remember and you'll smile, then you'll frown, and finally in the silence of that little room, you'll cry. You'll cry because it will all make sense then. Your wife will find you crying and she'll hold you and ask what happened. You'll look at her and see she's frightened. In all the years she's known you, through all the troubles you faced together, she's almost never seen you cry. You'll shake your head and simply say, 'Gwen.' She'll understand and the two of you will hold each other. You'll both cry and the moment will pass. It will be a good moment. Whatever was troubling you will be washed away by those tears and remind you of many things, some that you'll have forgotten about but shouldn't have, and that day will be the better for it."

Looking embarrassed, Hadrian turned to Royce and said, "Hear that, I'm going to have a wife."

"You deserve one," he replied, and was pleased to see Hadrian and Gwen each took his meaning differently. Words were rarely so accommodating.

Gwen looked back at the tavern. "It will take years to make it really presentable. I'll need to rip out whole floors and still I wonder if I will ever manage to clean the memories of Grue and Stane from it."

"Make it too pretty and you'll have to change the name," Hadrian said, grabbing his horse.

"Oh, I *plan* to change the name. I won't own a place called The Hideous Head."

"What are you gonna call it?" Hadrian asked.

"The Rose," she told him, and this caused a round of smiles. "I was thinking of clearing out that old kitchen storage room for you and Royce. It's back away from the public rooms. You could talk business there. Store your gear if you like. I'll watch over you as I did when we first met."

"How much?" Royce asked.

"How much, what?"

Royce approached her. "How much rent will you charge?"

Gwen looked stunned. "I won't charge you rent."

"That's not smart."

Gwen pivoted around the crutch with two petite hops to face him full-on. "I couldn't have bought the certificate to the tavern without you. If you hadn't come—" She looked away and took a breath. "If you hadn't come, Grue would have driven me out of business, or worse, and I honestly think it would have been the *or worse*. And who knows how many more Avons and Roses there would have been." She placed a small hand on his chest. "You changed everything. And I owe you that—how could I charge?"

"Okay, fine. You'll get a percentage."

"I don't want a percentage. Honestly, I'm offering the use of the room in the selfish hope it will keep you coming back."

"I don't think you need to worry about that," Hadrian told her with a wink.

Royce wanted to stab him, but then noticed her smile, and...was she turning red? "There's a risk to hosting thieves," he said quickly. "You could be arrested, have your holdings taken, your hands cut off, for Maribor's sake. I won't let you take that risk without payment. As long as we work out of your tavern, you'll get a cut of what we make."

"But I—"

"I won't stay otherwise."

She had her mouth open but slowly closed it. He longed to wipe away the smudge on her cheek. His hand moved partway before he caught himself. *What is it about her that makes me feel I can do such a thing?*

"You'll stay? You'll live here?"

Royce glanced at Hadrian and shrugged, trying his best to sound casual. "Be nice to have a safe place to come back to. But I insist you take a cut."

Hadrian chuckled. "If this is going to be Royce's permanent home, maybe you should call it The Rose *and the Thorn*."

Royce glared, but Gwen beamed. "I think I will. Yes, The Rose and the Thorn. It has a ring, don't you think?"

"Oh good, I caught you!" Albert came out of the House wrapping a robe about him and squinting at the bright sky.

"It's midmorning Winslow," Royce growled. "You're starting to act like a real noble."

"Thank you. I'm putting weight back on too. Now if I could only afford a decent coat I—"

"What did you want?" Royce asked, pulling himself up on his mount and snapping his cloak behind him.

"There's a party at Lord Harrington's tomorrow night that I thought I should attend."

"Uh-uh. Next outfit comes out of your share of the profit."

"It's not money. I was thinking that, well, I should call you two something. It's awkward to explain that I know *two men* who can arrange for *things to happen*. It sounds amateurish and I can't hope to establish referrals that way. I need a title, something people can remember, but of course nothing that would lead anyone to you. I don't want to use the word *thieves* either. The people I deal with won't like that. So I was thinking of giving you a name. How about the Two Phantoms or Specters—something like that?"

"The *Two Phantoms*?" Hadrian asked skeptically.

Gwen shook her head. "You need something special, something unique. Something short."

"How about *Riyria*?" Hadrian said, climbing onto his horse.

Royce smirked.

"Arcadius was right after all, don't you think?"

Royce shrugged. "Just don't tell him that."

"Who was right—about what?" the viscount asked.

"Nothing, Albert."

"So I'm to call you Rye-ear-ah? Is that correct?"

"Good enough," Royce said as he and Hadrian turned their horses.

Albert pursed his lips. "Well, I don't think it's as good as Phantoms, but it's something I guess."

"It's perfect," Gwen said.

"See you soon." Royce waved and began to ride down Wayward Street.

"Wait! What is it?" Albert called. "What is *Riyria*? What does it mean?"

"It's elvish...for *two*."

CHAPTER 25

THE VISITOR

"Did anyone see you come in?" Bishop Saldur asked, stepping back and opening the path to the coatrack. From the snow his guest was covered in, the bishop assumed it was still snowing.

"No, but is it a crime to visit a church?"

"Not yet, and with Novron's help, it never will be."

Two weeks had passed since the fire, but still Saldur had nightmares of the king drawing that sword of his. *How dare he threaten a bishop of the church!* His actions only showed how far Melengar had slipped into the mire of godless monarchy. This was the trouble reaped when men set themselves up as rulers—when they claimed a throne reserved for Novron's seed.

Saldur sat down and leaned back in his desk chair. He was the bishop of Melengar, and Mares Cathedral was bestowed to his care by the Patriarch and the archbishop of Avryn, but he spent most of his time in that tiny, cramped room at that miserable desk. It wasn't the life he'd imagined for himself when he took his vows.

"Novron was of little help this time."

"Have more faith." Saldur scowled. The bishop was used to disappointments. The church had a long history of waiting. For others a minor setback always felt like the end of the world. They just couldn't understand the scope. Everyone saw themselves as the hero of their story, as if the world rotated around them. Saldur knew the truth. Such impressions were only arrogance. Individuals never managed any kind of lasting change. Real change had to be built over generations. The church worked like drops of water on granite; the impossible was achievable only through sacrifice and time.

This just wasn't the time.

"It's still early," Saldur said, putting his feet up on the velvet stool before the little fireplace. "Eventually all the kings' heads will fall."

"What of Exeter's killer? And that girl—Rose—who hired him? They're still out there—still know about us."

"They know about *me*," Saldur corrected. "No one knows about *you*. No one could ever suspect you—not now, not after how things turned out. And I wouldn't worry about Exeter's killer. He's likely some hired thug or lovesick puppy who she enchanted with those wicked eyes. Even I was taken in by her apparent innocence. He and Rose are likely long gone. I don't expect to hear from them again."

"What about Richard Hilfred?"

Saldur almost laughed, but laughter was unbecoming a bishop in the office of his church. Instead he raised an eyebrow. "The man is dead. What's there to worry about?"

"He might have told others."

"No. Richard was a solitary soul, closed off to the world. He didn't trust anyone. That was why I chose him. He blamed the king for his lover's death, and I knew he was an ambitious man. No real loyalty in him either. Anyone could see that. I merely showed him the path he wanted to take."

"And gave him the blessing of the church. Knowing Novron is on your side always eases one's conscience, even when plotting murder."

Saldur didn't appreciate the disrespectful tone, but what did he expect from this one? "Killing isn't murder when done in the name of Novron. Everyone must die, and die they will—when Novron or his father Maribor decrees it. What difference does it make should the hand of Novron be a lightning bolt or a dagger? I was concerned about your ability to weather the storms necessary to take the throne and rule Melengar. Your age has always been a concern. You're very young. Perhaps I chose poorly?"

"No."

Saldur got up and placed another log on the fire. Feeding his own hearth was just one more indignity he had to endure, but he certainly couldn't allow anyone in his office during *this* meeting, and they couldn't meet in the high tower anymore. And it was cold. He hated winter. This looked to be a long, dark one, made colder by the fact that he'd expected to be spending it in the luxury of the castle.

"It seems like a defeat," Saldur said, trying to sound positive, "but we're actually closer. Much closer."

"Maybe."

"So skeptical."

This brought a smirk.

"The next time we won't miss. We'll wait a few years, let things settle down, let people forget."

"We can't have another fire. There's already been two."

Saldur considered this. "And we can't afford to miss again. We'll have to literally stab him in the back."

"If we do that, the people are going to want us to find the killer."

"That won't be a problem." Saldur smiled. "We'll just pin it on someone."

"Not another traitor. I'm not sure people will stomach that either."

"No, we'll find someone else. Someone without a name, someone unimportant and easy to attach the blame to."

"Like who?"

"A couple of thieves perhaps—that way nothing can go wrong."

GLOSSARY OF TERMS AND NAMES

ABBY: Prostitute at Medford House in the Lower Quarter of Medford

ALBERT WINSLOW: A landless viscount hired by Royce and Hadrian to arrange jobs with the gentry

ALRIC ESSENDON: Prince of Melengar

ALVERSTONE: Name of dagger used by Royce Melborn

AMRATH ESSENDON: King of Melengar

ANN ESSENDON: Queen of Melengar

APELADORN: The four nations of man, consisting of Trent, Avryn, Delgos, and Calis

AQUESTA: Capital city of the kingdom of Warric

ARCADIUS VINTARUS LATIMER: Professor of lore at Sheridan University

ARISTA ESSENDON: Princess of Melengar

ARTISAN QUARTER: The geographic region of Medford where most of the goods are produced

AVON: Former prostitute at The Hideous Head Tavern and Alehouse, killed by Stane

AVRYN: The central and most powerful of the four nations of Apeladorn, located between Trent and Delgos

BA RAN GHAZEL: The dwarven name for goblins, literally "Goblins of the Sea"

BERNUM RIVER: Waterway that joins the cities of Colnora in the north and Vernes in the south

BLACK DIAMOND: International thieves' guild centered in Colnora

CALIAN: Pertaining to the nation of Calis

CALIANS: Residents of the nation of Calis, with dark skin and almond-shaped eyes. An isolated people, not much is known about them in the northern and eastern kingdoms of Avryn, except that their women are among the most beautiful in existence, but the suggestion of their use of magic makes them reviled and outcast.

CALIS: Southern- and easternmost of the four nations of Apeladorn, considered exotic and strange as most in the north have little interaction with people from that part of Elan. The region is in constant conflict with the Ba Ran Ghazel.

CARTER: A person who makes their living by moving goods from place to place, usually employing a horse-drawn cart

COLNORA: Largest, wealthiest city in Avryn. A merchant-based city that grew from a rest stop at a central crossroads of various major trade routes.

CROWN TOWER: Home of the Patriarch and center of the Nyphron Church

DELGOS: One of the four nations of Apeladorn. The only republic in a world of monarchies, Delgos revolted against the Steward's Empire after Glenmorgan III was murdered and after surviving a goblin attack with no aid from the empire.

DIXON TAFT: Carter operating out of Medford and employee of Medford House

DROME: God of dwarves, second son of Erebus

DUSTER: Person (or persons) responsible for a gruesome set of murders one summer in the city of Colnora

ELAN: The world

EREBUS: Father of the gods Ferrol (god of elves), Drome (god of the dwarves), Maribor (god of men), Muriel (goddess of nature), Uberlin (god of darkness)

ERVANON: City in northern Ghent, seat of the Nyphron Church, once the capital of the Steward's Empire as established by Glenmorgan

ESSENDON: Royal family of Melengar

ESSENDON CASTLE: Home of the ruling monarchs of Melengar

ETHAN: Sheriff in the Lower Quarter of Medford

ETTA: Least attractive prostitute at Medford House in the Lower Quarter of Medford

GENTRY QUARTER: The geographic region of Medford where the wealthiest (usually noble or rich merchants) reside

GHENT: Ecclesiastical holding of the Nyphron Church

GLENMORGAN: Historical figure and a native of Ghent who reunited the four nations of Apeladorn 326 years after the fall of the Novronian Empire. He initiated the new Steward's Empire, founded Sheridan University, created the great north–south road, and built the Ervanon palace (of which only the Crown Tower remains).

GWEN DELANCY: Calian native and proprietor of Medford House

GWENDOLYN: Given name of Gwen DeLancy

HADRIAN BLACKWATER: Originally from Hintindar, he left home at fifteen, spent two years as a soldier (with multiple armies) and three years as an arena fighter in Calis

HEAD, THE: Nickname for The Hideous Head Tavern and Alehouse

HIDEOUS HEAD TAVERN AND ALEHOUSE: Brothel and tavern run by Raynor Grue in the Lower Quarter of Medford

HINTINDAR: Small manorial village in Rhenydd, home of Hadrian Blackwater

HOUSE, THE: Nickname used for Medford House

JOLLIN: Prostitute of the Lower Quarter working at Medford House

LADY BANSHEE: Large fishing boat operating out of Medford

LOWER QUARTER: The geographic region of Medford where most of the impoverished reside

MAE: Prostitute of the Lower Quarter working at Medford House

MANZANT: Infamous prison and salt mine, located in Manzar, Maranon

MARANON: Kingdom in Avryn, rich in farmland and known for breeding the best horses

MARES CATHEDRAL: Center of the Nyphron Church in Melengar

MARIBOR: God of men, third son of Erebus

MEDFORD: Capital city of Melengar. The town is divided into four distinct quarters: Artisan, Merchant, Gentry, and Lower.

MEDFORD HOUSE: Brothel in the Lower Quarter of Medford run by Gwen DeLancy and employing prostitutes who once worked at The Hideous Head Tavern and Alehouse

MELENGAR: Small but old and respected kingdom of Avryn ruled by King Amrath

MERCHANT QUARTER: The geographic region of Medford where most of the goods are sold

MERRICK MARIUS: Former best friend of Royce Melborn, known for his strategic thinking

MONTEMORCEY: Excellent wine imported through the Vandon Spice Company

MURIEL: Goddess of nature, only daughter of Erebus

NOVRON: Savior of mankind, demigod, son of Maribor, defeated the elven army in the Great Elven Wars, founder of the Novronian Empire

NYPHRON CHURCH: Predominant church of mankind. Worshipers of Novron and Maribor.

PATRIARCH: Head of the Nyphron Church, lives in the Crown Tower of Ervanon

PERCEPLIQUIS: Ancient city and capital of the Novronian Empire, destroyed and lost during the collapse of the Old Empire

PICKLES: Street urchin from Vernes and former companion of Hadrian

RAYNOR GRUE: Proprietor of The Hideous Head Tavern and Alehouse in the Lower Quarter of Medford

REUBEN HILFRED: Son of Richard Hilfred. After the death of his mother, he was raised by an aunt until the age of fourteen, when he came to Essendon Castle to live with his father and become a member of the castle guard.

RHENYDD: Poorest of the kingdoms of Avryn

RICHARD HILFRED: Father of Reuben, member of the king's bodyguard

ROSE: Prostitute of the Lower Quarter working at Medford House

ROYAL PERMIT: Legal paperwork allowing a proprietor to operate a business

ROYCE MELBORN: Thief, assassin, and former inmate at Manzant Prison

RUE: Nickname of Reuben Hilfred given to him by his father

SENTINEL: Inquisitor generals of the Nyphron Church, charged with rooting out heresy and finding the lost Heir of Novron

SERET: Knights of Nyphron. The military arm of the church, commanded by sentinels.

SHERIDAN UNIVERSITY: Prestigious institution of learning, located in Ghent

SIGHT, THE: Ability, usually possessed by Calian women to see the future

SONG OF MAN, THE: Poem that tells the history and mythology of mankind

SPADONE: Long two-handed sword with a tapering blade and an extended flange ahead of the hilt allowing for an extended variety of fighting maneuvers. Due to the length of the handgrip and the flange, which provides its own barbed hilt, the sword provides a number of additional hand placements, permitting the sword to be used similarly to a quarterstaff and as a powerful cleaving weapon. The spadone is the traditional weapon of a skilled knight.

SQUIRE: Errand runner or servant of a knight

STANE: Net hauler for the *Lady Banshee*, killed a prostitute of the Head

TENENT: Most common form of semi-standard international currency. Coins of gold, silver, and copper stamped with the likeness of the king of the realm where the coin was minted: 1 gold = 100 silver; 1 silver = 10 copper.

THREE CRUELTIES OF HUMANITY, THE: As described in the poem "The Song of Man," they are age, disease, and hunger

TRENT: Northern mountainous kingdoms of Apeladorn, generally remote and isolated

UBERLIN: God of darkness, born from the rape of Muriel by her father, Erebus

VERNES: Port city at the mouth of the Bernum River

WARRIC: Most powerful of the kingdoms of Avryn, ruled by King Ethelred

WAYWARD INN: A defunct establishment that used to reside at the end of Wayward Street in the Lower Quarter of Medford

WAYWARD STREET: Road leading to the most impoverished section of the Lower Quarter in Medford

WILLARD: Bartender at The Hideous Head Tavern and Alehouse in the Lower Quarter of Medford

WINTERTIDE: Chief holiday, held in midwinter, celebrated with feasts and games of skill

WOLVES: Street gang of children; Royce Melborn was once a member

extras

www.orbitbooks.net

about the author

Michael J. Sullivan is one of the few authors who have successfully published through all three routes: small press, self, and big six. His Riyria Revelations series has been translated into fourteen foreign language markets, including German, Russian, French, and Japanese. He has been named to io9's Most Successful Self-Published Sci-Fi and Fantasy Authors list as well as making #6 on EMG's 25 Self-Published Authors to Watch list. As of January 2013, his books have appeared on more than sixty-five "best of" or "most anticipated" lists, including:

- Fantasy Faction's Top 10 Most Anticipated Books for 2013
- Goodreads Choice Awards Nominees for Best Fantasy in 2010 and 2012
- Audible's 2012 5-star The Best of Everything List
- *Library Journal*'s 2011 Best Books for SF/Fantasy
- Barnes & Noble Blog's Best Fantasy Releases of 2011
- Fantasy Book Critic's #1 Independent Novel of 2010

Like many authors, Michael's journey to publication was a long one. In his twenties he became a stay-at-home dad and wrote while his kids were napping or at school. He completed twelve novels over the course of a decade, and after finding no traction, he quit writing altogether. During the next decade, stories continued to form, but he never put any of them down on paper. He finally relented and started writing again, but only on the condition that he wouldn't seek publication. He decided to write the stories that he wanted to read and expected to share them only with his family and close friends. His wife, Robin, had other plans.

After reading the first three books of The Riyria Revelations, she became dedicated to getting them "out there." Since Michael refused to jump back on the query-go-round, she took it upon herself and after more than one hundred query rejections, she finally landed an agent. After a year of submissions, without any interest, she switched to querying small presses and *The Crown Conspiracy* was signed to Aspirations Media Inc. They later signed the second book, *Avempartha*, but when they lacked the funds for the print run, the rights reverted and Robin started releasing the books at six-month intervals through her own imprint. When foreign language deals started to come in, she hired Teri Tobias to pick the right publishers and negotiate the deals. By the publication of the fifth book, Robin asked Teri to try New York again and the series received a much different reception. Out of the seventeen publishers they approached, almost half expressed interest and in less than a month, a deal was signed with Orbit (fantasy imprint of big six publisher Hachette Book Group).

After finishing The Riyria Revelations, and while waiting to evaluate the reaction to the series, Michael wrote two stand-alone novels: *Hollow World* (a science-fiction novel) and *Antithesis* (an urban fantasy). Work on these was temporarily suspended because of the public's demand for more Royce and Hadrian stories. In response, Michael wrote the two prequel novels (The Riyria Chronicles), which have been sold to Orbit. *The Crown Tower* will release in August 2013 and *The Rose and the Thorn* in September 2013. Find out more about the author at www.riyria.com.

Find out about Michael J. Sullivan and other Orbit authors by registering for the free monthly newsletter at www.orbitbooks.net.

if you enjoyed
THE ROSE AND THE THORN

look out for

PROMISE OF BLOOD

Book One of the Powder Mage trilogy

by

Brian McClellan

CHAPTER

1

Adamat wore his coat tight, top buttons fastened against a wet night air that seemed to want to drown him. He tugged at his sleeves, trying to coax more length, and picked at the front of the jacket where it was too close by far around the waist. It'd been half a decade since he'd even seen this jacket, but when summons came from the king at this hour, there was no time to get his good one from the tailor. Yet this summer coat provided no defense against the chill snaking through the carriage window.

The morning was not far off but dawn would have a hard time scattering the fog. Adamat could feel it. It was humid even for early spring in Adopest, and chillier than Novi's frozen toes. The soothsayers in Noman's Alley said it was a bad omen. Yet who listened to soothsayers these days? Adamat reasoned it would give him a cold and wondered why he had been summoned out on a pit-made night like this.

The carriage approached the front gate of Skyline and moved on without a stop. Adamat clutched at his pantlegs and peered out the window. The guards were not at their posts. Odder still, as they continued along the wide path amid the fountains, there were no lights. Skyline had so many lanterns, it could be seen all the way from the city even on the cloudiest night. Tonight the gardens were dark.

Adamat was fine with this. Manhouch used enough of their taxes for his personal amusement. Adamat stared out into the gardens at the black maws where the hedge mazes began and imagined shapes flitting back and forth in the lawn. What was...ah, just a sculpture. Adamat sat back, took a deep breath. He could hear his heart beating, thumping, frightened, his stomach tightening. Perhaps they *should* light the garden lanterns...

A little part of him, the part that had once been a police inspector, prowling nights such as these for the thieves and pickpockets in dark alleys, laughed out from inside. *Still your heart, old man*, he said to himself. *You were once the eyes staring back from the darkness.*

The carriage jerked to a stop. Adamat waited for the coachman to open the door. He might have waited all night. The driver rapped on the roof. "You're here," a gruff voice said.

Rude.

Adamat stepped from the coach, just having time to snatch his hat and cane before the driver flicked the reins and was off, clattering into the night. Adamat uttered a quiet curse after the man and turned around, looking up at Skyline.

The nobility called Skyline Palace "the Jewel of Adro." It rested on a high hill east of Adopest so that the sun rose above it every morning. One particularly bold newspaper had compared it to a starving pauper wearing a diamond ring. It was an apt comparison in these lean times. A king's pride doesn't fill the people's bellies.

He was at the main entrance. By day, it was a grand avenue of marbled walks and fountains, all leading to a pair of giant, silver-plated doors, themselves dwarfed by the sheer façade of the biggest single building in Adro. Adamat listened for the soft footfalls of patrolling Hielmen. It was said the king's personal guard were everywhere in these gardens, watching every secluded corner, muskets always loaded, bayonets fixed, their gray-and-white sashes somber among the green-and-gold splendor. But there were no footfalls, nor were the fountains running. He'd heard once that the fountains only stopped for the death of the king. Surely he'd not have been summoned here if Manhouch were dead. He smoothed the front of his jacket. Here, next to the building, a few of the lanterns were lit.

A figure emerged from the darkness. Adamat tightened his grip on his cane, ready to draw the hidden sword inside at a moment's notice.

It was a man in uniform, but little could be discerned in such ill light. He held a rifle or a musket, trained loosely on Adamat, and wore a flat-topped forage cap with a stiff visor. Only one thing could be certain ... he was not a Hielman. Their tall, plumed hats were easy to recognize, and they never went without them.

"You're alone?" a voice asked.

"Yes," Adamat said. He held up both hands and turned around.

"All right. Come on."

The soldier edged forward and yanked on one of the mighty silver doors. It rolled outward slowly, ponderously, despite the man putting his weight into it. Adamat moved closer and examined the soldier's jacket. It was dark blue with silver braiding. Adran military. In theory, the military reported to the king. In practice, one man held their leash: Field Marshal Tamas.

"Step back, friend," the soldier said. There was a note of impatience in his voice, some unseen stress—but that could have been the weight of the door. Adamat did as he was told, only coming forward again to slip through the entrance when the soldier gestured.

"Go ahead," the soldier directed. "Take a right at the diadem and head through the Diamond Hall. Keep walking until you find yourself in the Answering Room." The door inched shut behind him and closed with a muffled thump.

Adamat was alone in the palace vestibule. Adran military, he mused. Why would a soldier be here, on the grounds, without any sign of the Hielmen? The most frightening answer sprang to mind first. A power struggle. Had the military been called in to deal with a rebellion? There were a number of powerful factions within Adro: the Wings of Adom mercenaries, the royal cabal, the Mountainwatch, and the great noble families. Any one of them could have been giving Manhouch trouble. None of it made sense, though. If there had been a power struggle, the palace grounds would be a battlefield, or destroyed outright by the royal cabal.

Adamat passed the diadem—a giant facsimile of the Adran crown—and noted it was in as bad taste as rumor had it. He entered the Diamond Hall, where the walls and floor were of scarlet, accented in gold leaf, and thousands of tiny gems, which gave the room its name, glittered from the ceiling in the light of a single lit candelabra. The tiny flames of the candelabra flickered as if in the wind, and the room was cold.

Adamat's sense of unease deepened as he neared the far end of the gallery. Not a sign of life, and the only sound came from his own echoing footfalls on the marble floor. A window had been shattered, explaining the chill. The result of one of the king's famous temper tantrums? Or something else? He could hear his heart beating in his ears. There. Behind a curtain, a pair of boots? Adamat passed his hand before his eyes. A trick of the light. He stepped over to reassure himself and pulled back the curtain.

A body lay in the shadows. Adamat bent over it, touched the skin. It was warm, but the man was most certainly dead. He wore gray pants with a white stripe down the side and a matching jacket.

A tall hat with a white plume lay on the floor some ways away. A Hielman. The shadows played on a young, clean-shaven face, peaceful except for a single hole in the side of his skull and the dark, wet stain on the floor.

He'd been right. A struggle of some kind. Had the Hielmen rebelled, and the military been brought in to deal with them? Again, it didn't make any sense. The Hielmen were fanatically loyal to the king, and any matters within Skyline Palace would have been dealt with by the royal cabal.

Adamat cursed silently. Every question compounded itself. He suspected he'd find some answers soon enough.

Adamat left the body behind the curtain. He lifted his cane and twisted, bared a few inches of steel, and approached a tall doorway flanked by two hooded, scepter-wielding sculptures. He paused between the ancient statues and took a deep breath, letting his eyes wander over a set of arcane script scrawled into the portal. He entered.

The Answering Room made the Hall of Diamonds look small. A pair of staircases, one to either side of him and each as wide across as three coaches, led to a high gallery that ran the length of the room on both sides. Few outside the king and his cabal of Privileged sorcerers ever entered this room.

In the center of the room was a single chair, on a dais a hand-breadth off the floor, facing a collection of knee pillows, where the cabal acknowledged their liege. The room was well lit, though from no discernible source of light.

A man sat on the stairs to Adamat's right. He was older than Adamat, just into his sixtieth year with silver hair and a neatly trimmed mustache that still retained a hint of black. He had a strong but not overly large jaw and his cheekbones were well defined. His skin was darkened by the sun, and there were deep lines at the corners of his mouth and eyes. He wore a dark-blue soldier's uniform with a silver representation of a powder keg pinned above the heart and nine gold service stripes sewn on the right breast, one for every five years in the Adran military. His uniform lacked an officer's epaulettes, but the weary experience in the man's brown eyes left no question that he'd led armies on the battlefield. There was a single pistol, hammer cocked, on the stair next to him. He leaned on a sheathed small sword and watched as a stream of blood slowly trickled down each step, a dark line on the yellow-and-white marble.

"Field Marshal Tamas," Adamat said. He sheathed his cane sword and twisted until it clicked shut.

The man looked up. "I don't believe we've ever met."

"We have," Adamat said. "Fourteen years ago. A charity ball thrown by Lord Aumen."

"I have a terrible time with faces," the field marshal said. "I apologize."

Adamat couldn't take his eyes off the rivulet of blood. "Sir. I was summoned here. I wasn't told by whom, or for what reason."

"Yes," Tamas said. "I summoned you. On the recommendation of one of my Marked. Cenka. He said you served together on the police force in the twelfth district."

Adamat pictured Cenka in his mind. He was a short man with an unruly beard and a penchant for wines and fine food. He'd seen him last seven years ago. "I didn't know he was a powder mage."

"We try to find anyone with an affinity for it as soon as possible," Tamas said, "but Cenka was a late bloomer. In any case"—he waved a hand—"we've come upon a problem."

Adamat blinked. "You...want my help?"

The field marshal raised an eyebrow. "Is that such an unusual request? You were once a fine police investigator, a good servant of Adro, and Cenka tells me that you have a perfect memory."

"Still, sir."

"Eh?"

"I'm still an investigator. Not with the police, sir, but I still take jobs."

"Excellent. Then it's not so odd for me to seek your services?"

"Well, no," Adamat said, "but sir, this is Skyline Palace. There's a dead Hielman in the Diamond Hall and..." He pointed at the stream of blood on the stairs. "Where's the king?"

Tamas tilted his head to the side. "He's locked himself in the chapel."

"You've staged a coup," Adamat said. He caught a glimpse of movement with the corner of his eye, saw a soldier appear at the top of the stairs. The man was a Deliv, a dark-skinned northerner. He wore the same uniform as Tamas, with eight golden stripes on the right breast. The left breast of his uniform displayed a silver powder keg, the sign of a Marked. Another powder mage.

"We have a lot of bodies to move," the Deliv said.

Tamas gave his subordinate a glance. "I know, Sabon."

"Who's this?" Sabon asked.

"The inspector that Cenka requested."

"I don't like him being here," Sabon said. "It could compromise everything."

"Cenka trusted him."

"You've staged a coup," Adamat said again with certainty.

"I'll help with the bodies in a moment," Tamas said. "I'm old, I need some rest now and then." The Deliv gave a sharp nod and disappeared.

"Sir!" Adamat said. "What have you done?" He tightened his grip on his cane sword.

Tamas pursed his lips. "Some say the Adran royal cabal had the most powerful Privileged sorcerers in all the Nine Nations, second only to Kez," he said quietly. "Yet I've just slaughtered every one of them. Do you think I'd have trouble with an old inspector and his cane sword?"

Adamat loosened his grip. He felt ill. "I suppose not."

"Cenka led me to believe that you were pragmatic. If that is the case, I would like to employ your services. If not, I'll kill you now and look for a solution elsewhere."

"You've staged a coup," Adamat said again.

Tamas sighed. "Must we keep coming back to that? Is it so shocking? Tell me, can you think of any fewer than a dozen factions within Adro with reason to dethrone the king?"

"I didn't think any of them had the skill," Adamat said. "Or the daring." His eyes returned to the blood on the stairs, before his mind traveled to his wife and children, asleep in their beds. He looked at the field marshal. His hair was tousled; there were drops of blood on his jacket—a lot, now that he thought to look. Tamas might as well have been sprayed with it. There were dark circles under his eyes and a weariness that spoke of more than just age.

"I will not agree to a job blindly," Adamat said. "Tell me what you want."

"We killed them in their sleep," Tamas said without preamble. "There's no easy way to kill a Privileged, but that's the best. A mistake was made and we had a fight on our hands." Tamas looked pained for a moment, and Adamat suspected that the fight had not gone as well as Tamas would have liked. "We prevailed. Yet upon the lips of the dying was one phrase."

Adamat waited.

"'You can't break Kresimir's Promise,'" Tamas said. "That's what the dying sorcerers said to me. Does it mean anything to you?"

Adamat smoothed the front of his coat and sought to recall old memories. "No. 'Kresimir's Promise'...'Break'...'Broken'... Wait—'Kresimir's Broken Promise.'" He looked up. "It was the name of a street gang. Twenty...twenty-two years ago. Cenka couldn't remember that?"

Tamas continued. "Cenka thought it sounded familiar. He was certain you'd remember it."

"I don't forget things," Adamat said. "Kresimir's Broken Promise was a street gang with forty-three members. They were all young, some of them no more than children, the oldest not yet twenty. We were trying to round up some of the leaders to put a stop to a string of thefts. They were an odd lot—they broke into churches and robbed priests."

"What happened to them?"

Adamat couldn't help but look at the blood on the stairs. "One day they disappeared, every one of them—including our informants. We found the whole lot a few days later, forty-three bodies jammed into a drain culvert like pickled pigs' feet. They'd been massacred by powerful sorceries, with excessive brutality. The marks of the king's royal cabal. The investigation ended there." Adamat suppressed a shiver. He'd not once seen a thing like that, not before or since. He'd witnessed executions and riots and murder scenes that filled him with less dread.

The Deliv soldier appeared again at the top of the stairs. "We need you," he said to Tamas.

"Find out why these mages would utter those words with their final breath," Tamas said. "It may be connected to your street gang. Maybe not. Either way, find me an answer. I don't like the riddles of the dead." He got to his feet quickly, moving like a man twenty years younger, and jogged up the stairs after the Deliv. His boot splashed in the blood, leaving behind red prints. "Also," he called over his shoulder, "keep silent about what you have seen here until the execution. It will begin at noon."

"But..." Adamat said. "Where do I start? Can I speak with Cenka?"

Tamas paused near the top of the stairs and turned. "If you can speak with the dead, you're welcome to."

Adamat ground his teeth. "How did they say the words?" he said. "Was it a command, or a statement, or...?"

Tamas frowned. "An entreaty. As if the blood draining from their bodies was not their primary concern. I must go now."

"One more thing," Adamat said.

Tamas looked to be near the end of his patience.

"If I'm to help you, tell me why all of this?" He gestured to the blood on the stairs.

"I have things that require my attention," Tamas warned.

Adamat felt his jaw tighten. "Did you do this for power?"

"I did this for me," Tamas said. "And I did this for Adro. So that Manhouch wouldn't sign us all into slavery to the Kez with the Accords. I did it because those grumbling students of philosophy at the university only play at rebellion. The age of kings is dead, Adamat, and I have killed it."

Adamat examined Tamas's face. The Accords was a treaty to be signed with the king of Kez that would absolve all Adran debt but impose strict tax and regulation on Adro, making it little more than a Kez vassal. The field marshal had been outspoken about the Accords. But then, that was expected. The Kez had executed Tamas's late wife.

"It is," Adamat said.

"Then get me some bloody answers." The field marshal whirled and disappeared into the hallway above.

Adamat remembered the bodies of that street gang as they were being pulled from the drain in the wet and mud, remembered the horror etched upon their dead faces. *The answers may very well be bloody.*